MOUNTAINEER DREAMS

LAURALEE BLISS
IRENE B. BRAND
YVONNE LEHMAN

BARBOUR
PUBLISHING

Mountains Stand Strong © 2007 by Irene B. Brand
A Bride Idea © 2007 by Yvonne Lehman
Seneca Shadows © 2008 by Lauralee Bliss

ISBN 978-1-60260-489-6

Scripture quotations are taken from the King James Version of the Bible.

This book is a work of fiction. Names, characters, places, and incidents are either products of the author's imagination or used fictitiously. Any similarity to actual people, organizations, and/or events is purely coincidental.

Cover model photography: Jim Celuch, Celuch Creative Imaging

Published by Barbour Publishing, Inc., P.O. Box 719, Uhrichsville, Ohio 44683, www.barbourbooks.com

Our mission is to publish and distribute inspirational products offering exceptional value and biblical encouragement to the masses.

ECPA Member of the
Evangelical Christian
Publishers Association

Printed in the United States of America.

MOUNTAINS STAND STRONG

STRONG

Irene B. Brand

Author's Note

The herbs mentioned in this story were carefully researched and are authentic to the era. Some have since been found to be questionable or even dangerous. In no way do I advocate the use of any herb, medication, or curative without checking first with your medical doctor.

Chapter 1

Would the prospect of buying a new dress for the Fourth of July celebration compensate for all the drudgery and humiliation she had endured in this household?

As if Nancy Logan's thoughts had penetrated the ceiling into the bedroom above, her employer, Tabitha Clark, commanded from the top of the stairs, "Nancy, when Dr. Foster arrives, go to the door and ask him to come to Tommy's bedroom. And see that you greet him correctly."

Annoyed by her employer's tone, Nancy threw the feather duster on the floor and waited for the doctor's arrival. "A body's only got two hands and two feet," she muttered. "Nancy, do this. Nancy, do that," she said, mimicking her employer as she listened for a knock on the door.

In Nancy's opinion, Tommy didn't need a doctor. All the boy needed was a cup of mint tea and a poultice of lard and kerosene on his chest overnight. But Tommy's sniffles and shortness of breath provided a good excuse for Widow Clark to entertain the handsome young doctor who had come to Wheeling from Philadelphia a year ago. It was common knowledge that the widow was at least ten years older than Dr. Foster, but during the few weeks Nancy had worked in the Clark home, he had already come to see Tommy four times.

Nancy couldn't imagine why a smart man like the doctor couldn't figure out that Mrs. Clark was casting her net in his direction.

Nancy wouldn't mind having the doctor take notice of her, too, but she wouldn't pretend to be sick to snag his attention. *Though it would be nice if the good Lord would give him some reason to notice me,* she thought.

Several minutes passed before she heard a knock at the door. Mrs. Clark must have been watching for the doctor, for she alerted Nancy before he had time to get out of the buggy and tie his horse to the hitching post. Nancy straightened her white cap and dainty apron and forced a smile to her face.

"Come in, Doctor," she said, standing to one side and bowing as Tabitha had taught her to do.

Heath Foster stepped into the entrance hall, took off his hat, and handed it to her. "Good afternoon, Miss Logan."

Nancy hung his hat on the hall tree beside the door.

"Mrs. Clark wants you to come see Tommy right away. You know which room it is?"

"Yes, thank you."

Nancy watched as he walked up the stairway. On their first meeting, she had tagged the doctor as a compassionate person, which any man who wanted to be a doctor ought to be. And he was sure handsome, too! He wore his sandy-colored hair long, and it was thick and curled loosely around his nape. His face was lean and beardless except for the long sideburns. Dark brown eyes glimmered above his high-bridged nose. He was a man of medium height, so Nancy didn't have to crook her neck to look up at him like she did a lot of men.

Because she had been ordered to prepare tea to be served in the parlor before Dr. Foster left, Nancy went to the kitchen. Earlier in the day, she had set out the silver tray and shined it until she could see her face in it. Before she had left for her afternoon off, the cook had told Nancy how to prepare and serve the tea, but this was the first time Nancy had served in this capacity, and she was nervous about it.

She dropped another chunk of coal in the stove and moved the teakettle to the hottest part of the stovetop. While she waited for the water to heat, Nancy arranged slices of raisin bread and pound cake on a china plate. By the time she heard footsteps descending the stairs, she was ready. But she waited until she heard the soft *ding-a-ling* of a silver bell before she lifted the heavy tray, walked down the hall, and entered the parlor.

Keeping her eyes straight ahead, Nancy didn't see the duster she had earlier tossed on the floor, and she stumbled over it. The tray tilted in her hands, and the plate of bread and cake slid to the floor.

Jumping to his feet, the doctor took the tray out of Nancy's hands and placed it safely on the low table close to where Mrs. Clark sat. Nancy caught her balance and stood like a statue, staring at the food on the floor, knowing that if it hadn't been for Dr. Foster's quick thinking, the tea service would be there, too.

"Clumsy girl!" Mrs. Clark shrieked. Her mouth twisted in anger; her dark eyes were venomous. She pointed at the duster. "Not only clumsy but negligent, too! Can't you do anything right? Clean up this mess. Then get out of my house, and don't come back. You're fired!"

Nancy started shaking, and she felt blood rushing to her face. It was bad enough to be humiliated in front of Dr. Foster, whom she admired, but Mrs. Clark's words angered her. She jerked off the white apron and cap she was required to wear and dropped them on top of the bread and cake.

"Clean your own floor," Nancy said. She turned and rushed down the hall to the kitchen, grabbed her coat off the rack beside the back door, ran down the steps, and headed toward the alley behind the Clark home. Although it was April and the redbud and dogwood trees were blooming on the hills surrounding Wheeling, the wind from the Ohio River was brisk and cold. But Nancy didn't take time to put on her coat, for she wanted to get away from the Clark home as quickly as possible.

At the end of the alley, she turned left on Main Street, wondering what she should do. Her Christian duty was to return to the Clark home and apologize for her behavior. But she just couldn't—especially if Dr. Foster should still be there.

She walked blindly, knowing that she must get over her anger before she went home. Her father hadn't wanted her to work for Tabitha Clark in the first place. Mrs. Clark's brothers were his competitors in the steamboat business, and her father thought they looked down on him because he owned only *one* boat. He would cause a ruckus if she told him how the woman had talked to her.

Recalling her earlier thoughts, she muttered, "God, I wanted You to make something happen so the doctor would notice me. But did You have to go this far? I just expected a little miracle, not a thunderbolt."

Nancy didn't figure Heath Foster would forget her after what he'd seen and heard today. And the worst part of it was that she knew she was really at fault. She shouldn't have thrown that duster on the floor in the first place. Tears stung her eyes, and partially blinded by the bright sun, she stumbled along the streets of Wheeling with no particular destination in mind.

———◦∿◦———

Mrs. Clark sat in silence for a few moments, her face more crimson than Nancy's had been, but she soon said angrily, "The nerve of that girl! Talking to me that way! It's impossible to find good help these days!"

Heath tried to think of some discreet way to make an exit from this embarrassing situation. At a loss for words, he knelt on the floor and started picking up the food and putting it on the tray.

"Stop!" Mrs. Clark said. "You're a guest in my house. I don't expect you to clean the floor."

Heath finished picking up the food, noticing that Mrs. Clark made no move to help him. He set the plate on the table. "I think I should go now. You're upset, and it's better for you to be alone. Let me know if the medication doesn't help Tommy."

"Oh," Mrs. Clark pleaded, "don't leave. Don't go without your tea."

"Thank you, but I rarely take time for tea. And I do have other calls to make."

She followed him to the door, wringing her hands, begging him to stay. But he bowed himself out of the house with as much grace as possible. When he reached the street, he hardly knew which way to turn, but he walked to the left, looking for Nancy Logan. He had noted the girl's distress, and he didn't think she should be alone.

When he reached Main Street, Heath saw her walking slowly, her head down. "Just a minute, Miss Logan," he called, and she turned to face him. "Are you all right?"

Surprise and anger lit up her eyes. A blush spread over her cheeks, and she looked away. "Yes, I'm all right," she answered, "but I'm mad."

"I gathered that," he said, smiling.

She kept walking, and he turned, matching his steps to hers.

"I have a call to make in this direction. May I keep you company?"

"I reckon," she said. "But I won't be good company. I should have listened to Pa. He didn't want me to go to work in that house. He said Mrs. Clark's family is too stingy to buy slaves—that they just hire white folks and treat them like slaves."

"Who is your father?"

"Wendell Logan. We live at the waterfront. Pa owns and operates the *Wetzel*, a packet boat."

"Oh yes, it runs from Wheeling to Parkersburg, I believe."

They were walking past the headquarters of the *Wheeling Intelligencer* when three newsboys catapulted from the building like shells spewed out of cannons.

"Extra! Extra! Read all about it!" they shouted as they extended papers toward everyone on the street.

"Here, boy," Heath called. "I want a paper."

He reached into his pocket and dropped some coins in the boy's hand. Nancy crowded close to him, and when he unfolded the paper, he held it so that she could see the headline: CONFEDERATE TROOPS FIRE ON FORT SUMTER. Shock and disbelief knotted Heath's stomach, and his voice trembled as he read the opening sentence aloud: "Today at 4:30 a.m., Confederate troops opened fire on Fort Sumter in Charleston Harbor."

He lifted his head and in an agonized voice cried out, "Oh God in heaven! Have mercy on us. Have mercy on us."

"But what does it mean?" Nancy stammered.

"It means war, child," he said. "It means war!" Crushing the paper in his hands, Heath turned from her and walked away.

—⁓—

Although she was stunned by Dr. Foster's troubled voice, Nancy looked sharply at him. Child! Did he consider her a child? She'd been doing the work of a woman since her mother had died. At eighteen, she hardly considered herself a child!

The newspaper office was located in the center of Wheeling's business section, and people poured out of stores and offices. The streets filled with people running back and forth. Some were shouting. Others laughed. Many women were crying. Nancy walked among them, trying to make sense out of what they were saying. She didn't know much about the current political unrest in the country, except that South Carolina had seceded from the United States of America in December. Much to her father's disgust, delegates were now meeting in Richmond to decide if Virginia, too, would leave the Union.

"Let 'em secede!" Wendell Logan had shouted. "People here west of the mountains will be better off without 'em. The western counties won't leave the Union."

"But Pa," Nancy had argued, "we have to be part of a state, don't we? What would we call ourselves?"

"Oh, I don't know," her father had said impatiently, for he was long on opinions but short on facts. "I reckon we can be part of Ohio."

As she wandered in and out of the excited throng, Nancy heard someone call her name, and she turned as her friend Stella Danford ran toward her.

"Oh, Nancy! Isn't this terrible?"

"Seems like that to me," Nancy agreed as she pulled Stella to one side. "But most of these people act like they're happy."

Tears ran down Stella's face, and she swiped at them with her hand. "I'm not happy. Mama and Papa are talking about leaving Wheeling," she said. "Our kinfolks live in Alabama, and Mama wants to go home. I'm afraid."

Stella's words brought fear to Nancy's heart, too. Since she didn't think she would be affected one way or another, she hadn't paid much attention to the political discussions that had swirled around Wheeling like storm clouds the past few months. But this was serious. She and Stella went to the same church, and they had been friends since Stella's father had come to Wheeling to supervise the clothing factory his family owned. Nancy didn't want her friend to move away.

"What are you doing here by yourself?" Nancy asked.

"I heard all the shouting, and Mama sent me to find out what was going on."

"Everybody's talking at the same time, and I can't make much sense out of what they're saying. Let's walk down to the river where it's quieter."

Nancy shivered and realized that she was still carrying her coat. She put on the long woolen garment, buttoned it, and intertwined her arm with Stella's. They left Main Street and walked silently along the stone pavement of a side street. Two-story red brick houses with black chimney pots lined the street. Coal smoke from the chimneys filtered into Nancy's nostrils. As they walked, she told Stella about the flare-up at the Clark home.

"Mrs. Clark is one of Mama's friends. She's always so nice—I'm surprised that she treated you so mean."

"She's never shouted at me before, but she's always pushing me to do more work. I'm used to working, and I did what she said. I didn't have any choice, especially when I'm trying to make money to buy a dress with a hoop and everything that goes with it. Now I won't have a new dress."

"I'll let you have one of my dresses," Stella offered. "You could take the hem up to fit you."

While Nancy had always admired Stella's clothes, which the Danfords ordered from New Orleans, she wasn't tempted by the offer.

She shook her head. "Pa won't take charity. And he can't see any reason for a hoop skirt anyway. He said if I got one, I'd have to earn the money to buy it. And I don't have half of the money for the things I want."

"Do you need it for something special?"

"I'd like to have something new to wear to the Fourth of July celebration." Looking in disfavor at her dark cotton homemade dress, she added, "Until I start wearing grown-up clothes, people will never realize I'm not a girl anymore." *Especially Heath Foster,* she thought.

"We have more than two months before Independence Day. Maybe you can find another job."

As they walked, Nancy wondered how her life would change if there was a war. Her father had come to Wheeling when he was a boy, and he had witnessed its growth from a sleepy Southern town to a thriving industrial city of more than fourteen thousand people. Virginia was the only place she had ever lived, and she couldn't imagine leaving. Of course, it was different with Stella's folks.

"I wish you wouldn't move," Nancy said, and Stella wiped tears from her eyes with a linen handkerchief.

"I don't want to leave you," she said, "but Papa says if there is a war, Southerners won't be welcome here. The western counties of Virginia are different from the rest of the state, and he doesn't think this area will pull away from the Union. He intends to leave before fighting starts."

"Your father is right. We do have more in common with our neighboring states than we do with people east of the Allegheny Mountains or the states farther south."

They arrived at the riverfront and looked across a channel of the Ohio River to Wheeling Island. Nancy had learned as a child that in colonial days it had been called Zane Island after a family of early settlers in the area. Now a suspension bridge with abutments on the island spanned the water between the city of Wheeling and the state of Ohio.

Pointing to the small packet boat moored at the foot of Market Street, Stella said, "I see your father is at home. If we leave, I suppose we could travel partway with him." Sighing deeply, she continued, "I'd better go home. Mama will be worried about me and wondering what has happened. I didn't expect to be gone such a long time."

"I'll see you at church on Sunday," Nancy called as Stella ran down the bank to her home. Besides losing her best friend, she wondered in what other ways a war would change her life.

Chapter 2

As she always did after a day at the Clark residence, Nancy compared her modest home to the splendor of her employer's. Because the area was prone to flooding, her family's living quarters were on the second floor of a frame house—ten feet above ground level. They had survived many floods when their neighbors, who lived in one-story houses, lost their homes. But when the Ohio overflowed its banks, her father kept a johnboat tied to the porch of the second floor in case they had to evacuate. It was scary sometimes when the muddy floodwaters completely surrounded their home, but Nancy had grown used to it, and her brother always took advantage of the situation by sitting on their front porch and catching catfish from the backwater.

Her father was working on a boat engine in his machine shop on the first floor of their home, which also served as a warehouse. Nancy called to him as she started up the steep steps to the left of the house.

"Supper will be ready before long, Pa." He nodded that he'd heard her.

Nancy stoked the fire and pulled the pot of rabbit stew she'd made that morning to the front of the stove. She hurried into her bedroom and took off her coat and washed her hands. The Logan living quarters consisted of three rooms. The combination kitchen and sitting room fronted toward the river. She had a small bedroom to herself, while her father and only brother, Clay, shared a room. Nancy hadn't realized what a simple home they had until she started working for Mrs. Clark, at whose home she had experienced a taste of gracious living.

Nancy ground coffee beans and put them in the coffeepot to make a hot drink for her menfolk. By that time, the oven was hot, and she sifted dry ingredients and added milk to make biscuits. After she cut the soft bread into large circles, she dabbed each piece in a pan of hot lard, placed them in an iron skillet, and put the biscuits in the oven to bake.

As she worked, Nancy's thoughts rioted with all the things that had happened that day. From the time she was a child, she had kept house for her brother and father. Year after year went by without many changes. If the country did go to war, what difference would that make in their lives?

Clay was five years older than Nancy. He had never liked working on the river and had angered his father three years ago when he quit the river to take a job as night watchman at the Merchants and Mechanics Bank. But Nancy was pleased when he started working at the bank, for he had generously contributed to the household needs, which made her life easier.

Supper was ready when her father came upstairs and took his place at the head of the table. At forty-five, Wendell Logan was a handsome, muscular man, and Nancy often wondered why he hadn't remarried. She hadn't asked him, because she sometimes found it difficult to talk to her father, although she and her brother could talk about anything.

Clay was usually out of bed by now, but apparently he was still asleep. So Nancy called him, and soon he entered the kitchen. He yawned widely and stretched his tall, lean frame, then pumped water into a pan and washed his face and hands.

As she usually did when she looked at her brother, Nancy wondered why she couldn't have been tall like the men in her family, instead of being short and petite like her mother. Rather than sharing their dark features, she despaired of her medium-brown hair, light complexion, and blue eyes.

Nancy spooned the stew into three bowls and placed a plate of biscuits on the wooden table. She added a jar of strawberry preserves and a bowl of butter. After Pa prayed, the family ate with a minimum of conversation. When her father finished, he pushed back his chair and sipped his second cup of coffee.

"Lots of excitement uptown today," he said. "What was going on?"

Since Clay had slept through the afternoon, both men turned to Nancy.

"The Confederates in South Carolina fired on Fort Sumter early this morning. The *Intelligencer* put out an extra."

"The news must have come over the wire in a hurry. Did you bring home a copy of the paper?" Clay asked.

"No. I left my reticule at Mrs. Clark's house and didn't have any coins," Nancy answered, remembering for the first time that she'd failed to pick up the reticule when she ran from the house. She had about a dollar's worth of coins in that bag, which she probably would never see again. She wouldn't risk the woman's anger by going back after her money. So, she thought glumly, she no longer had a job and she'd just lost a dollar of her hard-earned money. She might as well kiss the new dress and hoop good-bye.

"What else did you hear?" Clay demanded, interrupting her thoughts.

"A big crowd gathered right away, and I walked around to listen. There was a lot of arguing going on—some thinking the Confederates had done right, others cussing them because they'd started a war."

"And there ain't nuthin' worse than a civil war," Pa said. "But though I hate to think it, that little incident might just be the spark needed to spur the western part of this state to break away from Virginia. We don't have nuthin' in common with them slave owners in the East anyway."

"To my notion, South Carolina did the right thing," Clay said. "The North has been pushin' the South around long enough. The whole South ought to take up arms against the northern bullies."

Slapping the table with the palm of his hand, Pa shouted, "Son, as long as you're under my roof, you can keep your treasonous ideas to yourself! I ain't liftin' a hand agin' the United States of America, and I forbid you to. Your great grandpappy was killed at Saratoga fightin' the British to get us our freedom. I ain't about to give it away by joinin' a bunch of rich slaveholders who want to destroy this Union."

Perhaps Clay knew this wasn't the time to defy his father, for he didn't answer. His face paled, and he left the table and went to the bedroom. Nancy hurried to spread the leftover biscuits with jam and wash an apple to put in his dinner bucket. She handed it to him when he came back into the kitchen ready to go to work. His face was clouded with anger, but he took time to bend over and kiss Nancy's cheek.

Her father was angry, too, and Nancy decided not to mention her fracas with Tabitha Clark. She washed the dishes while he stalked around the room muttering under his breath.

"I'm going down to the river, Pa."

He waved his hand in dismissal. "Be back before dark."

She walked to the wharf where the *Wetzel* was tied up. She climbed to the top deck and sat on a bench. The sun, filtering through dark clouds on the western horizon, had turned the waters of the Ohio to crimson. She never got tired of this view.

On the eastern side of the valley, a range of high bluffs towered over the town. In the gathering dusk, she saw smoke from the factories that were located to the north and south of the business and residential areas. For the most part, the trees lining the streets were just beginning to leaf out, but the willow trees along the riverbank had been showing green for a month. Nancy loved her home during all seasons of the year, but she was most partial to it during the spring. It seemed as if God, knowing how dreary the long winter had been, wanted to give His people a special treat.

When the sun dropped behind the clouds, Nancy left the boat. As she neared her home, she became aware that a rider was approaching. She wasn't surprised to recognize Heath Foster, for he often visited patients in the evening. But she was surprised that he reined in the sorrel horse when he came abreast of her.

"Miss Logan, I told my mother that you might be looking for work. She needs help around the house, and since I had a call in this direction, I told her I'd let you know. If you're interested, go to see her when it's convenient for you."

For a moment, Nancy was speechless, then she mumbled, "Well, thank you! Thank you very much." The possibility of a fancy dress with a hoop loomed again in Nancy's future.

Heath touched the brim of his hat and rode off, leaving Nancy staring after him. In spite of the incident with Widow Clark and the possibility of war, the day had turned out well after all.

"He's sure takin' notice of me for some reason," she said softly.

But Nancy started upstairs with another problem. How was she going to explain to her father that she no longer worked for Tabitha Clark? And how would he feel about her going to work for the Fosters? They were Quakers, and Pa didn't hold with their religious views. How could she change his mind if he put his foot down and refused to let her work for Mrs. Foster?

Chapter 3

Nancy knew she would have to downplay the incident or her father would storm over to Mrs. Clark's house and give her a bawling out that she wouldn't soon forget. Should she tell her father about Dr. Foster's offer? Or should she go and talk to Mrs. Foster first and then tell her father?

She had pleaded with Pa for weeks before he finally agreed that she could work for Mrs. Clark, and when she now told him how the woman had talked to her, he would throw a fit. But she had to tell him before he heard it from another source.

When she heard the clock in the kitchen strike the hour of five, Nancy slipped out of bed, washed quickly, and put on her clothes. Her father expected his breakfast to be ready when he got up, and she didn't want him to be irritated this morning.

Nancy stirred the coals in the iron stove, laid wood chips on the coals, adjusted the damper on the stovepipe, and soon had a hot fire going. She had laid out the cutlery, pottery cups, and plates the night before. She quickly filled the coffeepot with water from the pitcher pump that brought water from the deep well behind their house. It was a sore spot with Pa that water lines hadn't been run to their street yet.

When the stove was hot, she mixed up a batch of biscuits and shoved them into the oven. She cut thick slices of ham and put them in a skillet. The coffee was hot when her father came from the bedroom. Everything was just the way he liked it, so he should be in a good mood.

"Mornin', Pa," she said in her brightest voice.

"Best of the day to you," he said. "That ham smells good."

She poured a mug of coffee and placed it beside her father when he sat down. "I'll get the milk while your coffee cools. The food is almost ready."

Nancy hustled downstairs to the cellar dug below the level of the first floor. The Logans bought milk and eggs three times a week from an Ohio farmer. When she came out of the cellar with a pitcher of milk, Nancy saw Clay approaching the house.

"You got breakfast ready, sis? I'm starved."

"Just about."

"I'll wash up down here."

"No hurry. I've got to fry the eggs yet. How many do you want?"

"Three will be enough. That is, if you've got plenty of ham."

Nancy laughed over her shoulder at her brother as she hurried up the steps. She set the pitcher beside her father. "How many eggs for you?"

"Two."

To Nancy's relief, the civil unrest in the country wasn't mentioned while they ate. As soon as Clay finished eating, he said, "I'm going fishing before I go to bed—maybe I can catch a string of catfish for supper."

Clay left the house, and while she removed his dishes from the table, Nancy heard him whistling as he headed toward the river. Waiting for her father to finish his breakfast, she looked out the window. The heavy fog on the Ohio when she had gotten up had lifted considerably, and the sun was breaking through the haze.

Her father finished the ham and biscuits on his plate, and Nancy refilled his coffee cup as he pushed back from the table with a satisfied look on his face. He always said that if a man had a good breakfast, he could make it through the day. If there was a good time to approach her father about something that would irritate him, this was it.

Nancy perched on the edge of her chair. Pa sipped on his coffee, a remote expression on his face. She wished she knew what he was thinking about. She opened her mouth twice before she could speak a word.

"Pa." Her voice trembled a little, and she wondered if her father noticed it. He turned his attention to her and waited. "Mrs. Clark fired me yesterday."

A frown spread across his features. "Go on," he prompted.

"She was entertaining Dr. Foster. I carried in the tea tray and stumbled, and the bread and cake fell on the floor. She said I was clumsy and ordered me to clean up the mess I'd made. I got mad and told her to clean it up herself."

One corner of Pa's mouth twisted upward into a grim smile.

"She fired me then, but I intended to quit regardless. I don't like to work for her."

Nancy expected him to say, "I told you so." Instead he said, "Anything else I need to know before I pay Mrs. Clark a visit?"

"I stumbled over a duster I'd dropped on the floor when I went to the door to let the doctor in. So it was my fault, but I didn't like the way she hollered at me. I'd rather you don't say anything to her, but I don't suppose she'll pay me the money she owes me. And I left my reticule there with some coins in it."

Her father's expression grew serious, and Nancy waited breathlessly for his decision. Although his temper could be volatile at times, usually he deliberated before he took action. At length, the tense lines on his face relaxed.

"I'll bide my time on this," he said. "Since you were at fault and had the gumption to tell her off, that should be enough for now. But she *will* pay you what she owes you, and she'll return the bag and money." He turned a stern eye on his daughter. "Maybe this has taught you a lesson."

Nancy squirmed in her chair, and the beginning of a smile curved the corners of her mouth. "Not exactly."

"And what does that mean?"

"Dr. Foster stopped by last night and told me that his mother needs some help. I want to go see her today. I still need to earn some money for that new dress and hoop I've told you about."

A look of pure anger crossed Pa's face. He hit the table with the palm of his hand, which shook his cup and sloshed coffee on the table. He jumped to his feet and angrily strode around the room. "Why can't you be content with what you have? We have plenty to eat, a roof over our heads, and all the clothes we need. Why do you want to copy people who are better off than we are?"

Although her father's anger usually daunted her, Nancy held her ground.

"I don't know! That's just the way the good Lord made me. It's not just pretty clothes I want, but I want to learn things, too."

"I paid to send you to that female seminary for five years. You can read and write better'n I ever could."

Nancy struggled to maintain her determination. She knew instinctively that there was more at stake than the issue of working for Mrs. Foster. If she relented now, she could see the trend of her future. She would continue to keep house for her father until he decided it was time for her to marry, and he would choose her husband. Nancy realized that was the normal scheme of things for women, and perhaps it always would be, but she wasn't content to settle for the way things had always been if she could improve her circumstances. She wanted to earn some money. And she wanted to learn new things, for she'd had just enough education to realize how much more there was to know. And she wanted to choose the man she married—someone she could love.

She knew her father would scorn such romantic notions, so she said, "But I want to learn more. When I go to the library and check out a book, I see hundreds of books. How many books do we have in this house? One—the Bible. I want books I can call my own. I'd even like to have my own Bible. I don't like to be disobedient or defy you, Pa, but as long as I take care of you and the house, I don't see why I can't take time to do the things I want to do."

Surprisingly, amusement flickered in his eyes.

"Go right ahead, then. I never did think much of a woman who let a man run over her."

Nancy was stunned for an instant, finding it hard to believe that he had acquiesced so quickly. Then she galvanized into action and did something she hadn't done for years. She ran to her father, threw her arms around him, stood on tiptoe, and kissed his cheek.

"Thanks, Pa. I'll go see Mrs. Foster today."

"I'm warning you about one thing. I don't want you to be took in by the Fosters' religion. They're Quakers, and they have some farfetched ideas about what the Bible teaches. I ain't havin' my daughter spoutin' their heresy."

Nancy wasn't sure how the Quaker religion differed from her own, but she wouldn't argue the point now. She intended to follow up on her victory before he changed his mind.

He took some coins out of his pocket. "If you're goin' uptown this morning, bring home a newspaper. I want to see what Campbell has to say in the *Intelligencer* today. I don't like the way things are happenin' in this country. There's not much standin' between us and war."

Even the gloom on her father's face as he made this ominous prediction didn't dampen Nancy's anticipation of the day. She took extra care in washing the dishes and cleaning the house. Pa always put more fuel in the stove when he had a noon snack, so she put a pot of white beans on the back of the stove where they could simmer most of the day. She would make it a point to be home in time to fix the rest of his supper. Since he had been so nice about letting her work for Mrs. Foster, Nancy didn't intend to neglect him. She just hoped Mrs. Foster would like her work.

Nancy spruced up the kitchen as fast as she could. She carried a bowl of hot water into her bedroom and sponged her body, using a bar of honey-scented soap she'd bought at the store. Although she knew Mrs. Foster wouldn't see her underwear, she chose the best she had. She put on a linen chemise, a petticoat, and a pair of scarlet flannel drawers that came to her knees. She pulled the drawstrings tight around her slim waist before she stepped into her gray calico dress with a tight-fitting bodice and a gored skirt that flowed out gradually from her tiny waist to the wide hemline. She frowned at her image in the small mirror that hung over her dressing table. Her appearance didn't suit her, but it was the best she could do. Wrapping a white shawl around her shoulders, she hustled down the steps, paused at the shop door to call good-bye to her father, and headed uptown.

The Fosters lived in a modest, two-story, white frame house about halfway between the river and the high bluff behind the city. Nancy knew the location of the house, for she and Stella had walked by it more than once. Behind the house was a barn where Dr. Foster kept his two horses. A small building that had once been a garden house had been converted into his office. As Nancy approached the home, she wondered if she would see him today. She couldn't help wondering if her desire to work at the Fosters stemmed from a chance to make money to buy the dress or the opportunity to encounter the handsome doctor. She tried to put such confusing thoughts out of her mind as she walked up two steps to the porch and timidly knocked on the front door.

A tall woman with a gentle, wise countenance opened the door. She didn't bear any physical resemblance to Dr. Foster, so Nancy didn't know if she was his mother.

"I'm Nancy Logan. I came to see Mrs. Foster."

"I'm Hope Foster," she said in a soft and soothing voice and ushered Nancy into a small sitting room to the right of the entrance. "Sit down, Nancy. Would you like a cup of tea?"

"No, ma'am. I had my breakfast earlier, but thank you."

Nancy sat gingerly on the chair Mrs. Foster had indicated, thinking that she had never been offered refreshments in the Clark home and had never been allowed to sit anywhere except in the kitchen when the cook gave her a small lunch. She deduced that working for Mrs. Foster would be as different from working for Mrs. Clark as daylight was from dark.

In a quick glance she noted that her hostess's gray hair had been braided and wrapped around her head. A dainty white muslin cap sat on her head like a crown.

Sitting near Nancy, Mrs. Foster said, "My son tells me that you might have time to help with our housework."

"Yes, ma'am. I need to make some money."

"Tell me a little about yourself, Nancy."

"Did he tell you why I'm not working for Mrs. Clark?"

Mrs. Foster nodded, and her eyes seemed gentle and understanding.

"I live with my pa and brother on the riverfront. My mother died ten years ago when I was eight, and I've been doing for them since then. So I know how to do housework."

"I usually do my own work, but I've been having back problems. Heath wants me to slow down."

"I'd be glad of the chance to work for you. I could work a few days for free to see how you like my work. Mrs. Clark had me do a lot of things over—said I hadn't done them the right way."

A gracious smile overspread Mrs. Foster's face. "I'm sure that won't be necessary. It won't take long for you to learn how I want things done. Perhaps you can work for me four hours a day, three days a week. I could pay you thirty-five cents a day. Would that be satisfactory?"

Quickly Nancy calculated in her mind that she would make more than a dollar each week. She still had the better part of three months until Independence Day, which would allow plenty of time to accumulate enough money for the new dress and maybe some left over for other things.

"That sounds all right, but I'll have to ask Pa."

"Yes, of course. If he agrees, perhaps you could start day after tomorrow."

"Yes, ma'am." Nancy stood up because she didn't want to overstay her welcome. "If Pa doesn't like our arrangements, I'll come and tell you tomorrow. If he does, I'll come two days from now at nine o'clock."

Nancy had wanted to see the doctor, and she glanced covertly at his office as she left the Foster home. She didn't see him, and in spite of her excitement over landing another job so quickly, she went home slightly disappointed.

Chapter 4

When her father gave his blessing to Nancy's new job, she spent the next day cleaning every nook and cranny of their home. It was a sunshiny day, and she washed the bed linens and hung them out to dry. She made loaves of wheat bread. She brought jars of green beans and hominy from the cellar to have handy if some days she was late getting home. But she intended to leave the Foster home every day in plenty of time to put Pa's food on the table when he was ready for it.

The next morning, calling good-bye to her father, she hurried up the bank, noting the activity up and down the river as she walked. A new steamboat was being built at the shipbuilding yard. A small tugboat was heading upriver toward Pittsburgh with a load of bleating sheep. At the wharf nearest the suspension bridge that spanned the Ohio, a dozen hogs were tearing into sacks of grain. As she watched, the harbormaster came storming out of the dock building and tried to run the hogs away from the cargo, but they were still there when the scene disappeared from Nancy's view. The hogs were a nuisance, but they kept garbage from accumulating on the streets, and when they grew too plentiful, city officials gave permission for residents to slaughter them for meat.

Nancy was all atremble as she approached the Foster home. What if she couldn't do the work to please Mrs. Foster? Pa had always taught her to do the best work possible no matter what she started to do, but the Fosters were bound to want things done in a different way from how she'd been taught. Mrs. Foster appeared to be a kind woman, but Pa had often cautioned her that looks could be deceiving.

When Nancy reached the Foster home, she stopped for a minute before she stepped up on the porch. Panic-stricken, she momentarily considered going back home and forgetting about a new dress. Maybe Pa was right in saying that she shouldn't want to live like people who were richer than the Logans. But a spark of determination ignited a renewed desire in Nancy's heart to better herself. She straightened her shoulders and walked confidently up on the porch, but when her hand shook as she knocked on the door, she knew she wasn't as confident as she wanted to believe she was.

Mrs. Foster must have been watching for her, because the door opened immediately.

"Come in, Nancy," she said with a smile. "Let me take your coat." She hung the coat on a hall tree. "Would you like a cup of tea before you start working?"

"No, thank you, ma'am."

"Then let me take you on a tour of the house." Perhaps sensing that Nancy was nervous, she continued, "I'm sure you and I will get along fine. I don't expect perfection in anyone. Don't worry about making mistakes. We all do that."

The Foster home was not as large as the Danford house, but as they went from room to room, Nancy decided that she liked it better than Stella's home. From the narrow entryway, they moved to a large parlor on the left, and behind it was Dr. Foster's bedroom, which they didn't enter. Across the hall was a commodious kitchen connected to a dining room, which opened into the small sitting room where Nancy had sat the first day she'd come to the house. Three bedrooms were located on the second floor, where Mrs. Foster slept.

"Since my son is often called out at night, we decided it would be more convenient for him to sleep on the ground floor. I'm rarely disturbed at night when he has to go out.

"So you see," Mrs. Foster said, "the house isn't large, and it won't be difficult for you to take care of it. I will clean Heath's bedroom, and it isn't necessary to clean the two spare bedrooms more than twice a month. It will be quite easy for you to dust, sweep, and mop the rest of the rooms during your working hours. I'll do the cooking. I would like to have your help with the laundry and ironing, but I won't overburden you with work. Do you have any questions?"

"Not yet, ma'am, but I'm sure I will."

"Then let's start today by having you clean the sitting room."

The next weeks passed in a daze of happiness for Nancy—she felt as if she entered a new world when she went inside the Foster home. Simplicity and peace marked the atmosphere of the household.

The Fosters had brought the furniture from their Philadelphia home. Furnishings in the parlor had belonged to Dr. Foster's maternal grandmother. Nancy particularly liked the Chippendale, serpentine-back, mahogany sofa with its cabriole legs ending in claw-and-ball feet. Two upholstered chairs with side wings, wooden legs, and hand rests were placed in opposite corners. A cabinet held pieces of glassware. Although wallpaper was not commonly used in Wheeling homes, the parlor wall was papered with historical scenes of the Revolutionary War. But the presence of peace and love exemplified in the home had the most effect on Nancy. She felt as if she was one of the family, rather than a servant.

Nancy sometimes fantasized that Mrs. Foster was her mother, and at times she felt that the older woman treated her like a daughter. A portrait of two young girls hung over the mantel in the sitting room, and Mrs. Foster told Nancy that her daughters, both older than Heath, had died within a week of each other, victims of an epidemic of smallpox that had swept through Philadelphia. She said that although Heath could barely remember his sisters, their deaths had prompted him to become a physician.

Dr. Foster usually took the noon meal with his mother, and Nancy was invited to eat with them. Often, when it was time for her to leave, he was ready to visit patients, and he would ask her to ride with him to the foot of the street or even to her own home if he had a patient to see along the river road.

Nancy's admiration of Dr. Foster increased daily, and although she was afraid to even think of such a thing, she occasionally wondered if he was interested in her, too. At those times, she always chided herself for having a foolish imagination. Why would an educated man like the doctor be interested in a nobody like her? Her mind cautioned her to stop thinking about him as anything more than a man who was kind to everyone, but her heart rebelled and went its willful way. To put such foolishness out of her mind, she sometimes wondered how often Dr. Foster called at the Clark home.

Mrs. Foster worked right along with Nancy, and although at first Nancy made several mistakes, she soon learned how the Fosters wanted their house to look. The most enjoyable part of Nancy's job was when she was asked to dust the bookcases. One day, she counted the books. The Fosters had more than two hundred of them. Having so many books at her fingertips was inconceivable to Nancy. And the Foster books weren't for show as the books in the Clark home had been. There was always an open book on the sitting-room table beside the chair where the doctor sat.

Nancy handled the books lovingly and carefully as if she was in contact with the greatest treasure in the world. Mrs. Foster must have noticed Nancy's interest in the books, for one day, she said, "You're welcome to borrow any of our books you would like."

"Oh, ma'am," Nancy protested, "I might damage them or lose them. Thank you kindly, but I don't think I ought to take any of them home."

"Books aren't any good unless they're read. Borrow one at a time, and if there's anything in the books you don't understand, Heath will be glad to explain the passages to you. He's read all of these books—some more than once. I've never read as much as Heath and my husband. I read magazines more than books."

Nancy first borrowed *Jane Eyre*, and because she loved the novel, when she returned it, she borrowed *The Scarlet Letter*. Since her goal, however, was to improve her mind as well as to be entertained, she sometimes chose Ralph Waldo Emerson's writings. The days passed swiftly for Nancy. Despite the civil unrest in the nation, she had never been so happy—her work was rewarding, and she was also adding to her small hoard of money.

One day when Mrs. Foster had to visit a sick friend, she told Nancy she could go home early. Dr. Foster was waiting for her in front of the house when she finished washing the dishes and putting them in the cupboard. Holding the reins in his left hand, he extended the other one to help Nancy into the buggy.

"I have a call out in the country," he said. "Do you want to ride along with me? I get weary of the city and enjoy getting away from it for a while. I thought you might like a change of scenery, too."

Nancy hesitated. Although the doctor never called her "child" anymore, she hadn't detected that he thought of her in any other way, and this invitation confirmed it. She understood that social customs were more relaxed in the Trans-Allegheny region than in the eastern cities; still, men didn't often ask single women to go places with them without a chaperone. But Pa hadn't made a fuss about her riding along with Dr. Foster in his buggy, and she figured he would have told her if he didn't approve.

"Sure! I'd like that—and Pa won't be expecting me home yet."

"If I could practice my profession by living in the country, I wouldn't live in a town." He pumped the reins, and the horse moved away from the sidewalk. "But a doctor needs patients, and it's necessary to settle in a city, where the population is centered."

By now, she felt comfortable enough in his presence to ask questions.

"Wouldn't there have been more patients in Philadelphia?"

He grinned sideways at her. "Yes, but a lot more doctors, too."

When he reached Main Street, Dr. Foster turned left.

"I'll travel out of town along the National Road."

The National Road had had a great influence on the growth of Wheeling. The road, which ran from Cumberland, Maryland, across the state of Virginia, had reached Wheeling in 1818 and now crossed over the suspension bridge into Ohio. Pa often hauled freight on the *Wetzel* that came in over the road.

Mrs. Clark was sitting on the porch when they passed her home, and it gave Nancy a heightened feeling of satisfaction for the woman who had fired her to see her riding in the doctor's buggy. He touched his hat to Mrs. Clark, but she stared at them without responding. Nancy didn't say anything, but she wondered if Dr. Foster was thinking of the time she'd dropped the food on the sitting room floor. The incident was uppermost in her mind, and she felt a blush spread across her face. She sneaked a sideways glance at him, but he was keeping his eyes straight ahead.

Pedestrians crisscrossed the street without any notice, dogs raced from the alleys to bark at the doctor's horse, and they met a wide variety of vehicles and other riders on the street. He didn't speak again until they left the city behind them.

"But the real reason I left Philadelphia," he said, as if ten minutes hadn't passed since she'd asked the question, "was to find a slower pace so I can do what interests me the most. I'm fascinated by medical research. I want to find new medicines to treat diseases for which there aren't any known cures."

Nancy looked at him with heightened interest and respect. During her few weeks with the Fosters, she'd learned that they were compassionate people. Not only did Dr. Foster treat the sick, but Mrs. Foster spent a lot of her time visiting and helping bedridden adults in her neighborhood. Nancy had glanced through a pamphlet on the bookshelf, which indicated that throughout their history, Quakers had been known for their humanitarian activities of prison reform and the humane treatment of mental patients. She hadn't found anything that showed why her father objected to their religion until she read that the Quakers rejected war.

She turned her attention to Dr. Foster when he said, "I intend to visit residents of the western mountains to learn their folk medicines. That's one reason the current political situation distresses me. Now that Virginia has seceded from the Union, this area may become a battlefield. If so, it won't be safe to travel—even on peaceful pursuits."

"I'm worried about what's happening in our family, too," Nancy admitted. "Pa and Clay can't be together ten minutes before they start arguing about the war. I can't believe how our lives have changed in such a short time. Sometimes I can't sleep at night for fretting about it."

Heath looked at Nancy, conscious of her distress, longing to comfort this girl who was becoming more and more important to him. But he could find no words to reassure her when he was also disturbed over the evidences of war all around them. He drove in silence, thinking about the changes the war had already made in Wheeling.

In an effort to cut off supplies to the seceded states, Ohio had stopped eastward shipments over the B&O Railroad, which had caused a shortage of supplies in the city. A military camp had been set up on the island across from Nancy's home. Union sentiment in Wheeling was predominant, and Heath sensed that the state of Virginia wouldn't ignore such internal rebellion for long. United States flags waved throughout the city, and residents of any home that didn't fly the flag were subject to ridicule and harassment.

Nancy sighed, and her slender fingers twisted together. Her lips trembled, and Heath impulsively shifted the reins to his left hand. He laid his right hand over Nancy's stiff fingers and held them until he felt the lessening of her tension as her fingers relaxed.

They traveled the rest of the way to the farmhouse in silence.

After Dr. Foster secured his horse to a post, he helped Nancy step to the ground. She was perfectly capable of jumping out on her own, but she had come to enjoy the little niceties he showed her. For the most part, Clay and Pa took her work for granted. She had been impressed by Dr. Foster's courtesy toward his mother, and he treated Nancy in the same manner, always voicing his appreciation for what she did for his mother.

The little farm was located on a high knoll overlooking the Ohio River. While he went inside to see his patient, Nancy sat on the front porch and enjoyed the peace of the countryside. She watched a robin fly back and forth from her nest to the ground, where she looked for worms to feed her young. The bright-breasted bird would tilt her head toward the ground, listen, and hop to another location, until she finally found a worm. She then flew upward and disappeared into a clump of cedar trees growing between the barn and the residence.

Hens cackled in a log chicken house. A pig squealed occasionally. A flock of white ducks waddled up from the river, and a goat nibbled on the brambles growing near the garden fence. Enjoying the peace and tranquillity of this scene, Nancy found it hard to believe that war could ever touch their county. She looked southeastward. Although she couldn't see the mountains, she believed that even if war should come, they would serve as a barrier to keep the enemy from invading their territory.

Last night her father had read aloud from the seventy-second Psalm. The third verse—"The mountains shall bring peace to the people, and the little hills, by righteousness"—had suggested to Nancy that the mountains might provide a barrier their enemies couldn't scale. Still looking toward the mountains, she wondered if they *could* provide some protection for the western counties.

Her reflections ceased when a woman accompanied Dr. Foster to the door. "Let me know if your husband doesn't improve, and I'll make another call."

"Just a minute, Doctor," the woman said. She returned to the house and brought out a basket of eggs. "We don't have no money now, but I hope this will pay your bill."

"Thank you very much. I'll return the basket the next time I'm out this way," Heath said as graciously as if she had given him money for his services.

He put the eggs under the buggy seat, and Nancy said, "I'd better hold the basket on my lap. Otherwise, a lot of the eggs might break before we get back to town."

"Thank you—that will be best."

He took her arm and helped her into the buggy, and when she was settled, he handed the basket to her. Nancy waved good-bye to the woman on the porch, then took hold of the basket with both hands. She didn't ask what was wrong with the farmer, for she'd noticed that Dr. Foster never discussed his patients. But she'd also noticed that he often brought produce into the kitchen when he returned from patients who lived in the country.

Mrs. Foster was always pleased with the fresh farm produce, and once she had commented, "My husband owned a clothing factory in Philadelphia, and I'm thankful he left Heath and me reasonably well off. With our extra income, Heath can treat anyone who comes to him whether or not they are able to pay."

As they passed Washington Hall on their entrance into town, Nancy wondered how the decision made there a few weeks ago would change her future. Assuming that the Virginia referendum on secession would pass, delegates from several Virginia counties west of the Allegheny Mountains had met for a few days to discuss possible partition from Virginia. The formation of a separate state to be called New Virginia was becoming a possibility, although some delegates argued that it was unconstitutional for a new state to be formed within the jurisdiction of any other state. The convention had adjourned without taking action on a separate state, but the matter was widely discussed.

And while the counties of western Virginia delayed a decision about statehood, the twenty-third of May—the day set aside by the Virginia legislature for the referendum on the secession ordinance—loomed closer. The general opinion in town was that the majority of Virginia's legislators would favor secession.

"Do you think the western delegates will approve the secession amendment?" Nancy asked.

"Not a chance."

"Then what happens to the counties that are loyal to the Union? Pa says we ought to become a part of Ohio or Pennsylvania. Do you think that could happen?"

"I don't know, Nancy." A few times after she had started to work at the Foster home, Dr. Foster had called her Miss Logan or "child," but lately he'd been calling her by her given name. If he continued that, she wondered if she would dare to address him as Heath.

Instead of continuing toward his home, he turned toward the river. In a thoughtful voice, he said, "It troubles me that the delegates to the referendum convention are talking about statehood."

"How could that happen?"

"I'm not sure. But I'm convinced that Virginia won't lose a third of her counties without a fight. That's why I'm worried. If this situation turns into war, the major battles will no doubt be fought between Washington and Richmond. But the Union will be determined to keep the western Virginia counties loyal to them, and Virginia won't give them up willingly. We'll probably see our share of fighting."

When he slowed the buggy to a halt in front of her house, Nancy asked, "Are you sorry you left Philadelphia to come to Wheeling?"

His dark brown eyes studied Nancy's face for several moments, as if he were seeing her for the first time. A crimson flush spread across his dark skin, and Nancy blinked, feeling light-headed. She looked down and realized that her hands were gripping the rim of the basket until her knuckles were white.

Her mind reeled with confusion, and to relieve the tension building between them, she babbled, "Well, look at this! I'm still holding the basket. You should have stopped at your house with these eggs. I could have walked home."

"Take the eggs as my gift, please. I brought eggs home two days ago, and I know Mother has all she needs."

He stepped from the buggy and took the basket of eggs. Nancy jumped to the ground before he could help her. She couldn't bear the touch of his hands at this moment.

"Thanks for taking me with you today," she stammered. "It was nice to get out of town for a while. And thanks for the eggs. We buy produce from a farmer west of the river, but he hasn't been regular in his deliveries since the governor of Ohio issued orders prohibiting trade with a state that's planning to leave the Union."

"Shall I carry them for you?"

Nancy grabbed the basket from his hand. She wanted to get away from the doctor and think over what had happened today—especially in the past few minutes.

"No, thanks. I'll put them in the cellar before I go upstairs."

She turned and walked away from him, but paused and looked over her shoulder when he said quietly, "Nancy."

She waited breathlessly for him to continue.

"I didn't answer your question. No, I'm not sorry I moved to Wheeling."

Nancy watched as he stepped into the buggy, lifted the reins, and directed the horse away from her home. What was the meaning behind Dr. Foster's words and the slight smile lurking behind his mask of uncertainty? What impact would this moment they had shared have on her future?

Chapter 5

A few weeks later, the doctor came into the house just as Nancy finished her work and was putting on her coat to leave.

"Dr. Foster, do you mind if I take one of your Shakespeare books home with me? Your mother told me to borrow any of the books I wanted, but I notice that you read Shakespeare's works a lot, and I don't want to take anything you might want."

Nancy wondered about the expression that spread across his face. Was it humor, compassion, or adoration she detected in his eyes? Or a combination of all three?

"My dear Nancy," he said, "you can borrow any of the books you want to." She started to thank him, but he held up his hand. "On one condition."

"Oh!" she said, hardly knowing how to respond to his change in manner and the softness of his voice. Her lashes fluttered over her eyes momentarily, but she glanced up again as he continued.

"You can borrow any of the books you want to," he repeated, adding, "that is, if you'll stop addressing me as Dr. Foster and use my Christian name. It's Heath, you know."

Nancy lowered her gaze in confusion, and she felt a blush spread over her face. Her pulse seemed to be spinning out of control. But she sensed a peace and satisfaction she'd never experienced. She would have to wait until she was by herself to assess what had happened to her, but believing that she was on the brink of a closer relationship with Heath, she was determined to take advantage of it.

Her eyes searched his face for a few moments before she said bravely, "Yes, I know that's your name, and I've wanted to say it for weeks, Heath."

An eager look flashed in his eyes, and he stepped closer to her just as the back door slammed. With a feeling of frustration, Nancy knew that Mrs. Foster had returned from her errand.

When Mrs. Foster entered the room, Nancy was lifting a book from the shelves, and Heath was putting on his coat. "Mother, I'm going to walk downtown with Nancy to get a copy of the *Intelligencer*. I'll be back soon if anyone needs me."

Nancy said good-bye to Mrs. Foster without looking at her. When they stepped off the porch, she didn't know what she should say after that emotional scene between them, and perhaps Heath was also jolted out of his normal calmness, for they walked in silence to the newspaper office.

—∿∿—

The situation in Wheeling had been tense since an overwhelming majority of local votes were cast against the secession ordinance, and Heath waited anxiously for each issue of the newspaper. Only eighty-seven citizens had voted for secession, which caused local residents to eye one another with suspicion.

"Have any more Confederate sympathizers had trouble?" Nancy asked when they stopped in front of the newspaper office.

Heath shook his head. "There have been many demonstrations in front of the homes of secessionists, but since Mr. Campbell denounced those activities as mob rule in his newspaper, there hasn't been any more overt harassment."

"I'm upset about my friend Stella. Their house has been pelted with mud, rotten eggs, and vegetables, so Mr. Danford is afraid for Stella and his wife. He has closed his clothing factory, and they're leaving tomorrow with Pa on the *Wetzel*. Their home is in Alabama."

Heath's eyes registered concern. "I'd heard they were leaving, and I'm concerned for them, too. That's a long trip, and they'll be traveling through hostile country part of the way."

Nodding, Nancy said, "Yes, but he's willing to risk that rather than to stay here and endure insults or danger to his family."

"I can understand his reasoning."

The war was never discussed within the Foster household, and Nancy voiced a question that had worried her for days.

"Are you going to join one of the militia groups?"

Heath gazed at her, surprise on his face. "Why no! Quakers believe in nonviolence. I've dedicated my life to saving life—not killing people on the battlefield. I won't fight on either side. I assumed you knew that."

In a meek, quiet voice, she said, "I'm sorry. I had read that in a pamphlet at your house, but I'd forgotten. Excuse me for asking."

"You're welcome to ask me anything, Nancy—you should know that by now."

Momentarily, she has happy knowing that Heath wouldn't be going off to fight, but unease gnawed at her satisfaction. The majority of local citizens were living in euphoria because of the new state movement, so how would they react to a man who wouldn't fight on either side? Although he knew it meant war, her father had embraced the idea of a new, pro-Union state with patriotic fervor. She didn't think he would allow her to work for the Fosters if Heath made it public that he wouldn't fight to defend the Union.

Heath put his fingers under Nancy's chin and lifted her face.

"Look at me," Heath demanded.

She lifted her gaze to study his face. His dark eyes narrowed speculatively, searching her face as if he was trying to reach into her mind.

"Do you think I'm a coward—afraid to fight?"

She hesitated momentarily. She didn't think he was a coward, but she couldn't bear for other people to say that he was.

"No, I don't believe that for a minute."

He squeezed her chin gently and released her.

"Violence never solves anything," he said as they leaned against the building that housed the newspaper's offices. "Don't you remember what Jesus said when one of His disciples tried to defend Him with the sword? 'Put up again thy sword into his place: for all they that take the sword shall perish with the sword.'"

Nancy sensed the struggle Heath was having with his conscience, and she put her hand on his arm, hoping that her action would convey to him that whatever decision he made would seem right to her.

"My soul is burdened when I think of all the bloodshed that may occur before this war ends," Heath continued, and Nancy listened with rising dismay. "It's my opinion that thousands of men will be killed, maimed, and ruined during this conflict. I read a prediction this week that it might take four or five years before the Union can win the war. Four or five years! A generation of men could be wiped out. I find it hard to believe that people are rejoicing—rejoicing, mind you—that we are going to war. Why can't they understand what war will do to this nation?"

Several newsboys raced from the newspaper headquarters with the latest issue of the *Intelligencer*, and Heath bought a paper.

"I want one, too," Nancy called to a newsboy. To Heath she explained, "Pa gave me the money. He reads every word of it."

She tucked the newspaper under her arm. "I have to go home now. Pa is heading downriver in the morning, and he'll want to read the paper before he leaves."

"How long is he gone on these jaunts?"

"He goes as far as Parkersburg, and his return depends on how much freight he hauls, the number of passengers, and the depth and current of the water. He can make the trip in three days, but sometimes it's longer than that."

"And your brother works at night? You stay alone?"

"I always have," Nancy said, shrugging her shoulders. "I'm not afraid."

She turned away from Heath, called good-bye, and started home. She would have to hurry to have the meal on the table.

<hr/>

After supper, Pa returned to the *Wetzel* for last-minute preparations, leaving Clay and Nancy together at the table. He fiddled with his coffee cup, and Nancy, knowing her brother well, waited. He had something on his mind, and like his father, he wouldn't speak until he was ready. Habitually, Nancy spoke up when she had something to say, a trait she had apparently inherited from her mother. She took the last piece of corn bread and spread it with butter. She ate slowly, dreading to hear what Clay had to say.

Through the open windows, she monitored the everyday sounds around their home. On the evening air, a bugle call wafted from the military camp on the island. A towboat passed downriver, and the captain greeted the crew of the *Wetzel* with three loud blasts of the whistle. A wren perched in a nearby maple tree, and its rich, whistled notes, which sounded alternately like *sweetheart, sweetheart* or *teakettle, teakettle*, invaded the quiet room. These ordinary happenings should have heralded that all was right in their community, but Nancy knew better. Watching the play of emotions on her brother's face, she felt a wretchedness of mind she had never experienced before.

"Sis," he said at last, "sometimes a man has to follow his conscience, no matter how much it hurts other people." He took a deep breath. "I'm leaving tonight. My friend Alex is going with me. We're aimin' to join the Confederate Army."

A soft gasp escaped Nancy's lips, and her body stiffened in shock. Although she had known that such an action was a possibility, when she heard the stark, bald truth from Clay's lips, the horrible results of a civil war hit home.

Brother against brother! Father against son!

Clay bolted out of his chair, knelt beside her, and put his arm around her shaking shoulders.

"I'm sorry, Nancy, but I couldn't think of an easy way to tell you."

"What's Pa going to say?"

"Nuthin' I want to hear. That's why I'm leaving without tellin' him." He pulled an envelope from his pocket. "If I tell him to his face, we'll both say things better left unsaid. But I'm not leavin' it up to you to tell him. I've spent most of the day writin' a letter to him. Don't give it to him until mornin'. By that time, I'll be a long way off."

"But your job?"

"I quit yesterday."

Tears blinded Nancy's eyes and choked her voice, but she gulped, "Clay, please don't go. What are we going to do after you're gone?"

"I have to go. I'm an able-bodied young man. We're at war, and I'll have to fight on one side or the other. If I don't fight, people will call me a coward. I have to choose sides, and I believe the South is right. I don't hold with slavery, but every state ought to have the right to do as it wants to do. If the North makes the rebel states stay in the Union, that's just another kind of slavery. A man has to do what he has to do."

Nancy sat as if turned to stone while Clay went into the bedroom and returned with a bulging haversack. "I raided your bread box and cellar and took enough food to last us several days. We've heard that there's a Confederate Army as close as Barbour County, and we're headin' in that direction."

Clay continued to talk of his plans, but Nancy's mind was so numbed that she missed most of what he said. She only knew that he was leaving to fight with the enemy, but it was difficult to think of people in eastern Virginia or the Carolinas as enemies.

Dear God, what is going to happen to us? How will Pa react to his son's treason? And what about Heath? Will people think he's a coward? Will he be harassed?

Clay stopped beside Nancy, and she stood to put her arms around his waist. Tears glistened in his eyes, and she knew this hadn't been an easy decision for him.

"God bless you, brother. I'll pray for you every day."

As his steps receded into the distance, Nancy wondered if she would ever see him again. Her father wouldn't take his son's treason lightly. If Clay survived the war, she doubted he would be welcomed home.

Taking the sealed envelope with her, Nancy went into her bedroom and closed the door. As upset as she was, if she encountered her father tonight, he'd be sure to notice that something was wrong. She pulled a chair close to the window and wrapped a blanket around her shoulders. The wind off the river was cool, but Nancy's nerves were atwitter, which, rather than the cold air, probably accounted for the trembling of her body.

When she heard her father come into the house and go into his room, she undressed and got into bed, savoring the comfort of the feather tick as it closed around her. She dozed intermittently during the night, but at first light, she got up and made breakfast preparations. A sense of desolation swept over Nancy as she laid only two table settings. She kept Clay's letter in her pocket. She wouldn't give it to her father until he'd finished his breakfast.

She cooked a pot of oatmeal and raisins and had a large bowl of it by Pa's plate when he came into the kitchen. He greeted her briefly as he always did. He took no notice of Clay's vacant chair, for Clay didn't always come straight home after he left the bank. When he finished eating, Nancy refilled his coffee cup and laid the letter beside his plate.

She felt his questioning eyes on her, but she refused to meet his gaze. She crossed the room and stared out the window with unseeing eyes. She couldn't watch her father's expression when he read the news that would break his heart. Despite their differences, she had never doubted that a strong sense of respect and affection existed between father and son. The heavy silence in the room seemed as loud as a clap of thunder. Nancy realized that she was clenching her hands and her nails were cutting into her flesh. She relaxed her fingers.

After clearing his throat, Pa said huskily, "Have you read this?"

She turned toward him and shook her head.

"Then read it and burn it. He's a traitor to his country, but I won't turn him in."

"He's only doing what he thinks is right."

Her father lifted himself wearily from the chair, and he looked as if he had aged ten years. "I know, but he's brought shame upon the family. Don't mention his name to me again."

"But Pa. . ."

"I no longer have a son—you don't have a brother. With the strong Union feelings in this town, he couldn't come home if I wanted him to. Forget him."

He went into the bedroom and closed the door.

She snatched up the letter and read the brief message:

> *Dear Pa,*
>   *I don't want you to hate me, but I can't set around and watch the country go to the dogs without tryin' to help. I know you will think I joined the wrong army, but I have to do what's right for me. Please pray for me and try to forgive.*
>
>

Your lovin' son,
Clay

Tears nearly blinded Nancy, but she read the message again before she lifted the stove lid and dropped the letter on the hot coals. As she watched it burn, she said good-bye to her beloved brother. Automatically, she cleared the table and washed the dishes. She was hanging the dishcloth and towels behind the stove to dry when the bedroom door opened and her father leaned against the jamb. Whether he was enraged or mournful about Clay's decision, her father seemed to have conquered his emotions.

"I don't know what to do about you," he said. "You can't stay here alone while I'm away on the *Wetzel.*"

"But Clay was hardly ever home at night! Nothing has changed."

Pa shook his head. "Everything has changed. There's an army camp on the island. Mobs are threatenin' people all over the county. When word gets around that Clay has joined the Confederates, we might have trouble. And I hear a Union army is coming here from Ohio. I can't leave you alone."

"I could stay with one of the neighbors at night."

He continued as if she hadn't spoken. "The trouble is, I don't have much room on the *Wetzel* this time, or I'd take you with me. The Danfords are takin' a lot of boxes and suitcases with them."

"I want to see them off. I told Mrs. Foster I wouldn't come to work until the boat left."

"Do you suppose she'd let you stay with her at night while I'm gone?"

Surprised that her father had made this suggestion when he hadn't wanted her to work for the Fosters, Nancy said slowly, "She probably would. She's good to me, and I like her. They have two spare bedrooms."

"I don't have time to get somebody to stay with you this time, but I'll delay leavin' until I get you settled. I'll tell the crew that we may be a little late but to have everything ready when I get back."

Nancy had to trot a few times to keep up with her long-legged father as they walked to the Foster home. Nancy always opened the door and went in, but when they arrived at the house, Pa strode up the steps and knocked. Heath came to the door. He glanced from father to daughter quickly before he said, "Come in."

"No," Pa said. "I ain't got time for that. My son is away from home, and I'm ready to leave on my weekly trip to Parkersburg. I don't want to leave Nancy alone while I'm gone. I wonder if your mother would let her stay here. I'll come up with some other plans before my next trip."

"Why, I'm sure that will be all right. Just a minute." He turned and called, "Mother, will you come here, please?"

Mrs. Foster soon appeared at the door. Nancy watched her father size her up one side and down the other. Seemingly satisfied, he repeated what he had said to Heath.

"I'd love to have Nancy's company," Mrs. Foster said, and no one could doubt her sincerity. "She can stay here as often and as long as she wants to anytime. You won't have to make other arrangements."

"Just the nights I'm out on the boat. I'll pay."

"But that isn't necessary—"

Pa raised a hand to interrupt her. "If I don't pay, she don't stay."

Mrs. Foster smiled. "I'm sure we can agree on a reasonable rate for her keep." She turned to Nancy, "Are you staying now?"

"No, ma'am. I want to go back and say good-bye to Stella. She's leaving on Pa's boat. I'll be back after that."

"Bring what you need for a few nights. We'll be glad to have you."

Nancy had a feeling that Heath was watching her, and she slid a glance in his direction. She thought she detected approval in his eyes. She wondered briefly how it would seem to be a part of the Foster household.

Her father shook hands with the Fosters and shepherded Nancy off the porch. She looked back over her shoulder and waved to them.

An hour later, she stood on the dock waving good-bye to Stella and the rest of the Danfords as the *Wetzel* slipped away from the dock and accessed the deep channel of the river. To lose her best friend and her brother in such a short time was heart wrenching. She was thankful she wouldn't have to stay alone in the house for the next two nights.

By the time she was ready to leave for the Fosters, it was noon, so Nancy put jam on a biscuit and ate as she hurried uptown. She was heartbroken over the loss of Clay and Stella, but her heart rejoiced that, for a short time, she would be a part of Heath's family life.

Chapter 6

Heath had occasionally joined Nancy and his mother for the noon meal, which they ate in the kitchen, but she had known that the Fosters ate their evening meal in the dining room. Since she was a paid servant, Nancy wondered if she would be invited to share the evening meal with them or if she would still sit in the kitchen.

Mrs. Foster assigned Nancy the task of cleaning the three upstairs bedrooms. The room Nancy was to regard as her own, according to Mrs. Foster, was a small dormer room. The furniture was made of rosewood and had deeply cut, spiral-turned legs. The dresser had a white marble top. The high-backed bed and dresser filled up most of the floor space. Nancy had always admired the patchwork quilt made with patterned silk fabrics, one that Mrs. Foster had made when she was a girl.

Nancy had learned that the Fosters always "dressed" for their evening meal, and just in case she was asked to join them, she had brought her church clothes—a white linen dress with a short dark blue jacket—that Clay had bought for her last birthday. She hung her garments on the clothes tree and tried to smooth out the wrinkles with her fingers.

When she went downstairs after cleaning the bedrooms to her satisfaction, Nancy walked through the dining room on her way to the kitchen. Three place settings had been laid at the table. She smiled, and her heart lifted. Her dismay at Clay's leaving lessened a degree.

Nancy was acutely aware of the differences in her family background and Heath's when she sat at the dining-room table and compared it to her own home. The table was covered with a linen cloth, several pieces of silverware surrounded the china plate before her, and a sparkling crystal glass was filled with water. Lighted candelabra shed a rosy glow over the table.

Heath sat at the head of the table and prayed before he served the food. Nancy was given the first portions as if she was an honored guest instead of a servant. He laid a thick slice of roast pork on her plate. "Would you like a larger serving of meat?"

"No, thank you."

"Please ask for seconds if you want more," he said as he put a dollop of potatoes on her plate and covered them with a thin layer of creamy gravy. He spooned a portion of his mother's pepper relish beside a slice of wheat bread that Mrs. Foster had baked in the afternoon. He passed the plate to Nancy and turned to his mother.

"How large a portion dost thou want?"

"The same size portion as thou gave Nancy will be fine, but not quite as many potatoes, please."

Throughout the meal, Nancy noticed, as she had before, that when Heath or Mrs. Foster spoke to her, they used the pronoun *you*. It was only when they addressed each other that they used the words *thee* and *thou*.

While Nancy washed the dishes that Mrs. Foster then dried and put in the cupboard, she said, "I've often wondered why you and Dr. Foster don't use *you* when you're talking to each other."

Mrs. Foster laughed softly. "The words *thee* and *thou* were used in earlier times. You will have noticed these words in the Bible."

"Yes, I remember that the Bible has those words, like when Jesus said, 'Thou shalt love thy neighbour as thyself.'"

"Some Quakers use the old pronouns when they're talking to other members of their faith or when they're speaking to members of their immediate family. They're also used as a term of endearment by sweethearts or between man and wife."

"I suppose I ask too many questions."

"And how else would you learn new things if you didn't have an inquiring mind! You may ask me anything you like."

Mrs. Foster took off her apron. "It's too early to go to bed, so you may join Heath in the sitting room." She picked up a plate she had filled with food and wrapped in a warm cloth. "I'm going to take supper to my neighbor down the street. I'll be back soon."

Nancy went down the hall and timorously entered the sitting room. Heath sat in a chair close to a light, reading, and she wondered if he would resent her presence. He looked up and smiled.

"Come in and find a comfortable place to sit. Mother says you like to read, so choose any book you like from the shelf."

Nancy took *Uncle Tom's Cabin* from the bookcase. She had noticed the book several times when she was dusting. She wanted to read it because an article in the *Intelligencer* had referred to the book as a cause of the war. She bypassed the chair where Mrs. Foster sat when she was reading or sewing and sat on the couch opposite Heath. He stood up and brought a lamp from the mantel and placed it where the light would fall on the open pages of her book.

He started to return to his chair but stopped when a knock sounded at the front door. Nancy thought he was probably being summoned on a sick call, and she was disappointed because she had looked forward to spending the evening with him.

Heath opened the door. "Good evening, Richard," he said. "How nice of you to stop by. Come in. Mother will be back soon."

A robust man past middle age entered the room, and Heath said, "Richard, this is Nancy Logan, who's staying with us a few days while her father and brother are away. Nancy, this is our neighbor Richard Donovan."

The visitor gave Nancy a brief smile while Heath pulled a rocking chair into the circle of light and invited him to be seated. "May I take your hat?"

Mr. Donovan shook his head, seated himself, and twisted his hat around and around in his hands. Heath took the book he'd been reading out of his chair, laid it aside, and sat down.

"What can I do for you?"

The visitor swallowed a few times. "This isn't an easy errand for me, Heath. But my mind is troubled, for we've been friends since you moved to Wheeling. I need to ask you some questions. I've denied some things I've heard about you over the past few days, and I want to set my mind at ease." Mr. Donovan looked at Nancy. "It might be better if we were alone."

The tension in the room was overpowering, and half rising off the davenport, Nancy murmured, "I'll go upstairs."

"Not unless you want to," Heath said.

She knew instinctively that Mr. Donovan wasn't the bearer of good news, and she didn't want Heath to hear it alone. She eased back on the couch and laid her book aside.

Donovan squirmed in his chair, but he took a quick breath and looked directly at Heath. "I've heard that you've been asked more than once to join one of the military companies forming in town and that you've refused."

"That's true," Heath answered without further explanation, and his mouth spread into a thin-lipped smile.

"I can't believe it!" Donovan said. "Does this mean you're a secessionist? Are you going to fight with the Confederates?"

Nancy had considered Heath one of the calmest men she'd ever known, but she saw a muscle contract in his jaw and sudden anger light his eyes. His voice was strained when he spoke. "We *have* been friends for a long time, and I pray that we can continue that friendship. Therefore, I'll answer your question. I'm a loyal Union man. I do not like slavery, nor do I respect the hotheads who have pulled this country into war. I have already signed the oath of allegiance to the United States of America. But. . ."

He paused, and his words were slow and distinct when he continued. "I will not join a militia. I will not go into the army. In an extreme case, I would consider violence. If someone should break into this house tonight and threaten Mother or Nancy, I would meet violence with violence. But I've dedicated my life to healing, not killing, and I will not enlist in the army. Before this conflict is over, doctors are going to be needed as much as soldiers. The people of Wheeling may be glad to have a resident doctor."

Donovan stood. "I guess I've heard what I came to find out. I suppose you have to live with your conscience, and I won't let your decision come between us as friends. But I think I should warn you that you and your mother may be in danger. Please be careful."

Heath closed the door behind his visitor and returned to his chair with dragging steps. He sat down and lowered his head into his hands. Nancy sat as if she'd been turned to stone. She longed to comfort him, but what could she do? What could she say?

After several minutes, she knelt beside Heath's chair, but she didn't touch him.

"I'm sorry," she whispered.

He looked up as if he'd forgotten she was in the room.

"Let's not mention this visit to my mother, please. She will hear soon enough. I've been getting the cold shoulder from several men the past few days, so I knew what to expect." He smiled wistfully in her direction. "Do you think any less of me than you did a few hours ago?"

She briefly touched his hand that lay on the arm of the chair and shook her head violently. "No, this hasn't changed my opinion of you at all. A man has to do what he has to do. My brother said that to me last night about this time."

His eyes questioned her.

"I guess it's time to tell you why Pa wished my company on you. My brother left last night to volunteer in the Confederate Army. Pa's afraid to leave me alone while he makes his run to Parkersburg and back. He figured I'd be safer with your mother."

"I'm not sure you're any safer here, but you heard what I said. I'll protect Mother and you with my life, if necessary, but I can't willingly take a man's life. I hope you understand."

The back door opened, and Nancy knew Mrs. Foster had returned. She jumped up from the floor and hurried to the couch.

"No matter what decision you make, I know it's the right one," she whispered. His glowing eyes thanked her.

Chapter 7

The next few weeks were like a nightmare to Nancy. She couldn't believe that her life had changed so drastically in such a short time. Vigilantes roamed through the northern panhandle of the state, carrying United States flags, threatening death to all who refused to salute the banner. In Wheeling, the lines between secessionists and pro-Union adherents had been finely drawn. The news spread quickly that Clay Logan had joined the Confederates, and in spite of the fact that her father flew the national flag on the *Wetzel* and from the roof of their home, one night a group of masked men surrounded the Logan house, shouting invectives and calling for death to all traitors. Pa didn't go to bed all night. He stood at the door, his rifle ready to shoot the first man who put a foot on the steps to their living quarters. Nancy went to bed, but she didn't sleep.

The attackers withdrew a few hours before daybreak. When Nancy went to the kitchen, her father had already stoked the fire and had a pot of coffee perking. He sat at the table, his head in his hands.

"Did you sleep at all, Pa?"

He lifted bloodshot, worried eyes and shook his head.

"What are we going to do?"

"Not much we can do but wait it out and pray that these hoodlums get tired of their meanness. They're a bunch of no-gooders who've found an excuse to cause trouble. We'd be better off in the hands of the Confederates, at least as long as they're headed by General Lee. He won't put up with such carrying-on."

He stood and stretched as if his muscles had locked during the stressful night he'd spent protecting his home and his daughter.

"I'll fix your breakfast right away."

"I've tried to find some woman who would come in and stay with you when I take the boat out, but I can't find anyone. We'll have to impose on the Fosters awhile longer."

"Mrs. Foster doesn't mind, Pa—really she doesn't. She's good to me—treats me like family."

"Fact is," Pa said as he poured hot water into a tin wash pan, stood in front of a mirror on the wall, and started shaving, "I'm not sure you're any safer there than you are at home. If Doc Foster won't sign a paper refusing to give aid to

Confederate sympathizers, he's bound to be bullied, too."

"I heard him tell his mother that he took an oath to never turn away anyone who needed help, and he intends to doctor anyone who comes to him and not question that person's political beliefs. He's also being ridiculed because he won't join the local militias."

"And I hold that agin' him," her father said, his eyes hard as agates. "Time comes when a man has to fight!"

"From what I've overheard, he would fight to protect his mother and others who are weak, but he won't go to war."

Her father shook his head. "I don't expect you to soak up any of their heathen doctrine. Even our Lord oncet took up the whip and drove the money changers out of the temple."

Nancy didn't argue any more—her father had enough on his mind now without adding a rebellious daughter to his problems.

"I'm gonna walk with you to the Fosters' this morning, and I aim to stop by Widow Clark's and get that money she owes you. You're goin' with me."

Although she dreaded facing Tabitha Clark, when her father used that tone, Nancy knew it was useless to argue with him.

As they hurried along the streets to the Clark home, Nancy wondered if her father had heard the rumors that Mrs. Clark had been spreading. Last Sunday at church, one of the women had pulled Nancy aside and whispered, "I don't like to spread gossip, but I thought I ought to tell you what Mrs. Clark is tattlin' around town. She's sayin' that you've been stayin' with the Fosters because you want to be near the doctor. And she's also tellin' what a poor worker you are, and that Mrs. Foster's only keepin' you on because she feels sorry for you."

That information had alarmed Nancy so much that she had nearly passed out, wondering what her father would do if he heard the tittle-tattle, too. But why, when he'd let weeks pass and hadn't confronted Tabitha Clark, had Pa taken a sudden notion to see the woman? Nancy's steps lagged behind her father's. If Mrs. Foster learned what was being said, would she lose her job? With a sense of dread, she figured she would soon have an answer to all of her questions.

Nancy stood half hidden behind her father when he pounded on the front door of the Clark home. Nancy wondered who would answer their knock. Had Mrs. Clark replaced her?

Tommy opened the door. "Hi, Nancy," he said, and she smiled at him. She'd always gotten along fine with Tommy.

"I want to talk to your mother," Pa said.

Tommy ran toward the rear of the house, and Mrs. Clark soon strolled down the hallway. Pa stepped aside so that Nancy was no longer hidden. Mrs. Clark stopped suddenly, and a cold expression settled on her face.

"What are you doing here?" she said. "I told you not to come into this house again."

"She's not comin' in the house, but I will if you don't give me the four dollars she earned workin' for you, which you didn't pay, *and* the bag she left behind when you kicked her out."

"As clumsy as she was, she cost me more than four dollars by breaking some of my china."

"Get the money," Pa demanded and stepped inside the hallway.

Mrs. Clark turned on her heel, and with her back as rigid as a post, she walked toward the kitchen. Tommy crawled up on the stairs and looked as if he was going to cry. In a few minutes, Mrs. Clark returned. She threw Nancy's reticule and four gold dollars on the floor at Pa's feet. "Now get out of my house."

"I'm not finished yet. Count the money in your bag, Nancy, and be sure it's all there." When Nancy knelt to get the money and her reticule, he turned steely dark eyes on Mrs. Clark. "I've been hearin' some lies you've been spreadin' about my girl, and I'm warnin' you if they don't stop, I'll be standin' on your porch again."

"Don't you dare threaten me," she shouted.

"Stop the tale bearing!" Pa said and turned his back on her.

"Don't come here again, or I'll have you arrested," Mrs. Clark shouted, then slammed the door shut.

Ignoring her, Pa asked Nancy, "Do you have all your money?"

"As well as I can remember." Nancy dropped the gold coins into her bag. "Let's get away from here."

As they walked down the street, she said, "I've got enough to buy the dress I want. Is it all right to go ahead and buy it now?"

"As far as I'm concerned. You earned the money. It's yours to spend."

Over the next few weeks, the war drew closer to home for Nancy. Enlistment offices were opened in the city. Companies were organized, and she often saw militia drilling in open fields on the island, where a rope corral held hundreds of horses that had been bought for the use of the army.

She continued to stay with the Fosters while Pa was gone, until the loyal forces commandeered the *Wetzel* to haul supplies to the troops quartered at the camp on the island. This placed a financial burden on her father, for although he received a voucher to pay for use of the boat, the banks wouldn't honor the funds because of their lack of money.

Patriotic fervor that had prevailed after local political leaders began a new state movement declined considerably when General Lee moved troops into the counties west of the mountains with the goal of keeping them loyal to the state of Virginia. With the army camp on Wheeling Island, those living near the Ohio River should have felt safe, but Nancy's father hinted at things going on in the army camp he didn't like. She was forbidden to cross to the island. But to add to the security of the western counties, Union troops from Ohio commanded by General McClellan crossed the river and set up camp downriver near Parkersburg.

Near the end of May, Colonel Kelley's regiment in the camp was ordered to leave the city and move east to stop an invasion by Confederate troops. Nancy and her father joined other local residents at the train depot to give the soldiers a joyous send-off. Nancy tried to be cheerful to encourage the soldiers, but she was really downhearted.

"Why such a long face?" her father asked as they turned toward home after the train had departed.

Nancy sensed that the Fosters' nonresistance attitude had influenced her, but she didn't dare admit that to her father.

"The soldiers seemed happy now and confident, as if the country is safe in their hands. But Pa, most of them are just boys. They don't seem to realize that war is more than glory. It's wounds, sickness, death, and hardship. Will they be so happy when they come home again?"

"No. And they won't be boys, either. War soon turns a boy into a man! What worries me is that the Confederates are targeting the B&O now, and the trains can't get through to Baltimore. These boys could be killed before they ever see a battlefield."

"The war is getting closer to us all of the time," Heath told Nancy the next day at noon. "And very few troops remain in the area. The general feeling is that Lee's campaign to take control of the renegade counties and stop the mass meetings and conventions being held to protest secession may be successful."

Looking around to be sure Mrs. Foster wasn't nearby, she asked, "Do you suppose Clay might be with him? Wouldn't it be terrible if the Confederates invade Wheeling and he fights against people he's known all of his life?"

"Yes, it would be terrible, but I've been praying that it won't come to that. Lee's full army may not be coming this way, but he has ordered a small regiment under command of Colonel Porterfield to advance on Wheeling and put a stop to the protests against secession."

"What will we do if this happens?"

"I've been wondering about that. I know a few people across the Ohio, and I think they would take Mother and you in."

Nancy didn't comment, but she wouldn't flee to safety and leave Pa and Heath behind in the danger zone. As the weeks had passed, Nancy had noticed that her thoughts were changing. She didn't think like a girl anymore. A few months ago, she would have been ready to run from the enemy at the first sign of danger. Now she felt like a full-grown woman ready to fight alongside her men.

But less than a week after Kelley's troops left town, his troops met the Confederates commanded by Porterfield in the first land battle of the war near the little town of Philippi. Two days after the battle, Heath made an early morning call to a home near the federal building, heard about the Union success, and hurried home with the news.

"Oh my," Nancy said when she heard the news. "I wonder if Clay was in the fighting."

"Even if he was, you're not to worry. The report is that there were no deaths and only a few wounded. Colonel Kelley was shot through the chest, but he's expected to recover."

"I didn't dream the war would come this close to us."

"Remember, we're involved in a little civil war in the midst of the big conflict. The northern states are determined to bring the South back into the Union. And Virginia is going to fight rather than allow the western counties to join the Federalist cause. Unfortunately, I believe that it will get worse before we see an end to this conflict."

The next afternoon when Nancy left the Foster home, Heath went with her as far as the *Intelligencer* office to pick up a copy of the paper. The usual crowd was gathered around the newspaper building, waiting for the papers to be released. Because her father was always interested in the war news, Nancy tarried to buy a copy of the paper, too. When the newsboys bounded into the streets, the crowd surged forward.

"I'll get a copy for you," Heath said.

Nancy was watching his straight shoulders when she sensed that a man crowded close to her and pushed a piece of paper into her hand. Startled, she turned toward him, but his hat was pulled low over his forehead. She didn't get a look at his face before he disappeared into the crowd. She looked quickly at the scrap of paper and slipped it into her pocket. She started trembling, and her face must have revealed her tension, for when Heath came back with two copies of the paper, he asked, "What is it? Are you ill?"

Nancy shook her head, but Heath took her arm. "I'll walk a little farther with you." He directed her toward the riverfront, and they sat on an empty bench facing the water.

"Can you tell me what happened?"

The strength of his shoulder as it pressed against hers relieved Nancy's tension to a degree. She took the slip of paper from her pocket and told him how she had received it.

"Have you read it?"

She shook her head. "No. I don't think the messenger wanted anyone to know he'd given it to me. And he apparently didn't want to be recognized."

"If you want to keep it a secret, I'll leave you. I just wanted to know what had alarmed you." He stood, and she tugged on his coattail.

"Please stay. I don't want to read it alone."

He sat again. It was a small sheet of paper. There was no address on the outside. Nancy unfolded the paper and scanned it quickly. There wasn't a salutation or signature, but she recognized her brother's writing.

"Clay," she said.

"I sensed as much."

"But how did it get here?"

"I understand that messages pass back and forth between the secessionists and their exiled families. Women are often the messengers."

"A man brought this paper."

"Or a woman dressed in men's clothing. What does he say?"

Glancing around to be sure they were alone, Nancy said, "I'll read it to you:

"We got as far as Harper's Ferry. I've joined the Confederates and was with Colonel Jackson there. Now I'm takin' orders from Colonel Porterfield, and we're guardin' the trains around Grafton. General Lee has got to keep control of the railroads. Ain't seen much action."

Voicing the idea that had been in her mind since her brother had left home, she said, "Clay might have fought some of the boys he's known all of his life at Philippi!"

"That's why we call it civil war, my dear. You'd better burn the letter to keep it from falling into the wrong hands."

She nodded. "I'll burn it as soon as I get home. I don't know if I feel better or worse. I've wanted to hear from Clay, but now that I know where he is, I'll be worried about him." She stood. "Thanks for being with me when I read this. I'd like to tell Pa about Clay, but he told me to never mention his name again."

Heath watched her as she slowly walked away with her head down. His soul rebelled at the prospect of war in the same world as Nancy Logan, who had become very important to him. And there were times when he sensed that she considered him as more than a friend and mentor. His mother had often thrown out hints that she would welcome grandchildren, but Heath had never intended to marry. His profession consumed so much of his time that he hadn't felt it was wise to encumber himself with a family. But when had he started wondering if marriage to Nancy would be an encumbrance?

Why had she snagged his interest more than the numerous other women he'd met? Her beauty was more captivating than the average woman's, yet it wasn't physical traits that drew him to her. Rather, he admired her capacity to love more than any woman he knew except his mother. Nancy loved her father and brother without qualification, and he was sure this same type of love would be showered upon her husband and children. She had unlocked his heart and soul, and he shared thoughts and concerns with her that he wouldn't have told anyone else. Perhaps more than anything else that made him realize that she was the only woman in the world for him were those few times when Nancy's gaze had mysteriously met his and his heart had turned over in response. Heath wasn't ready to admit that he loved her, but he sensed that a few more weeks of her company would prove that he was.

———

As soon as Nancy reached home, she read Clay's message one more time and dropped the paper on the hot coals of the kitchen stove. She mixed enough crust for a rhubarb pie and prepared it for baking. Pa liked warm pie with thick cream on it, and the cream had just been delivered this morning, so it would be fresh. She scrubbed small red potatoes and cooked them with fresh peas and fried a young rooster she'd bought at the market. While she had the oven hot to bake the pie, she stirred up a pan of corn bread and shoved it in the oven.

Her father didn't often compliment Nancy on the food, but after he finished eating, he said, "You're a good cook, girl. More 'n' more, you remind me of your ma. She was a good woman, and you will be, too."

Nancy blushed and stammered, "Thanks, Pa."

While Nancy washed the dishes, her father sat at the table, picked his teeth, and read the newspaper. When she heard him lay aside the paper, Nancy's hands hovered over the water. Without turning, she said, "Clay is all right. He's in Grafton under command of Colonel Porterfield."

Nancy held her breath, wondering how her father would react. He seldom lost his temper with her, but perhaps she'd pushed him too far this time. After all, he'd told her never to mention Clay's name again. Silence filled the room, and the clock ticked off the minutes. When he didn't speak, Nancy continued washing the dishes and drying them. Ten minutes or more must have passed before she poured the dishwater down the drain and hung up the dish towel.

"How did you find out?" Pa asked, and Nancy drew a deep breath.

"You're better off not to know."

He got up from the table. "Thanks," he said quietly, then walked to the door and went downstairs.

Nancy buried her face in her hands, and hot tears rolled down her cheeks.

"Thank You, God," she whispered. "He hasn't cast his son aside. He still loves him. But God, have mercy on us."

Chapter 8

Nancy counted her money again and with resolve walked into a store on Main Street. How she wished Stella were here to advise her! Most of the dresses were made to order, but the proprietor always had a few gowns made ahead. Nancy hoped she had enough money to buy what she wanted. Today was the first of July, and there was no time to have a dress made especially for her.

Now that the country was at war and she had seen firsthand how much it cost to wage war, Nancy wondered if she wasn't being selfish to spend her money on clothes. But a big Independence Day celebration was planned on the island, and since she had worked so hard and saved to have a new dress, she decided she might as well go ahead and buy one.

Clutching her reticule tightly, Nancy approached Pearl Martin, the saleswoman. She would choose the dress first and see how much money she had left for accessories.

"I want to buy a readymade dress."

Pearl measured Nancy's height, around her waist, across her shoulders. "We only have two that will fit you," she said apologetically. "Our supply is very low. I used to order my material from Richmond, and that isn't possible anymore. I order from New York now, and it takes longer for shipments to arrive. I have this dark green silk."

Nancy shook her head. "I don't think so. I wanted something in a light color."

The second dress couldn't have pleased her more if she'd placed an order for it.

She tried on the white silk petticoat and overdress of white crepe, which was trimmed with three rows of pinked ruffles in a light blue. "I'll need to put a tuck or two in the waist if you want this one," Pearl said. "It's a bit long, but if you wear a hoop, the length will be all right."

"I don't have a hoop. Do you have any for sale?"

"Yes, and at a good price, too."

After she paid for the dress and hoop, Nancy had to choose between a new pair of shoes and a hat. The dress was long enough to conceal her old shoes, so she used the rest of her money to buy a leghorn bonnet with a wide white ribbon and a bunch of violets on the left side. Pearl made a few tucks in the waist of the dress and buttoned the dress up the back. As Nancy tied the bonnet in place, Pearl turned her to face the wide, floor-length mirror. Nancy could hardly believe it was her image looking back at her.

"I'm sure you'll enjoy these clothes. They've turned you from a girl into a grown-up lady," Pearl said. Her words encouraged Nancy, for sometimes she believed that Heath still thought of her as a child.

The saleswoman wrapped Nancy's purchases in white paper and smiled as she opened the door for her. Nancy hurried toward home. She couldn't wait for Heath to see her in such finery. But her steps slowed when Nancy remembered that the Quakers were plain people. Considering the simple, unadorned dresses that Mrs. Foster wore, Nancy wondered if she had chosen the right garments to snag Heath's attention. But she put these worries aside and counted the minutes until the great day.

The celebration wasn't scheduled until three o'clock, but Nancy and her father left the house soon after noon because they wanted to find a shady place to sit. They crossed a small swinging bridge to the island and walked to the army camp, where the festivities were to take place. When she'd modeled her new garments for her father, he'd looked her over carefully and shrugged his shoulders. "If you're happy to be dressed that way, it's okay with me."

Considering his lack of praise, she wasn't as happy with her appearance as she'd expected to be.

Although she'd looked forward to this occasion for months, she felt ill at ease. When she saw Colonel Kelley, who was still recuperating from his wounds, and the other soldiers sitting in places of honor on the platform, Nancy again questioned if it was unpatriotic for her to spend all of her money on clothes she didn't need. She was tempted to go back home and change, but a lot of people had already seen her. Besides, the ceremony was ready to start, and she didn't want to miss any of the speeches.

Nancy sat on a blanket with several girls who attended her church. Her father joined a group of men standing near the platform. Most everyone had a flag pinned on his or her clothing.

After speeches by the town's dignitaries and a few words from Colonel Kelley, a bugler played a favorite hymn. The words found lodging in Nancy's heart, and as she listened to the gentle strains of the instrument, she prayed the words in her heart as her fondest hope for her country:

O God, our help in ages past,
Our hope for years to come,

Our shelter from the stormy blast,
And our eternal home.

The celebration ended when the national flag was hoisted to the top of the pole. Church bells started ringing in the city. Rockets soared high above the assemblage. Drums sounded. Men and boys shot rifles into the air. The crowd applauded and cheered heartily. Nancy's heart swelled with love and pride of her country, and it was difficult to believe that the nation could be divided.

Nancy had looked around several times to see if Heath had come to the celebration, but she hadn't seen him. So her dream of playing the elegant lady in his presence had backfired. *Pride goeth before destruction,* she silently chided herself as she tried to get up off the ground in her billowing skirts.

Giggling, one of her friends pulled on her right hand while Nancy held her skirts in place. In an attempt to hide her embarrassment, Nancy smiled broadly. She walked across the field toward her father and came face-to-face with Heath, who stared at her as if he was seeing her for the first time.

"You're beautiful," he murmured huskily.

"Oh! I didn't know you were here."

"I had a sick patient here on the island. I was late, so I stayed in the background rather than interrupt the program. May I walk you home?"

"I guess that will be all right. I'll tell Pa."

Her father had gone onstage to shake hands with Colonel Kelley, but when he turned toward her, she pointed to Heath and waved. Pa interpreted her message and agreed by nodding.

Many people were leaving the army camp, so they weren't alone, but Heath said quietly, "Perhaps I spoke out of turn, but I've never seen you in such elegant garments. They become you."

"Thank you. I've wanted a dress like this since I saw the pretty clothes Stella wore. Pa didn't object, but he said I'd have to earn the money to buy a new dress. That's why I went to work for Tabitha Clark. But I haven't enjoyed wearing them today. When our country is at war, I shouldn't have spent so much money on fripperies."

"I'm sorry you feel that way. The dress and hat are perfect for you."

"That makes me feel better."

They crossed the small bridge single file. Heath's horse was tied to a post along the wharf, but it was only a short distance to the Logan home. He walked with her, chatting about the celebration.

Since the army had commandeered the *Wetzel*, Nancy's father was home at night, and Heath had missed his talks with Nancy.

As if she'd read his thoughts, Nancy said, "Pa has had some good news. The army has released his boat so he can start making his usual runs. He'll be busy for several weeks delivering the shipments that have backed up in the warehouses."

"Does that mean you'll be staying at our home while he's gone?"

"I don't know. After the Union victory at Philippi, it seems like everything has calmed down, so he may tell me to stay at home."

"Mother and I like your company."

"Thanks."

"Have you heard anything more from your brother?"

"No, and it worries me. I'd like to know that he's all right. Do you think the war will end soon?"

Heath frowned and threaded his hair with his long, slender fingers. "I can't say this to anyone else without being taken for a traitor, but I don't believe there will be a speedy resolution of this conflict. Some of our country's best generals have joined the Confederacy, and they'll be fighting a defensive war."

"I don't know what that means."

"All the South wants is to be left alone. And I believe they have the man- power to keep the Federal armies out of their states. It's easier to defend what they have than for the Northern armies to invade a hostile territory. The fighting could drag on for years."

They had reached Nancy's home and paused at the foot of the steps. "Pa will be home soon if you want to wait."

He shook his head. "I have some work to do, but I've enjoyed our walk."

He lifted her hand, kissed her palm gently, turned abruptly, and left. He had noted surprise and confusion on Nancy's face, and he wondered if she had resented his caress.

—∿∿—

Although the citizens of Wheeling had come together to celebrate Independence Day, much unrest still filled the city. The local authorities attempted to keep a tight rein on crime, but Pa worried about Nancy's safety. "Because your brother joined the Confederate Army, some people are suspicious of us. I don't like for you to be alone, even in the daytime. The attitude of people in this town changes according to who's winning the war, and right now, the Confederates seem to be."

"I heard Dr. Foster say that people are afraid the Confederacy will be vic- torious in its attempt to establish a separate country, and if it is, Virginia will invade its rebellious northwestern counties and force us to stay with the mother state."

"And it could happen. I'm a loyal Union man, but everybody's got a right to live accordin' to the dictates of his own conscience. Even if I don't agree with a man, I ain't gonna burn down his house or deny him his freedom. If I was a bettin' man, I'd wager that before the year is out, secessionists in this town will be arrested. And when Doc Foster keeps on treatin' Confederate sympathizers the same as he doctors anybody else, he'll probably end up in jail, too. That just ain't right."

Her father's prediction worried Nancy, but the days passed, and Heath wasn't arrested. Never knowing when he might be put in jail, Nancy cherished every moment she was with him. They didn't have many opportunities to be alone, but during those few times, a delicate thread of magnetism formed between them. He sometimes held her hand, once he had kissed her on the forehead, and when he knew she was worrying about Clay, he gathered her gently into his arms, holding her until the bad moment passed. A tangible bond brought them together, and she often wondered what the future held for them.

As the heat of summer invaded Wheeling, the Fosters spent more time on their front porch. While Mrs. Foster and Nancy prepared sewing kits for soldiers, Heath pored over the latest edition of the *Intelligencer*. He also subscribed to *Harper's Weekly*, and the week after Wheeling's Independence Day celebration, he said, "Wheeling made headlines in the *Weekly*."

Willing to rest her eyes for a moment, Nancy laid aside her sewing and looked up. "Good or bad news?"

Grinning, Heath said, "That depends on the reader, I suppose. This is the July 6 issue. They have an illustration of the third floor of the district federal courtroom of Wheeling's U.S. Custom House."

He passed the newspaper to Nancy as he continued to explain. "In an earlier issue, *Harper's* highlighted the May meeting when delegates met in Wheeling and called for a new state of Virginia—one loyal to the Union. This article mentions the Second Wheeling Convention, convened after a majority of Virginians voted for secession."

Nancy's eyebrows puckered thoughtfully. "I understood that the delegates want a new state."

"They do, and the Congress of the United States is apparently willing to approve a separate state, but the Constitution provides that a state can't be formed within a state unless the mother state approves. The Richmond legislature would never give their consent, so our lawmakers intend to create a reorganized Virginia government, which *will* agree to form a separate state."

"Sounds like that might not be legal," Nancy said.

Heath laughed, for he liked the keenness of Nancy's mind. "You've hit the nail on the head! Some of our delegates agree with you. That's the subject of the article—you can read it."

Nancy read a few paragraphs, then turned to Heath, perplexity wrinkling her forehead.

"It would feel strange to live in the same city but be a part of a new state. What would the state's name be?"

"Several have been suggested. Let me name some of them, and you can decide which you like best." Listing them on his fingers, he said, "Allegheny. Augusta. Kanawha. New Virginia. West Virginia."

"I was born in Wheeling, and I've always been a Virginian. I think I'd choose a name that had Virginia in it. West Virginia sounds good to me. Will this happen right away?"

"It will probably take a year or so before all the political decisions are made. And a lot can happen before then."

"But if the Confederacy takes control of the western counties again, we would stay a part of Virginia."

"Yes, and we would be fighting a civil war in our own state. A lot of blood will be shed if that were to happen, and the very thought distresses me."

In less than a month, Nancy realized that Heath's prediction about the length of the war was probably true. The Confederates' stunning victory at the Battle of Bull Run brought the grim reality of war home to Wheeling families, when several of their sons were killed and sent home in wooden coffins. Fearing the reaction if the Confederates won the war, some of Nancy's neighbors moved into Ohio. And when she had no further word from Clay, Nancy worried that he might have fallen in battle and that she would never know.

Perhaps concerned about the same thing, her father became morose and bitter. And his worries increased when the packet business declined after factories closed because their workers were drafted into the army. The only peace Nancy found was in the Foster home, and she was there often after her father was hired by the army to use the *Wetzel* to haul supplies. He was away from home several nights each week, but while the country seemed on its way to being torn apart, the emotional relationship between Nancy and Heath continued to grow.

Chapter 9

One November evening as Heath and Nancy walked slowly along the street in front of the U.S. Custom House, she said, "Even though it's been talked about for months, it's still hard for me to believe that people in that building are making plans for the counties west of the Allegheny Mountains to form a new state that would be loyal to the Union."

"It is rather amazing," Heath agreed. "But it isn't as easy as it sounds. The formation of a new state may not be constitutional."

"Yes, I remember we talked about that several weeks ago."

" 'No new State shall be formed or erected within the jurisdiction of any other state; nor any state be formed by the junction of two or more States, or parts of states, without the consent of the legislatures of the states concerned as well as of the Congress.' "

Nancy's mouth dropped open, and she stared wide-eyed at him. "Imagine! Being able to quote part of the federal constitution from memory!"

With an apologetic smile, Heath said, "I wasn't trying to flaunt my knowledge. But I've been studying that section for a week or two—trying to figure out if the steps we're taking to organize a new state are legal."

"But you would favor such a move?"

Heath continued to talk as they moved toward the Logan home. "Yes, I think it's the only logical step our delegates can take. The two sections of the state have very little in common. Not only are we separated from the Tidewater counties by rugged mountain terrain, but there are economic, political, social, and cultural differences, as well."

They wandered on toward the river and sat side by side on a bench. Nancy buttoned her coat, for although winter was late in coming this year, the nights were cool.

With a smile, he asked, "Are you sure I'm not boring you with all of this?"

"Oh no," Nancy hastened to assure him. "It's important for me to know why we want to form a new state. Clay was so convinced that the government in Richmond was right in its decision to secede that he was willing to give up his family and home to fight for what he believed in. When I ask Pa about the political situation, he starts ranting that Virginia shouldn't have seceded, but he never says why. Tell me all you can."

"I'll make it brief. Because the mountains prevented easy trading with the eastern seaboard, Virginians in the west found markets for their goods in Ohio and Pennsylvania, while the eastern section shipped to the northern and southern states."

"I remember studying in school that the people are different, too," Nancy added. "The mountaineers, mostly Scotch-Irish and German, are more democratic and less aristocratic than the residents along the seaboard who can trace their ancestral roots to England."

"That's true. I didn't know much about the Appalachian region until I moved to Wheeling, but I've learned that the people who live here are a breed apart from those along the seaboard. Both areas were settled by Europeans, but from varied backgrounds."

A steamboat traveled past, going downstream, and the captain blew the whistle in greeting. The sound had been familiar to Nancy all of her life, and she waved to him, wishing she could go back to those carefree times of her childhood. She acknowledged sadly that because of this conflict waging around them, the old ways were gone forever. But the fact that she was accepting these changes and changing with them indicated that she was leaving her childhood behind.

"Perhaps slavery is the greatest difference in the sections now," Heath continued. "The Tidewater counties depend on slave labor for their livelihood. In comparison, there are very few slaves in the Trans-Allegheny regions. The rugged country has developed into small farms, making slave labor impractical."

"But slavery doesn't cause any trouble in Wheeling."

"That's because there are fewer than fifty slaves in the town. Most of them are household servants and treated well. And if they should be mistreated, it's easy to cross the Ohio River and be in free territory." Heath stood. "It will be dark soon. I'll walk you home."

As autumn passed into winter, Pa's temperament rose and fell depending on how much work he had to do. He was cranky through most of November. His usual runs to Parkersburg and his trips for the army were disrupted by a lack of rain that kept the channels closed to river traffic. Nancy was down in the dumps, too, for she hadn't had much opportunity to see Heath. For a couple of weeks he was busy with a bout of sore throats and lung inflammation in Wheeling and the countryside, and with her father at home, it hadn't been necessary for her to spend nights with the Fosters.

Nancy realized that she was becoming too serious about Heath. Except for a few times, he hadn't given any indication that he had any more consideration for her than any other woman. But a week of hard rains in early winter raised the river level, and the week after Thanksgiving Nancy's father made a run to

Parkersburg. Upon his return, he stopped to pick up Nancy at the Foster residence. Heath happened to be home, and Pa asked to see him.

"Come in, Mr. Logan," Heath said when he came to the door.

"No, thankee. I've got to do some repair on the *Wetzel*'s engine before I head back downstream." Nancy came to the door with her satchel, and Heath opened the door for her and followed her out on the porch.

"Nancy mentioned that you want to talk to somebody who practices herbal medicine."

"Yes," Heath said eagerly. "I've long been interested in finding new medicines. Because of the restrictions of war, my plans to talk to herbalists living in the Appalachian region have been thwarted. I can't very well go into the mountains when there's a civil war going on."

"You don't have to go to the mountains," Pa said, looking pleased about the information he had to share. "There's a woman as close as Parkersburg, who's supposed to be an expert on herbs. Her home is in the mountains south of the Kanawha River, but there's so much fighting going on there that she moved to Parkersburg to live with her daughter. If you've a mind to, you can ride with me on the *Wetzel* free of charge."

"I certainly want to take the opportunity to talk to the woman," Heath said eagerly. "Most of my patients with colds and other ailments are better now, so I can probably leave for a few days. When will your next trip be?"

"Not until I get the engine fixed on the *Wetzel*, which I hope ain't more'n five or six days, for I've got a lot of freight to haul. I'll send word by Nancy."

Heath glanced at his mother, who had come to the door and heard. "I don't know of any reason I shouldn't go. Do you?"

"I've been taking turns looking after our sick neighbor, but if both of you are gone, I'll stay home to look after Nancy."

"Don't need to change your plans, ma'am," Pa said. "Nancy can ride along with us on the boat. There's a little cabin where she can sleep. She goes with me sometimes when I'm not crowded."

Nancy couldn't think of anything she would enjoy more than a trip on the steamboat with Heath. And the opportunity had been dumped into her lap without any effort on her part. Nancy felt Heath's eyes on her, but she didn't look at him. Was it possible that her father was matchmaking?

When the *Wetzel* weighed anchor five days later, Nancy and Heath, shoulders touching, stood at the bow looking at the riverbank where leafless deciduous trees gave a gaunt appearance to the landscape. Nancy scanned the hills where a few evergreens added some color to the countryside. Sunrays highlighted the rugged bluffs behind the city.

Nancy shivered when a cold wind swept around them. "The hills are pretty even after the leaves fall."

"During the first year after I moved here, I wondered if I would ever get used to the hills. I'd always lived in Philadelphia, and I didn't know much about the rest of the country. I've learned to love this area, though, and I wouldn't be happy to live in the East again."

"I'm happy to hear that," Nancy said. "I would miss you and your mother if you left Wheeling."

Heath didn't answer, and he stared moodily at the water. When he left Philadelphia, he had thought his future was well defined. Knowing the demanding hours of a physician right from the beginning, he had decided that a medical practice and family life didn't mix. He had chosen medical research and the practice of medicine as his priorities.

He glanced at Nancy, half annoyed because meeting her had disrupted his plans. When he had his life ordered, why had he become so enamored with this young woman, ten years younger than he, which in itself presented a problem? Although many men married women much younger than they were, from a doctor's standpoint, he didn't approve of it. He'd seen too many young widows left with a passel of children to raise by themselves. And he had no idea what she thought of him. How could she stand there so calm and serene as if this were an ordinary day, when he hadn't been able to sleep the night before because he'd been contemplating the few days they would have together?

He looked up toward Wendell Logan in the pilothouse as he steered the *Wetzel* into the deepest channel of the Ohio. In a few succinct words, Wendell had once made it known what he thought of Quakers. So considering the differences in age and spiritual beliefs that stood between Nancy and him, why couldn't he put her out of his mind?

But knowing that two or three days with Nancy would be an opportunity he might not have again, Heath put his somber assumptions aside. As Wendell unerringly steered the *Wetzel* toward Parkersburg, Heath settled down to enjoy the trip. His problems could be resolved after they returned to Wheeling.

—∕∿∕—

Because of a late start from Wheeling, which necessitated an overnight stop, it was noon of the second day before the *Wetzel* arrived in Parkersburg. After giving his crew orders about unloading the cargo, Wendell walked with Heath and Nancy up the riverbank toward the town of Parkersburg. Nancy looked with interest at the general stores and a few restaurants, not unlike the buildings they had at home. Wendell stopped in front of a two-story brick building with HOTEL painted in large gold letters across the front.

"The owner of this hotel is the one who told me about the herb woman. We can eat in the hotel restaurant, and I'll see if I can find out where she lives."

The hotel was near the waterfront, and compared to the elegance of the McClure House in Wheeling, Nancy considered it to be a little shabby. Heath held the door for her, and Nancy stepped inside. Her eyes were immediately drawn to a young woman standing in the lobby. The shock of discovery stopped Nancy in her tracks, and she took a quick breath of utter astonishment.

"Stella?" she murmured, and at her voice, the young woman looked her way. It *was* Stella.

Nancy ran toward her friend. "Why, Stella! I supposed you would be in Alabama by now. What are you doing here?"

Tears formed in Stella's eyes, and she threw her arms around Nancy. "Because we don't have any other place to go," she said bitterly. "You'll never believe all the things that have happened to us."

Nancy felt a hand on her shoulder.

"I'm here," Heath said, and Nancy's heart lifted, as she realized that he would know what to do and say in this situation. Her father was talking to the hotel clerk and apparently hadn't noticed Stella's presence.

"We're going to eat dinner here, Stella," Heath said. "Where's your family? Could all of you join us?"

Nancy gave him a grateful look. His calm presence helped to steady her erratic pulse, and she prayed that she could be of some help to her friend. Tears cascaded down Stella's face, and Nancy put an arm around her. Nancy and Heath exchanged concerned glances over Stella's shaking shoulders.

"Has something happened to your parents?" Nancy asked.

Stella shook her head. "No, they're safe. But we've had a horrible time—just horrible!"

"Let's sit over here on this divan," Heath said. "You can tell us about it."

Nancy turned Stella toward a quiet area near the stairway. When they sat down, Nancy pulled a handkerchief from her reticule and wiped the tears from Stella's face as she continued to hold her hand firmly.

"Tell us what has happened," Nancy insisted.

Pa joined them, surprise on his face. Stella seemed to take courage from his presence, for she had once admitted that she felt more comfortable around Nancy's pa than she did her own father.

"We left Parkersburg a week after you brought us here, Mr. Logan. Everything went well enough until we got to Cincinnati and learned that Federal troops had closed the river to all southbound traffic. They wouldn't let any boats pass Cincinnati unless they agreed to stay on the northern Ohio. And even the northbound traffic was at a standstill for weeks."

Stella had calmed considerably by now. She glanced from one to the other of the three sympathetic faces before her. "You can't imagine how good it is to see you."

"Why did you wait so long to come back?" Heath asked.

"Papa was determined to go to Alabama. He tried to find overland passage, but Kentucky is a battleground, too, just like Virginia. It wouldn't have been safe, even if we could have found someone to take us. Train travel into the Confederacy has stopped." She started crying again but continued in a quavering voice. "Just because we talked like Southerners and wanted to go to Alabama, people treated us like spies. We waited around, thinking that the Confederate Army might open the river, but that didn't happen. We spent all the money Papa had, and he sold Mama's jewelry to get enough money to pay our passage back to Wheeling."

Heath and Nancy exchanged troubled glances. The way distrust was accelerating against secessionists in Wheeling, Nancy doubted that the Danford family would receive any better treatment there.

"Will you take us with you when you go home?" Stella asked Pa.

"I'm not sure I can take you this trip. We'll have to tie up at night, and Nancy is sleeping in the cabin."

"That's okay, Pa. I'll share the room with Stella and her mother. Or I can sleep in the pilothouse with you."

"Let me go and bring Papa to talk to you," Stella pleaded. "He's awful worried about Mama. She cries all the time and covers her face when we're out in public—she says all she wants to do is go inside her house and never see anyone again."

"I'll tuck you in somewhere," Pa agreed.

Giving him a grateful smile, Stella hurried up the stairway.

"Ain't that a shame!" Pa said. "Why didn't the hotheads who started this war look ahead and see what their flying off the handle would cause? We had a good country, so why did they have to tear it apart and ruin the lives of good people like the Danfords?"

"And I didn't have the heart to tell Stella that their home has been confiscated by the army," Nancy said. Hearing footsteps on the stairs, she turned around.

She couldn't believe that the stooped, defeated man walking toward them was Sinclair Danford. She had always stood in awe of Stella's father, who wore only the best, tailor-made garments and whose bearing proclaimed that he was proud of being a self-made man. Stella loved her father deeply, but Nancy had always considered him a dominating man, whose attitude had probably turned Stella's mother into the weak-willed woman she was.

Mr. Danford shook hands with Heath and her father and nodded in Nancy's direction. His gray eyes were dismal. His usually trim beard was scruffy, and his hair didn't look as if it had been combed for days. He straightened his shoulders, but that gesture did little to disguise his defeated attitude.

Addressing Wendell, he said, "My daughter says you will take us back to Wheeling."

"Yes. It will be crowded for your womenfolk, but I'll make them as comfortable as possible."

"We came here from Cincinnati on a boat pushing two barges loaded with cattle. Your accommodations can't be any worse than that. When are you leaving?"

"Probably day after tomorrow. Doc Foster has some business to take care of here in Parkersburg, and I'll be loading cargo tomorrow. I'll let you know."

Mr. Danford turned away, and Heath invited, "Will you and your family have dinner with us as my guests?"

Danford rejected the invitation with a cold smile. "We don't have to take charity yet. Besides, my wife is indisposed. I'll send Stella down if she wants to share your meal."

Chapter 10

Mattie Sawyers was like no one Nancy had ever seen. After a mile's walk outside the city limits, they located the mountain woman at her daughter's home. The wizened, stooped woman was about five feet tall. Her frowsy gray hair framed a face as wrinkled as a monkey's, but the hooded black eyes that peered from under bushy gray brows gleamed with an inner fire of mystery and intelligence.

"So ye want to learn my secrets, do ye?" she said with a cackle when Heath sat near her on the porch of the modest frame cottage.

"I'm a doctor, Mrs. Sawyers, and I'm interested in learning anything and everything that will bring healing to the sick and wounded. I'm convinced that herbal remedies are superior to some of the patent medicines I can buy."

She nodded her head emphatically. "You're right about that. I'll gladly tell you what I know, for there ain't many folks want to learn the old ways," she said. "My young'uns would druther buy a bottle of Dr. Flint's Quaker Bitters from peddlers than take a dose of my wild ginger tea that will fix them up after a few teaspoonfuls."

"My mother and I grow a small garden of herbs, and I sometimes use those in treating my patients, but with your experience, you must know more about native plants than I do. I'll be obliged if you will share that knowledge with me."

"I will, sonny. I ain't gonna live much longer, and it will do my heart good to know that a fine young man like you will carry on my healin' know-how."

Nancy sat in the background during the next two hours, content to listen as Mrs. Sawyers, in her quaint mountaineer voice, explained the secret of nature's healing to Heath. She talked slowly, and he quickly recorded what she told him.

Nancy recognized that some of the remedies were made from familiar plants. She was surprised to learn that salves could be made by boiling chickweed, plantain, water lily roots, and sour dock. Tansy was used for sick headache, chamomile was good for a tonic, dandelion and fennel for colic, marigold blossoms would cure colds, and mashed catnip leaves could relieve the itching of hives. Taken altogether, Nancy considered it a profitable visit for Heath, and after they left the woman's home, he agreed that the knowledge he'd gained from Mrs. Sawyer would be helpful in his research.

"I learned more from her in a few hours than from many of the classes I took in medical school. I'll have to study all of this information and decide how I can adapt it to treating my patients. I have a book that lists different plants in the United States, some of them growing in other climates. Hopefully, when this war stops, I can travel to look for them. In the meantime, I'll search for the plants growing in the Wheeling area. Will you help me look for these herbs?"

"Yes, I like to wander around in the woods and fields. I recognized some of the plants she named."

"I wouldn't prescribe any of these herbal treatments to my patients until I've done a great deal of research on them and discussed them with my learned colleagues, but I've always been interested in learning more about herbal medicines. There's so much about curing the human body that we don't know." He continued to discuss what he'd heard from Mrs. Sawyers, and although Nancy was interested in what they'd learned and hesitated to interrupt him, she was troubled about Stella and her family. Heath paused in thought about the time the houses of Parkersburg came into view, and Nancy asked, "Should we tell Mr. Danford that his home has been confiscated by the army to store supplies for the army camp on the island?"

Sighing, Heath answered, "He needs to know before we get to Wheeling. I'm hoping your father will tell him."

"Wonder what they'll do—where will they live?"

"He owns a few cottages down near his factory. They may have to move into one of them. Perhaps he'll start the factory again, although he may not have enough raw materials to resume operation, for he depended on cotton from the South to make his products. Now that the Ohio and Mississippi river valleys have become battlegrounds, there won't be much raw cotton available in the North."

"Nobody considered all of those things when the war started, did they?"

"People in general didn't think at all—only irrational people would want a war."

Nancy didn't comment, and she wouldn't tell her father what Heath had said, for they seemed to be getting along all right now. She hadn't heard Pa mention Heath's Quaker heresy for several weeks, and she didn't want to remind him of Heath's views on the war.

———

Heath took a room in the hotel overnight, but he had supper with Wendell and Nancy before they went to the *Wetzel*. Before they parted from Heath, Nancy said, "Pa, are you going to tell Mr. Danford before we get to Wheeling that they don't have a home?"

He threw up his hands. "Not me! They ought to know, all right, but I don't speak Danford's language. Doc, you can talk to him."

With a resigned shrug of his shoulders, Heath said, "I suppose there's nothing else to do. I hate to hit a man when he's down, but he must be told."

***

The return trip to Wheeling held none of the serenity and pleasure for Nancy that she'd enjoyed with Heath as they had traveled to Parkersburg. Mrs. Danford spent all of her time in the small room that Nancy had occupied, and Stella stayed with her. Their spirits were so low the first day that Nancy was depressed, too, and she stayed several hours on deck with Heath. It seemed that every time she glanced toward the pilothouse, her father was watching them. When darkness approached and the boat docked for the night, she spread some blankets in the pilothouse where her father slept.

The air was cold, but Nancy and Pa weren't sleepy, so they sat alone on the hurricane deck as darkness fell around them. Nancy's thoughts lingered on the Danfords' problems, and she wished she could do more to help Stella. Her father was less talkative than usual, and Nancy wondered what was on his mind. When he spoke, she was sorry to learn what he was thinking about.

"Daughter, I'm worried about you seeing so much of Doc Foster. I wish I hadn't brought you along on this trip. He's got his good points, but I can't trust no man who ain't willin' to fight for his country. Besides, he's gonna end up in prison for helping the enemy. You're gonna have to stay away from him."

"But Pa," Nancy protested. Pa raised a hand to silence her.

"I ain't finished. I won't keep you from going to work for Mrs. Foster in the daytime and helpin' with her work for the soldiers, but you can't stay at night. And I don't want him drivin' or walkin' you home like he's been doin'. I've been kinda lax in that because of the differences in your ages, but it appears to me that you're growing up mighty fast lately. And if the matter should happen to come up, I want you to know how I stand on any courtship between you and Doc Foster."

Nancy dropped her head and bit her lips to stop the quivering. So much for her wondering if her father was matchmaking between Heath and her!

He stood up and headed toward the pilothouse. "It's time to go to sleep," he said, and although Nancy wanted to beg him to change his mind, she knew it would be useless. She went inside and lay down on the pallet she'd prepared earlier. Her father wrapped a blanket around his shoulders and lay near the door.

After Nancy heard his even breathing and his usual cacophony of snoring, she gave way to the sobs she'd been stifling since her father's ultimatum. She knew now that she loved Heath, and to be deprived of his company would be heartbreaking.

Why did she have to lose everybody she loved? She'd lost her mother when she was only a girl. Clay was gone, and she wondered if she would ever see him again. Now she was forbidden to have anything to do with Heath, who had brought more pleasure into her life than anyone she had ever known. But she would have to obey her father, or he would go to Heath and tell him that he didn't want his daughter keeping company with a coward.

Nancy cried until her eyes burned and her nasal passages were congested. She sat up and gasped for breath. She leaned against the wall and waited until morning. If she could only pray, it would have made the hours pass, but there seemed to be a wall between her and God.

Her father had said she could continue working for Mrs. Foster, but Nancy knew she couldn't. Pa didn't realize that Heath was in and out of the house all day long, so she couldn't obey her father if she still worked there. She faced a dreary existence, for not only was she losing Heath, but she was also giving up the friendship of Mrs. Foster, whom she regarded almost as a mother.

When daylight came and Pa stirred, Nancy threw the blanket aside, stood, and walked outside and gulped the fresh morning air. Pa walked by, and apparently unconcerned over the emotional blow he'd tossed into her life, he said, "I'm gonna get some breakfast. We'll be under way in no time and home by midafternoon."

Nancy didn't answer, trying to think of some way she could avoid Heath until they reached Wheeling. She stayed on the upper deck until the *Wetzel* pushed away from the bank and accessed the deeper waters of the river. She didn't know where Heath had spent the night, but keeping an eye out for him, she scuttled down a rear stairway that led to the galley to get some breakfast for Stella and her mother. Her own stomach was queasy, and she didn't feel like eating.

"Hi, Tom," she said quietly, relieved to see that the cook was alone.

The cook's face spread into a toothy smile. "Hi, lil' Nancy."

Tom, an aging, brawny man, had worked on the *Wetzel* several years, and he still considered her a child. He was a jack-of-all-trades, but he always did the cooking.

"You hungry?"

"No, but I'd like some food for Mrs. Danford and Stella."

He wagged his shaggy white head. "Poor folks. Too bad about them. My boy worked for Mr. Danford—he treated his workers right."

Tom lifted a tray from the cupboard. "I'll put some batter cakes, honey, and sausage on here—enough for all three of you." He peered keenly at Nancy. "You look a little out of curl, this mawnin'. What's wrong?"

"I'm all right. Do you have any tea?"

He scratched his head. " 'Fraid not, missy. We don't carry womenfolk very much. All I've got is coffee."

She had tasted Tom's coffee once, and she knew Mrs. Danford would turn up her nose at the strong brew. "I'd better take a jar of water, then."

Tom poured water into a jar, capped it, and put it on the tray.

"Careful!" he admonished when Nancy lifted the tray with trembling hands. "Maybe I'd better carry it for you."

"No, I'll manage. Thanks, Tom. I'll bring the tray back."

Heath was standing at the bow of the *Wetzel* when Nancy rounded the corner. He moved eagerly toward her, but she shook her head at him and dodged into the small stateroom, where she intended to stay until the steamboat reached Wheeling. The room was stuffy, and Mrs. Danford's sighs nearly drove her to distraction, but that was better than facing Heath. Yet didn't he deserve an explanation? After a few hours, she came to a decision.

"Stella," she said, "I want to write a note, and I don't feel very well. Will you go to Pa's office and see if you can find a sheet of paper and a pencil? I'll stay with your mother."

Stella had been sitting on the floor and leaning against the cot where her mother lay, but she jumped up eagerly.

"Yes, I'd be glad to." With a worried look at her mother, she whispered, "Thank you for asking—I don't think I could have endured another moment in this room. I need a breath of fresh air."

"Take your time. It will be awhile before we reach Wheeling."

———

Heath chose a seat where he could watch the door to the cabin. When Nancy didn't show up, he impatiently decided that if she didn't come out soon, he would knock on the door and ask about her. He stood quickly when he saw a woman come out of the cabin, but frowned in disappointment when he recognized Stella.

The bright sun must have blinded her momentarily, for she stopped, leaned against the rail, and shaded her eyes. Heath hurried toward her and lifted his hat.

"And how is your mother, Stella?" She jumped slightly, and he apologized for startling her. "I'm willing to help if she needs medical treatment."

Stella shook her head, and he saw tears glistening in her eyes. "Thank you, but she isn't physically ill. Her whole world has been destroyed, and her heart is broken. You don't have a pill for that kind of sickness, do you?"

"Unfortunately, no."

She turned away, and he said slowly, "Is Miss Logan still in the cabin with you?"

"Yes, and she must have realized that I was almost near the breaking point, too, for she asked me to run an errand for her while she stayed with Mama."

"Then she isn't sick?"

"I don't know. She looks sad and awful peaked. But that room is so stuffy, it's no wonder she looks sickly. Mama won't let us keep the door open. Nice to talk to you, Dr. Foster, but I have to go."

"When you go back, will you tell Miss Logan that I'd like to see her?"

Stella nodded her head and turned toward the stern of the steamboat.

Heath sensed that something was wrong, for he thought that Wendell had avoided him this morning, too. He looked speculatively at the pilothouse where Nancy's father stood, both hands on the wheel, eyes intensely focused on the river in front of him. What could have happened in such a short time to make the Logans evade him?

Too restless to sit down, Heath paced the main deck, keeping his eyes on the cabin door. The *Wetzel*'s whistle sounded loudly, indicating that it would soon be docking, and when the boat rounded a small curve in the Ohio, he caught sight of the taller buildings in Wheeling. Just as he had given up hope of seeing Nancy, he saw Stella approaching. He turned eagerly toward her. She walked close to him and slipped a piece of paper in his hand before she hurried away. Amazed, Heath stared at the note. He unfolded the wrinkled paper.

Heath, please forgive me for avoiding you today. It would be too embarrassing to tell you why I had to do this. I won't come out of the cabin until you leave the boat. Tell your mother that I can't work for her. Try to understand. Don't hate me.

Heath read the message again, trying to make sense of it. He knew from her brief message that the decision had been made by Wendell Logan rather than Nancy. Why? When the war started, Wendell had been very curt with Heath about his political views, but as the war effort had intensified, he believed that Wendell had changed his mind. Sentiment in Wheeling, however, was becoming more biased against secessionists and pacifists, and it wasn't wise for anyone to befriend them.

He was the first one to walk down the gangplank when the boat docked, and he hurried toward his home without a backward glance. In that moment when Heath knew he had lost Nancy, he realized that he loved her. He had tried to tell himself that he didn't want a family to interfere with his plans to devote his life to medical research. He had argued with himself that he was ten years older than Nancy, although he felt younger when he was with her than at any other time. But now that he knew she was lost to him, none of those arguments were convincing.

My God, he prayed silently, *I can't violate my conscience just to get the woman I love. But now that I've learned the full blessing of love, how can I live without her?*

If I would swear complete allegiance to the Union cause, it would please Wendell Logan, and he wouldn't be opposed to my courtship of Nancy. But, dear God, how can I choose between my convictions and the woman I love?

Chapter 11

Spring 1862

Nancy breathed deeply of the mild spring air as she and Stella walked along the banks of the Ohio. Although it was the middle of May, a few dogwood trees were still blooming on the hills, and the trees were almost in full leaf. The goal of statehood for western Virginians loomed ever closer, for just a few days ago the Reorganized Government of Virginia had approved the creation of the new state with forty-eight counties. Believing that eastern Virginia wouldn't lose a large portion of the state without a fight, Nancy's father still worried about invasion by Confederate raiders.

"It's hard to believe that a year has passed since the war started," she said.

"It seems like more than a year since my life *ended*," Stella commented bitterly. "A year ago we were rich and happy. Today we're poor and miserable. I hate this war and the trouble it's brought us."

Nancy had been through this before with her friend, and she wanted to retort, "The Southerners started it." But she knew that Stella's life was miserable. Although she was tired of hearing her friend's complaints, Nancy wouldn't add to Stella's misery.

Mr. Danford had eventually reclaimed their home, but most of their furniture was gone, and they were living in dangerous and impoverished conditions. Mr. Danford was operating his factory on a small scale, using the hoard of raw cotton he had stored before the war. But lacking a steady supply of cotton, the output wasn't half what it had been prior to their disastrous flight from Wheeling. Because cotton goods were scarce in Wheeling, residents didn't let their dislike of Mr. Danford's Confederate sympathies keep them from buying his products. They needed to replenish their sheets, towels, and clothing.

Even so, the Danfords' lifestyle had changed completely. They couldn't afford any household servants, and new clothes were a thing of the past. Stella and her mother wore the clothing they had taken with them on their aborted flight at the beginning of the war.

"Although it's against his conviction," Stella continued morosely, "and he feels like a traitor, Papa got a Union flag and put it on the front porch. He did it for Mama and me. But the local residents know what we believe, and rowdies file past our home about every night shouting and calling us bad names. They're still throwing rotten eggs and vegetables at the house, too."

"The Fosters are having similar problems. Heath is happy to fly the flag because he's a loyal Union man, but he's still harassed because he doctors secessionists. Since that new doctor moved into town from the eastern panhandle, Heath has lost a lot of patients. Even Papa sympathizes with him, so that may be why he insisted that I go back to work for the Fosters."

Stella slanted a sly glance toward Nancy. "And you've been a lot happier since then, too. I wish I had a beau as handsome as Dr. Foster."

Nancy felt her face growing warm, and she didn't answer. Her feelings for Heath were too precious to share with anyone, even her best friend. Stella had assumed the reason she had stopped working for the Fosters was because Pa feared that the Fosters' secessionist sympathies might cause him to lose his hauling contracts with the Union Army. Nancy hadn't corrected her assumptions.

"Dr. Foster is a fine man," Stella continued. "He comes to see Mama every week, and he knows that Papa doesn't have much money to pay him. I'm glad your pa came to his senses about the Fosters."

"So am I. Pa would never admit it, but I think he realizes now what Heath and his mother are going through. Pa is as loyal to the Union as Abe Lincoln himself, but just because my brother is in the Confederate Army, a lot of people shun us. And the army has stopped giving him any shipping business, so we don't have much money, either."

The two girls walked in silence, and Nancy recalled how miserable she'd been during the two months and eleven days she hadn't gone to the Foster home. Being unable to see Heath was about the worst thing that had happened to her, and she moped around the house day after day. Her pa must have thought the same thing, for one morning in February, out of the blue, he said, "If you want to go back to the Fosters, it's all right with me. I'll go with you to see Mrs. Foster tomorrow morning."

Without questions or reservations, Mrs. Foster had welcomed Nancy back. They didn't ask why she had stopped working for them, but she figured Heath suspected the reason. Nancy missed their rides and talks together, but Heath didn't touch her or seek her company unless his mother was present.

Interrupting Nancy's musings, Stella said, "Papa has heard that there's going to be an attack on the Clark home tonight. Now that Mrs. Clark's two brothers have sneaked out of town and joined the Confederate Army, she's suspected of being a spy. People are saying that when she left Tommy with the housekeeper and was gone three days last week, she took information about what's going on in Wheeling to her brothers. There's a rumor flying around that they will guide an army in here to take over the town."

"That's probably a bunch of nonsense. I don't believe Mrs. Clark is brave enough to do that. But because the Union seems to be losing the war, even Pa is fretting what will happen to us if the Confederacy wins. Virginia troops will take over our town if they possibly can and treat us like traitors."

"I hope not," Stella said. "I don't wish that on anyone—not even the people who've been mean to us."

Nancy had long ago forgiven Tabitha Clark for the way she'd treated her, and on her way home, she wondered if she should go and warn Mrs. Clark about the planned attack. Still, the woman had ordered Nancy and Pa to get out of her house and warned them to stay away. Nancy wasn't quite brave enough to risk her anger alone, but she was determined to tell Pa about it. He would know the right thing to do.

―――

Nancy placed a dish of white beans, a platter of corn bread, and a bowl of chopped onions on the table. She took a chair beside her father and waited until he said the blessing.

Her father didn't like to talk as he ate, so Nancy fidgeted until he ate two bowls of beans and onions with several chunks of corn bread. When he pushed back from the table and held up his cup for a coffee refill, she said, "Stella has heard that a mob is going after Mrs. Clark tonight."

As was his way, Pa looked at Nancy to see if she had finished. When she didn't speak, he threaded his graying hair with his fingers, none too clean after a day's work in the shop.

"Don't surprise me. She's too uppity and makes enemies of the wrong people."

"I reckon she's got a right to her own beliefs same as anybody else."

Pa nodded agreement. He never mentioned Clay's name unless Nancy brought up the subject, but when he sat on the steps for several hours in the evening, looking eastward as if he was trying to see what was going on beyond the mountains, Nancy was convinced he was thinking of his son. She figured that was one reason he had mellowed toward the secessionists.

"I thought about warning her, but I didn't want to cause you any trouble."

Knowing that her father would give serious consideration to such a touchy situation before he made a decision, Nancy started clearing the table. She stored the leftovers and then washed and dried the dishes and placed them in the cupboard before she sat at the table again.

"It's a problem, all right, and I don't rightly know what to do about it," her father said. "I don't like the woman because she's too highfalutin, and I fault her for the way she treated you. But I don't like hoodlums, either—'specially when they prey on a woman and a boy. Wonder if she's the kind to defend herself."

"There's a rack of guns in the hallway. I suppose they belonged to her husband, but I don't know if she can use them."

Pa took his hat from the coatrack beside the door and jammed it on his head. "The Good Book says we're supposed to do good to them that despitefully use us, so I'm goin' to help the woman."

"I want to go, too."

"You might as well," Pa said. "I don't know when I'll be back, and you ain't got no business bein' alone." He took a shotgun off the wall, stuck a handful of shells in his pocket, and reached in a cabinet drawer for a pistol.

"You'd better take the handgun," he said. "Your brother taught you how to shoot it, didn't he?"

"Yes."

"It's just for your protection, mind you. I don't want you shootin' at nobody unless you're forced into it. We'll wait till dusk to go. I don't want to be seen totin' all of this hardware along the streets."

———

Frogs croaked along the riverbank, and a slight breeze wafted the scent of wild plum blossoms from the island. The sound of a bugle carried on the night air brought memories of her brother. As they started out on their warlike mission, Nancy wondered if her father was thinking of Clay, too.

"It's hard to believe that evil is afoot on such a nice night," Nancy murmured, and her father nodded.

"Step lively," he said.

Pa stopped when they were a block from the Clark home. "We'd better go to the back door. I'd like to talk to someone other than the widow first. Does she have any live-in help?"

"I've heard that Nora Lively, one of her poor relations, came to live with her after I left."

"It's worth checkin' out," he said, circling the house to the backyard.

A light still burned in the kitchen, and the curtains were drawn, but they detected movement as if someone moved back and forth in the room. Motioning for Nancy to stay in the background, Pa strode up on the porch and tapped softly on the door.

The door opened slightly, and a quavering voice asked, "Who is it?"

"Wendell Logan," he said quietly. "I want to talk to Mrs. Clark right away. I've come peacefully."

She quickly closed the door and locked it.

"You think she'll talk to you?" Nancy asked.

"I don't know." Pa stared into the darkness that had settled over the city.

"It's too quiet to suit me. If she don't show up soon, we're gettin' out of here."

The door opened a few inches. "You're not welcome here, Mr. Logan," Mrs. Clark said in her haughtiest voice.

"That may be, but Nancy heard today that your house is gonna be attacked tonight. We came to help."

Tabitha peered into the darkness. Nancy moved so she could be seen in the dim light from the kitchen.

"A likely story! Do you think I'd trust you after the way you talked to me?"

Pa stepped forward, shoved on the door, pushed Mrs. Clark aside, and walked into the kitchen. He motioned for Nancy to follow him.

"Leave my house at once."

Pa ignored her and strode toward the front of the house. "It may be a false alarm, but a lot of secessionists are being attacked now, and you being without menfolk, I ain't gonna stand by and see a bunch of riffraff burn your house. Men that attack and pillage in the night are usually cowards, and if they see you're not alone, that might scare them off."

"Take charge, then," Mrs. Clark said meekly.

"Where's your boy?" Pa asked as he walked through the hallway.

"Upstairs in his room."

"Good. That's the safest place for him."

In the dim candlelight, Nancy saw a woman huddled on the stairway, wringing her hands and moaning. Her father must have sensed that she wouldn't be any help, for he said to Mrs. Clark, "Send her to stay with the boy."

"Nora, please go upstairs and look after Tommy. Don't let him out of his room."

The distraught woman jumped to her feet and scurried up the steps.

To Pa, Mrs. Clark said, "He likes to think he's the man of the house, but he's only eight and a sickly child at that."

"You're right to protect your own," Pa said. With Tommy's safety taken care of, Pa laid out his plans.

"Nancy, be sure the back door is locked, then open the window and watch for anybody who comes up the alley." To Mrs. Clark, he said, "I'm not aimin' to shoot nobody, but it won't hurt to be prepared. Do you know how to shoot any of them guns hanging on the wall?"

"One of them."

"Then load up and be ready. Keep a candle burning so we can see to move around inside, but blow out the other lights. Set by an open window. I'll be out on the front porch, and if I open fire, shoot up in the air. You, too, Nancy," he called quietly. "Be sure you don't hit nobody unless they rush the house."

"Shouldn't the police know about this?" Mrs. Clark asked.

"They're all pro-Union and would likely refuse to help."

"Rather than fighting for a lost cause, I can't understand why my brothers didn't realize that they were needed here," she said in a harsh, raw voice. "We're going to lose everything—our business, our wealth, our homes."

"So you don't think the Confederates will win the war?" Pa asked, and he sounded surprised.

"How can they? The North has railroads, factories, money. Southerners have slaves, cotton, and bravado, none of which is worth much in fighting a war. I sympathize with the secessionists, but old Abe Lincoln has the determination of a bulldog, and he won't give up. Unfortunately, I couldn't make my brothers realize that. Our boats are sitting idle while they're off fighting."

In a tone Nancy had never heard from Mrs. Clark, she added, "Mr. Logan, in light of our past differences, much of which was my fault, I truly appreciate your help tonight. Most of my neighbors don't feel kindly toward me because of my secessionist views. I don't know what I would have done without you and Nancy tonight. I'm thankful you came." She extended her hand, and Pa grasped it without hesitation.

"You've got a right to your political beliefs same as anyone else. Just because I don't believe the same as you do won't keep me from doing what I can to protect you and your boy."

In a trembling voice, Mrs. Clark said, "Whatever happens tonight, I won't forget your kindness."

Pa stepped out on the porch, and quietness settled over the house. Nancy scurried to her post in the kitchen and monitored the passage of time by the clock on the wall. When it struck midnight, as if that was a signal for action, she saw two men sneaking up the alley.

Nancy stepped into the hallway. "Mrs. Clark, tell Pa they're coming the back way," she said. Her heart was hammering, but it was gratifying to know that her voice sounded normal.

Mrs. Clark turned from her post at one of the windows. "And I see a small group of men coming up the street, too. Some of them are carrying torches. Be careful."

At that moment, Nancy saw Tabitha Clark in a new light. If she had thought about it, she would have guessed that Mrs. Clark would be cringing in a corner with her head covered. But there was a steel edge to her voice, and Nancy was convinced that the woman wouldn't hesitate to fire the gun she held if anyone tried to enter the house. Despite her other faults, the woman loved her son devotedly, and she would fight for him like a lioness defending her cub.

The two men moved from the alley, and Nancy heard their steps on the back porch. They pushed on the door, and Nancy turned in that direction, her back against the kitchen wall. If there was any shooting, she figured Pa should start it, but she pushed the pistol in front of her and held it with a steady hand. If the men tried to break in, she would fire.

She moved closer to the door and heard a man's voice mumble, "Pry it open with the crowbar, and don't make no noise."

God, what should I do? I don't want to kill anyone, Nancy thought.

Suddenly she remembered when Heath had told his neighbor that if someone tried to break into the house and harm his mother and Nancy, he wouldn't hesitate to defend them.

Recalling that was enough for Nancy. She tilted the pistol and without warning pulled the trigger. The wood at the top of the door splintered, and one of the men yelled. She was sure she hadn't hit him, so the surprise must have caused him to shout. Nancy stood to one side of the door in case they returned her fire. But no shot sounded, and the men must have thrown the crowbar away, for it hit the side of the house. She heard the rapid beat of footsteps leaving the porch.

As if her shot was a signal, a barrage of gunfire sounded from the street.

"Are you all right, Nancy?" Mrs. Clark called.

"Yes. I shot through the door and scared the attackers away."

For the time being, Nancy decided the back door was safe. She scurried into the front hall and peered out a small window near the place Mrs. Clark knelt.

"So far, they've been shooting in the air," she said quietly.

"I haven't heard Pa's gun. I figure he's mad because I fired, but a couple of men were trying to break in through the kitchen door."

"Hey, secesh," a voice taunted. "You want a quick trip to the Confederacy? We'll ride you out of town on a rail."

Coarse laughter greeted his remark. No doubt this attack was fueled by liquor, for in spite of the town's efforts to control the sale and use of alcohol, it was still available. A man separated from the crowd milling in the street and started toward the house.

When he put his foot on the bottom step, Pa shouted, "That's far enough," and unloaded a volley of shotgun pellets to the right of where the man stood. "The next load of grapeshot will be for real. Get out of here."

"There's only one man—we can take care of him," the man on the step shouted.

Mrs. Clark fired. Pa's gun sounded again, and the advance halted as the attackers huddled together, talking angrily in the middle of the street. Nancy opened a window, knelt beside it, and braced herself for another attack.

—✥—

Heath yawned, tempted to stop the horse and take a nap in his buggy. He had been at a farmhouse ten miles out in the country for several hours, his patient in labor. Now the baby was delivered, the mother was resting, and he was finally on his way home. He shook his head, slapped his cheeks lightly, relaxed his shoulders, and kept going.

When he arrived in town and drove down Twelfth Street, he noticed a glow a few blocks away. He halted the horse and heard the sound of gunfire. Heath had a sense of uneasiness about what was going on. The Clark home was down that street, and pressure was being put on all secessionists right now. Heath pumped the reins, and the horse picked up speed.

As he drew closer, Heath saw the men milling in front of Tabitha's home. He knew that she and Tommy were alone, with only a weakling cousin for company. A shotgun blast echoed over the street, but he couldn't tell if it came from the house or from the attackers.

He lifted the reins, and with a silent apology to the horse, which had also had a long day and night, he touched its flanks with the whip.

"Giddyup," he yelled, flicking the reins and heading straight toward the rabble. Unaccustomed to the sting of the whip, the horse lunged into action and plowed through the middle of the mob. A few men were knocked down by the wheels, but most of them dove to safety when they saw the buggy bearing down on them. By the time Heath slowed the animal and turned around, the street was empty.

―⁓―

Nancy hurried out on the porch just as Pa stood up, took off his hat, and tossed it into the air. He burst into laughter. "I don't believe I've ever seen a funnier sight. They scattered like a covey of quail."

"Who ran them down, Pa?"

"I don't know. Everything happened so fast, I couldn't take it all in. Whoever it is has turned the vehicle and is coming our way."

Cradling the gun under his arm, Pa walked off the porch.

"Why, it's Doc Foster!" he said.

Heath halted his horse and jumped out of the buggy. "What's going on here?"

"Not much. But there might have been a lot of action if you hadn't arrived when you did." Pa grabbed Heath's hand and pumped it up and down. "You're all right, Doc. You're all right."

As soon as the ruffians had scattered and Heath had come to help, Nancy hurried to the kitchen to light the oil lamp. Now that Pa knew Heath wasn't a coward and would fight when forced into it, a glad song sang in her heart. Would Pa be less concerned about her relationship with Heath?

―⁓―

Surprised not only by his own action but to find Wendell Logan defending the

Clark home, Heath stepped inside the hallway. Mrs. Clark hurried out of the parlor and, with a glad cry, ran to Heath, threw her arms around him, and laid her head on his shoulder.

"Oh, I might have known you would come to help me," she cried.

Before Heath could extricate himself from her embrace, he heard footsteps approaching. He looked to the rear of the hallway just as Nancy entered, carrying a lighted lamp. She stopped abruptly and stared. Her features contorted with shock and anger, soon replaced by a look of disappointment and sadness. She set the lamp on a long table and brushed by Heath and Mrs. Clark.

"Let's go home, Pa," she said in a resigned voice. "We aren't needed here any longer."

With Mrs. Clark still holding him tightly, Heath watched the Logans walk away from the house. He removed himself from her arms and turned to follow Nancy.

"Mama, are you all right?" Tommy called from the top of the stairs in a tearful voice.

Mrs. Clark went to the stairway and motioned for Tommy. He ran to her, and she hugged him.

"Everything is all right now. Thanks to the Logans and Dr. Foster."

"I wanted to help, but I don't feel good."

Knowing that Tommy was a fragile child, Heath decided he had better check the boy's heart before he left. Innately, he realized that this wasn't the time to talk to Nancy. In that brief moment when Nancy had found him in Mrs. Clark's embrace, a range of emotions that he hadn't seen there before had flitted across her face. Was it possible that Nancy loved him? With a sigh of resignation, he walked out to his buggy and picked up his medical bag. He would have to mend his fences with Nancy at a later time.

Chapter 12

Between the late hour when she went to bed and the sleeplessness that plagued her when she thought of Mrs. Clark in Heath's arms, Nancy overslept the next morning. The scent of coffee awakened her. She jumped out of bed, washed hurriedly, struggled into her clothes, and went to the kitchen. Her father was at the table, eating a bowl of oatmeal.

"Sorry, Pa."

"I wanted you to sleep as long as you could. I ain't gonna do much today. I was proud of you last night. If you hadn't guarded the back door, the outcome might have been a lot different."

Flustered over this unexpected praise, Nancy stammered, "I expect Mrs. Clark won't be too happy with me for splintering the door."

"I ain't so sure. She struck me as bein' a lot more sensible than I credited her with. I would have expected her to throw a fit and crawl under a bed when the mob attacked. Instead, she shot into the street. She didn't touch a man, but her shot scattered them. Then the doc added the final touch."

"Is it likely that the mob knows that you and I were there? Will this cause us trouble?" Nancy asked, thinking how ironic it would be for the Logans to be further harassed because they'd helped, of all people, Tabitha Clark.

"I don't know, and I don't care. It's time the citizens of this town remembered that we're all Americans and stop labeling people as traitors because they have family members fightin' on the other side."

"You'd better be careful saying things like that. Now that the army has taken over the Athenaeum Building for a military prison, people considered disloyal to the Union are being put away. I don't want you to end up in prison. Heath goes there to see patients, and he says that the conditions are terrible."

"And he's gonna end up in jail, too, if he don't stop doctorin' the enemy. I've heard threats agin' him," Pa said. "I remember you saying that the Widow Clark was makin' up to Doc Foster. I figure that's all on her side. I notice he didn't take kindly to her throwin' her arms around him last night. He looked kinda taken aback—she probably hadn't done that before. The woman's barkin' up the wrong tree. She needs a forceful man to curb her spirit—not a meek man like the doc."

Her father's words encouraged Nancy, who had dreaded encountering

Heath. But after her father's assessment of the situation, she forced herself to meet Heath as usual, and the incident faded into the background during the increasing lawlessness and unrest that continued to plague the city.

———⁓———

Feeling guilty, although he hadn't done anything to encourage Tabitha Clark, Heath delayed approaching Nancy for a few days, but he could sense her displeasure with him. Finally, he decided he couldn't let the incident pass without comment. But how could he indicate to Nancy that the infatuation was wholly on Mrs. Clark's side and not appear egotistic? Glancing out his office window, Heath saw his mother disappearing down the street, carrying a meal to a soldier's impoverished family. Deciding to face the issue, he hurried across the small section of lawn that separated his office and the house. Nancy was in the kitchen, washing dishes.

Needing to keep his hands busy while he explained, he lifted a dish towel and picked up a plate to dry. Over and over, Heath had debated the best way to broach the subject with Nancy, and he wasn't particularly comfortable with his decision when he said, "I expect you to keep this information in confidence, but Tommy Clark's health isn't good. He has a weak heart, and his mother sends for me many times when the boy isn't really sick. Because of his condition, I can't refuse to go there. I never know when he might have an attack, and it's only for Tommy's sake that I go to her house."

He put the plate he had dried in the cupboard and looked directly at her. "Do you understand?"

"Yes," she murmured, and her lids lowered until he couldn't read the expression in her eyes, but a tender bond of affection escalated between them. He stepped behind her and placed his hands lightly on her shoulders.

"I did nothing to invite Tabitha's embrace that night. I've been attentive to the woman out of pity because I know she may lose her son, but there is nothing more between us—at least on my part. Do you believe me?"

Nancy's heart was singing, and she knew how easy it would be to make a slight turn and be in his arms. She had a feeling he wouldn't reject her if she did, but she wouldn't stoop to Mrs. Clark's tricks.

She nodded her understanding. He squeezed her shoulders and stepped away.

———⁓———

"It's starting to rain again," Nancy complained as she set food on the table for their evening meal. She jumped as a blast of thunder sounded nearby and a streak of lightning illuminated the kitchen.

Her father didn't answer as he filled his plate. No answer was needed. And it wasn't even news, for it had been raining for weeks. They had watched the river for several days as muddy water overflowed its banks and inched closer to their home. They'd lived in this house fifteen years, and the water had never reached the second floor, but no one could tell what the Ohio River might do.

While they ate, the rain increased steadily until it sounded as if buckets of water were being dumped on the house. The wind whistled around the eaves. When Nancy peered out the front window through the haze of rain streaming over it, she saw whitecaps on the river that looked like the waves of the Atlantic Ocean she had seen pictured in one of Heath's books. Willow trees along the riverbank bent double from the force of the wind and dipped their branches into the muddy Ohio.

Her father finished his meal and came to stand by her side. After one look, he galvanized into action. He pulled on a pair of gum boots and took a raincoat from a rack by the door.

"I'm gonna check on the *Wetzel*. The way that water is churnin', the boat might be set adrift. And if it breaks loose, I want to be on it."

"Oh, Pa, be careful!"

He nodded, pulled a hat firmly on his head, and hurried out the door.

Feeling the need to keep busy, Nancy cleared the dishes from the table and washed them. She had just finished and was hanging the dishcloth and towel behind the stove to dry when the persistent ringing of the bell on the top deck of the *Wetzel* caused her heart to skip a beat.

Pa was in trouble, or he wouldn't be ringing the bell like that! Pausing only long enough to put on a coat and hat, Nancy ran through the rain, sloshing through water puddles that soaked her shoes and stockings before she got to the river.

She raced up the gangplank of the *Wetzel*.

"Pa! What is it? Where are you?"

He shouted from the pilothouse, but she couldn't hear what he said. She took the steps to the hurricane deck two at a time.

"What's wrong? I thought the *Wetzel* was adrift," she shouted. When she reached her father, he was leaning against the railing, peering through the mist and rain.

Her eyes followed his pointing hand. "See that boat? It has run aground, and there's a heap of men on it. It's probably the one from Pittsburgh bringing soldiers to join the army in Parkersburg. The pilot must be a stranger to this part of the river and didn't know about the sandbar that makes the eastern channel too shallow for navigation. Or maybe the buoy washed away in the storm. You keep ringin' the bell while I run uptown to get help."

Nancy's arm was tired of ringing the bell by the time several wagonloads of men arrived on the riverbank. Gradually, the strength of the storm lessened as it moved eastward. The steamboat was floundering in the waves generated by the aftermath of the storm. Men were diving from the sinking boat and swimming toward the bank. Those on shore helped them up the slippery bank. Nancy saw her father approaching the *Wetzel*, and she hurried to meet him at the gangplank.

"Was anybody drowned?"

"The boat's captain says they're all safe. Since they landed on that sandbar, the water was shallow, and most of them waded ashore. But a few are wounded, so I sent a man after Doc Foster."

"Thank God they weren't all killed."

Shouting from the doomed boat intensified. Nancy looked toward the accident scene just as the boat toppled into the deepest channel of the river.

Pa shook his head. "Poor fellers! They lost all of their gear and their supplies. I suppose they'll have to stay here until they get some equipment."

"And the camp already has more soldiers than they can handle."

"Could you rustle up something for them to eat and drink?"

Aghast, Nancy turned to him. "How many are there?"

"I counted about forty."

"Forty!"

Nancy stared at her pa, but when he didn't act as if he'd made an unreasonable request, she said, "I'll see what I can find," and hurried off the steamboat.

"What can I fix in a hurry?" Nancy mumbled as she rushed toward the house, bending her head against the wind that still held some rain. "I'd better get hot water to boiling first so I can make coffee."

After she filled a teakettle and a big pot with water and set them on the stove, she hurried down to the cellar. She always laid by enough goods in stone jars to last for a year, so she put two jars of pickled peaches and a chunk of smoked ham in a basket. When she came out of the cellar, Mrs. Foster was walking toward the house. Nancy hurried toward her.

"I've never been so glad to see anyone in my life. Pa asked me to fix something for the shipwrecked soldiers to eat. We don't have enough food in the house to feed that many men."

Mrs. Foster squeezed Nancy's shoulders. "When I heard what had happened, I came with Heath to see if anyone needed nursing. He says that none of the men have severe injuries. I wasn't needed there, and your father asked me to come give you a hand."

"I made two loaves of bread yesterday, and we can make sandwiches with this ham, but that won't be a drop in the bucket to feed so many."

"We won't have to do it all by ourselves. Soldiers have arrived from the island. The army cook has started a fire, and he's making coffee. Two island women rowed across with their men, and they went home to prepare some food, too. Just like when Jesus fed the five thousand—we'll have food left over when they're all fed."

Mrs. Foster and Nancy were used to working together, and Mrs. Foster soon adjusted to the more primitive conditions in the Logan kitchen. In a short time, they filled two large baskets with sandwiches and slices of cake that Nancy had made the day before. They covered the baskets with pieces of oilcloth to keep the intermittent rain from spoiling the food. After they prepared a large peach cobbler and put it in the oven to bake, they carried the baskets to the riverbank.

Pa saw them coming and hurried to take the basket from Mrs. Foster's hands. "That was quick," he said approvingly.

"I see they already have tents set up," Mrs. Foster said.

"Yes, ma'am. One is for the cook, and one for the doc to check out the wounded. The officer in charge at the army camp has already sent a detachment to find six or seven tents. They ought to have them in the clothing factory that's makin' uniforms and other army supplies. They're goin' to be here a spell, for they lost everything."

Nancy handed her basket to a young soldier dressed in homespun garments, whose only sign that he was a soldier was the short-billed, blue Union cap he wore. His wet clothes clung to his slender body, and he shivered in spite of the humid air. His face was a mask of fear and pain. He didn't appear to be more than twelve or thirteen years old, and Nancy wondered why he had ever enlisted in the army.

Mrs. Foster's eyes, too, were full of pity as she surveyed the discouraged men. She motioned to the two island women who had arrived with baskets of food. When they joined Nancy and her, Mrs. Foster said, "We need to do something for these soldiers. If you can organize the women on the island to gather up items for them, I'll get my friends and neighbors to do the same."

"What'd you have in mind?" Nancy asked.

"The army will provide clothes and blankets for them. We can gather soap, towels, needles and thread, and medication and put them in cloth sacks that they could carry along when they leave. We could make cookies, too."

"Maybe we can find a few Bibles," Nancy said. "I know we won't be able to get a Bible for everyone, but they can share."

"This ain't gonna be a short war, to my thinking," one of the women said. "Let's keep up this good work even after we send these men on their way."

"That's an excellent plan," Mrs. Foster said and shook hands with the two women. "God will reward you for your goodness. Nancy, why don't you come home with me, and we'll organize my neighbors to help."

"I'll ask Pa."

Within a week, the soldiers were on their way eastward to an uncertain destiny, but Nancy believed they were encouraged by the attention they'd received from the women of Wheeling. She joined a large crowd at the depot to cheer them on the way, pleased that the misfortune of those soldiers had encouraged her and other local women to help needy servicemen and their families.

Chapter 13

Throughout the summer, drunkenness in the city of Wheeling increased lawlessness to the point where her father wouldn't let Nancy go anywhere, day or night, unescorted. The city council passed an ordinance prohibiting the sale of liquor to soldiers, who devised all sort of plans to smuggle booze into the camp on the island. Pa didn't mention it to her, but Nancy learned from her friends that after the city passed an ordinance suppressing houses of prostitution, many of the women had taken refuge at the army camp. Pa relied increasingly on Mrs. Foster to provide a safe environment for her.

Nancy often wondered if either of their parents was aware of the emotional bond that was growing steadily between Heath and her. Or did they approve of a closer relationship? After that night on the *Wetzel*, Pa hadn't mentioned again that Heath was an unfit suitor for her, and she welcomed every moment she spent with Heath and his mother.

"Mother," Heath said one evening when the Fosters and Nancy were enjoying a quiet time together after their evening meal. "The city authorities are cracking down on a lot of lawlessness among the soldiers, but I wonder if they aren't going about it the wrong way."

Mrs. Foster removed her glasses and looked up from the socks she was knitting.

"What does thee have in mind?"

"Is it ever satisfactory to meet force with force? Jesus taught that we're to do good to all men. Every week, trains come into Wheeling from Illinois and Ohio, transporting soldiers to the battlefields. Many of them are hardly more than boys. I'm sure they're scared and homesick, and that may be the reason they get drunk and disorderly."

"It is quite a problem, though, for liquor is easy to get," Nancy said. "Pa has heard that farmers hide spirits in the hay or straw carried on the wagons they take to the army camp, and grocers sneak in liquor when they're taking supplies. Besides, people back in the hills make moonshine and sell it to the soldiers. When Pa is home, he hardly ever sleeps at night but keeps going back and forth between the house and the *Wetzel*. That's the reason I stay over here so much. He says he can't protect me and our property, too."

Mrs. Foster smiled fondly at Nancy. "You've become an important part of our household. I don't know what we'd do without you." She turned to Heath. "If these young men don't have something positive to do, they are bound to get into trouble. And several families in this town are in need, too. Husbands and fathers have gone off to war, leaving their families destitute. The soldiers send money home when they can, but they don't get paid regularly, and that leads to stealing. Our sewing circles are busy making clothes. But what else can we do?"

While Heath deliberated, Nancy said, "I don't know what we can do for the ones in the army camp, but a lot of the soldiers from the West just stop over in Wheeling for a few hours. Why couldn't we set up a welcome center down at the station and give them coffee and cake?"

"That would be a good start," Heath approved. "With our industry disrupted like it is, I'm sure there are some empty warehouses you could use."

The next day, Nancy and Mrs. Foster formulated plans to add entertaining these soldiers to their activities. They also enlisted the help of Tabitha Clark, who, since the time Nancy and her father had come to her rescue, had joined the women's sewing circles. Pa had commented, "That doesn't surprise me. Widow Clark has lots of possibilities—she just needed to wake up."

Nancy was happy to be helping the Union soldiers, but she often remembered Clay, wondering if Confederate women were providing his needs.

Heath entered the portals of the Federal Court Building and joined a line of other citizens who had been summoned to appear before the judge to answer to charges of disloyalty.

Lord, he prayed silently, *my attitude is wrong. Give me the grace to speak as Thou would have me speak—that I might not answer hostility with hostility. Help me to be gracious even as Thou wast in the midst of persecution.*

He had been astounded two days ago when he had received the summons to appear in court. He supposed he shouldn't have been surprised, because he had been aware that citizens were no longer judged on their past contributions. There was no middle ground—either you took an oath of allegiance, or you were a traitor.

He had taken the oath of allegiance months earlier, and the Union flag was displayed on a staff on his front porch. But in the patriotic fervor of the moment and with the fear of Confederate invasion, past performances counted for little. Other pacifists had been harassed, so now it was his time.

The men in line didn't exchange glances with anyone else, and talking was subdued and at a minimum. No one wanted to be here, nor did they want to be seen in this company. Heath's turn came at last. He stood before the judge, who riffled some papers on his desk and looked up.

"Dr. Foster, my apologies for calling you away from your humanitarian work, which is well-known in the area. However, charges of disloyalty have been brought against you. I'm sure you will agree that in these troubled times, it is imperative for this court to examine all accusations."

"Even when the charges are unfounded?"

The judge turned steely eyes upon Heath. "That is for the court to decide." He looked again at his papers and handed a sheet to Heath. "This is an oath of allegiance that all male citizens are required to sign."

"Which I signed several months ago."

"Some revisions have been made in the oath."

Heath was aware of the changes, and he had no intention of signing the paper, but he scanned it quickly. The only change from the previous oath was the addition of the words, "and will neither directly nor indirectly give aid or information to the enemies of the United States, and will not advocate or sustain, either in public or private, the cause of the so-called Confederate states."

Heath handed the paper back to the judge, who refused to take it.

"I won't sign this paper. If I did, it would supersede the Hippocratic oath I signed when I became a physician. I refer to the words, 'I will apply dietetic measures for the benefit of the sick according to my ability and judgment; I will keep them from harm and injustice. . . . Whatever houses I may visit, I will come for the benefit of the sick.'"

The judge's expression was stern, his voice sarcastic. "I'm sure the famed Hippocrates would have held the defense of his beloved Greece higher than his devotion to the sick."

In Heath's opinion, this comment didn't deserve an answer. Instead he said, "But from the Holy Bible, I have a mandate that supersedes my medical oath. Jesus indicated that His people would be those who fed the hungry and helped the stranger. I have particularly heeded His words, 'I was sick, and ye visited me: I was in prison, and ye came unto me.' He ministered to Samaritans and Romans, as well as Jews, and if confronted with our present crisis, I'm sure our Lord wouldn't have made a difference between Union and secessionists in His healing ministry."

The judge's eyes were cold and proud, and he continued as if he hadn't heard Heath. "I understand that you have visited the homes of many secessionists, which has caused suspicion, and that you go to the prison to treat Confederate soldiers. How does anyone know whether you went to treat the sick or to discuss treasonous measures toward our nation?"

"When they need medical attention, a Confederate sympathizer or a Unionist looks alike to me."

"You still refuse to sign?"

Heath dipped a pen in the inkwell the judge pushed toward him, scratched out the words that offended him, signed the paper, and gave it back to him. The judge scrutinized the form.

"You may go now, Doctor, but your activities will be watched."

Heath expected to be arrested every time he attended a person who was known to favor the Southern cause, but the months passed and no one challenged his activities. He wondered if he was spared because of his mother's humanitarian help to soldiers and their families. If his mother helped Confederate sympathizers, he didn't want to know.

Chapter 14

Nancy slipped her hand in her pocket as she and her father walked home from worship Sunday morning. Looking for a handkerchief, she was surprised to feel a piece of paper instead. Intuition told her it was a note, for she knew the paper hadn't been there earlier. She had no idea when or by whom it had been placed in her pocket. Heart pounding, Nancy hurried up the stairs and into her room, closing the door behind her. She pulled the paper from her pocket and unfolded it.

I'm hurt bad and don't know if I'm gonna make it. I've been travelin' for weeks, wantin' to get home before I died. I know Pa wouldn't want me to come home, so I'm hidin' in Wetzel's Cave. You know where it is. I'd like to see you.

The message wasn't signed, and although the writing was hard to decipher, she was sure it was from Clay. It had been thirteen months since he had left home, and this was the first message they'd had from him for almost three months.

She hadn't been there for several years, but Nancy was well aware of the location of Wetzel's Cave. On a hill overlooking Wheeling Creek, the cave was the legendary home of Lewis Wetzel, a backwoodsman who had roamed the countryside during the latter part of the eighteenth century when settlers first came into the upper Ohio River valley. During her childhood, Nancy had gone to the cave several times with her friends until her father found out about it and abruptly stopped her cave excursions. She wasn't sure she could find the cave now, yet she had to try. But how could she get away without Pa knowing?

That afternoon when her father was contacted by the army to make an unscheduled trip on the *Wetzel*, Nancy thought his departure was divine providence, until he told her to spend the night with Mrs. Foster. But since Mrs. Foster didn't know she was supposed to be there, Nancy could slip away to see Clay without anyone knowing about it. She had to be careful. If the authorities discovered Clay's hiding place, he would be locked up in the military prison, where he would surely die since he was badly wounded. In spite of Heath's efforts to heal the Confederate prisoners, many of them had died.

Nancy packed a basket with food and medicines. She put on heavy shoes and her oldest dress because she would be climbing over rough terrain before she reached the cave. She would stay off the main streets and take alleys until she found the path that she could follow up the hill to the cave. She filled the lantern with oil and settled down to wait for dark, trying to remember the way to the cave.

Loud talking and hilarity across the river told her that someone had smuggled in another batch of liquor. She didn't want to be apprehended by a drunken soldier, so when semidarkness approached, Nancy left home and walked stealthily, all of her senses alert to detect the first sign of danger. She reached the National Road without meeting anyone she knew; she believed her escape was going without a hitch, only to be brought up short when she heard a buggy approaching behind her. She turned quickly. It was Heath, and her shoulders slumped in despair. He halted his horse, looking at her with a probing query in his eyes.

"I noticed that the *Wetzel* was gone and you hadn't come to our home. What are you doing out here?"

After one quick glance at Heath, Nancy looked away, unwilling to meet his eyes. She knew she could trust him, but she didn't want anyone to know where Clay was. Not only would Clay be in danger, but anyone who harbored a Confederate soldier was subject to arrest. Heath was already in enough trouble with the local authorities. Why hadn't she started five minutes earlier and avoided this meeting with him? Tongue-tied, she looked piteously at him.

Gathering the reins in one hand, Heath held out his right hand to her. Torn between uncertainty over what she should do and the relief of confiding in Heath, she took his hand and stepped into the buggy. He gazed curiously at the heavy haversack she dropped at her feet and at the unlighted lantern she carried.

"We'll drive around for a while."

Leaving the thoroughfare, he turned right into the industrial section of Wheeling. He slowed his horse to a slow gait and traveled along a quiet street. When she remained silent for the better part of fifteen minutes, he asked softly, "Is it Clay?"

Nancy nodded, but knowing he probably couldn't see in the dim streetlights, she said quietly, "Yes." Glad now that she had someone to share her burden, she told him about the note she'd received.

"I didn't know how I could go to Clay without Pa knowing, and I felt like God had arranged for him to leave to give me the opportunity to see my brother." Her lips trembled. "He said he's dying, but I brought some medicines and things to help him if I can."

Heath asked for directions to the cave and turned his horse and buggy.

"We'll go home so I can stable the horse, and I'll go with you."

"I don't want you to get into trouble."

"I'm always in trouble. Even if he weren't your brother, I'd try to help him. And if he is dying, you shouldn't have to suffer through it alone."

She knew how dangerous it was for him to come with her; still, his presence would be a comfort. The exigencies of war had made her more self-reliant, but it was heartening to have Heath share her burden. He stabled the horse and asked Nancy to wait in his office. He went into the house and soon returned dressed in a pair of loose trousers and a short wool jacket. He had changed his shoes for a pair of brogans. He carried his medical bag in one hand and balanced the haversack on his shoulder as they set out. Nancy carried the lantern.

"Tell me about this cave."

"There are several caves in the hills around Wheeling, but this particular one was the hideout of Lewis Wetzel, a backwoods scout. Wetzel dedicated his life to protecting the settlers from Indian raids. That's where Pa got the name for his steamboat. When we were children, we played on these hills and in the caves."

"You go first and I'll follow," he said.

"I haven't been to the cave for a long time, but I think I can find it. The path used to be well traveled, but it may be hidden by underbrush now."

Nancy led the way out of town, plunged into the wild plum thicket that concealed the entrance to the path, and headed uphill. Surely God's hand was leading the way, for the path she followed seemed familiar.

Time passed quickly, and when she finally paused for a quick breath, she said, "We're almost there. We go downhill for just a short distance, and we'll find the cave—I'm sure of it."

They approached a large stone slab, and she pointed. "That must be it. This entrance is small, but once we're inside, the cave branches out into several small rooms. We called one of the rooms the hideout. I figure that's where Clay will be."

She crawled through the opening and peered anxiously ahead to where the cave branched into more than one room, but she didn't see anyone. Bending low, Heath entered the cave.

"Wait here," he said. "I'll check everything out first."

<hr/>

Heath gave Nancy a quick embrace as he moved past her and looked into a small room. His head barely cleared the ceiling, but he held the lantern high and glanced around the damp, cool room. The room had a musty smell, but his medical instincts also picked up a fetid stench, the odor of mortifying flesh. Was Nancy too late to see her brother?

"Clay," he called quietly. "Clay Logan, are you here?"

A low, eerie moan was his only answer, but he moved toward the sound.

A man lay on his back, covered with a ragged blanket.

"Come on in, Nancy," Heath called.

When she rushed to his side, he said, "There's a man here, and it's probably your brother."

Still hesitant, Nancy moved in the direction Heath indicated and looked down. Heath turned up the wick of the lantern, and she knelt beside the man. Could this emaciated, bearded, dirty man be Clay? But on closer inspection, she looked up, tears glistening in her eyes.

"It's Clay," she said. She touched her brother's arm. "It's Nancy. I've come to help you."

The man tried to sit up but fell back on the dirty pallet. Heath knelt on the other side and found a feeble pulse. He lifted the blanket and replaced it quickly before Nancy saw the blood-soaked garments.

Nancy took a bottle of water from her pack. "If you'll hold him up, I'll give him some water."

Heath carefully lifted Clay into a reclining position and propped him against his knees. Clay groaned and gasped. With a shaking hand, Nancy lifted the bottle to her brother's mouth. She managed to force a few swallows between his parched lips before his head rolled to one side.

Heath lowered him to the ground. "He's passed out. He has a bad wound in his side."

Nancy touched Clay's face. "He's awful hot."

Heath nodded. "His temperature is high. Why don't you wash his face and hands? I'll try to revive him long enough for you to talk to him."

"You think he's going to die?"

Heath looked away so he wouldn't have to see the impact on his beloved when he answered, "Yes."

"I wish Pa was here."

"I'd go after him, but I don't think there's time. The bad odor from his wound indicates that gangrene has set in. If we can rouse him, I'll give him a morphine tablet to dull the pain."

She shook her head. "Pa won't be home until tomorrow morning."

Nancy kept washing her brother's face, and once when he roused, they forced a morphine tablet down his throat. He seemed to sleep after that. Nancy held his hand while Heath sat beside her, his arm around her waist, her head resting on his shoulder.

Once, when the misery in Nancy's heart boiled to the surface and she started crying, Heath wiped away her tears with his handkerchief and kissed her lips softly.

"How I wish I could have spared thee this trouble. Thou art precious to me, and I hate to see thee suffering in this way."

Heath's words gave Nancy the courage to face what problems Clay's return and his death would cause her family. She remembered the time when Mrs. Foster had told her that Quakers used the old form of *you* when they spoke to fellow believers, to close members of the family, or to those they loved. She wasn't a Quaker, and she wasn't a family member, so in this gentle way, when she needed encouragement more than any other time in her life, Nancy knew that Heath loved her.

Clay slept peacefully for an hour, and when he woke up after a bolt of pain seemed to slither through his body, his eyes opened and focused on Nancy and Heath.

"What—," he said. He started to sit up, gasped, and fell back again. Heath put Nancy's knapsack under his head.

"Where am I? What are you doing here, sis?"

"You're in Wetzel's Cave. I don't know how you got here. I brought Dr. Foster to help you."

Monitoring Clay's pulse, Heath shook his head. Nancy knew that Clay was sinking fast, and if they were to learn what had happened to him, he needed to talk now. "How were you wounded?"

Slowly, with many pauses to catch his breath, Clay gasped out the facts of his injury.

"I've been fighting with one Confederate general after another in northeast Virginia most of the time I've been gone. Mostly, we've been trying to keep control of the B&O Railroad. The Federal troops are better equipped than we are, and it seemed like bad luck plagued us from the first. I was shifted from one unit to another, fighting around Harper's Ferry and other mountain areas. I was hit by sniper fire. The army doctors don't have much to work with, and I didn't get any better. I wanted to come home to die, and another soldier and me headed west. I didn't figure Pa would take me in, so I crawled up here." Turning his attention to Heath, he asked, "How much time do I have, Doc?"

"A few hours."

Clay nodded. "Well, I made my choice. I lived with it, and now I'm a-dyin' with it. I'm not sorry. I could have gotten wounded no matter which army I joined. But the whole war was a big mistake. I see that now. We had a great country. I don't know why we couldn't get along. I did what my commanding officers told me to, but it just didn't seem right to be shooting at other Americans—men who spoke the same language we do, men who worship the same God."

The morphine was having its effect, and he slept again. Heath put his arm around Nancy, and they leaned against the damp walls of the cave. Daylight was seeping into the tunnel when Clay wakened again.

"Nancy," he said, "you know I ain't been too bad. I've always helped out any-body in need. Do you suppose God will have me?"

Knowing she was out of her element when it came to discussing eternal salvation with her brother, Nancy looked helplessly at Heath.

Placing his hand lightly on Clay's forehead, he spoke tenderly, "Spending eternity in heaven with God doesn't depend on the things we have done or haven't done. The way to eternal life was made possible because of what Jesus, God's Son, did when He died on the cross for the sins of all mankind. After we've accepted Jesus as our Savior, then we're expected to live good lives, but there's nothing we can do to save our souls. Jesus took care of that at Calvary."

"Nobody in our company had a whole Bible, but we passed scraps of the New Testament around among us. There was one word I couldn't understand. Somethin' like that Jesus was the propicheation for our sins. Do you know what I'm talkin' about?"

Heath answered softly, "Yes—that's one of my favorite passages in the book of Romans. 'For all have sinned, and come short of the glory of God; being jus-tified freely by his grace through the redemption that is in Christ Jesus: whom God hath set forth to be a propitiation through faith in his blood, to declare his righteousness for the remission of sins that are past.' *Propitiation* means that through His death, Jesus became the means by which people's sins can be forgiven."

Sweat popped out on Clay's face. Heath felt his pulse and spoke quickly.

"Have you taken that step in your relationship with God? Have you accepted Him as your Savior?"

A beautiful smile momentarily erased the suffering on Clay's face. "I did that a long time ago, Doc."

"Then you need no other assurance that God will indeed have you."

"Tell Pa I'm sorry I disobeyed him and went to fight with the enemy. Do you think he'll forgive me?"

"He already has," Nancy assured her brother. "When you left, he told me never to mention your name to him, but anytime I've had news of you, I've told him, and he was glad to hear."

"I thank God for that." With an effort, Clay lifted his hand and patted Nancy's cheek. "I've always looked after you, little sister, but now somebody else will have to take care of you." Lowering his hand, he looked significantly at Heath.

Clay lived on until midmorning, but he didn't speak again. Nancy held her brother's left hand; Heath held his right one; and as the minutes passed, they felt life slowly leaving his body. The smile that had spread across Clay's face when he confessed his belief in Jesus as his Savior faded at last.

———∿∿∿———

Nancy lifted her eyes to Heath's. He nodded and drew the blanket over Clay's face. Her brother had moved from this troubled world to a place where he would feel no more pain. After witnessing his hours of suffering, she couldn't be sorry that he had died.

"What do we do now?" she asked quietly.

"I've spent the last hour trying to decide if we should just bury him here in the hills and not tell anyone about his death. If we take his body to be buried in Wheeling, you and your father may be hounded more than you have been."

"I think Pa ought to know—he should make the decision."

"Then one of us will stay with Clay. The other will go and tell your father."

"I wish you would go and tell him. I don't think I could bear to break the news to him. For all of their differences, Pa and Clay loved each other. He should be home by the time you get there."

"That probably is best, but I don't like to leave you here alone."

"That's the only way."

Heath stood up, saying wearily, "Yes, I suppose it is. I wish I could have spared thee this trouble, my dear."

He came to her and gathered her snugly into his arms. Gently he rocked her back and forth. Softly his breath fanned her face. She pulled back slightly and looked at him. He first kissed her with his eyes, and then she felt his lips on hers as light as a whisper.

"I love thee, Nancy. Dost thou feel the same for me?"

"Forever and ever," she promised softly. He kissed her again and released her.

"I'll be back as soon as I can," he promised and exited the cave.

Nancy felt an immeasurable peace and satisfaction. Perhaps this cave, with her brother lying dead at her feet, was a strange place for Heath and her to declare their love, but she knew Clay wouldn't have minded. She sat down again and removed the blanket from her brother's face. All through her life, Clay had been her protector—now he had given her into Heath's care.

Chapter 15

As he hurried away from the cave and made the long walk into town, Heath agonized over what he should do first and how he could approach Wendell about the loss of his son. The *Wetzel* was docked at the foot of the street. As he approached, he saw that the crew was still unloading freight, so they hadn't been in port long.

God, I don't know how to break this news. Give me the wisdom to approach Wendell in the right way about the tragedy that has struck his family.

A deckhand told Heath that Wendell was in his office, and he headed in that direction. Wendell looked up, startled, when Heath tapped on the door. Perhaps Heath's expression warned Wendell that something was wrong, for he clenched the handful of freight bills he held. "Is my girl all right?"

"Oh yes, Nancy is fine," Heath hastily assured him, "but I do have bad news."

He quickly related how Nancy had received the note, how they had gone to the cave, and how Clay had subsequently died.

"Since it's against the law to harbor or give aid to a Confederate soldier or sympathizer, Nancy and I discussed burying Clay in the hills without telling anyone. But she believed that decision should be left up to you."

Wendell dropped the freight bills into a desk drawer, took his hat off the rack, and pulled it low on his forehead. When he started out the door, Heath asked, "What are you going to do?"

"I'm goin' after my boy, that's what! I ain't no Confederate sympathizer, but Clay's my boy. I'm bringin' him home to be buried beside his ma. I'll get my men to build a coffin, and we'll carry him off the hill. If my neighbors don't like it, that's too bad—it won't matter to me." He paused and looked directly at Heath. "I thank you for helpin' Nancy out, but your part don't need to be made public. No need for you to be arrested for aidin' and abettin' the enemy. I'll take it from here."

Heath nodded his thanks. But when Wendell and his deckhands arrived at the cave with the hastily built wooden coffin several hours later, Heath was waiting with Nancy. And he followed along as the small cortege carried the body of Clay Logan out of the hills and to the cemetery to be buried beside his mother.

The news must have circulated rapidly, for a crowd of more than fifty people had gathered at the cemetery, including Mrs. Foster, Tabitha Clark, and the editor of the *Intelligencer*, Archibald Campbell, to mourn with Nancy and her father. The next day, Heath brought a copy of the newspaper to Nancy.

"I guess Mr. Campbell's editorial has summed up the feelings of most Wheeling residents today," he said as he read the headline: "NATIVE SON DIES FOR HIS COUNTRY."

With tears seeping from her eyes and drizzling over her cheeks, Nancy read,

"Yesterday in Wheeling, a truce was declared. There was no North or South—no Confederates or Yankees. Confederate sympathizers, loyal Union men and women, and grieving neighbors, some with no particular political beliefs, gathered to pay their last respects to Clay Logan, who died for the cause he held dear. All mankind looks the same in God's eyes. The preacher summed up the feeling of Wheeling's citizens yesterday by quoting from the book of Galatians: 'For ye are all the children of God by faith in Christ Jesus. For as many of you as have been baptized into Christ have put on Christ. There is neither Jew nor Greek, there is neither bond nor free, there is neither male nor female: for ye are all one in Christ Jesus.' I applaud those who risked persecution and harassment to honor a fallen soldier."

When Nancy finished reading, Heath pulled her into a close embrace and held her until she stopped crying.

———

A week after Clay's funeral, Heath brought Nancy home in the buggy, and she asked him to stay for supper. He had a call to make on one of her neighbors, but he promised to return for the evening meal. Nancy was atwitter as she prepared stewed chicken and dumplings, potatoes, and green beans to her satisfaction. The biscuits turned out golden and flaky. She opened a jar of pickled cucumbers. Heath not only complimented her on the meal, but ate as heartily as he did at his own table.

After they finished eating a slice of chocolate cake, Heath pushed back from the table. "Wendell," he said, "I have another call to make soon, but now seems as good a time as any to ask for your permission to court Nancy."

Nancy gasped, and her face flushed. Since the time he had declared his love in the cave where Clay had died, she had felt sure that Heath would approach her father, but she hadn't expected it so soon.

"I realize that Nancy is mourning her brother, so I wouldn't expect to marry right away, but I do love her. I'd like to have your permission to marry her eventually, and to keep company with her until that time."

Wendell took a big swig of coffee and looked from Nancy to Heath.

"And what does Nancy think about that?"

"I didn't want to ask her until I'd discussed it with you, but I'm sure she shares my feelings."

"Nancy?"

She sensed her father's gaze on her, and she knew he would press for an answer. She couldn't lift her head, and she was tongue-tied. The silence grew in the room until she nodded her head and sneaked a quick look at her father. The room seemed deathly still as her father deliberated.

"I know you don't approve of my political beliefs," Heath said, "but I can't understand why that will keep me from being a good husband for Nancy."

"I ain't necessarily agin' this marriage, but there are things to consider. Nancy, look at me. Do you want to marry the doc?"

Nancy lifted her head and unwaveringly met her father's eyes. "Yes."

He nodded and looked at Heath. "I ain't agin' havin' you court, but speakin' as man to man, it might be well for Nancy to get used to the idea gradually."

"I understand what you mean, and as I said, I don't mean to rush into marriage. For one thing, Nancy is sad now about Clay's death, and she should be happy at her wedding."

Nancy flashed a grateful smile in his direction, marveling that he understood her so well.

"Now that I have your permission, I want to build a house. My mother will probably insist that we live with her, but every woman should have her own home. There's an empty lot on the same street where we live, and I've got an option to buy it. Nancy can plan the house the way she wants it, and by the time the house is built, we should be ready to marry."

Her father nodded approvingly and cleared his throat. Nancy noted a mist in his eyes. "You have my blessing."

Nancy walked downstairs with Heath when he rose from the table and shyly received his kiss. As she watched him drive away, Nancy had never been happier. When she returned to the kitchen, her father still sat at the table.

She put her arms around his shoulders. "Thanks, Pa. You've made me very happy."

"He's a good man, and he'll take care of you. I can't ask for more."

<hr />

Nancy walked slowly along Market Street on her way to the Foster home. The months that had passed since Clay's death had brought death and tragedy to many families in Wheeling, and sadness seemed to hover over the city. The concern about Southern sympathizers in the city had taken second place to the guerilla warfare occurring in the counties west of the Alleghenies. Several raids had been conducted by Virginia raiders determined to block the new state movement and to keep the western counties as part of the Confederacy.

Because Wheeling was the most important city in the west, many of these expeditions attempted to reach their area. Nancy had been worried when the city was placed on alert several times, but so far, none of the guerilla bands had reached Wheeling. The news, however, was disturbing, for while lawmakers continued to make decisions that would eventually change the political map of Virginia, the military outcome seemed to favor the Confederacy.

Sometimes her father worried that the Union might actually lose the war. Once, he'd said to Nancy, "If that happens, we'll have to move into Ohio or farther west. Or maybe Heath will take you back to Philadelphia."

"I don't think so," Nancy said. "He likes it here, and he believes the Union will ultimately win. He takes a lot of magazines and newspapers, and from what he reads, he says that the Union Army is getting stronger—that all they need now is a general who will fight instead of retreating every time they lose a battle."

But in spite of the bad news from the war front and the threat of invasion by Southern troops, Nancy was happy in her love for Heath. Lacking a mother, as soon as Pa gave permission for their eventual marriage, Nancy approached Mrs. Foster for guidance.

"I love Heath very much, but it will take more than that to make me the kind of wife he needs. Working for you has taught me to how to keep house the way he's accustomed to. But I want to improve my mind so I can discuss subjects that interest him. Will you help me?"

"Of course I'll help you. During the winter months, you'll have more time to read. I'll point out his favorite volumes on the bookshelves, and you can read those. By being in our home, you've already learned much about our customs and our ways. I have no doubt that you'll fit graciously into his life. He's made a good choice."

Chapter 16

January 1863

Heath let in a cold blast of air when he arrived home from his daily calls. Nancy hurried to help him take off his heavy overcoat, and he bent to kiss her.

"Your face is cold," she protested, but he kissed her anyway, took off his gloves, and placed his cold hands on her face. She shivered.

"It's cold outdoors. All of us can't stay inside where it's warm," he joked.

He waved a copy of the *Intelligencer*. "It's happened at last."

"What has happened?"

He unfolded the paper and read, " 'In spite of opposition from half of his cabinet, on December 31, President Lincoln signed the bill favoring the admission of West Virginia into the Union.' "

Entering from the kitchen in time to hear the news, Mrs. Foster said, "It's about time. It's been months since the statehood bill was introduced by our senators."

"There was a lot of maneuvering back and forth, trying to decide what was legal and what wasn't," Heath agreed. "But after Senator Willey made a proposal last July concerning statehood that was passed by the U.S. Senate, there wasn't much doubt that we would be a separate state. After a lot of deliberation, President Lincoln finally got around to signing the bill."

"Does that mean we're a new state?" Nancy asked.

"Not yet, but we're getting closer. The West Virginia Constitutional Convention will meet to adopt a few changes made to the original proposal; then the voters will have to approve the constitution as amended. It will still be several months."

He put the paper aside. "But enough political discussion," Heath said. "You can read the paper later. It's time to have the plans drawn up for our home, and I want to know what kind of house you want."

"I can't get excited about a new home when the war effort is going against the Union. After the Confederates won the Battle of Fredericksburg in December, everybody expects General Lee to head our way. If the Confederacy wins, the first thing they'll do is retake our counties, and probably those of us who are pro-Union will lose everything we have."

Heath took her hand and led her to a map of the United States on the wall with the state of Virginia highlighted. "You shouldn't fret about that. In the first place, the Confederacy isn't going to win. It's true that they have great generals and valiant soldiers, but the Union does also."

"But the Confederates have won the most battles." Wanting to prepare for the time when she would be Heath's wife, Nancy read all of the newspapers and magazines that came into the Foster home, and the predominant news was about the war. "The Union lost two battles at Bull Run. And when they tried to conquer Richmond along the Virginia peninsula, they had to retreat."

"I'll admit," Heath said, "that the losses are embarrassing, but the Union seems to have trouble finding the right leadership. Now that Robert E. Lee is in command of the Army of Northern Virginia, it won't get any easier."

"If we could have had Stonewall Jackson on our side, it might have helped. He was a native of the western counties, so I don't know why he had to fight with the Confederacy."

Always willing to discuss political matters with Nancy, Heath delayed talking about the new house plans.

"The Union Army has made a poor showing in the attempt to take Richmond, but we need to look to the West. We've made great gains in the Mississippi River area."

Indicating places he had marked on the map, Heath said, "Union victories at Fort Henry and Fort Donelson gave the nation a new hero in Ulysses S. Grant. A subsequent Union victory at Shiloh and the capture of New Orleans gave us control of the Mississippi River and cut the Confederacy in two."

"But the Confederates are still in Vicksburg."

Heath laughed and playfully chucked her under the chin. "Why are you so pessimistic tonight—throwing cold water on all of my ideas? The Southerners are tough, but they can't compete with the military and industrial might of the North. Our navy has thrown a blockade around the South. They can't ship their cotton. They can't get any armaments, medical supplies, or food through the blockade. England and France haven't recognized the Confederacy as a separate nation, and they aren't likely to."

"You're looking at the situation on a larger scale than I do."

He nodded. "Right from the first, the Union has waged an offensive war, and they're always harder to win. As a physician, I deplore the loss of human life, and the longer the war drags on, the more men are going to be killed. I wish I could change that, but I can't."

He took her hand and drew her forefinger along the crooked chain of mountains dividing the proposed state of West Virginia from the eastern seaboard. "If all else fails, these mountains will stand strong. They provide a good barrier between us and an invasion by enemy forces. We can wage a war on this side of the mountains and still keep our state free."

Nancy looked at him with wondering eyes. "*We* could wage a war? Do you mean you would fight if it comes to that?"

"I hope I'm never forced to, but I've always said that I would defend my home and my loved ones against the enemy. Does that answer satisfy you, my little one?"

She stood on tiptoes and kissed him. "I won't say again that I think we'll lose the war."

"Good! And don't think it, either," he said as he gathered her into his arms and returned her kiss. "Let's make plans for our dream house."

"When I forget about the war, I get excited about our wedding. But I hate to leave Pa alone."

"I don't figure your father will be alone very long. He's not an old man, and he's a good catch. He'll probably take a wife."

Nancy's eyes widened. "I've wondered for years why he never remarried, and I finally figured he never would, whatever the reason."

"Would it bother you?"

"I don't think so. Mama has been gone a long time, and I wouldn't want him growing old alone."

"Do you have any ideas about our house?"

"I like that little brown house on Byron Street."

"You mean where the Baxters live?"

She nodded.

"It's small."

"But at first, I wouldn't want a big house." She waved her hand to indicate his present home. "A house this size would be too big for me to take care of by myself, and I'd still want to help your mother with this one. Wouldn't it be better to build a home with four or five rooms and add more rooms when we have a family?" She blushed and looked away from him.

He lifted her chin, and she met his eyes. "Then you do want to have children."

"Of course—that's just the way it happens. You get married and you have babies."

"But some women don't particularly want a family. I'm glad to know that you do."

<center>~~~</center>

Conscious of the fact that in a few months she would leave her father's home, Nancy took three trips on the *Wetzel* with him during the months of February and March. Those journeys drew Nancy even closer to her father, but she was looking forward to her marriage. When she was with Heath, they made plans for their coming wedding and new home. With a few modifications, Heath had an architect draw plans for the kind of house Nancy wanted. Their dwelling was under construction by April 20 when President Lincoln announced that the act passed by Congress to admit West Virginia into the Union as the thirty-fifth state would take effect in sixty days.

"Will our house be finished by then?" Nancy asked.

"It should be. Why?"

"Let's get married the same day, on June 20."

Heath picked her up and swung her around the room.

"That sounds wonderful to me. We can always celebrate two great occasions on the same day."

When she left the Foster house the next afternoon, Nancy detoured to go by the Danford home. Stella ran to let her in. "It's so good to see you. It's been a raw day outside, and I haven't gone out. Mama is in the kitchen."

As she walked with Stella down the hallway, Nancy remembered how beautiful this house had been before the war, and it saddened her to think of all the heirloom furniture that had been destroyed. "Mama is making a pie out of canned blackberries," Stella whispered, her eyes sparkling.

To everyone's amazement, Mrs. Danford, who had always been a lady of leisure supposedly suffering from ill health, had become a completely different woman in the aftermath of the family's financial losses. With Stella's help, Mrs. Danford had taken over the cleaning and operation of the household. And to her own surprise, she enjoyed cooking, and in no time, she was turning out excellent meals. Her contributions to church fellowship dinners were as popular as food prepared by longtime cooks. And there wasn't a healthier woman in all of Wheeling.

The luscious smell of baking pastry wafted down the hallway, and Nancy smiled at Stella. Mrs. Danford was just lifting the pie from the oven as the girls entered the room. Thickened berry juice oozed from vent holes in the flaky crust.

"That's a masterpiece," Nancy said. "I'm sure it tastes as good as it smells and looks."

Mrs. Danford hugged Nancy. "Sit down and tell us the news while the pie cools, and I'll let you sample it."

"You look mighty happy," Stella commented.

"I am. Heath and I have set June 20 as the date for our wedding."

"That's less than two months away," Mrs. Danford said.

"Stella, will you stand up with me?"

Stella squealed and hugged Nancy.

"Yes, yes," she said. "I'm so happy for you."

"Are you going to have a big wedding?" Mrs. Danford asked.

"No. With the war still going on and everybody so hard up, we intend to keep everything simple. But we are going to be married at the church and invite any of our friends who want to come. Pa is going to stand up with us, too."

"Isn't that that the date Papa said West Virginia will become a state?"

Nancy nodded happily. "That's the reason we chose that day."

As she moved around putting pieces of steaming pie in bowls, Mrs. Danford said, "You should have a new dress anyway. I'd like to make it for you."

"Now that Mama has learned to sew, she always wants to make new clothes."

"That would be wonderful," Nancy said.

"Perhaps Mrs. Foster will want to make your dress," Mrs. Danford said with some disappointment.

"I'll ask her, but she's so busy with the soldiers' canteens and knitting items for the needy that she wouldn't have enough time."

"We'll go shopping next week to see if there are any dry goods in Wheeling. If not, we can rip up some of our dresses and make it. I had a ball gown in the long ago, and I have no use for it anymore," she added without resentment. "We might use that."

Stella's mother had come a long way, Nancy thought and looked fondly at the woman who had lost so much in wealth and position, but had gained much more in things that really mattered.

With the completion of their home, the making of the wedding dress, and Nancy's involvement in the war effort, the two months passed more rapidly than she could have believed. During the last week that she would spend in her home on the banks of the Ohio, Nancy walked from one room to the other, touching the items that had always been a part of her life. How would it seem to move into a home where she couldn't even see the river?

Perhaps sensing that she was having difficulty coping with the changes marriage would bring, two days before the wedding, Heath suggested that they take a picnic lunch and spend the day by themselves.

Taking a deep breath as they drove away from the house toward the bridge that would take them into the state of Ohio, Nancy said, "Oh, it is good to be alone with you. I want our wedding day to be wonderful—something we can look back on the rest of our lives. And everything seems to be going wrong."

"What's troubling thee, sweet?" Heath asked. "I brought thee away from town to set thy mind at ease. But we might as well talk about whatever is troubling thee so we can put it behind us. Go ahead and tell me."

"The current talk is that Confederate forces are going to invade Wheeling to stop the inauguration of Governor Boreman. They've captured two towns in the eastern panhandle, and the commanders of state militia have been alerted to mobilize their troops."

"We're a long way from those towns."

When Heath turned to access the bridge that led to the state of Ohio, they saw that a barrier had been placed across the bridge, and two armed militiamen held up a hand to stop them.

"Whoa!" Heath said, muttering under his breath, "What's going on?"

Nancy clutched his arm.

The man who approached the buggy must have recognized Heath, for he said, "Where're you going, Doc? Somebody sick?"

"No. Nancy and I are going for a drive."

"We can't let you cross into Ohio. You'll have to do your drivin' somewhere else. You don't have a reputation of bein' favorable to the Union cause anyway."

Nancy had seldom seen Heath display anger, but he raked the man with a withering stare. He opened his mouth to speak but apparently changed his mind. He backed the horse a short distance until he could turn around and start eastward.

"I don't understand," Nancy said. "Why won't they let us go into Ohio?"

"I don't know," he said in a choked voice. "Dost thou have any idea where we can go now?"

"Let's walk down the river from our home to where there's a hickory nut grove with plenty of shade. We pick up a year's supply of nuts there every fall. There's a pretty view of the river."

In silence, they drove back to Nancy's home, and Heath tied his horse in the shade. Pa was working on steamboat equipment in his shop, and he looked surprised when they stopped in the doorway.

"Short picnic," he said.

"No picnic at all. The bridge into Ohio is blockaded—we weren't allowed to cross," Heath said.

Pa whistled and wiped his greasy hands on a rag. "Rumors have spread around that that was going to happen."

"Why?" Nancy asked.

"Two days ago, President Lincoln called for one hundred thousand troops from Pennsylvania, Maryland, Ohio, and West Virginia. Our state's quota was ten thousand." With an ironic grin, her father continued, "Wheeling folks who were awful patriotic two years ago have seen what war's like, and they want no part of it. Seems like a lot of local men tried to leave town yesterday to avoid the draft. The officials aim to stop them, or they won't get enough soldiers to fill the quota."

"That does seem like a lot of men from our few counties," Nancy said.

"There's more to it than that," Pa said. "The Army of Northern Virginia is as strong as it's ever been. After that big Confederate victory at Chancellorsville, General Lee is headin' north with his army. They might intend to take the federal capital, but the general feeling is that Lee plans to raid one of Pennsylvania's munitions factories. The Army of the Potomac is staying between the Confederates and Washington, so Lee is angling westward. It won't surprise me if there ain't a big fight in Maryland or Pennsylvania. The war is comin' closer to home now!"

"Yes, and that's why local residents aren't as enthusiastic about fighting as they were two years ago," Heath said.

"They ain't so worried that they've stopped gettin' ready for the big shindig they're throwin' two days from now. I was uptown yesterday and saw the large platform they're buildin' in front of Linsly Institute."

"That building will be the first statehouse. The program will be held there at eleven o'clock after the fourth and fifth regiments of the West Virginia militia march from the McClure House to the institute."

"After your weddin' at nine o'clock," Pa mentioned.

"Yes," Nancy answered. "Mrs. Foster is serving wedding cake and coffee at her home afterward, but that will still give us time to attend the inaugural ceremonies."

"We'll go to the hickory nut grove for our picnic," Heath said, "if it's all right to leave my horse and buggy here."

"I'll keep an eye on 'em. You won't have any trouble with soldiers down on the point, but the locusts might pester you. I've never seen such swarms as we're havin' this year."

"I like to hear them sing," Nancy said.

"I don't call it singin'," Pa complained. "Just a humdrum buzz that gets on my nerves. Besides, they eat up too many leaves and gardens."

"All right," Nancy said, laughing. "I won't listen to them."

"You can't help it," Pa said, but he grinned. "Go on and enjoy yourselves."

Heath picked up the basket his mother had packed. The locusts' incessant humming did accompany them as they walked, but the sound of songbirds and the quacking of ducks on the river overpowered the locusts when they reached the shaded grove and spread out the food on a tablecloth.

"Even the president's call for more troops hasn't stopped the excitement of the launching of our new state," Heath said. "According to the paper, the hotels are already filled with visitors and dignitaries. The *Intelligencer* is full of ads. The stores think they can sell a lot of merchandise to make up for the loss they've taken during the hard times of the past six months."

The peace of the area tended to quell many of Nancy's concerns about the war, their coming wedding, and the change in her life. "Two days from now, we'll be married," she said with a tinge of sadness in her voice.

Heath reached for her hand. "Surely thou aren't having second thoughts!"

"No, but I've always dreaded change. I love you, and I want to marry you, spend the rest of my life with you—but there's a little sadness, too, that the first twenty years of my life have ended. I suppose everyone feels that way."

He kissed the fingers he held. "I'm sure that all brides do, but it's been that way since the days of Adam and Eve when God told His first creation, 'Therefore shall a man leave his father and his mother, and shall cleave unto his wife: and they shall be one flesh.' God will bless our union; I'm sure of it." Attempting to direct her attention away from the past, he asked, "And how's the wedding dress coming along?"

"It's beautiful," she said happily "I can't believe that Mrs. Danford could take two of her old dresses and come up with such a beautiful gown. It's made out of cream taffeta trimmed with flat pleating, deep fringe, and large ribbon bows. And she fashioned a short veil out of a lace curtain." She didn't mention the ruffled pantalets and embroidered chemise that his mother had helped her to make.

"I hope I won't be too plain for thee," he said, his eyes twinkling. "I'm wearing my best black suit, which is only a year old, but Mother is making a new shirt for me."

"I know you'll look as handsome as always," she said. Moving close to him, she touched her lips to his. "I'm going to like being your wife."

———

Nancy sat wide-eyed beside the open window, breathing in the dank smell of the river and the droning of night insects, wondering if she would sleep at all. In spite of the anticipation of tomorrow, when she would marry Heath and when West Virginia would officially be admitted into the Union, she knew that the political situation of the nation would have its effect on the happiness they should enjoy as newlyweds.

The future of the new state was uncertain, for it was generally believed that Virginia would not willingly give up its western counties. And with Lee's army on the march, it was difficult to predict the future. She knelt beside her bed for a long time, asking God's blessing on her marriage to Heath, as well as His mercy on the nation.

Although she had only a few hours of sleep, Nancy got up at the usual hour, and when Pa came from his bedroom, she had a breakfast of oatmeal and eggs ready for him.

"You didn't have to cook for me this morning," he protested.

Her father was not a demonstrative man, and when he came to Nancy and put his arms around her, she started crying.

"Now! Now!" he said, patting her head, which she'd pressed against his chest. "I didn't mean to make you cry. But I want you to know how proud I am of you and thank you for bein' such a dutiful daughter. You've picked a good man, and I can't ask for nuthin' more than that you'll be the kind of wife to him that your ma was to me." He held her at arm's length and kissed her cheek. She noticed moisture in her father's eyes that she hadn't seen except at the funerals of her mother and brother. But he grinned through his tears, saying, "Now git busy and put my breakfast on the table. We don't want to keep your man waitin'."

Chapter 17

Nancy had left her wedding clothes at the Danford house, and at her father's insistence, she let him wash the breakfast dishes while she hurried to their house.

Mrs. Danford greeted her at the door. "I've already filled the tub with water. And I bought a bar of fancy soap yesterday," she said. Nancy followed her into the kitchen. "You don't have to hurry. Mr. Danford went to the factory for a short time, and Stella and I won't disturb you. There's a fresh towel on the rack."

As Nancy reveled in the warm water, sniffing the violet-scented soap, she missed not having her own mother with her on her wedding day. "But I shouldn't complain," she said to herself. "Both Mrs. Foster and Stella's mother have been so good to me that I really won't miss a mother's love today."

Heath's mother had made her dainty linen nightgowns. And they had nice furniture for their home. Heath had bought new oak furniture for their parlor, and Mrs. Foster had insisted that he take his bedroom suite from her house. She had also divided some of the crystal and china that had been in the Foster family for several years. Nancy had been particularly pleased with the gift of a Boston rocker that she'd used often during her hours in the Foster home.

"Are you about finished?" Stella called. "It'll take awhile to get into our new dresses."

Nancy stepped out of the tub and dried quickly. She didn't want to be late for her own wedding.

———————

Shortly before nine o'clock, Nancy and Stella walked downstairs to join the Danfords for the short walk to the church. Mr. and Mrs. Danford wore two-year-old clothing like everyone else in Wheeling, but they appeared as elegant as they had looked when they were wealthy as they followed Nancy and Stella down the street to St. Matthew's Church.

Nancy had been pleased with her appearance after she'd surveyed herself in the floor-length mirror in Stella's bedroom. And she was even more gratified when people they met on the street paused to stare at her.

"We're getting a lot of attention," Stella whispered, and her brown eyes glistened with merriment. "It won't be long now," she added as they walked into the church.

Mr. Danford escorted the girls to the front pew where Heath and Pa sat. Nancy picked up the bouquet of white roses that Mrs. Foster had prepared for her. An unseen organist started playing softly, and the minister entered the sanctuary from a small door to the left. He shook hands with the members of the wedding party and motioned for them to stand. He asked Heath and Nancy to join hands.

Starting with God's creation of man and woman in Genesis, the pastor discussed the importance that God had placed on marriage. He mentioned some of the more memorable wedded couples in the Bible—Ruth and Boaz, Hannah and Elkanah, John and Elizabeth, Joseph and Mary. He closed the biblical meditation with a quotation from the book of Ephesians: " 'Let every one of you in particular so love his wife even as himself; and the wife see that she reverence her husband.' "

After they took their vows, Heath slipped a simple gold band on Nancy's ring finger. The minister closed his Bible and concluded the service. "It has been my privilege to preside at this ceremony uniting Heath Foster and Nancy Logan in the bonds of sacred matrimony. What God has joined together, let no man put asunder." Smiling benignly, he added, "You may kiss your bride, Heath."

With hands that trembled slightly, Heath lifted Nancy's veil, and their kiss sealed for eternity the vow they had taken.

Stella's parents, Mrs. Foster, and several of their friends, including Tabitha Clark, quickly gathered around the wedding party to congratulate them. "All of you are invited to a wedding breakfast at our home," Mrs. Foster said, "which we can enjoy and still have time to get in place before the inauguration ceremony starts."

During the short walk to the Foster home, Heath held Nancy's hand. "It's a proud day for me, but also one that has humbled me. I don't have the words to tell thee how much it means to me that thou actually want to be my wife. While the preacher talked, I made my own private vow, promising God that I would never let thee be sorry you married me."

Clouds had gathered by the time they finished their breakfast, and Heath must have noticed that Nancy was worried about getting her wedding dress wet. Before they left the house, he picked up a large umbrella from the hall tree. "This will keep us dry," he promised. The sun peeked in and out of the clouds as the wedding party hurried to the roof of a store building near Linsly Institute to watch the festivities, but Nancy was trusting that it wouldn't rain.

The new state officials sat on the platform in front of the institute. Eager spectators crowded every rooftop, nearby streets, and private yards. When Reverend J. T. McClure stepped to the podium and removed his hat, a sudden hush fell over the noisy crowd.

Nancy's own heart and mind echoed the words of the minister as he prayed, "Almighty God, we pray that this state, born amidst tears and blood and fire and desolation, may long be preserved, and from its little beginning may grow to be a power that shall make those who come after us look upon it with joy and gladness and pride of heart."

When Governor Pierpont, who had so skillfully and patiently guided the Reorganized Government of Virginia, gave his farewell speech, he said, "My desire is to see West Virginia free from all shackles. I pray that she may from this small beginning grow to be the proudest member of the glorious galaxy of states that form the nation."

The crowd cheered when Arthur I. Boreman stood to take the oath of office as the new governor. Nancy looked at him with interest. It was rumored that the new governor was an unyielding man, but Heath had said that was a necessary attribute for any man taking over the reins of a new state with such a stormy background. A man in his late thirties, Boreman had a stern face dominated by a long black beard, and Nancy was impressed by his appearance and his acceptance speech. She especially liked his pledge to establish a system of education that would give every child, whether rich or poor, an education to fit them for responsible positions in society.

After the speechmaking ended, men removed their hats and the crowd stood at attention. Thirty-five girls representing each state in the Union sang the "Star-Spangled Banner," accompanied by the band. Overcome by pride in her state, as well as the nation, Nancy wiped her eyes with a lace handkerchief.

A captain of the militia stepped forward. "Let's hear three cheers for the state of West Virginia," he called.

The cheers were deafening, and Nancy wished they were loud enough to be heard all the way to Richmond.

"Now three more cheers for the United States of America."

Again the sounds of rejoicing echoed from the bluffs east of Wheeling and across the river to the hills of Ohio. When the ceremony ended, Heath and Nancy mingled with the crowds milling around the streets of the city, waiting for evening to come when they could watch the fireworks display. Although they had seen a lot of Tabitha Clark in the past year, to Nancy's knowledge, her father had never taken any notice of her, but when Tabitha took hold of Pa's arm and they wandered off together, Nancy quickly exchanged a surprised glance with her new husband. Heath grinned at her and lowered his left eyelid in a significant wink.

By six o'clock, Nancy thought she couldn't walk another step, and it was still four hours before the fireworks started. Perhaps noting her fatigue, Heath said,

"Let's go home, Nancy. We can have supper, rest awhile, and come out again for the closing celebration."

"Yes," she said. "My wedding clothes are hot, and I'd like to change into something cooler."

Their family and friends had been lost in the crowd, and they turned toward their new home alone. Nancy went into the bedroom and changed her wedding gown for a white linen dress she had brought to the house the day before. While they discussed the events of the day, she served the supper that Mrs. Foster had prepared. Mealtime had been a silent time in the Logan home, but Nancy and Heath discussed the day's festivities, as was the custom of the Foster family.

When it started to get dark, Heath said, "It's time to go now."

Nancy sat on the sofa and bit her lip. When she didn't answer, Heath persisted, "Or dost thou not want to see the fireworks?"

"Not really. Do you?"

He replied by pulling her up into his arms, and Nancy surrendered to his embrace. She was shy about the intimacies of marriage awaiting her, but she loved Heath and looked forward to whatever the future held for them.

Epilogue

April 1865

N ancy had just finished nursing her two-month-old son when she heard the back door open. She didn't want to waken Clayton, so she continued rocking slowly in the Boston rocker.

"I'm home," Heath called as he always did when he returned from a call.

"I'm in the parlor," she said quietly.

He bent to kiss Nancy and touched Clayton's tiny fingers curled on his mother's breast.

"I love thee," he whispered. "Both of you."

She smiled at him. "If you'll take the baby and put him in his cradle, I'll finish supper."

He laid the newspaper he carried on the table beside her and took Clayton from her arms. Wondering at his significant look, she picked up the paper and read the prominent headline: LEE SURRENDERS TO GRANT AT APPOMATTOX.

"It's finally over," Heath said.

Nancy didn't know whether to shout with joy that the war had ended at last or weep in remorse over the tragic events that had torn the country apart. As she worked at the stove, finishing preparation of the food, she reflected on the things that had happened since they had been married.

Not long after their wedding, two events had struck the death knell of the Confederacy. After months of siege, Vicksburg had finally surrendered, which paved the way for the Union's complete control of the Mississippi River. And on that same day, July 4, 1863, the Confederate Army started the slow trip back to Virginia after being defeated at Gettysburg, Pennsylvania. Even then, the Confederacy held on, and the months since then had cost the lives of thousands of young men. Knowing how she had mourned her brother's death, Nancy's heart was burdened daily for families who were experiencing the same sorrow that she and Pa still felt.

Grateful for the good news, Nancy whispered, "Thank You, God, that the war has finally ended. Have mercy on us as a nation and heal our wounds."

Coming into the kitchen, Heath said, "Theoretically, we're one nation again."

"And I thank God for that," she said, "but how long will it take to heal the wounds inflicted by four years of warfare?"

As he sat at the table, Heath said, "Longer than it took to fight the war. There's too much ill will and hatred on both sides now. I tremble for what the future holds. Our people have lost the innocence they had at the beginning of the war."

"I'm certainly not the girl I was when the war started."

"I know," he said with a grin as he served her a helping of beef stew. Switching from *thee* to *you* in his conversation as he often did, Heath continued, "Instead of the sassy girl who stood up to Tabitha Clark, you have become a devoted wife, mother—an attractive matron who's up on all the current news and can discuss the classics as if you grew up reading them. You're quite a challenge for me to live up to."

"Disappointed?" she asked.

Suddenly serious, he said, "Not at all. Thou art all I could ever have dreamed for in a wife. You have made me very happy."

She blew a kiss across the table. "Now that other doctors will be returning from the war, maybe you can proceed with the medical research you came to Wheeling to do."

"I intend to." As he helped himself to another serving of stew, he speculated, "I thought that was my reason for coming west, but now I know that God sent me here to meet you. I never forget to thank Him for that."

"Tabitha stopped by today," Nancy said, "to bring a blanket she made for Clayton. After turning out to help your mother and the rest of us make items for the soldiers—Union soldiers, mind you—she's become a good knitter. She said Pa's taking the *Wetzel* out in the morning." Reminiscently, she added, "I think that of all the surprises I've had over these years, the most amazing was when Pa and Tabitha got married."

"That didn't surprise me," Heath said. "I told you Wendell wouldn't stay single long after you left home." He slanted a teasing look at Nancy. "I'm still curious why their marriage didn't bother thee."

Giving him a minxlike smile, she said, "After having such a happy marriage with you, I think everyone should enjoy wedded bliss. Besides, I forgave Tabitha long ago for the way she treated me. If she hadn't been so mean, you probably never would have noticed me. I couldn't be mad at her when she's made Pa happy. And it does my heart good to see the way he dotes on Tommy."

"The way Tommy has taken to life on the river may have saved the boy's life. He's much stronger since he's been traveling on the boat with Wendell."

She walked to the oak sideboard and brought the Bible to him for their nightly reading. "I'm thankful that God has brought an end to the war and that

Wheeling wasn't overrun by the enemy. Can you think of something to read that will sum up the last four years?"

"I know exactly what I want to read. For weeks when it was obvious that the war would end soon, I've thought many times about the incident when His disciples asked Jesus to give a sign of His second coming. He said, 'And ye shall hear of wars and rumours of wars, see that ye be not troubled: for these things must come to pass, but the end is not yet.'"

Turning to the Old Testament, Heath said, "God hates conflict, but I suppose we will have wars until Jesus returns to earth for His followers. But I always take comfort in the words of Isaiah when he talked about the latter days.

" 'And he shall judge among the nations, and shall rebuke many people: and they shall beat their swords into plowshares, and their spears into pruning hooks: nation shall not lift up sword against nation, neither shall they learn war any more.' I believe that Isaiah was prophesying about the second coming of Jesus. So no matter how many wars come our way, we have that to look forward to."

"I pray that our country will never be divided again and that all wars will cease."

"Amen, darling! That's my wish, too. But I don't foresee that happening in our lifetime." He laid the Bible on the table, stood, and pulled Nancy into a tight embrace. "But as long as we face the future together, I'll be content, for I love thee."

Snuggling close to him, Nancy gave herself freely to the promise of his kiss.

IRENE B. BRAND first aspired to be a published author when she was eleven years old, the same year she gave her heart to the Lord and became an active member of the local Baptist church. During the past twenty-five years she's had the privilege of seeing forty-one of her inspirational fictional books (contemporary, historical, and suspense) published. She's also the author of several novellas and nonfiction books, and her works have been reprinted in many anthologies. Irene and her husband, Rod, have had many happy years of marriage. They've visited 35 foreign countries, as well as all 50 states. They attend writers' conferences throughout the United States.

A BRIDE IDEA

Yvonne Lehman

Dedication

Dedicated to the members of my writers' group who patiently allowed me to brainstorm with them and who offered their valuable opinions: Lori, Michelle, Debbie, Phoebe, Ann, Aileen, Gloria, David, and Steven.

Chapter 1

West Virginia, 1916

WANTED: A bride of convenience for one year. A strong, young woman to marry an established man. Care for and be a companion to an incapacitated woman (no nursing experience necessary). The position requires some cooking and management of other employees. Respond by mail to DNMC, General Delivery, Post Office, Sunrise, West Virginia.

Olivia Easton never would have read such an advertisement in the Sunday *Sunrise Gazette* had she not been visiting her aunt, Stella Easton Kevay, in Canaan Valley. "Stella, look at this. It has to be a joke."

Her aunt's shoes pattered against the hardwood floor as she stepped gingerly from the stove to the kitchen table. She set her coffee cup down and looked over Olivia's shoulder.

Olivia tapped on the ad.

After reading for a moment, her aunt gasped. Then she read the entire ad aloud. Olivia watched her step back and plant her hands at the sides of her trim waist. "Well, I've seen some fantastic things in my travels as an actress, but this beats all." She shook her head of copper-colored curls, cut in the latest short style. "How desperate a man must be to advertise for a wife." She picked up her cup and walked around the table.

Olivia nodded. "And how ridiculous a woman would be to consider such a thing."

"True," Stella agreed. She sat across from Olivia on the long bench. "Here, let me see that again."

Olivia handed the paper across to her.

"Hmm," Stella mused. "The man can't be too stupid, using words like 'established,' 'incapacitated,' and 'respond.' If he wrote the ad, he must be educated."

"He may be educated, but he's got to be too old or ugly to get a wife."

"Maybe." A gleam of mischief appeared in her green eyes. "But ugly can be overlooked if he's rich. This does say he's established."

Olivia wrinkled her nose. "That means rich?"

"Well, it means he's not poor. He has a job or a business. He probably owns

119

a restaurant or a hotel. Now that's an interesting thought."

"Maybe. But there's also an incapacitated woman." Olivia thought for a moment. "Incapacitated? But she doesn't need a nurse?"

Stella waved her hand. "Oh, he'd have a nurse for her since he's a man of means."

Olivia lifted a finger for emphasis. "*Ugly* man of means, remember. But why would he want a wife for one year? I know." Widening her eyes, she spoke in an ominous tone. "He marries a woman for a year, incapacitates her, and then seeks another."

Stella leaned over the table, speaking dramatically. "We have a killer here. Like Jack the Ripper or the ogre, Iago, in Shakespeare's *Othello*."

Olivia loved this silly game they were playing. As far back as she could remember, she'd admired her colorful, fun-loving aunt who was considered the outcast of the family. Her father's stories of Stella's escapades were supposed to dissuade her from wanting to pursue an acting career, but they only made Olivia more determined to be like her.

That's what got her in trouble with her father who finally said, "All right. Go spend time with your aunt this summer. See how different her life is than ours and ask yourself if you want to end up like her."

She'd been here for a month now. She saw how Stella lived and preferred her aunt's cozy cabin more than her father's rambling, lonely big house in the city. She'd rather be like her warmhearted aunt who encouraged her dreams instead of like her father who stifled them.

Olivia searched for more job opportunities. "There's an ad for a telephone operator and a nurse in Sunrise and factory workers in the city." She sighed, feeling defeat settling upon her. She'd hoped to find a job in Canaan Valley and live with Stella so she could save her money. Sunrise was ten miles up the mountain, too far for her to travel back and forth, especially since the roads would be too treacherous in winter months.

"There's nothing in Canaan Valley for me. I can't be a logger or become a blacksmith." Trying not to sound morbid, she added, "Too bad there's not an opening for a stagecoach driver."

That sparked Stella's interest. "Oh, but wouldn't that have been fun? Too bad stagecoaches aren't really used anymore. Being on the road is never dull."

"Oh, Stella. You're such fun."

Her aunt grew serious. "Your visiting with me these past weeks has been wonderful, Olivia. Much of my time is spent being alone, living with my good memories of the past."

"At least you have those. Since Mama died, I haven't had many good experiences to make good memories."

"You're young, dear. And your father is right in wanting you to be sure about your future."

"Father thinks I should find a man and make a home for him." She made a face to show her disdain of that idea.

Stella laughed. "You don't want that?"

"I don't want to live my life for a man. I want to live it for me. Isn't that what you did?"

"Yes, but Kev was an actor. We were on the road together. I would like for him to be here with me now that my acting days are over."

Olivia noticed the familiar melancholy look that came to her aunt's face whenever she talked about her husband who had died several years ago. Stella had truly loved George Kevay, or "Kev," as she always called him.

"Since Kev, I haven't met anyone I want to settle down with."

Olivia sighed. "Maybe I'm condemned to a life of tragedy as a spinster schoolmarm or a piano teacher and living with my father for the rest of my life. I just can't do that."

"Well, it looks like you're as stubborn as I am."

Olivia agreed. "That's what Father says."

Stella laughed lightly. "What he doesn't realize is that he's more stubborn than the two of us put together. But don't despair," she added in her optimistic way. "Tomorrow we'll hit the shops in town again. We'll even go to the logging companies."

—✦—

Olivia tried to be optimistic on Monday through Thursday mornings when she sat beside Stella in the wagon. The old gray mare pulled them along the dirt roads until they came to the gravel streets of the town and its stores. She loved spending time with Stella, walking down the streets and frequenting all the shops. But being told there were no job openings finally wilted her spirits.

By Friday morning, she'd given up. Barely touching her breakfast, she moaned, "Oh, Stella, I'm doomed to a dreary, lackluster life. I'll have to go back to Father and do exactly what he says. I finished college like he asked, but he refuses to pay one penny on my acting career. What am I going to do?"

Stella didn't make a quip this time but looked very serious. "It's not easy, Olivia, doing something your family doesn't approve of. And actresses don't have the greatest reputation, you know. There are hard times and heartaches."

Olivia nodded. "But isn't it that way with everyone? Father lost his wife. I lost my mother. I have friends who did what their parents demanded, and some are not happy. Oh, Stella, I want to be happy."

Stella put her arm around Olivia's shoulders. "Hon, the life of an actress isn't always fun, either. And sometimes a person has to laugh, even at herself, to

121

keep from crying. But in being an actress, you can escape into the personality of another character. I love that. But you have to love it more than anything and know it's right for you."

"Oh, it is, Aunt Stella. I have to be an actress, or I'll never be happy. Father let me visit with you this summer to get the idea of acting out of my system. But it's in my system even more."

"It has to be your decision, Olivia. But you know you can stay with me as long as you like. You're a big girl now, and Herman needs to recognize that."

Olivia nodded. She didn't want to think badly of her father. "He means well. He really wants the best for me. Now that John and Sarah have married and moved to Wheeling, I'm sort of all he has." Her hand flew to her mouth. "Oh, I don't mean—"

"I know, dear. Herman has me as a sister but doesn't want me. He has such a stiff neck."

Olivia saw the sadness that appeared for a moment in Stella's eyes before she quickly recovered and smiled. "You owe your father respect, but you're not obligated to sacrifice your life for him."

Olivia felt torn. She'd lost her mother, and her stillborn sister, at an early age. She didn't want to lose her father, too. That would leave her only family as her brother, John, and his wife, Sarah. And she wasn't really close to them, either.

Despondency settled in, but Stella had the cure. "Did you forget? This afternoon you get to see me shine. Now let's make sure our duds are ready, and we'll go paint the town."

That afternoon, Olivia sat in the nickelodeon audience. Stella's exuberance at the piano, playing the background music for the movie, was more entertaining to Olivia than the action on the screen. Especially during the automobile chase scene.

"You were wonderful," Olivia said on the way home.

"Honey," Stella said, "this is nothing compared to the stages I've played on, where there are voices attached to the action."

"Oh, but the audience loved you. And all of them wanted your autograph."

"Three people wanted my autograph. But thanks just the same." Stella flicked the reins, and the mare trotted faster. "I'm more fortunate than most actresses in their forties, especially since movies are becoming more popular than the stage. I can't keep up with all the young actresses vying for the movie roles, much less for the roles on the stage. I'm afraid my days of 'kicking up my heels' are over."

"Humph. I've seen you wind up your phonograph and kick up your heels."

Stella laughed. "All right, so maybe I can, but the audience and the producers want young people. You need to know these things."

"I'm young," Olivia said. "And the stage would be okay. But I want to train to be a movie actress." She sighed. "All I need is a job."

Saturday's paper showed no promise. Olivia tried to count her blessings. At least she had this time with Stella.

Olivia liked sleeping late on Sunday morning and having a leisurely breakfast while reading the newspaper. "Oh, that ad is in here again from the man wanting a wife." Olivia sighed. "I guess that poor man just can't find one."

Stella laughed. "Not poor, remember. He's a man of means." When there was nothing fun going on, Stella made her own fun. "You know, we need to check out that man. Like you said, he may be a killer. It's up to you and me to catch him."

Eager to get her mind off her failure to find a job, Olivia joined in. "What could 'DNMC' mean? Does he have four names?"

"Oh no, it's some kind of code. Like. . .Dinner Nightly at My Castle."

"Or," Olivia said menacingly, "it may be a warning, like Do Not Marry Crazy. Remember, he's a murderer."

Stella nodded. "I'm not going to be satisfied until I find out what this is about."

"Are you—"

"Maybe I am crazy," she said, finishing Olivia's sentence. She laughed, as if "crazy" were a most desired state of mind. "This is too good to pass up."

Olivia's heart raced at the prospect of doing something so adventurous, maybe even dangerous. "We can't let somebody like that think we're serious."

"Of course not. We won't use your real name. And we'll put our address as General Delivery in Canaan Valley. We have to satisfy our curiosity, don't we?"

There was only one answer. "Yes, we do." She laughed with her aunt. "Now, what name will we use?"

Stella tapped her cheek, and her green eyes gleamed with mischief. "Well, for this Romeo, what else but. . .Juliet?"

Chapter 2

On Tuesday, Dr. Neil McCory picked up a letter from General Delivery. He had received two letters the week before and had promptly torn them into small shreds and deposited them in the post office trash can. The letter writers eagerly accepted his invitation of marriage.

One, a not-so-young grandmother, vowed she was young inside, needed the job, had managed a household of thirteen children, and could cook anything over a fireplace, including possum.

The other came from a woman who told her story of loneliness for all of her thirty-five years, was strong since she had grown as large as her lumberjack brothers, and always prayed she'd someday be established. Except for having copied the word "established," her vocabulary indicated she hadn't had a day of schooling, and he could barely make out the scrawl.

He dreaded opening this letter. At least his address on the envelope was neatly printed. If only he could have found a solution other than advertising for a wife.

After a furtive glance around, he turned toward the trash can in the corner. Sighing, he tore open the envelope, took out the sheet of paper, and read the brief note.

Dear DNMC:
> *I am interested. Please send more information.*

> *Sincerely, Juliet Kevay*
> *General Delivery, Post Office*
> *Canaan Valley, West Virginia*

At least this one had enough sense to question the sanity of the situation and want some clarification. He could appreciate that.

His slim ray of hope was immediately dispelled, however. Why in the world would any decent, respectable, halfway lucid female consider such an arrangement?

Olivia and Stella rode to the Canaan Valley post office on Wednesday, only to find they had received no mail. Afraid their fun was over, Olivia shook her head. "I knew that couldn't be serious. Somebody put that ad in the paper as a prank to see if any silly person would answer it."

"We only posted the letter on Monday. Give it time. Now let's prance down Main Street and go into every shop and pretend we might buy out the stores."

Olivia laughed. "Not being a woman of means, I can practice my acting."

Stella shook her head of curly red hair that Olivia admired so much. "Ah, my dear, you're my niece. And contrary to what some relatives might think, I've made some wise moves. After Kev was killed in that bar brawl, I had sense enough to begin saving for my old age. Not a lot, mind you, but I'm not destitute." She leaned over and whispered, "Don't tell ol' Stiff Neck."

On Thursday, Olivia stayed in the wagon while Stella went inside the post office. Soon Stella hurried out, her skirts bustling, waving the letter in the air. "It's from Sunrise." .

"Open it," Olivia said. "I can't wait to see what a desperate man—or a killer—has to say."

"We must do this right," Stella said dramatically. "Let's sashay up to the restaurant."

Olivia hopped down from the wagon, hardly able to contain her excitement.

"This is better than any play I've acted in, Olivia. But we have a lot to figure out, so let's get a cup of coffee and mull this over."

They scurried along the sidewalk, drawing some questioning looks from passersby.

Stella asked for the corner table at the window. After the waitress brought their coffee, Stella used the handle of the coffee spoon to cut along the edge of the envelope. She took out the sheet of paper.

Olivia scooted her chair around to see it as Stella read the typed words.

Dear Miss Kevay:

Thank you for your interest. I will be glad to meet you at a place of your choosing for an interview.

Sincerely,
DNMC
General Delivery, Post Office
Sunrise, West Virginia

Olivia balked, dubious about the whole thing. "But of course we can't do that."

"Oh, you shouldn't have said that word," Stella wailed.

"What word?"

"*Can't,*" Stella said. "When anyone says, 'I can't'—" She broke off her sentence and began to laugh. So did Olivia. The whole thing was so hilarious. And

Olivia knew that Stella had always been a daring person. She wasn't surprised when her aunt laid out a plan.

"Let's take the wagon and go up to Sunrise." She squeezed Olivia's hand. "Isn't *sunrise* a beautiful word? It's like. . .a new beginning. The start of a new day."

Stella's enthusiasm and optimism were winning. And if Olivia was going to be like her aunt, what better time to start? "Well, I guess it wouldn't hurt to look around."

"Exactly."

"But," Olivia cautioned after the bill was paid and they were hurrying toward the wagon, "you know I could never consider marrying anyone for a job."

Stella stopped and faced Olivia. "Of course not." Then she grinned. "But I could. And maybe this man of means would let you work there, too. And I'm sure, Olivia, you and I together could overcome that murderer."

The mountains seemed to echo with the sound of their laughter. But Olivia thought Stella might really consider this. She was in her forties but looked and acted young and was beautiful. She made anything seem possible.

On the ride up and around the mountains, Olivia marveled at the beauty of the lush green mountainsides forested with pine, sugar maple, oak, and spruce. One peak rose above another. Rhododendron, laurel, and wildflowers flanked the narrow dirt road.

"Look behind you," Stella said.

While Olivia looked, Stella explained. "Canaan Valley was once as lush and green as this. Now the lumber companies are stripping the land, cutting the trees. It's sad. But logging has become such a huge industry." She sighed. "That's called progress."

Olivia nodded. "Yes, like the tree trunks that are in the bigger cities with electric lines on them so we can light up our homes. It is nice being able to pull a chain or flip a switch and have light."

"Yes, it's not all bad. If it wasn't for some of those cut trees, I'd be in a pickle." She smiled over at Olivia. "Mom and Dad had a small sawmill on this land up here. When they died, your father inherited it. To his credit, he gave me a tract of land, but he kept the mill. I sold some of the land but still have my little cabin, and nobody's going to cut those trees around it."

Because Stella lived in it, Olivia could honestly say, "I like your cabin better than our house in Davidson."

Stella nodded. "So do I. That's something Herman can't understand. About me. . .or you."

By midmorning they came upon a sign: SUNRISE, WEST VIRGINIA, POP. 2,013.

"Let's drive around and see what this town offers," Stella said. They passed cleared areas and sawmills and railroad tracks and a black, smoking train, huffing and clanging around a mountain.

They rode past a church, a school, a hotel, and a hospital. After returning to Main Street, Stella led the horse and wagon to a livery stable where the mare could be watered and fed. Across the street was a lovely white, two-story house with a sign outside with the words LAUREL BLOSSOM BOARDINGHOUSE.

"Hmm." Stella expressed what Olivia was thinking. "Living and working there wouldn't be the worst of fates."

Olivia agreed. "The worst would be married to a maniac."

"Quite an astute observation," Stella said, as they began to walk along the sidewalk. "And of course we can't go inside the boardinghouse or the hotel in case I decide to apply for the job."

Olivia liked the charming town where ladies, gentlemen, and a few children walked along the sidewalks and entered shops. Several blocks revealed a saloon, shops, a restaurant, a grocery, a bank, an attorney's office, a medical clinic, and a post office. Farther down stood the depot.

"Years ago, when Kev and I were married, we came through here with an acting troupe."

Olivia detected a moment of sadness in Stella before her aunt whispered, "That's my future husband."

The man was tall and skinny, wearing a top hat and dark suit, and eighty years old if a day. He was an aristocratic-looking man, but Olivia had a hard time picturing him as Stella's husband.

"Or him." Olivia nodded toward a man on the other side of the street.

"Oh, you mean Humpty Dumpty?"

He did rather resemble a picture-book drawing Olivia had seen of a short, oval Humpty Dumpty.

Stella sighed. "The good-looking ones have women with them. Oh well, let's go into the Soda Shoppe and drown our sorrows with a Coke or a milkshake."

Olivia soon discovered her aunt had something in mind far removed from sorrows. "Here's what we should do in the name of common decency," she said. "In case our man of means is not filled with common decency, it's up to us to put a stop to it."

Olivia felt a nervous giggle coming on. Stella continued, "You can't go to acting school yet because you don't have the money. Herman would kill me if I paid your way." Her words were tinged with regret. "Besides, you have to want this enough to work for it. And you need to be able to give it up at any time without feeling obligated to anyone. You understand that?"

"I do."

"All right," Stella said. "Just in case this might be a job for you, here's the plan. Let's at least have an interview with this man with four names. Oh." She perked up. "The four names thing probably means he's either very wealthy or royalty and has 'de' or 'van' in his name. Now what were those initials?"

"DVMC? DMNC? Something like that."

Stella slapped the table with such force Olivia thought the straw might fly right out of the glass. "Aha! See? He could be either 'de' or 'van' or both."

"Yes." Olivia played along. "De Van of Many Corpses. I'll bet he's a mortician."

"We have to know. It is a job. And it's worth checking out."

In a matter of minutes, Stella had Olivia believing that man might have a good reason for wanting a temporary wife. "And you know I wouldn't let you get mixed up in anything objectionable."

Olivia knew that. But she also knew what one person considered objectionable, another considered perfectly reasonable. Hadn't her own father called her unreasonable for wanting to be an actress?

But the possibility of just seeing the man was too big a temptation to resist. After all, Stella said she would do the interviewing as the "mother." Olivia wouldn't even have to speak to the man or let him know she was in any way connected with Stella. Ignoring the butterflies in her tummy, she marched alongside her aunt to the post office.

Stella asked if there were paper, pen, and an envelope available for her to respond to an ad in the paper. The middle-aged clerk, obviously taken with Stella's good looks and charm, gave her everything she asked for free of charge.

After writing the note, making sure she got the initials correct, Stella handed it to Olivia to read.

Dear DNMC,

Thank you for your note. Please meet me at the Canaan Valley Restaurant Saturday at 10:00 a.m. I would like to question you before allowing you to interview my daughter. Please bring a book with you so I might identify you.

Sincerely,
Juliet Kevay's Mother

Olivia swallowed hard. Maybe this was the answer to her dilemma. Although she didn't really believe that for one moment, she nodded.

Stella looked pleased, folded the letter, addressed the envelope, licked the gum on the stamp and made a face, then handed it to the smiling clerk.

Olivia had the feeling she had reached a point of no return.

Chapter 3

Needing a break after a busy morning, Neil left the clinic and walked across the street and down the sidewalk to the post office.

There was a letter, again neatly printed. He almost smiled upon seeing that the letter was signed by the interested applicant's mother. He could appreciate a mother's caution. And he could appreciate a young woman who would confide in her mother about something this preposterous. He'd never let a daughter of his consider such a thing.

On second thought, one never knew what he might consider. Although he knew that mail-order brides had been an acceptable practice in some parts, Neil hadn't an inkling he would ever advertise for a wife—until now.

Nevertheless, despite self-reproach, anxiety, and a sense of helplessness, on Saturday morning at 10:00, he tied his horse, Sally, to the hitching post at the side of Canaan Valley Restaurant.

He'd already given himself every conceivable lecture. He willed himself to put one booted foot in front of another and go inside. As Mrs. Kevay had requested, he placed a book on the corner table at the front window and sat down.

The book he brought was the Bible, hoping that Mrs. Kevay's reaction to it would give him an indication about her and tell her something about him, too. He ordered a cup of coffee and, upon lifting it to his lips, marveled that his hand was steady in spite of his quavering insides. A man, especially a doctor, needed to be in control at all times. Even the worst operation hadn't affected him like this.

Three gentlemen were seated at a table near him. Snippets of conversation sounded like a business discussion. Two fashionably dressed young ladies waltzed in and sat at a table beyond the gentlemen. He doubted those young ladies would need or want to apply for his job—unless they did it as a lark. That could be, since they were whispering and giggling.

Never before having been one to be self-conscious, he now thought he glowed like a bonfire. The sunshine streaming through the window made him uncomfortably warm. He preferred a dimly lit corner, but it was occupied by a young woman. She was staring at a magazine through spectacles. When her chin lifted as if she might look his way, he lowered his cup and his head.

His ears seemed to ring with the mingling of male voices and the young women speaking to the waitress. He was acutely aware of the distant rattle of dishes and muted voices from across the room. However, all other sounds faded away when he heard the turn of the door handle, the *swoosh* of the door opening, and the rustle of a woman's skirt approaching him.

Swallowing hard, he put his hands on the edge of the table and forced his gaze to travel up the dark blue dress and into the face of a woman. Thanks to instinct and having been taught good manners, he stood. "Mrs. Kevay?"

She extended a gloved hand. "Mr.?"

He briefly shook her hand. "M–McCory."

"Mummacory," she repeated.

"No, no." He hated this but rushed around to pull out the chair for her. "Just"—he forced himself not to stumble over his own name—"McCory."

She sat in the chair, looked up at him, and said without smiling, "Thank you."

Neil stared for a moment. What beautiful green eyes. He'd never seen eyes that color. He returned to his seat and folded his hands in front of him on the table. "The name is D–Dr. McCory."

"Dr. McCory."

Was she trying not to laugh? Some sense of reality returned when the waitress came over and he watched the interaction between her and the woman.

Mrs. Kevay's skin was exceptionally clear except for the dark circles beneath her eyes and a black mole on one cheek. Her navy blue dress was plain, and her dark brown hair was pulled back into a tight bun.

While waiting for the waitress to bring her coffee, Neil tried to act normal. "It's a nice day."

"Yes," the woman said. "The days are cooler now that fall is almost upon us." She removed her gloves, which revealed graceful-looking, long-fingered hands.

He stared, then looked up and saw that she stared at him. He sincerely thanked God that the waitress brought her coffee and refreshed his.

The woman dropped two lumps of sugar in the cup, picked up the spoon, and stirred. He opened his mouth to say some other inane words—he knew not what—when he suddenly caught his breath. It occurred to him that this woman might be the one applying for the job. He was in his early thirties. She could possibly be in her early forties. Yes, she could have a young daughter. But the only way to find out was to get on with the interview.

Just as he opened his mouth to speak, she patted the Bible. "I see you must be a man of. . .of the Holy Bible."

"Yes, ma'am." That helped. "Are you a woman of faith?"

"Oh." Her eyes closed for a moment. Then she looked back at him with a sweet expression. "Where would we all be without God?"

He nodded. "Exactly."

"Well," she said, "I am glad to hear that you are a man of the Holy Bible."

Neil felt that put a little perspective on the situation. He'd prayed that if this was not God's will, then nothing would come of it. He must simply lay on the line what the situation was and interview this woman, and daughter if she had one.

"Mrs. Kevay," he said. "I am a Christian. I have a medical practice in Sunrise. My grandmother owns the Sunrise Inn. This is difficult for me, and I would like to tell my story only once. Could I speak with you and your daughter together?"

The woman stared at the table thoughtfully. He felt sure she would confess that she was the job applicant. However, she looked over her shoulder and wiggled her finger at the girl in the corner.

The young woman hesitated so long, Neil wondered if Mrs. Kevay was trying to force her daughter into something against her will. That would not do.

Finally, the girl stood and began to walk toward them. He tried to size her up without being obvious. Describing her as "demure" would be an exaggeration. She looked rather prim with her hair in a bun at the back of her head. He couldn't get beyond taking in the wire-rimmed spectacles to see her face. Her high-necked, plain gray dress covered everything from her feet to her wrists. Just as she seemed not to have a face, she seemed not to have a figure.

Neil stood. The girl put her hand on the back of the chair, so he made no effort to step over and pull it out for her. The young woman did not look directly at him, nor did she smile, but quickly removed her gloved hand from his after a brief handshake.

Although he suspected this girl was not the one to help in this situation, perhaps he could help them in some way. They must be in dire circumstances.

At least, even if he could consider hiring her, he didn't need to be concerned—not that he was—about any attraction between this spectacled young woman and himself.

—∿∿—

Olivia sat, and upon seeing the Bible, she figured he must want to make a point of believing in God. She expected most everyone did, but she'd never had much experience with church life until the past few years when they'd moved to the city and her father insisted they go and hear a preacher occasionally, especially at Easter and Christmas or when he was meeting with a churchgoing businessman.

She had expected DNMC to be an undesirable man with whom Stella would converse and say this was not the position for her daughter. But Stella had given the nod, a signal that this might really be a job for Olivia. But how could any of them even consider the job of. . .marriage?

All right, she would act like the demure daughter of Stella Kevay. They could laugh—or cry—about this later. She had to admit that while sitting in the corner, she watched this man and thought him quite handsome. However, her vision was rather blurry since she had to look through the spectacles. Any man who advertised for a wife had to have something dire wrong with him.

"Would you like for me to bring your coffee over here?"

Olivia stared at the waitress as if she'd spoken a foreign language. DNMC and Stella seemed to be doing the same. Oh, they were all crazy as loons. Olivia shook her head. "No, I'm fine."

The waitress said, "I'll bring your bill over here."

Watching the waitress walk away, Olivia wondered what happened to the sense of fun she and Stella had when talking and planning this. This wasn't a game. She knew she would have to call upon her amateurish acting ability, and then some, to keep up the charade. She'd like to take the pins from her hair, shake it loose from that silly bun, and let this man see that she was not a woman desperate for a husband. There was more than one marriage-minded man in the city who had taken a liking to her.

"Miss Kevay," she heard but did not raise her gaze from the table. She dared not look at Stella, not knowing if she'd laugh, cry, or run. "I want to tell you and your mother," he said, "why I advertised for a wife. Then I would like to know why you would consider becoming my bride for a year."

Olivia had every reason not to look at him. She certainly was embarrassed at what she and Stella were doing. And how in the world would she answer his question as to why they answered the ad in the paper? She wouldn't have to pretend that she was speechless.

Maybe she could kick Stella without being seen and have Stella say she had fits or something that would make this man not want her as a wife. Not that she would ever even consider it.

They were all silent a moment longer until the waitress brought the bill for her coffee. She reached for it, but DNMC got it when her hand was only a fraction of an inch from his. They didn't touch, but she felt that if they had, she would have been shocked with an electric streak.

He laid the bill beside him, away from her. This man of means was going to pay for her coffee. Proving there was something wrong with him, he might even offer her a job. . .unless she did something even more drastic than look plain to prevent it.

Chapter 4

Much of this has to do with my grandmother," Neil began. He felt he needed to tell as much truth as he could without going into unnecessary details. A little family history might be in order.

"My only family," he said, "is my grandmother whose husband owned Sunrise's first sawmill. When the demand for lumber increased, my grandfather grew quite wealthy and built a big house in Sunrise. Their son. . ." Neil looked at Mrs. Kevay who seemed interested and at Miss Kevay who wasn't looking at him.

He continued. "Their son, who was my dad, married and brought his wife into my grandparents' home at their request. The men ran the sawmills, one for softwood and the other for hardwood. The women took care of the house and turned it into an inn since so many newcomers were settling in Sunrise and needed places to stay while looking for homes or building their cabins."

"I understand that," Mrs. Kevay said. "Here in Canaan Valley, the sawmills have about stripped the land of trees. Communities have sprung up overnight."

Neil nodded, but he needed to get to the situation at hand. "My mom and dad planned to have many children—girls to help run the inn. But I was their only child, and I became a doctor."

He wasn't one to disclose his personal life but felt some of it necessary. "My parents died in a flu epidemic when I was young. My grandfather was killed in a train wreck when I was in medical school. That brought me back to Sunrise to help my grandmother who had raised me."

Thinking that his once-vital grandmother was now an invalid wrenched his heart. "Now my grandmother has had a stroke, and she has a weak heart. The specialists don't expect her to live another year."

"I'm sorry." The soft words came from the young Miss Kevay.

Neil was taken aback by her sympathetic tone of voice. He looked at her and was immediately again struck by the sight of those spectacles that partially hid her face. How in the world did she keep them on her small nose? But what struck him even more was that he knew she cared. Anyone who took this job would have to care, not about him, but about his grandmother.

"Your ad said she's incapacitated," Mrs. Kevay said.

"Not entirely, but I didn't want to go into detail for the ad. My clinic and the hospital are near the inn. I live in the inn and could get a nurse at a moment's notice. But I do want someone to take her food to her when she doesn't feel like getting up. Someone to make sure she takes her medications and to do personal things for her, such as ensure she's all right in her bath."

Neil waved away the waitress who neared with the coffeepot. This was no time for refills. Neither he nor Mrs. Kevay had touched his or her cup after the conversation began. He lowered his voice to make sure no one away from the table could hear. Mrs. Kevay leaned slightly toward him. "She's known as Mama McCory," he said. "Her dream is to see me married, which she feels will ensure that the home they turned into an inn will continue to serve the people and tourists of Sunrise."

"That's a worthy goal," Mrs. Kevay said.

Apparently he hadn't alienated her, but he couldn't tell about the daughter. He really didn't care to look at the younger woman and think about a stranger becoming his wife. She was probably thinking something similar. But he'd gone this far, and they hadn't left the table. "Mama McCory knows I don't have time to supervise the running of the inn."

"Why, Dr. McCory, can't you hire someone for that?"

"Hired help comes and goes. A couple who has been with us for years wants to retire. My grandmother needs a companion—someone to make her last days pleasant and give her a hope for the future of her family and home. You see, to make her happy, I need a wife to keep the name of McCory and the inn alive. I want to give my grandmother her dying wish since she cared for me most of my life and paid for my medical school training."

He felt it time to get to the point. "I need someone to pretend to be my wife for a year, be a companion for my grandmother, live in the inn, learn to manage it, be paid a weekly salary, be content with a marriage of convenience, and agree to an annulment after a year."

Having finished, he knew if something like this ever got out, he'd be finished in more ways than one and be the laughingstock of the county. He leaned back, just then realizing he had been sitting quite straight and stiffly. He spread his hands. "That's my story."

Mrs. Kevay's eyebrows lifted. "Why, Dr. McCory, I would think a respectable, nice-looking, established man like you could find several decent women who would jump at the chance to marry you."

Neil wasn't sure if that was a compliment or condemnation, so he didn't thank her. But he did feel he needed to defend himself, lest they think he was totally undesirable. "Well, there have been a few who might have married me, had I asked. But I didn't care to make a permanent commitment with any of them."

"Ohh." Mrs. Kevay clicked her tongue, and he detected a gleam in her eyes. "You're one of those confirmed bachelors? Why, Dr. McCory, why ever so, might I ask?"

He might as well spill the whole pot of beans. These two now knew more about him than he liked to admit to himself. "I came close to marriage once, Mrs. Kevay. But my intended decided that living in a mountain town was not for her. She was a city girl and could never adjust to my backwoods way of life." He felt the sting of that. "We parted amicably."

"Oh, that must have hurt your heart, having to choose between your grandmother and your fiancée."

Neil felt quite warm from the sun beating through the window against the back of his vest. He felt it all the way through his white shirt. For a long moment, he pondered her statement. In reality, he hadn't thought of it as a choice between the two women. He'd simply known a wife of his must love his grandmother and be a part of life in Sunrise. Now he felt like the sun was shining on his face instead of on his back and head. "Well, just as my fiancée wasn't ready for life in a mountain town, I wasn't prepared for a life as a city doctor. As long as she is alive, I will take care of my grandmother."

"But after Mama McCory. . ."

The sympathetic expression on Mrs. Kevay's face and in her voice led Neil to nod. "Who knows?" he said, not wanting to think of facing life without his beloved grandmother. He liked the way Mrs. Kevay had said his grandmother's name. "I want to make her happy as long as I can."

Mrs. Kevay nodded. "Dr. McCory, would none of those young women you mentioned consider this arrangement?"

He shook his head. He knew his face had to be red. "No, ma'am. They wouldn't consider a—" He stopped his words. Men didn't discuss some things with ladies. "They wouldn't consider what I stipulated in the newspaper ad."

"Oh, I see." Her voice had become singsong. "Well. This is quite. . .interesting, to say the least."

He cleared his throat and dared a glance at the young woman behind the glasses. "Miss Kevay," he said gently, lest he frighten such a passive creature—or was she embarrassed? "Will you tell me why you would consider this arrangement? And something about your background?"

The poor girl closed her eyes for a long moment, then barely opened them but did not look at him or her mother. Was she deaf, dumb. . .or both? Or. . . something worse? Like. . .deranged?

He wouldn't be surprised if she had a fit. He felt like having one himself.

With eyelids at half-mast, Olivia slid a sideways glance at the man Stella called

"Dr. McCory." What kind of doctor was he? An animal doctor or a people doctor? She couldn't very well ask if he had a pill that might make her disappear. What had she and Stella gotten themselves into?

Strangely, she had begun to think of this interview as real. His story about the loss of his parents and his love for his grandmother touched her heart. She wouldn't mind having a sweet old grandmother. Actually, she'd begun to wish she might have applied for the job legitimately.

But she hadn't. She thought of her father's having said that acting was the worst kind of job for a decent woman. Wouldn't he squirm to know about this! Well, he'd made her squirm enough times. She took a deep breath, wondering what to say, and shot a helpless glance at her aunt.

Stella patted Olivia's arm. "Dr. McCory, it's difficult for my daughter to talk about her papa, whose livelihood comes from the mining town beyond Sunrise."

Olivia wondered what her aunt might say. She'd better listen carefully in case it became her new identity.

"Juliet and I live in a little cabin here in Canaan Valley. Before that," she said, "Juliet's life was difficult living in the mining area beyond Sunrise."

He spoke quietly. "Yes, I know something of the difficult life in mining towns."

Unexpectedly, Olivia felt the pain of having lost her mother. How could she say that her father was a wealthy man who owned several mines and logging companies? When she was growing up, they lived in a big house away from the mines—quite a contrast to the little box houses in which miners lived. After her mother died in childbirth, she and her father moved to the city.

Stella was painting a true picture of her wanting to leave the mining area. But she knew this doctor assumed she had led a life of poverty and misery. She hadn't lived a life of poverty—only misery.

But it was too late to tell the truth. This man had revealed his heart to her and Stella. That couldn't have been easy, especially since they were strangers.

If she considered this job, she never wanted him to know that she and Stella had begun this as a joke, a fun adventure. This man would not think it funny.

She decided to speak lest he think her not qualified for the position. "Dr. McCory," she said, still not meeting his eyes, "I did get a college education in Davidson, and contrary to what your fiancée preferred, I don't want to live in the city." That was certainly true. She wanted to be in New York long enough to attend acting school. Then she wanted to be an actress traveling the United States, maybe even the world.

"And you asked why I would consider this job. Only one reason, sir." She stared at the table. "The reason is money."

Chapter 5

The young woman's articulate way of speaking surprised Neil. She obviously knew how to be quiet and let her mother talk, but he felt she had no problem providing information. Her words were few, but she had expressed them well.

Was there a possibility this might work? Of course this one meeting wasn't enough for any of them to make a commitment about the job offer. "If you are seriously considering this," he said, looking from one who met his gaze to the other who didn't, "I want to invite you to visit the inn and meet my grandmother. If either of us decided against the arrangement, I can say you were applying for a job. However, if all goes well, I can then surprise her by announcing my. . . um. . .our. . .engagement."

He wouldn't blame them if they backed out. Their feet might be as cold as his about this situation, so he quickly added, "After you come to the inn, if you don't want the position, then I will simply go on with my life as usual."

Mrs. Kevay gave a brief nod. Her daughter said, "Thank you. I would like to see the inn. . .and your grandmother."

"Miss Kevay, we will need to be on a first-name basis when you come to the inn." He took her silence as assent. Remembering the name on the first letter, he said, "I should address you as Juliet, right?"

When she nodded, he tried to lighten his mood. "I'm often called Dr. McCory, Doc, or Mac. But I think you would prefer calling me Neil."

Neither of the women laughed, but Juliet nodded.

If pigs sweat, he'd be sweating like one. Heat rose to his face again at what he must say. He dared not look at Juliet but kept his focus on Mrs. Kevay. "There is the matter of dress. I will be glad to provide the cost of clothing. I. . ."

His voice trailed off when Mrs. Kevay's eyebrows lifted and her eyes widened. "You mean," she said, "you want someone who looks like a citified fiancée?"

He hedged. "Not exactly." But his grandmother would never believe he fell in love with this plain creature with grotesque spectacles, even if she did have a nice way of speaking.

"Well," Mrs. Kevay huffed, and he thought he'd completely alienated the two women. Her stiff manner now reminded him of a stern schoolteacher who had looked down her nose at him when he was a boy and scared the wits out of him.

"Just because we live in a small cabin in Canaan Valley and have spent part of our lives around the poverty of the mining area, Dr. McCory. . ."

He was already nodding, bracing himself for a cup of coffee being slung into his face, the thump of the Bible smacking him on his head, or a tongue-lashing.

The woman stared. She did have striking, unusual green eyes. They were extremely large. He swallowed hard. She drew herself up, and her upper lip seemed to curl slightly. Juliet, or maybe he should revert to thinking of her as Miss Kevay, appeared to inch back from the table.

"Dr. McCory, we will not take one penny of your money without giving one minute's work. We are honorable people, sir. And I have been in a city or two in my life and have observed young women and their clothing. You can believe I know how to fix up my daughter in the proper uniform for the job for which she is applying."

The younger woman seemed to become strangled on something, but she hadn't even a glass of water. Probably, like he, she felt about ready to choke on this entire situation. "About a uniform," he said. "I wouldn't want her to look like a waitress, although I do need someone who can cook or can learn."

Mrs. Kevay reached over and patted his hand. The length and curve of her fingernails surprised him, as did the softness of her hand. He would expect her to have the rough hands of a hard worker. But of course, there were many kinds of hard work. He put in more time as a doctor than many men he knew, but that didn't give him the calloused hands of a miner or a logger.

"Dr. McCory," she said sweetly, "my use of the word 'uniform' was just a figure of speech. I understand you want someone attractive enough that your grandmother, and your acquaintances, would believe you'd fall in love with her. And at the same time, she must be a sweet, kindhearted girl who doesn't want the fancy trappings of city life but would capture your heart with her goodness." She patted the Bible.

Neil felt a sense of fear and trembling that God might not be in on this. For what seemed like the umpteenth time, he cleared his throat. Mrs. Kevay was an astute woman—more so than he would have thought upon first look. But then, she did have those fancy fingernails. He'd like to have a look at Juliet's fingernails, but he surmised from the movement of her arms that she might be twisting her hands beneath the table.

"I don't mean to be insulting." He turned his head toward Juliet, and she as quickly turned hers away from him. "And this is not only about looks. It's about meeting the proper requirements for a job."

"I quite understand, Dr. McCory. The work presents no problem. And I think my Juliet can meet with your approval after I fix her up. And, too," she said with acuity, "I realize your grandmother would need to approve your choice. But there are two sides to this. I and my daughter will need to be certain that she will be happy and treated well in this position." She added very quietly, "If she is interested in you as an employer."

At that, Mrs. Kevay slapped her hand on Juliet's coffee receipt and slid it toward herself. He did not insist upon paying, since this woman's act displayed principles. Juliet ducked her head and had to push her glasses up to keep them from falling off her face. He wished they had. However, he said, "Very well. When would be a convenient time for you to visit the inn?"

Mrs. Kevay began pulling on her gloves. "This afternoon," she said and stood.

"Fine. If you will meet me at my clinic, I will escort Juliet to the inn from there."

After finalizing the plans, Mrs. Kevay said, "We will be there, Dr. McCory." She paid her bill and led her daughter out.

⸻

"Is this wrong?" Olivia moaned and removed the spectacles from her face as soon as she and Stella were heading away from town. Had she not been hiding behind them, she never could have gone through that fiasco of an interview.

"Wrong? For who? Dr. McCory advertised. He needs a temporary wife, his grandmother needs a companion, you need a job, and I need—" Stella grimaced, looking over at Olivia with a puppy dog expression in her eyes. "I needed. . .to stay out of things?"

Olivia burst into laughter, shaking her head. That helped release the tension she'd felt from the moment Dr. Neil McCory walked into that restaurant with a Bible. "It's a little late to stay out of things, don't you think?"

Stella laughed then, and having driven out of town, yanked off the brown wig and handed it to Olivia. She shook her head while the curls bounced back to life. "Well, we did it. You're on your way to being a married woman."

"Oh, don't say it that way. I'm on my way to a job."

"But," Stella emphasized, "the job is acting like a married woman."

"How do I do that?"

Stella glanced at her and grinned. "Just pretend you love. . .Neil."

"Love?" Olivia shrieked. "I've never been in love in my life."

"Oh yes, you have," Stella contradicted. "Remember Coco?"

"My dog?"

Stella nodded. "You loved him. He had shiny, dark brown hair, and you wanted to name him Hot Chocolate, but your mama talked you into calling him Coco for short."

"Yes, Coco was my best friend and confidant."

Stella reached over and patted Olivia's arm. "There you have it. That look on your face right now is precious. When you look at Neil in front of other people, just pretend he's Coco and treat him like he's your dog."

Olivia huffed. "I'm not about to look for fleas and ticks on any man!"

They could still laugh and joke, but it was becoming too real and too personal. "Maybe we should forget this whole thing."

"Fine," Stella said. "You want to go back to Daddy?"

Olivia felt caught between a rock and a hard place. "Oh, Stella."

"Just call me Mama."

Olivia moaned.

After they returned to the cabin, Stella stood in front of her and held Olivia's hands. "Honey, if you don't want to do this, then it's all right. We'll look for something else."

"It's not that," Olivia admitted. "Now I kind of wish I had applied for the job legitimately. I don't like this deception."

"Don't think of it as deception, Olivia. Think of it as pretending—acting. Even if Neil McCory knew we responded to that ad as a lark, the two of you would still be pretending to be married and pretending in front of his grandmother."

That was true. "But what if something happens and I don't want to be committed to being there for a year?"

Stella smiled. "No problem. You can walk away at any time."

"But we'll be legally married."

"Only if you marry him under the name of Olivia Easton. But to him, my dear, your name is Juliet Kevay. The marriage will not be legal. You can walk away at any time. Now," she said, letting go of Olivia's hands, "let's get you ready to take a job of being an engaged woman, pretty enough to become Mrs. Dr. Neil McCory."

Chapter 6

Mrs. Kevay certainly wasted no time. Neil told himself he mustn't either. After having sat in that hot seat all morning while the sun rose higher, he'd have to bathe and be ready to convince his grandmother that he was either considering hiring a maid or that he had become an engaged man.

After riding Sally up the mountain, he made a quick stop at the clinic. "Carter, everything all right?" he asked his young assistant when Carter looked up from the desk in his office.

"Couldn't be better," Carter said with a smile. "Other than taking a look at the stitches in Billy Hooten's hand, it's been a slow day."

"Great," Neil said with a force that caused Carter to give him a questioning look. "I mean, I'll be tied up the rest of the day."

Carter shrugged. "This is Saturday, you know. My day for doctoring. Like you always say, 'Don't call on me unless there's a dire emergency.'"

Neil nodded. "A couple of women are to meet me here later today. Just wanted to let you know." He left the office and walked back through the waiting room and outside to unhitch Sally. There was a "dire emergency," and this doctor wasn't sure what to prescribe for it. But he had to quit questioning this. When he picked up Miss Kevay at the clinic, where Mrs. Kevay would bring her—fixed up—he could change his mind before anything became legal.

Yes, that made sense, even if nothing else had since he'd put that ad in the paper. Upon arriving at the inn, he rode Sally out back along the cobblestone path and to the stable where Bart was tending the horses. "Hey, Bart," Neil said. "I'm going to need the buggy in a couple hours. Can you make sure it's ready? And see that Sally is hitched to it."

"You don't mean the doctor's buggy?"

"No," Neil said. "This is something personal."

"How personal?" Bart said with a gleam in his eye.

Bart had worked for Neil's grandfather and his dad and had been a pretty good substitute after they'd died. "You'll know soon enough. Just practice being on your best behavior."

"I'm always on my best behavior." As Neil walked away, Bart called, "But I can't say the same for Hedda."

Neil could agree with that. Not openly, however, and as soon as he entered the kitchen from the back door, gray-haired Hedda began her interrogation. "Where've you been all day?"

"Where am I most of the time?"

She put her hands on her ample hips. "Out doctoring, even on your days off. That's all you do. You had anything to eat since that biscuit you swiped this morning?"

"Not a thing. Are there any left?"

"None of my biscuits are ever left," she said proudly. She went to the cupboard, took a tea towel off a basket, and handed him a muffin. "Blueberry," she said. "You want coffee?"

"Maybe after I've cleaned up. I suppose Grandmother is resting." She usually did after lunch.

"Yes, she was outside this morning. But she didn't stay out long. She's just not herself anymore."

"I know," he said. Since her stroke, she seemed to have given up on life. "Hedda, if she's not awake before I leave, would you tell her I might be bringing a guest home this afternoon?"

"A guest?"

"Hedda, it's not certain. But I'd appreciate it if you'd make tea, then serve it in the parlor. Oh, and include some of those little cookies."

She was nodding with a sly grin on her face. "I'll be here. I wouldn't miss it."

Neil mentally reprimanded himself for feeling like a nervous man about to meet the woman to whom he might become engaged. He felt both bad and good about Mrs. Kevay's saying she knew how to dress her daughter appropriately, but no amount of dress could make up for those grotesque spectacles. Maybe he could ask her to remove them. If she couldn't see, she could take his arm. He hoped Mrs. Kevay wouldn't clothe her daughter in the kind of revealing attire some young women wore. But he felt he needn't worry—that wouldn't fit with quiet Juliet who hadn't even looked him in the eye.

No, this wasn't going to work anyway, was it?

Finally, running out of time, and since this was an afternoon affair, he decided to wear casual tan slacks, a white shirt, and a brown vest. With his wavy hair still damp, he peeked into the parlor, which was empty.

Neil tapped on the bedroom door, and his grandmother called for him to come in. He stepped inside and went over to the bed where she was propped up against pillows. She laid aside a magazine and smiled at him. Yes, she looked more rested than she did most days. "Looks like your being outside in the sunshine was good for you, Grandmother."

"I feel fine," she said. "But what's this about you bringing home a guest?"

"I may be bringing a young woman home for you to meet."

Her mouth opened and her eyes widened. "Oh, Neil. Who? Where did you meet her? Why have you not said anything?"

Not wanting to be any more Machiavellian than necessary, he stated as much truth as he could. "I met her in Canaan Valley."

"Oh, tell me all about her."

He lifted her hand, conscious of how cold it felt, and warmed it with his own. "I'll let you see for yourself. If I can't have your blessing, then. . ."

"Oh, Neil. You know how happy it would make me for you to marry, carry on the McCory name. Oh my." She shook her head, and a look of pity came into her eyes. "It's about time you got over pining away for Kathleen."

He didn't think he'd exactly "pined away." Kathleen had been everything an up-and-coming young doctor could want. She was blond, beautiful, fun, educated, and the daughter of a prominent doctor in Wheeling. "Well, Grandmother, you know Kathleen wasn't the kind of woman to live here and manage the inn. It's my home, and I couldn't leave it. That's why this young woman is coming here— to find out if this is the kind of life she can live. I'm bringing Juliet—"

"Juliet?" Her eyes brightened further. "What a beautiful name. Oh, she must be lovely."

He lowered her hand to the afghan she had spread over her. "Haven't you taught me that looks aren't everything?"

"That's right. But it's. . .something. Is she unattractive?"

"Well, no. But she sort of has a. . .an eye problem."

"Crossed?" She chuckled.

Come to think of it, he wasn't sure. Maybe her eyes were crossed. That would explain why she hadn't looked directly at him—she couldn't. He had that throat-clearing problem again. "I'll let you judge for yourself."

"Well, I've had only one grandchild, and he turned out to be the most handsome man around. I'll be happy if my great-grandchildren have your looks and Juliet's lovely insides." She glanced up at him. "She is lovely inside, isn't she?"

What else could he say but, "What else but?"

She laughed and looked happier than he'd seen her look in a long time. "I know you're joshing with me, Neil. You've always been attracted to the most beautiful girls around. And they to you. I can hardly wait to see her."

Neil felt he could wait. But he'd invited Miss Kevay to the inn to meet his grandmother, and he'd see it through. Maybe Juliet wouldn't like it. Or maybe his grandmother would tell him that Miss Kevay wasn't his type.

After all, she wasn't.

At 3:00, Neil pulled the buggy up to the side of the clinic where he had told Mrs. Kevay he would meet them. He parked in the spot reserved for his doctor's buggy. Either the wagon next to him belonged to Mrs. Kevay, or they were running late.

He hitched Sally to the post, thinking that it wasn't just the midafternoon sun that made him sweat. He pushed open the door, telling himself that a doctor shouldn't be having that kind of throat problem. But the kind of remedy he'd need didn't come in a little brown bottle one could buy off the shelves at the pharmacy.

He closed the door after entering the waiting room. Apparently the Kevays were running late. Carter was talking with two women. They must be new in town.

Then Carter turned, his eyes wide as saucers and his smile reaching from ear to ear. "Neil," he said. "I've just met your friends." His head was bobbing, and he seemed to have lost any other words that might be forthcoming.

Friends? Neil looked at the two women.

"Neil, you have a fine clinic here," the middle-aged woman said. "And Dr. Carter has made us feel right at home." She extended her gloved hand, and he had no choice but to take it and plant his lips on it. She had the same voice and brilliant green eyes as Mrs. Kevay, but her hair was short, curly, and red. There were no circles under her eyes nor a mole on her cheek.

"Oh, I'm so sorry. You probably don't recognize me, fixed up and all. Wigs are the in thing, you know."

Oh, so the red hair must be a wig. But it made her look more...citified than she had this morning. Her dress with a jacket seemed fitting for a stylish, yet conservative mother. He was almost afraid to look at the younger one who had stepped aside as if she, too, were reluctant.

"Juliet," he said with effort, taking the opportunity to catch a glimpse of her. She didn't extend her hand, and his hands were rubbing themselves together in front of his vest.

Not allowing more than a lingering glance, he, however, had the impression her white blouse had rows of lace in front and lace at the high neck and long sleeves. Kathleen dressed much fancier, but he was not looking for another Kathleen. He wasn't one to keep up with women's latest styles but thought Juliet was dressed modestly but quite acceptably for a young lady's daywear.

He dreaded looking at her face, but when he did, he felt like a weight had lifted. She was not wearing the spectacles. Her hairstyle looked quite pretty—parted in the middle and fastened in a roll from the sides of her head and curved to the back of her neck. He didn't think those little tendrils had fallen along the sides of her face this morning, but he couldn't be sure. What he wanted to see was her eyes, but she kept her eyelids lowered. He felt sure she was cross-eyed. As long as she didn't look straight at people, she'd be acceptable. He reminded himself that no one was perfect.

After Mrs. Kevay's exuberant good-bye to Carter and Juliet's quiet one, Neil nodded at Carter, who winked at him and grinned like some kind of hyena. This morning they had decided Mrs. Kevay would meet them at the Sunrise Restaurant after Juliet's visit to the inn.

When they walked around to the side of the clinic, Mrs. Kevay spoke seriously. "Neil," she said, "I've thought about this and decided I can't simply let Juliet ride away with you. After all, you are a stranger to us. We don't even know that there is a Sunrise Inn."

That shocked him. But he saw her point. "Please, Mrs. Kevay, along with your daughter, accept my invitation to the inn."

"I'd be delighted. Shall I leave Not-to-Be here?"

"Not-to—? Oh. You mean the horse? We wouldn't want to chance a horse thief coming by. You and your daughter—"

"Juliet," she corrected.

The throat again. "Juliet. You and she could ride behind me in the wagon, or she could ride with me, if you feel that is proper."

"I believe it is proper for a man's fiancée to ride with him. I'll follow."

Neil took hold of Juliet's arm just as she stepped up to get into the buggy. Her foot seemed to slip slightly, but she recovered immediately. Had she been startled by his touch? That was the gentlemanly thing to do.

"Do you have any questions, Miss. . .um, Juliet?" He thought she might ask about the town they were driving through, or his clinic, or the inn, or his grandmother.

"No, sir."

The *clip-clop* of Sally's hooves on the cobblestone street sounded unusually loud. So did the silence. After driving a bit farther, he thought a little instruction might be in order. "You do know you should address me as Neil when we get to the inn."

"Yes, sir."

He noticed she looked back a few times, as if making sure her mother was following, in spite of the obvious clunking of wagon wheels against the road.

He attempted conversation again. "You don't talk a lot, do you?" He glanced over at her.

She seemed pressed against the side of the buggy as if afraid of accidentally touching him, and her gloved hands lay on her lap, one over the other. She did not look at him but spoke in that clear tone he had noticed that morning. "Since the job calls for me to be a companion for your grandmother, do you think she would like for me to talk a lot, or should I be less than verbose?"

Verbose? Well, she had said she went to college. Maybe she was trying to sound educated. "Just. . .be yourself," he said.

145

He turned his head toward her as he turned the buggy to his right. She turned her head away from him.

Yes, Juliet. Just be yourself. Your quiet, retiring, less than verbose, cross-eyed little self.

Chapter 7

*B*e *myself?*

Olivia wished she had a script to read, telling her just who "herself" was. Only a couple of days ago she'd been Olivia Easton, a motherless girl looking for a job so she could become an actress.

Now she'd become an actress before getting the job. She must be Juliet Kevay, who had a mother named Stella Kevay. Her job was to marry a stranger and pretend to be his wife but not really be his wife. So she would be pretending to be pretending to be his wife since she'd be married under the name of Juliet Kevay. They would not be legally married.

If she had anything to feel good about, that was it.

And if this doctor, who carried a Bible around with him, thought this was all right, then it must be. He was trying to give his grandmother the best year of her life by giving her hope of a granddaughter-in-law who would give him children and carry on the name of McCory.

She was doing this for a good cause, too—to make money to go to acting school so she could do what she'd been born to do. If she didn't like the grandmother, or the inn, or didn't want to go through with the marriage, then she could simply take the stand that Dr. McCory's former fiancée had taken and say that she preferred city life or felt she couldn't manage an inn.

Olivia was startled when the doctor spoke. She'd been lost in her thoughts and the rhythmic sound of wheels and hooves against the road. "Pardon?" she said.

"Our property begins here," he said and gestured toward a sign beside the road that read Sunrise Inn with an arrow pointing to the right. The horse and carriage turned to the right, and the horse gracefully clopped along the road that was bordered by stately pine and lush, green rhododendron.

They rounded a curve, and only for a moment did the large white house beyond register in Olivia's consciousness. Her attention was drawn to the people on the level stretch of lawn that looked like green velvet.

A woman and young lad were watching intently while a man knelt to show a little girl how to hold a mallet. The child, who looked to be about three years old, hit the croquet ball, and it rolled a few feet across the lawn.

A laugh of approval sounded from the doctor, and Olivia couldn't hold back her own small laugh as she remembered her father teaching her to play croquet.

"Look, Daddy. It's Dr. McCory," the lad said.

"Whoa, Sally." Neil drew to a stop as the family walked toward the carriage. The little girl had lagged behind, having picked up the orange and yellow ball. She held it close, as if it were some kind of treasure.

"My friends, the Martins, who have just arrived for a stay," Neil said. "I should introduce you." He turned to step from the carriage.

"Should I step down?" Olivia asked.

"No, that won't be necessary." He nodded to Stella who drew up beside them on the wide driveway.

"Samuel, great to see you." He walked out onto the lawn, shook the man's hand, and accepted an embrace from the smiling woman. "Melanie. And who is this tall young man?"

The boy ducked his head slightly. "I'm Chad."

"Chad? My, how you've grown. And Mary," he said when the man picked up the little girl. "You're still the prettiest girl around."

The girl grinned, clutching the ball close to her dress, and lay her head against Samuel's shoulder.

Olivia watched as they greeted each other in such a friendly manner. For a long moment, she was able to look at Neil McCory's ruggedly handsome face, the kind she preferred over the smooth, citified type. His skin was bronzed, like he spent a lot of time in the sun—the sun that now brushed his dark brown hair with gold.

Neil introduced the family to Olivia. "This is my friend, Juliet Kevay." After their polite greetings, Neil walked them over to Stella and introduced her.

The man and woman both looked at Neil with happy faces and excitement in their eyes. Neil had not said she was his fiancée, but the sly look in Samuel's eyes and the wide smile on Melanie's face indicated they thought she was more than a "friend."

After the family returned to their game and Neil jumped up into the carriage, the horse drew them nearer the big house. While he explained the relationship to his friends, Olivia took in the impressiveness of the Federal style house nestled against the backdrop of lush, green mountains rising into the clear, late-summer sky.

"Samuel, Melanie, and I grew up together," Neil was saying. "They married and settled down in Sunrise. A midwife delivered Chad, but Melanie had such a hard time she wanted me to deliver Mary. That bonded us even more. Then they sold their house and moved to the city where Samuel is now vice president of a large bank. They come back every year to visit friends and relatives, so they stay here."

"You seem to have a way with the children," she said as he drove around the curved drive and stopped in front of the house.

"Especially with those I help bring into the world." He jumped down and came around to her side of the carriage. She already had one foot on the ground, so he took her hand as a polite gesture.

Olivia caught the whiff of some musky fragrance, possibly a shaving lotion. She thought it rather tantalizing.

Just then an elderly man came down from the porch and said he'd tend the horses. Neil introduced him as Bart Henley.

The inn was slightly larger than her father's house in the city, and it was just as impressive with its white columns that reached to a second-floor roof and black shutters that flanked the windows. Noticing one of the black rockers moving while the others were still, she knew that's where Bart had been sitting.

She turned to see what he would see and caught her breath. The view was a family laughing and playing on that vast green lawn that stretched to the grove of stately trees that seemed to meld with the fantastic view of mountain ranges.

"That is one beautiful sight."

"Thank you," Neil said. "It's only one of many around here. God has truly blessed this area."

Enthralled by the view, Olivia hadn't realized Stella had stepped up onto the porch until her aunt touched her on the shoulder. When Olivia turned, Stella gave her a smile of encouragement.

Neil opened the screen door, and Olivia, with Stella right behind her, stepped into the spacious foyer, formed by rooms on the right and left. A staircase ran along the right wall, ending at a small landing. On the landing stood a corner table, graced by a tall vase of wildflowers. The stairway then took a sharp left, extending to the second-floor hallway. A crystal chandelier hung from the high ceiling.

"Neil, this is lovely," Stella said. "It feels like a home instead of an inn."

"That's what Grandmother wants—a home away from home for the guests."

"I suppose that's where guests check in." Olivia gestured toward the area beneath the staircase.

"Yes, it is."

She nodded, since he was behind her. "It gives the impression of someone's private library."

He laughed lightly. "I have spent some time back there, reading or writing."

Olivia could understand why. A lamp, ledger, and telephone sat on a huge desk in front of a big leather chair. Behind the chair and along the paneled walls were shelves, some with decorative items and pictures but most filled with books.

"Grandmother," Neil said suddenly, and Olivia's attention was drawn to the movement on her right.

A white-haired woman, using a cane for balance, moved slowly toward them. "Thank you for the nice compliments," she said. "And welcome to my home."

A tremor raced along Olivia's spine. She felt like turning and running. This was not just an inn, but a woman's home. This was *the* grandmother—the one who would decide Olivia's future.

As if knowing what she was thinking, Stella lightly touched Olivia's arm. The touch served as a reminder that she wasn't invading this woman's home under completely false pretenses. She was being interviewed for a job.

The elderly woman's kind smile formed deep lines in her face, which was lovely and surrounded by wavy, snow white hair brushed back into a roll at the back of her head. She was dressed in a fine pink dress with lace and buttons. A rose-colored shawl lay around her shoulders. She obviously had been a beautiful woman in her younger days. She stood shorter than Olivia or Stella and appeared rather frail, but there was something elegant and confident in her demeanor.

"I could not wait in the parlor," she said in a slightly breathless voice, like one who had walked hurriedly rather than slowly across the carpet. "I've been watching from the window."

As soon as Neil finished the introductions, the woman said, "Call me Mama McCory. Everyone does, except Neil, of course."

Olivia held out her hand. Mama McCory ignored it, handed Neil her cane, and embraced Olivia. The woman's fragrance was like sweet lavender with a faint aroma of talc or face powder.

At that moment, Olivia thought she knew something of how Neil felt about his grandmother. Her smile was sweet, and her eyes, dark and as intelligent as Neil's, expressed love and acceptance.

Mama McCory released her and stepped up to Stella. She looked into her face for a long moment, then opened her arms to her. "Shall I call you Stella?"

"Please do. Since early childhood, even Juliet usually addresses me as Stella."

Although Olivia knew Stella said that in case she erred and called her Stella, she wondered if Mama McCory might think that much too forward.

The older woman stepped back, took hold of Stella's hands, and held them as she laughed softly. "I can imagine that was adorable when she was a little one." She looked over at Olivia then. "She's certainly adorable now. And those eyes are the most beautiful and expressive I've ever seen." She looked at Stella again. "There's no wondering where she gets them. Eyes like the two of you have are unforgettable."

"Thank you," Stella said at the same time Olivia said it softly. Both she and Stella often heard comments like that.

"Now," Mama McCory said, "come into the parlor. Hedda has gone to fetch our tea." She took her cane. Neil crooked his arm, and she wrapped her frail arm through it.

When they came to the door of the parlor, he stopped. Mama McCory walked on in. Neil gestured for Olivia and Stella to go ahead of him.

Mama McCory went to an armchair. "I like a chair with arms," she said. "That makes it easier for me to get up. Please, sit on the couch."

After they sat, Neil took a chair across from them, on the other side of the coffee table.

"Oh, this is Hedda," Mama McCory said when an older woman, wearing a long apron over her dress, came in with a silver tray and set it on the coffee table. She introduced Stella and Juliet.

"Very nice to meet you," Hedda said and straightened. She smiled at Juliet. When she looked at Stella, her breath seemed to halt for a moment. "Have we met before?"

Juliet watched Stella study the woman then smile demurely. "I can't say. Where do you think we might have met?"

Hedda shrugged. "You're not from Sunrise, are you?"

"No," Stella said, still looking at her and smiling as if waiting for another question.

Olivia knew she and Stella both would have found something like this funny at any other time. Stella was probably finding it humorous now. She simply played the part of a modest woman being questioned by the hired help.

As if realizing that herself, Hedda's cheeks pinked and she turned to face Mama McCory, who said, "Thank you, Hedda."

"If you need anything, I'll be in the kitchen." Hedda hurried from the room.

"Would you like for Juliet to pour?" Stella asked.

"Please," Mama McCory said.

Olivia looked at the silver tea set and the china cups. She'd been taught etiquette as far back as she could remember. She knew the routine. She wasn't concerned about asking if anyone preferred sugar, one lump or two, cream, or just taking it plain. She knew what to do with napkins and cookies.

Removing her gloves, however, she felt self-conscious, wondering what kind of interrogation might follow. If a servant asked a personal question, what might Mama McCory ask?

Chapter 8

Neil saw Juliet hesitate only slightly after pouring his tea last. Hoping she would get the signal to keep it plain, he said quickly, "I'll have one of those small cookies, please."

She laid a cookie on the side of the saucer, picked it up, along with a napkin, and walked over to him.

The tea sloshed over the rim of the cup and into the saucer when Juliet handed it to him. He looked up at her. He hadn't enough breath to say it was his fault—his hand was the one that shook. Earlier, when his grandmother had said Juliet had beautiful eyes, he had thought that was one of the few times she had erred like that. One shouldn't say crossed eyes were beautiful, no matter what their color.

Neither of the women had seemed insulted. Now he knew the reason why. Speechless, he stared up into the most beautiful eyes he'd ever seen. They were a deeper green and even more stunning than her mother's that had so impressed him.

He looked down quickly, holding a firm grip on the saucer, hoping it wouldn't crack under the pressure. If he wasn't careful, both his grandmother and Stella might think he was so taken with Juliet that he couldn't keep his eyes off her.

But that was what his grandmother was supposed to think, wasn't it? No doubt she would notice the color he felt rise to his face. She was an observant woman, but who could tell if the color in one's face was from some romantic emotion or from what one was feeling—humiliation and surprise?

The sound of a cup lightly touching a saucer and the faint sound of a voice and laughter on the front lawn, wafting through the open windows where the breeze stirred the lace curtains, was enjoyable. Stella appeared perfectly at ease. Juliet appeared tense. He would have thought it strange had she not appeared so.

Stella commented on the tea and cookies being quite good, and Juliet agreed, then blotted the sides of her mouth with a napkin and laid the cup, saucer, and napkin on the tray.

For a while, Mama McCory and Stella commented on the good weather they'd been having. Stella then mentioned the piano between a window and the corner. "Do you play?" she asked his grandmother.

"Not often. I have rheumatism so bad in my hands anymore. Sometimes when my fingers allow, I'll pick out a tune. But it's an effort, and my fingers don't flow over the keys like they once did."

To Neil's surprise, Stella asked his grandmother, "Would you like Juliet to play something for you?"

Neil watched his grandmother's eyes light up as she looked at Juliet. "Oh, would you, dear?"

After a moment, Juliet rose from the couch and walked to the piano. She sat with the straight back and grace of a young woman who had been trained to play in a drawing room. That reminded him of many young women he'd known, some who played well and some who played poorly.

Where would a girl who grew up in a mining town learn to play the piano? But she had been in the city, too, at college. Maybe she had learned from Stella who did not fit his picture of a miner's wife. Perhaps she and her husband had been incompatible, like he and Kathleen.

He had no idea what to expect, but he certainly didn't expect what happened after a long moment of Juliet's sitting there, poising her hands over the keyboard. She began playing "In the Good Ol' Summertime."

His grandmother couldn't conceal her pleasure. She began to nod and in her thin, somewhat trembling voice began to sing along. Stella chimed in. That woman had a good voice. Juliet didn't sing; she just continued to play while staring at the wall beyond her as if she were playing classical music in the finest of drawing rooms.

After finishing the song, she rose from the bench. His grandmother motioned for her. "Come here, dear."

Juliet walked over to her.

His grandmother's eyes were teary. Grasping Juliet's hand, she patted it affectionately. "You couldn't have played anything I liked better. That was one of my and my husband's favorite songs, oh, seven or eight years ago when we first heard it." She smiled wanly and let go of Juliet's hand. "He died six years ago."

"I'm sorry," Juliet said and touched her shoulder.

"Oh, don't be sorry about the song. Sometimes I get teary thinking about Streun McCory, but I like to remember our times together. A lot of people change the subject when I say his name, as if he should never be mentioned. I don't feel that way."

"I can understand that," Stella said. "I've lost loved ones, and I, too, prefer to recall the good times."

Mama McCory nodded and looked fondly at Stella. "You and I could have some good talks. But for now," she said, "would you like to see more of the house?"

Both women reacted warmly. Neil was glad his grandmother mentioned it. For a moment, he seemed to forget this was a time for Juliet and her mother to discover if this job was right for Juliet.

For a couple of moments, when he'd looked into Juliet's eyes, then watched her play and saw the pleasure on his grandmother's face, he too had forgotten this was about a job. Instead, he had delighted in the feeling that his grandmother liked this young woman he brought home for her to meet.

"I'll leave the tour to you women," he said. "I'll just duck out and see what's going on with Samuel and his family."

First, he went into his study, opened his safe, and took out a small box. He whispered a prayer, "God forgive me if I'm wrong."

———

"I don't climb stairs anymore," Mama McCory said, leading Olivia and Stella from the parlor and into the hallway next to the part of the stairs that formed the landing. "Those rooms are in use now anyway." Lifting her cane, she pointed to the room on the left. "That's my bedroom," she said. "Next to it is now part of the dining room. We tell guests to use the hallway on the left to reach the dining room. We'll go this way."

Olivia and Stella followed her past the parlor. She gestured to her left. "We had this wall put in since this is our family area. Over here is Neil's bedroom," she said when they passed a closed door to the room next to the parlor. "The one next to it is his study."

She opened the door to that one. Olivia liked it upon sight. There was a patterned love seat and an ornate desk smaller than the one in the foyer. The wall was paneled halfway up to a chair railing. Above that was light beige wallpaper with a hint of a maroon-striped pattern. The curtains were maroon. It had not only a masculine look, other than the love seat, but it had a masculine smell, like that musky fragrance of Neil and leather and furniture polish.

"He has a telephone in here, too," Mama McCory said with a sense of pride.

"I'm sure he needs one," Stella said. "His being a doctor. A lot of the homes are getting them now, but I don't have one in my cabin in Canaan Valley."

Mama McCory was somewhat familiar with Canaan Valley, and they talked briefly of places they all knew. "Hedda and I used to go down there. I'd go to that bakery on Main Street, buy some of their muffins, and come back and try to figure out what all was in them."

Stella laughed as they reached the kitchen. "I used to work in that bakery. I could tell you a few things about ingredients."

"Oh," Mama McCory said, "we must talk."

Hedda apparently overheard. "That may be where I saw you."

"I don't know," Stella said. "I haven't worked there in several years." She changed the subject. "I love this kitchen. And I see you have all the modern conveniences."

Mama McCory nodded. "It's amazing we ever ran an inn without them." She sighed. "But nobody knew any different. I remember when we used wood in the stove instead of coal. And when we used to have to go to the well for water instead of it being pumped into the house. And when electricity came..."

"Even I remember that," Olivia said.

"Yes," Stella said, "it's amazing the progress that has been made in just a few years."

Mama McCory agreed. "Telephones—did you see the one in the foyer? Why, I can pick that up and talk to my friends anytime I want. Well, to those who have one."

Olivia got the impression that might be Mama McCory's favorite convenience until she added, "And inside bathrooms. Of course, we're more fortunate than most. For a long time I've felt it my Christian duty to share what I have with others."

Stella asked, "What do you think about the automobiles?"

"Oh, don't get me started." Mama McCory huffed. "They are a nuisance—noisy, smelly, don't go half as fast as a horse. They won't last."

Olivia didn't bother to say that horses could be quite smelly, too. Her father had a roadster and loved it. She hadn't minded riding in it, but she preferred taking a leisurely ride in an open carriage and taking in the views. Also, horses didn't tend to break down or get stuck in the mud like those horseless carriages.

Just then Neil made his appearance. "I think the cities are adjusting to the horseless carriage," he said. "But in a town like Sunrise, with the mountain roads and steep inclines, horses do a better job."

He smiled, and Olivia thought, *Is that my husband-to-be?*

"If you ladies have finished your tour, you might enjoy seeing more of the grounds," he said.

"They haven't seen the dining room," Mama McCory said. She touched Stella's arm. "If you two would like to stay over, you're welcome. We can set up a cot for Neil in his study, and you two could take his bedroom."

"We do need to get back down to Canaan Valley." Stella's voice held regret. Olivia wondered if she was pretending or if she would really like to stay here.

Olivia liked Mama McCory. She would love to be her companion. Olivia could understand why Neil loved her enough to try and give her hope in her final months.

The dining room was spacious. A long table sat in the center of the room. Four smaller round ones were placed around the room and extended to the area next to Mama McCory's bedroom. There was a fireplace, and windows on two walls.

After they thanked Mama McCory and bade her good-bye, they walked down to the stable, where Bart said the horses had been fed and watered. Neil asked if they might walk around the grounds a bit before returning to town.

I'm supposed to feel this way, Olivia told herself. *This is acting practice, so I should experience what it's like strolling along between my mother and my fiancé.* She was much more aware of that than how the flower gardens looked or the bench beneath a sugar maple.

"Mama McCory seems lonely," Stella said as they walked into a grove of apple trees where the remaining leaves shook in the breeze.

Olivia knew how those leaves felt—much like her heart did when the sleeve of Neil's shirt lightly brushed against the sleeve of her dress.

"Yes," Neil said, answering Stella. "That's one reason I want a companion for her."

"Is Hedda not a companion for her?" Stella asked.

"To a great extent. But Hedda has her husband, Bart. They aren't here every day, and they go home at night. They would like to retire, but out of friendship and loyalty, they've stayed on. I can get temporary and part-time help, but none have ever stayed very long. Hedda is her friend," he said, "but Grandmother needs someone she feels is. . .family."

He stopped and seemed to examine a small green apple. "I could tell Grandmother liked you both." A long moment passed, and it felt like even the wind was holding its breath. Finally, he said, "Juliet, do you think you could accept the job?"

Olivia looked at Stella, who after a long moment nodded and said, "I think Mama McCory is delightful. I am in agreement if my daughter is."

Olivia knew her options. This job was a good opportunity, with the promise of more money than any job she had been able to find in the area. But there was the thought of being married to Neil, even if it was in name only—at least in fake name only.

When she didn't answer right away, Neil spoke again. "I do have two requests if you take the job. One is that you attend church with me on Sunday."

"Sunday?" Olivia said.

"Yes," he said simply. "And the other request is that you wear my mother's ring. That way everyone will know we're engaged and talk will spread."

Olivia nodded. She felt rather in a daze. The next thing she knew, they were back in the flower garden near the bench.

"Mrs. Kevay—" Neil began.

"Stella," she corrected.

He nodded. "Stella, could I speak with Juliet alone for a moment?"

"Of course," she said. "I'll wait at the stable."

When Stella was out of earshot, Neil turned to Olivia. "Would you sit down, Juliet?"

Olivia sat on the bench, then scooted over when he made a move to sit beside her. He reached into a small pocket of his vest and took out a ring. With the ring lying on his upturned palm, he said soberly, "Juliet, will you accept my. . . proposition of becoming my wife for a year?"

He smiled gently at her, and it took all her acting ability not to melt on the spot. She had to look away from his captivating dark brown eyes that seemed to dance with a golden spark. The sun winked through the branches of the sugar maple, turning the color of his hair from dark brown to honey gold.

She'd never met a man she wanted to propose to her, even though a few had alluded to it. She rather wished this were real, that she and Neil had met under different circumstances.

Staring at the beautiful diamond ring, she had that trembling feeling again along her spine. She knew that sometimes one could get caught up in a play or a book and it seemed real. That's what this felt like, as if she were really a prospective fiancée of a handsome doctor. That's what she was supposed to feel. That was the job.

Job. That's what she must dwell upon. She would be committed for a year, and then she'd have her freedom. No more fights with her father. She could live her life as she pleased.

She swallowed hard. "Yes," she whispered.

"Your left hand, please."

She untangled her left hand from her right one and held it out. The touch of his fingers did to her hand what that tremor had done to her spine. With his slight push, the ring slipped over her knuckle and seemed to be a perfect fit.

Olivia looked long into his eyes, feeling warmth travel through her body and settling in her face. She lowered her gaze to the ring. Her hand was against his as if he were holding it for her to see the sparkle of the diamond. She didn't know how it was possible to feel like two people. One was happily engaged to a handsome, appealing doctor. The other would pretend to be married to the doctor, but it wouldn't be real—just a job.

Wasn't that what acting was all about—being yourself and also being a different character? The trouble was that at times she began to feel she didn't know which one of her was the real one and which was the actress.

Neil let go of her hand, and his voice invaded her contemplation. "Thank you," he said solemnly and stood, squinting as he lifted his face toward the sky. "I'm beginning to think this is God's will for my situation."

Really? Olivia wondered at that. Then maybe God wasn't as stuffy as she had thought.

Chapter 9

I'm not even going to think about the haste of this, Neil," his grandmother said after Juliet and Stella left in the wagon and he told his grandmother that he and Juliet were engaged. "I trust your judgment, and from all I see of Juliet, she is lovely." She smiled. "And that Stella is a delight. I really like her. I think she's very smart."

"Really?" Neil didn't say he thought so, too. But he got the feeling that Stella was in control of this whole situation and not he. But, on second thought, shouldn't a mother be the controlling one in a situation where her daughter would commit herself for a year to a man as his wife of convenience? He could only hope, when the year was out, she would not try and make trouble.

Right or wrong, he was committed, and his grandmother was happier than she'd been in a long time. That's what he wanted.

His grandmother took hold of his sleeve. "I know you had to bring Juliet to the inn, and both of you feel she can be content here. I suppose you see now that Kathleen wasn't the girl for you."

Neil nodded. If a woman could not understand his obligation to his grandmother and his responsibility to care for her in her own home, then she wasn't right for him.

On Sunday morning, Neil stood in the churchyard with several men, including Samuel and Bart. Many people walked, and some came in wagons and others on horseback.

He'd told Stella and Juliet, before they left the inn, that the church he attended was back from the first road before driving into Sunrise. There was a village, and the church would be obvious by its position on an incline and the steeple on its roof.

He was reluctant to mention his engagement to the men around him in case Stella and Juliet kept the ring and never showed up again. If so, he couldn't report it to the authorities. Who would believe such a story?

He felt a sense of relief, and shame for having doubted, when they drove up in the wagon. "My fiancée," he said.

"I expected as much the other day." Samuel gripped his shoulder. "She's a beautiful young woman."

Bart laughed. "I knew it when I saw the sparkle of that ring on her finger.

But I wasn't going to say anything till you did."

Neil reached up and took Juliet's hand to balance her as she stepped down. She was not dressed as finely as Kathleen would have been. But she looked respectable and quite smart in a conservative dark blue suit and a light blue blouse. She wore a pert blue hat with a dark bow at one side. Many of the women would be more plainly dressed. He was not embarrassed to present her as his fiancée. Besides, anyone who looked into those arresting eyes, which he tried not to do too often, would find her—as Samuel had said without exaggerating—beautiful.

He took Stella's hand for her to step down. She was wearing a large hat decorated with big, colorful flowers. Her red curls peeked out beneath it. Her green suit, the color of grass, was rather fancy, too, but no fancier than the bank president's wife or the wife of Mr. Johnson who owned the general store in town. She was just. . .more colorful.

How could he ever have thought these women were plain?

Well, they had been, but after his conversation with Stella, she had said she knew how to dress her daughter like a city girl. She did indeed, and not so anyone could find fault as far as he could see.

He held out his arm. Juliet tucked hers around it, and they walked together toward the church door. Others were looking, and some whispers stopped as they passed. He nodded and thought Juliet was smiling, with her head slightly bent, looking appealingly modest.

After they entered the church, he led the way down the single aisle, then stood aside for Juliet and Stella to sit in the pew where his grandmother was already seated.

"That's a lovely hat," Stella said, moving to the end of the pew to sandwich his grandmother between her and Juliet.

"It's fine for an old lady," his grandmother said. "Mine's quiet though. I like the way yours speaks."

Neil heard Stella ask, "What does it say?"

"It says, 'I'm a leader, and I want to live life to its fullest.' "

"Are you a psychologist?"

"No. Just a wise old woman."

He liked the way his grandmother and Stella related. His glance fell upon Juliet who glanced over at him and smiled as if she had been thinking the same thing. Then her cheeks looked rosier and she looked down at her hands. Of course, she wouldn't be thinking what he was thinking then—that it was amazing how the expression in beautiful eyes tended to reach into the soul.

Trudy Simms began to play hymns on the piano, the sign for everyone to come inside and be seated. Soon Pastor Whitfield stepped up onto the raised stage and stood behind the podium.

As always, he welcomed guests and asked them to stand for introductions. Samuel's family, on the left side of the aisle, stood. So did Neil, Juliet, and Stella.

After Samuel expressed his delight at again being in the area, Neil turned slightly, since they were on the fourth row from the front. "I'm pleased to introduce Miss Juliet Kevay and her mother, Stella Kevay, from Canaan Valley. And I hope Milton back there will reserve us a table for lunch at his restaurant."

"Out of my control," Milton shot back. "You'll have to talk to the waitress."

The people laughed, but he saw nods from the members as they looked at Juliet and Stella. He'd been to many big churches in the city and had visited the bigger one in town, but he preferred this informal, friendly kind of worship place where he'd grown up. Most were simply folks with big hearts.

"I know we're all glad to see Mama McCory back with us," the pastor said. Several amens followed.

Neil shared his hymnal with Juliet, but she didn't sing. His grandmother didn't stand, and he thought it was nice of Stella to remain seated and share the hymnal.

Neil listened carefully to the sermon, wondering if God might have a particular message for him about what he was doing, but he heard nothing that confirmed or condemned.

After the service, it seemed all the women came up to welcome Juliet and Stella and to tell his grandmother how good it was to see her at church. He escaped to the front yard where he received congratulations.

Later, when he entered the restaurant with the three women, he discovered Milton had gone ahead and reserved a table for them. He particularly gushed over Mama McCory. "It's good to see you here again," he said.

"I feel like a new woman, Milton. The engagement of my grandson has put new life in me." Others came up to the table to speak and be introduced. If the whole town didn't already know of his engagement, they would know before sundown.

Later, at the inn, Neil checked his grandmother's heartbeat and thought it sounded stronger. But she was tired and wanted to rest.

He asked Juliet and Stella to make wedding preparations. He would come to Canaan Valley as soon as he could, possibly the following afternoon, to discuss the plans for him and Juliet to be married in Stella's cabin.

After the two women left, Neil felt he had done this before with his ex-fiancée. They had talked of marriage and her living at the inn. When it ended, he'd felt jilted, and from the reactions of those who knew him, they thought he had been, too. They were all right.

This time he would be legally bound for a year. Then after a year there would be an annulment that would look to others like a divorce. Although he didn't like the stigma of divorce, it would be easier because he'd planned the whole thing out.

This time emotion wasn't involved.

This time. . .it wouldn't hurt.

***

"I now pronounce you man and wife." The pastor smiled at Neil. "You may kiss your bride."

Olivia reminded herself she wasn't really going to melt in the arms of her husband. This was act one, scene one in a play called *You're Now Mrs. Dr. Neilson Streun McCory*. Olivia turned toward Neil and felt his hand lift hers, which now felt heavy with the weight of the wedding band he'd slipped on her finger. She felt his breath and then the touch of his warm, firm lips against the top of her hand.

She lowered her hand, and the only thing she could think to do as a wife was to lift the bouquet of marigolds to her nose. Stella had thought of flowers at the last minute. She'd picked them from her bed by the front steps and tied them with a strip of white ribbon.

The pungent odor of the marigolds, thankfully, overwhelmed the musky aftershave she'd caught a whiff of when Neil had kissed her hand. She needed to keep her wits about her, and that scent seemed to steal them away.

She must surely look the part of a shy maiden as Neil expressed as much. "Pastor, we prefer our kissing to be done in private."

Olivia dared not look at Neil. She stared at Stella and saw the gleam in her aunt's eyes. She glanced at the pastor's wife whose face had turned a deep pink as she fidgeted with pulling on her gloves.

The pastor glanced at his wife with wide eyes, then coughed lightly and said, "Um, yes, well, I can appreciate that. Young people nowadays are getting too forward. But it's a part of the ceremony. The kiss means a joining of the soul, so to be married in the sight of God, it would be a good idea. We can look the other way."

They all turned away. Olivia visualized kissing Neil and lowered the bouquet of marigolds. Oh, he would think he was kissing a skunk. Why hadn't Stella picked wildflowers? Slowly, she lifted her face toward his and then her gaze.

His eyes met hers for an instant before she saw a furrow form where his eyebrows almost met. He looked over her head. "We've. . .finished," he said after a long moment.

Finished?

The pastor turned toward them. "Congratulations to the bride and groom." He walked over to the coffee table and signed the marriage certificate. His wife and Stella signed as witnesses. "I suppose we're. . .about done here." He looked from Neil to Stella and back to Neil.

"I'll walk you out," Neil said.

After the sound of wagon wheels and horses' hooves faded, Neil opened the screen door and stepped inside. He walked over to the table, looked for a moment at the license, and picked it up. Glancing at Olivia, he said, "Thank you again, Juliet. Stella. If there's nothing else, I'll be on my way to the convention in Wheeling. I will call and leave a message at the general store if I need to get in touch with you. If you need me—"

"Yes," Stella said, "we know how to reach you at the Wheeling Hotel."

"Juliet"—he faced her—"you are legally my wife, and I will do my best to be a good husband."

"Thank you," Olivia said. "For the. . .job."

His words, "I'll return on Sunday," were accompanied by his retreating footsteps, soon followed by the sound of Sally making a hasty retreat after he unhitched her from the carriage.

Walking to the door, Olivia watched until he rode out of sight. Her husband would ride to the depot, take the train to Wheeling, and attend a medical convention. He had said he wanted particularly to visit with the heart specialists whom he had consulted about his grandmother's stroke and weakened heart.

She wondered if he would rent a carriage there or if he would hire an automobile. Had he ever driven an automobile? She didn't know a lot about this man she would pretend to be married to for a year. Something in her wanted to. Would he see Kathleen while there? If so, would he tell her about his marriage? Would he be sorry he'd done this?

Stella's voice brought her back to reality. "Throw those marigolds in the yard," she said. "They're pretty, but they sure can stink up a place."

Olivia removed the ribbon from her wedding flowers—yellow and orange marigolds. She threw them—not to a bridesmaid who hoped to be next to fall in love and marry—but into the yard where they would fade, wither, and die.

Returning, Olivia sat on the couch beside Stella and read what she'd already read twice that morning—the contract entitled "Marriage of Convenience."

The agreement was much like Neil had outlined in the newspaper ad and when he had talked with them that first morning at the Canaan Valley Restaurant. "It will be annulled after a year," she said, "and I will return the rings to Neil."

Stella didn't open her eyes. "This sounds like you've landed a good job, Olivia."

Olivia felt as drained as Stella looked. They'd both had a hectic few days, making arrangements for a wedding. Olivia hadn't wanted to wear white, so she wore a simple fawn-colored skirt and matching blouse that they felt was befitting one being married in the morning at home in a simple ceremony. Stella had gone far up the mountain to find a preacher she thought would not know her or would not have heard of Dr. Neil McCory.

Thinking Stella might be asleep, Olivia murmured, 'Well, I guess I'm on my honeymoon."

All of a sudden Stella opened her eyes. "I have an idea. Let's go celebrate your marriage—I mean, your job. We can have lunch in town." She looked tenderly at Olivia. "I didn't rope you into something against your will, did I, Olivia?"

Olivia thought. "Maybe at first, but I could have backed out at any time, and you did keep saying that. There's an upside and a downside to this."

Stella sat straighter. "What's that?"

"One," Olivia said with a feeling of joy, "I can send a telegram to my father and tell him I have taken a job and am able to make a life for myself." She felt her smile fade, and she pursed her lips for a moment. "The bad part is I'll be leaving you to go and live in Sunrise."

Stella patted her arm. "We'll be closer than when you were in the city and going to college. Also, I didn't feel too welcome at your father's home. But we can see each other often at the inn. Now"—she rose from the couch—"let's hitch Not-to-Be to that carriage and go paint the town."

"But. . .what if someone from Sunrise sees me? I'm supposed to be with Neil on my honeymoon."

Stella scoffed. "Not to worry. Who would ever recognize you in the blond wig that's been lying useless in that trunk for way too long?"

Olivia was glad to laugh. She hadn't done much of that lately. "I need to wash my hands. The marigold smell is driving me crazy."

She went into the bathroom, and the light caught the gleam of the diamond ring. She stared at her hands, outstretched. Neil McCory believed she was his wife. He had kissed her hand. "Stella?"

Stella came to the doorway. "Yes, dear?"

Slowly her head turned toward her aunt. "I've had a few boys kiss me. But I never felt anything. . .special. Can kissing. . .really be like that?"

"Depends on who you're kissing." Stella patted her shoulder. "Obviously, you haven't kissed the right person."

Chapter 10

Four days later, Neil was hitching Sally to the carriage when Juliet walked out the doorway of Stella's cabin and stood on the front porch at the top of the steps. "Hey," she said softly.

He didn't know what else to say but "Hello." Saying, "Good afternoon," would sound too formal to one's wife. "Sorry I had to call and say I'd be later than expected," he said like a dutiful husband. "I suppose you got the message?"

"Yes, Stella and I checked with the general store every day."

"The rain didn't stop for two days in Wheeling," he explained. "There was flooding, and automobiles were stuck in the mud at the sides of roads. One was stalled on the railroad tracks. Thank goodness the word got to the depot before the train left and they could get the auto off the tracks. That's why the train was delayed."

"It rained here, too, but not that much."

After his quick glance took in her appearance, he focused on Sally and the carriage. To make conversation, he said, "The carriage isn't where I left it a few days ago."

"Oh, were we wrong to take it into town?"

He glanced up. Her hand, which he had come to know was as graceful as her mother's, lay against the delicate pink lace at her throat. His gaze lingered for a moment. A ray of late afternoon sun slanted across her auburn hair and turned it to reddish gold. Her cheeks were flushed as if she thought she'd done something wrong. "No," he said. "I just noticed and. . .said it."

Relief washed over her face. "We did take it into town. I mean it's so much nicer than that creaky old wagon."

"I. . .don't mind."

"You look like you mind. Your eyes squinted and your mouth sort of looked funny."

He stared at her. "Funny?"

"Oh, I'm sorry. I don't mean ha-ha funny. I mean. . .like you're troubled."

"No. Not exactly."

"Well, if you don't want me to ever take the carriage, just tell me." Her hands fluttered in front of her. "I don't know how to act like a wife. I've never been married."

Neil quickly finished what he was doing. He walked up and propped one foot on the step. "I've never been married either. Do you suppose this is what's called—" He'd almost said, "A lover's spat." Quickly he changed it to "What's called. . .our first argument?"

After a moment of her incredible green eyes staring into his, her expression softened and she smiled. "I think it might."

He straightened and stood on both feet. "But you were right. Something did concern me. Not that you took the carriage, but that someone might recognize you."

"No, no. I wore a wig."

"A wig?"

She nodded, her face aglow with the slanting sun. "A blond one."

He tried to picture her as a blond. Kathleen was blond. Kathleen's eyes were light blue, not green. "You do that often—wear a wig?"

"No. It's Stella's. She has. . .wigs."

Neil felt himself nodding like a willow branch in the wind. The first time he saw Stella she had brown hair pulled back in a knot. The next time she had copper-colored curly short hair to just below her ears, like some of the doctors' wives wore theirs. Well, he would not concern himself with whether or not a woman wore wigs. "Is your mother in Sunrise?"

"My?" She looked as if she hadn't understood the question. "Oh," she said after a moment. "Yes. She went up right after lunch to help your grandmother and Hedda prepare for the reception tomorrow."

He walked up onto the porch. "Let me wash up, then we should be on our way." She went inside ahead of him. After washing up, he saw that she'd put on a gray jacket that matched her skirt. The gray and pink looked nice together. "Oh," he said, "I see you're wearing those pointed shoes."

"Is something wrong with that?"

"No, no. I saw some of the city women wearing that kind."

"Stella keeps up with the latest styles." She picked up a shoulder bag and a small travel bag.

"Do you have anything else to take?" he asked.

"Stella took my luggage."

He took the bag from her, and soon they were on their way up the mountain. "Sorry to be driving Sally so fast," he said. "But darkness comes quickly once the sun has dropped behind the mountains."

"Good idea," she agreed. "After all the rain, there may be potholes in the roads. By the way, did you get to see people you knew in Wheeling?"

People I knew? Have I mentioned that Kathleen's father was a doctor? "Yes. Yes, I did."

Her asking that question surprised him. But if she went away for several days, he would certainly ask questions. After all, they are married, even if it is a marriage of convenience. "Kathleen's father was one of my mentors. He invited me to his home." He did not say that Kathleen had been most cordial, was still single, and managed a boutique in Wheeling that catered to stylish women.

"Did you tell them you are married?"

"No. No, I didn't mention it."

"Well, I suppose there's no reason. After a year, you won't be."

That surprised him, too, as if she knew his thoughts. He didn't know what he would do when his grandmother was no longer with him. "It was a good convention. And I spoke with Dr. Maynard who gave me some recent reports on stroke and heart disease. He thinks there are some new medications that might at least make Grandmother more comfortable. I also consulted with a couple of doctors who will give me information that might help ease her rheumatism."

"Oh, I hope so. I was with her for only a short while. But I can see why you love her so. She's so nice, and I would love to have a grandmother like her."

"You do," he said quickly. "That's what this is all about—making her dreams of my marrying come true, for however long—"

The sudden sway of the carriage sent them both trying to keep their balance, and for an instant he was afraid the wheel might come off or get stuck in the muddy pothole. Sally knew her business, however, and pulled them right out.

After having been thrust against his arm, Juliet straightened and emitted a small laugh. "If that had been an automobile, we'd still be back there, wouldn't we?"

He agreed. "That's why we don't have many autos up here. And I wouldn't want to get stuck on this road at night. There's not much traffic on it now that the trains run daily."

"Yes," she said, "most of the people in Canaan Valley are loggers' families. They're stripping the land, which is a concern about what will happen to the town when there are no more trees. I know that's progress, but it seems to me there should be some kind of restrictions. I've heard talk that stripping the land of trees means the town could flood when there's a hard rain."

They discussed that for a while. Neil was pleasantly surprised that she would converse about the logging or even care about it. Whatever happened to that demure little spectacled creature he met that first day? He formed an answer—the same thing that happened to that demure, middle-aged, plain mother of hers. They were. . .different. And he liked the difference.

They reached Sunrise as darkness fell. Bart appeared almost as soon as Neil helped Juliet down from the carriage. Bart hugged him and welcomed him back. "Nice to see you again, Mrs. McCory."

"Just Juliet," she said and smiled.

"Thank you, ma'am. And I'm just Bart to everybody. Don't think anybody knows my last name anymore. And I've about plumb forgot it myself. But that might be old age. I'll take care of Sally."

Neil noticed that, contrary to what Bart said, he lingered, patting Sally and talking to her. He knew the reason when he and Juliet walked up the steps to the porch. The door opened, and they were bombarded by his grandmother, Stella, Hedda, and Edith Whitfield laughing and throwing rice at them.

He and Juliet were laughing, too. She was shaking her head and trying to dig out the rice stuck in her thick roll of hair. He began to help pick the rice out and brushed some off the shoulders of her jacket. Some of the pins came out, and her hair began to come loose. Her gaze met his, and he felt his laughter catch in his throat at what he was doing.

Her laugh seemed forced this time. "Why do they throw rice at weddings anyway?" She looked around at the women.

When they all shrugged, or admitted they didn't know, Neil offered the information. "Comes from a pagan ritual. Offering grain to the gods is a. . .um. . .fertility rite." Now he wished he'd kept silent. He gave a quick laugh. "There's also a ritual of throwing shoes at a couple. No, none of that," he said when Bart laughed and reached for his shoe. He looked at the women blocking the doorway. "May we come in?"

They shook their heads.

Suddenly it dawned on him that there was another tradition besides rice throwing. Juliet's head turned toward him, and her eyes widened with understanding.

He knew this would end in an annulment, but he quickly swooped Juliet up in his arms. She squealed, and her arm cradled his neck as if she thought he might drop her. His greatest worry was that he might not let her go.

The women stepped aside, and he carried her over the threshold, aware of how easily he had lifted her and held her. He could feel her softness against his chest, her arm over his shoulder and around his neck. He wondered if that faint fragrance was her natural odor, something like women dabbed behind their ears, or her hair that brushed against the side of his face as he set her on the floor and made sure she was balanced. He'd never seen anyone prettier as she stood there, a blush on her cheeks and her hair in disarray.

"I know why a man carries his bride over the threshold," his grandmother said, and he was grateful for the diversion. "The saying is that if she trips or falls, she'll have bad luck for years to come."

"Here are the bags," Bart said. "I'll get a broom and sweep up the rice. That gets wet, and we'll all slide down the mountain on it."

"Thanks." Neil turned to get the bags. He would not dare meet Stella's eyes.

Everyone there should think he found his wife. . .attractive. Everyone except Stella, his wife's mother.

He'd dreaded what questions might be asked them but soon realized they had none. He supposed it wouldn't be fitting to ask how things were on one's honeymoon. They simply mentioned the rain, and he told of the train's delay. Soon Hedda, Bart, and Edith left.

"We can't have Stella going back down the mountain tonight, Neil," his grandmother said. "I had Bart set up that old bed that was in the attic down there in your study. I didn't think you'd mind."

"Yes, that's the hospitable thing to do. You know I don't use the study very much. We certainly should do this for Juliet's mother."

He felt a sense of relief, having supposed he would have to sleep on the love-seat in the study or on the floor. That had to be more than coincidence. More like divine providence. God must be approving this "union" with Juliet. . .and Stella.

Later in the evening, when Juliet and Stella were unpacking Juliet's things, his grandmother took hold of his hands and stood in front of him. Her dark eyes were more alive than he'd seen them in a long time. "Oh, Neil," she said, "I know I can't live forever on this earth. But it's so wonderful having family again. This is the medicine I need. I didn't even feel my rheumatism today."

When she was ready, he listened to her heart, kissed her forehead, turned out her bedroom light, and closed the door. Next he walked down the hallway to his—no, Juliet's—bedroom.

"I'll have all my things out of here as soon as I can," he said. But for the moment, he retrieved a few items of clothing, bade them good night, and went through the bathroom between the rooms and into his study/bedroom.

Later he lay in the darkness, without any light coming through the window because the sky was overcast. Wind moaned lightly through the trees. His grandmother was right. He'd almost forgotten how it felt to have family around. Tonight had felt like family. He'd made his grandmother happy.

He pulled the quilt closer around his shoulders. Faint voices and an occasional laugh sounded from his former bedroom. For a while tonight, while going through the motions of being a married man and holding his wife in his arms, he'd almost believed it. But he dared not forget that the woman in his home, in his room, in his bed, and wearing his mother's ring was not his wife.

She was his *employee*.

Chapter 11

Olivia sat straight up in bed. Light pressed against the curtains. "Stella, should I be making breakfast?"

Stella moaned then mumbled, "I'm not hungry. I'm not even awake." She turned to lie on her back and pull up the covers Olivia had just flung aside. Her aunt blinked several times. "You never make my breakfast anyway."

"I mean for the guests. And for Neil and Mama McCory."

Stella dragged herself upright against a pillow and fluffed out her curls. "That's taken care of. Hedda supervises things when Mama McCory can't. And there's a cook who comes in early. Your role will be to take Mama McCory's place. You're the lady of the house, not the hired help."

"But I am the hired help."

"Yes, but secretly. Openly you're the mistress of the house. As far as everyone knows, except me, you, and Neil, you're married to the doctor in this town. So you must act like it. And today, after church, you and Neil will be the celebrated newlyweds at a reception that Mama McCory, Hedda, and Edith planned for you. I've been working with them on it, too."

"Who's cooking?"

Stella laughed lightly. "Everybody. We were doing that yesterday, but all the women know if they come to the reception they bring a dish of food. They do that all the time here."

"There was a dinner on the grounds at the church in the city one time, but I never went."

Stella nodded. "The only one I went to was a church picnic in a play. We didn't get to really do it, just donned our duds and picked up an empty basket and exited the stage." She laughed. "But this is real, child. You'd better get yourself into that claw-foot tub and get ready to meet the town as Mrs. Dr. Neil McCory." She jumped out of bed. "I'll go to the kitchen and say you and Neil want breakfast in bed. How's that?"

"You're a lifesaver."

Stella grinned. "I know."

Olivia felt a strange stirring in her stomach, and it wasn't hunger. "Stella, what will I do after you leave here?"

Stella looked at her with one of her loving, serious expressions. "Olivia," she said with a note of confidence, "you will rise to the occasion."

Olivia wondered if she could rise to the occasion of being welcomed by the town as Neil's wife. At least she knew how to dress appropriately and wore the same outfit she'd worn the night before in coming to Sunrise, with the addition of a small gray hat trimmed with a band of pink ribbon and a pink bow on one side.

At church, Pastor Whitfield had them stand, and everyone applauded the newlyweds. He announced that since the weather had cleared up, the reception would be on the church lawn.

Right after church ended, most of the men went to their wagons and the women walked away. Olivia's heart sank, thinking they weren't staying for the reception. However, in the next few moments, men were setting up tables they took from their wagons. Some brought doors and set them on sawhorses. They even brought benches. By the time some women put tablecloths on the tables, others were bringing dishes and boxes of food from nearby homes.

As soon as the feast of every imaginable food was spread on the table, Edith said she and Neil must go first. They were followed by Mama McCory and Stella. Olivia kept marveling that the church members and even some townsfolk were doing this for her and Neil.

As soon as she put her plate on a table, she took off her jacket and hat and laid them across her lap. Most of the women were dressed in plain skirts and shirtwaists. She wanted to identify with them. In a way, this reminded her of the times she wanted to play with the miners' children but her father wouldn't allow it, as if she were better than they. She wasn't, and she knew all of these people were better than she. They were not pretending.

People she'd never met came by the table where she sat to congratulate and welcome her. She was glad Stella could keep conversation lively and ongoing. It felt wonderful to be accepted as their beloved doctor's wife. But she felt guilty because it was all fake.

To her surprise, people started singing "O Perfect Love." Edith Whitfield and Stella were walking toward her, holding a tall cake. They put it on the table in front of her. Hedda brought a sheet cake and set it alongside it. Neil joined her as several men brought trays of pitchers and glasses.

Olivia began expressing her delight. She looked at Neil who had a funny look on his face. His eyes seemed to hold a warning. Had she done something wrong?

"You know the tradition, don't you?" asked Mama McCory.

Dumbfounded, Olivia shrugged. "I've seen the bride and groom feed each other a piece. Is that it?"

"Hardly," said Edith.

Stella's eyes gleamed with mischief. She knew.

"The bride and groom must kiss over the cake," Edith said. "That's for future prosperity."

Now Olivia knew what that look on Neil's face was all about. But women and men were gathering around. Those nearby were cheering them on. They began to clap in unison. Little children joined in.

Neil got on his knees on the bench across from her. "I guess we're outnumbered."

She had no choice but to make the best of this. . .job. "I guess it's my wifely duty." She got on her knees across from Neil, braced her hands on the table, and leaned over the cake.

She closed her eyes and pursed her lips, hoping she wouldn't fall in the cake when he kissed her.

All of a sudden, she knew when it was about to happen. The sweet fragrance of cake icing was replaced by the aroma of musky aftershave, the smell of Neil's clothing. Then she felt his warm breath. Like a feather, something touched her lips. Then she felt the warm, soft, firm touch of his lips on hers. His lips didn't move and neither did hers. But as quickly as it happened, it ended.

The people all applauded. Olivia opened her eyes and saw Neil back away, so she did, too. Someone handed her and Neil glasses with small amounts of lemonade in them. While others were getting their glasses and Neil walked around to her, Olivia whispered, "What's this for?"

Her heart beat fast at the idea of kissing over the glasses. These people certainly had interesting customs.

"We'll all clink our glasses together."

"Why?"

He grinned. "To keep the devil away."

Oh dear. When the pastor lifted his glass and shouted, "To the bride and groom," everyone clinked their glasses and then took a drink of lemonade. Looking into Neil's eyes, Olivia had that strange feeling again of being his wife, belonging to him—and these people.

Maybe he should go into acting, too, because something in his eyes seemed to hold hers. She could even imagine he forgot for a moment, too, that they were pretending.

But he believed she belonged to him legally, so he could look at her as if he. . .approved of her. . .if he wanted to.

Staring into his eyes and hearing the congratulations, laughter, and people moving around, she took another sip of her lemonade. Maybe—since the devil seemed to be playing with her mind—she should ask if they might clink again.

After eating a piece of the cake that Edith cut, Olivia started to get up with her plate. Mama McCory reached over and touched her hand. "No, you're not allowed. You're the guest of honor."

Olivia smiled and looked down. Honor? Was this honorable? It seemed so. People were happy. Mama McCory was feeling better than she had in a long time. She'd only wanted a job. But what about when this ended?

Seeing a glint of light, she realized she was twisting the diamond ring that sparkled in the sunlight. She looked up and straight into the eyes of Mama McCory. Their gazes held for a long moment. Olivia tried to conceal the feelings of guilt and concern she felt inside.

Then Mama McCory smiled. That was a sweet smile of complete warmth and acceptance from this woman who thought Olivia was her granddaughter-in-law.

Olivia smiled back, hoping Mama McCory knew she was not acting like she liked her. She didn't want this woman to die but couldn't bear the thought of her knowing this marriage was not real. That would break her heart.

Oh, and wouldn't these people all despise her when this was over?

Chapter 12

"Mrs. McCory, will you pray for Janie?" Mary Clayton asked on Tuesday morning when Neil took Juliet with him to visit church members in the hospital. He'd removed the little girl's tonsils on Monday.

Juliet's hand played with the lace at the neck of her blouse. Her glance at him held uncertainty. He nodded, and they all bowed their heads and closed their eyes.

"God is great, God is good. Let us thank Him for. . ."

Neil's eyes popped open and his head came up. They were not at a table, getting ready to eat. They were at the bedside of a pale, six-year-old girl lying in a hospital bed.

When they'd come into the room, Mary Clayton had hugged Juliet as if she were a long-lost friend. "How sweet of you to come and see my Janie." she said. "I mean, you being a newlywed and all. I wouldn't expect you to even think of her."

George Clayton also expressed his appreciation.

Their greeting her so warmly seemed to be another confirmation that he'd done right in marrying Juliet. Neil was a doctor and a grandson, expected to tend his patients and care for his grandmother. But his "wife" showing concern was special.

Now what would they think of Juliet thanking God for "the food" at a time like this? Even if there was any food in the room, Janie couldn't eat it.

Her parents didn't look up, and Janie's little hands were folded beneath her chin. The child's smile spread across her face as Juliet continued, ". . .for this pretty little girl, with the beautiful name of Janie. Thank You for Dr. Neil who took out her tonsils. And thank You for ice cream that will help make her well. Amen."

They all said, "Amen."

Mary looked hopeful. "You said she could have ice cream today, didn't you, Doctor?"

"Sure did."

George said he'd run down and get some for Janie.

Mary turned to Janie. "Now see what Mrs. McCory has done for you?"

"Please call me Juliet," she said, and Mary smiled.

Janie stretched out her arms. Juliet began to sing in a clear, musical voice,

"Oh, you beautiful doll, you great big, beautiful doll. Let me put my arms about you. I could never live without you. Oh, you beautiful doll." Then she put her arms around the little girl, who was obviously charmed by her.

"You were wonderful with Janie and the other patients," Neil said after they left the hospital and headed for the clinic.

"I wasn't sure what to do. But I remembered you told me to 'be myself,' so that's all I could do."

"Yourself is. . ." What could he say? Surprising? Beautiful? Admirable? He decided on, "good enough."

Since the clinic wasn't full of patients, he could take his wife to lunch. He felt good walking down the sidewalk with his smartly dressed wife. Passersby nodded or spoke.

If he had to say so himself, when they stopped for her to admire some purses in a shop window, he thought the reflection of that couple was quite handsome. She wore her tailored suit and a pert little hat with a feather in the band where the brim turned up. The gentleman accompanying her looked dapper in his suit coat and tie.

"Oh, I love that one." She pointed to a small black bag adorned with jewels.

"You want it?"

He watched her reflection as she studied the purse for a long moment. "I'm saving my money."

He wondered what for but had no right to ask. "I would be glad to. . .get it for you."

"No," she said quickly and turned from the window.

"Sorry." Of course a man shouldn't offer to buy a gift like that for a lady unless they were engaged or married. Knowing what to do or say at times wasn't easy. He was bound by a marriage license but also a legal contract saying the marriage was a temporary one in name only. She was not really. . .his.

Hesitantly, he asked, "You will allow me to treat you to lunch, won't you?"

His heart skipped a couple of beats when she looked up at him and smiled, like a lady being courted by a gentleman. "I'd be delighted."

After Milton brought their food, Neil said, "Would you say the blessing?"

"Sure."

With bowed head, he peeked as she said, "God is great. God is good. Let us thank Him for this food. Amen."

"Amen," he said, unfolding his napkin to put on his lap.

"Why are you grinning like that?"

He looked across at her. "I'm happy."

Seeing the skepticism in her gorgeous green eyes, he ventured to ask, "Are you?"

She picked up her fork. Mischief lay in her glance before she looked down at her plate. "Who wouldn't be with green beans and red potatoes staring us in the face?"

—⁓—

Olivia looked out the kitchen window when she heard the sound of wagon wheels against the cobblestones. "It's Stella." She hadn't seen her in three weeks, but it seemed like a lifetime.

"Run out and see what she's up to," Mama McCory said. "I would, if I could run."

Olivia laughed, rushed outside, and hugged Stella. "I'm so glad to see you. I didn't know you were coming today."

"Two reasons," Stella said. "Good news and not-so-good news."

"Something happened?"

"No. Just a letter from that stubborn ol' brother of mine."

Olivia groaned. "My father. What's he done now?"

Stella took a letter from her pocket. "I didn't read it. But knowing Herman, it won't be good." She handed the letter to Olivia. "But the good news is that I called your dad's housekeeper and asked her to send some of your personal items and clothes. I thought you'd need mainly skirts and shirtwaists."

"Thank you." Olivia tore open the envelope and read aloud.

Olivia,

I've always wanted the best for you. I'm sorry we don't agree on what's best. Apparently you will no longer listen to me, but to your aunt Stella. You must learn your lessons the hard way. I hope you will come to your senses and realize an acting career is not right for a young lady.

I can't imagine what kind of job you've taken since you didn't say. Maybe one like Stella, playing in a honky tonk. Was your college education and good upbringing all a waste?

Sorrowfully,
Your father

"Oh, honey," Stella consoled.

"It's all right." Olivia stuffed the letter into her skirt pocket. "I've felt rejected by my father since I first mentioned acting. Let's go inside, where I'm accepted for my acting ability."

Olivia loved the way Mama McCory took to Stella. The two of them sat at the kitchen table, sipped coffee, and talked.

"Juliet is becoming quite a cook." Mama McCory cast an approving glance at Olivia.

"What? Juliet a cook?"

"See for yourself." Olivia took the Peach Brunch Pie from the icebox. She cut Stella a piece, and after one bite, Stella agreed it was wonderful. Mama McCory decided to have a small piece, although she'd already had breakfast.

"Not only is Juliet learning to cook, and not just breakfast," Mama McCory said, discussing her as if she weren't there, "but she's learning to manage this inn. Still, she does have a problem."

Olivia caught her breath. What was she doing wrong?

Stella looked concerned, too.

Mama McCory took a sip of coffee to wash down the pie. "She has trouble giving instructions to our cleaning ladies. When Juliet sees something that isn't dusted or cleaned well enough, she does it herself."

Olivia smiled at that. Her father had a housekeeper and a cook. They knew their jobs, and he was great at giving orders. She walked over to get their empty plates. "I don't want to run them off. You and Neil, and Hedda, too," she said, taking the plates to the sink, "have talked about the trouble you've had keeping workers."

"Everything is running smoothly," Hedda said, beginning to wash the plates, "now that you're here."

Maybe it was her imagination, but Olivia felt there was an edge to Hedda's voice. It was accompanied by a sidelong look at Stella. A small silence followed. Mama McCory seemed not to notice.

In case Hedda was simply complimenting her, Olivia said, "Thank you."

Stella, however, looked directly at Hedda. "Does that mean you'll be retiring soon, Hedda?"

Hedda scrubbed the plate harder than necessary. "When I'm sure Juliet has learned enough. She's doing a good job, but she's still new at it."

Olivia pretended to be looking at a recipe for a dish she wanted to try. Hedda didn't mean anything by using the word "job," did she? No, of course not. Everybody said things like that.

"You have a point," Mama McCory said. "Juliet is still a newlywed. With her learning all this and Neil doctoring, they don't have much time together."

"You are so insightful, Mama McCory," Stella said. "She and Neil should take a day off."

Olivia told herself that the expectation welling up in her was simply excitement over getting out and seeing more of the spectacular views of these panoramic mountains, not anticipation of being alone with Neil. But they were supposed to be giving the impression that they were a married couple.

Stella and Mama McCory kept making their plans.

"Carter is on duty at the clinic on Saturdays," Mama McCory said.

"A good time might be when the leaves are at their peak."

"But that's our busiest time, Stella," Olivia responded.

"I can cook, change beds, do laundry, and clean house. And I'd love to be up here when the leaves peak. I do have something to do Friday afternoons in Canaan Valley, but I could come after that."

"Oh," Hedda said, just as the plate she was drying slipped out of her hands and thumped onto the rug in front of the sink. She examined it. "It's not broken. I'm so clumsy today."

Mama McCory waved her hand. "No bother, Hedda. Over the years, you and I both have broken enough dishes to make up several sets."

Hedda nodded and smiled. She set to washing the plate again.

Mama McCory returned her attention to Stella. Hedda came over to finish going over the recipe with Olivia. She said softly, "You make Mama McCory happy."

Olivia thought Hedda's eyes were watery. "Thank you." She could imagine that Hedda would be sad to leave the inn—and Mama McCory. Wouldn't anybody?

Olivia joined them at the table. "Now, have you two finished planning my life?"

Laughing, Mama McCory patted her hand. "For now. You and Neil must get away when the leaves are at their peak."

"I'll come that Friday evening," Stella said, "weather permitting. I'll stay for the weekend and go to church with you on Sunday."

Mama McCory leaned toward Stella. "Did Juliet tell you she's playing the piano for the church now?"

Stella's "No" sounded more like disbelief than response to a simple question.

Mama McCory told the story. "Trudy didn't show up for church two Sundays ago. We found out later she was ailing. When Pastor Jacob asked if anybody wanted to volunteer—"

"She volunteered me," Olivia interrupted, and the three of them laughed.

"Well, I've heard you play," Mama McCory said. "Most of our members haven't had the opportunity to learn. When Trudy came back, she heard that Juliet had played in her place, and she wanted to sit and listen. After she listened, she said she would play the opening music and Juliet could play the hymns."

"How nice," Stella said in an exaggerated tone. "My sweet girl playing the piano in church."

"Stella plays better than I do." She decided to play a little of her aunt's game. "Why don't you come up this Saturday, stay the night, and play for us in church on Sunday?"

"Oh, please do," Mama McCory said, looking expectant.

"I'd love to come up but not play. I play by ear, not notes."

"How does that work?" Mama McCory asked curiously.

"I can hear a song," she began to explain, "and the tune stays in my mind. My fingers and that tune work together when I sit at the piano. Sometimes I can play the tune the first time. On more complicated pieces, I might have to pick it out or hear it more than once." She shrugged as if that were simple. "But once the key matches what's in my mind, my fingers know what to do."

"Amazing," Mama McCory said. "Before you leave today, I want to see Juliet play from my sheet music or the hymnal and watch you do that."

Olivia knew that Stella had heard and played church songs in some of her performances. "Yes, you should play for us Sunday, instead of me."

Olivia felt Stella's hand find her arm beneath the table and pinch it.

Chapter 13

On Sunday morning, Pastor Whitfield greeted them at the church door. "So pleased to see you again, Mrs. Kevay." He smiled broadly. "Your daughter is a gift from the Lord. She's the best pianist we've ever had." He put his finger to his lips and cast a furtive glance around. "Don't tell Trudy I said that."

Mama McCory laughed lightly. "Juliet says Stella plays even better than she does."

Stella protested, like one too modest to admit her talent.

"It's true," Olivia said.

"Please play for us," he said. "God gives us talents to be shared." He looked beyond them, so they moved on. Mama McCory stopped to speak to another woman.

"How could you do this to me?" Stella said. "I didn't think Mama McCory would remember your talking about that."

"Mama McCory doesn't forget a thing. Besides, don't worry. If I can act like a wife, you can act like a church pianist."

Stella stood for a moment and listened to Trudy. Then she smiled broadly and strutted down the aisle to take her seat.

After Trudy finished, Olivia walked up and sat on the piano bench. Pastor Whitfield took his place in the pulpit and looked out over the congregation.

"You all know how pleased we are that the Lord has provided us with Mrs. McCory, a gifted pianist. Well, this morning, after she plays our first hymn, we have another treat. Her mother will honor us with some special music. Now, let's turn to page 158, stand, and sing 'Nothing but the Blood.' "

When they finished, Stella walked up. "Kind of slow, wasn't it?" she whispered as Olivia rose from the bench.

Oh dear! Olivia felt like a pitcher of cold creek water had been poured over her head. For an instant she froze, seeing Stella's hands poised over the keys. What had she gotten them into? Before Olivia could return to her place between Mama McCory and Neil, the rafters were already ringing with a rousing rendition of "Mine Eyes Have Seen the Glory."

Stella's whole body was into it, and her fingers were playing notes in between any notes that had ever been written for that hymn. Olivia knew that would be a hit for an outdoor crowd—even in a nickleodeon. But in a church?

Was Stella ruining everything? She was supposed to be the mother of Juliet Kevay McCory, the respected wife of the town's beloved doctor.

This should light a fire under the members any minute. The first movement was a woman's head turning. Then she saw that the woman was Hedda, with eyes popping and mouth agape.

Olivia was afraid to look at Neil. He must be terribly embarrassed. Pastor Whitfield sat in his chair on the platform, staring at Stella like she was one of the great wonders of the world. In fact, Olivia reckoned she was.

Not only were the rafters ringing, the pew seemed to be shaking. Feeling like people were looking at her, too, Olivia peeked to her left. Mama McCory was shaking while covering her mouth with her hand. Was she laughing? Well, becoming the laughingstock might be a little better than being tarred and feathered.

Stella was almost bouncing off the bench.

"Hallelujah!" came a voice from the back. A couple of male voices roared, "Amen!" A woman said, "Praise the Lord!" A woman down front stood and lifted her arms toward the ceiling. Then one on the other side of the aisle did the same. Heads were bobbing and bodies were bouncing.

"More, more," someone yelled when she finished with a flourish. Stella slapped her hands on her thighs and faced her audience with a look of triumph while they said amen and applauded. Olivia wondered if Stella had led them down the path of wickedness and turned this place into a honky-tonk.

Pastor Whitfield walked a few steps over to the piano with his hands outstretched. "Please," he pled. "One more."

A wide smile spread across Stella's glowing, beautiful face. "Everybody," she shouted and began pounding out a fast version of "When We All Get to Heaven." They all stood, began to clap and sing and sway—except Hedda. Then Bart poked her and she stood. Before long, she was moving, too.

Even Mama McCory was standing, clapping, and singing. Olivia looked at Neil. His gaze met hers, his eyebrows lifted, but he grinned then and stood, so she did, too. Soon the two of them joined in.

Amid applause and Pastor Whitfield's high praise, Stella returned to her seat. Mama McCory reached over and held Stella's hand for a long time.

Pastor Whitfield said that was a hard act to follow. It was indeed, and Olivia didn't know what his sermon was about. Her concern was what Neil might say. Although it had been entertaining, he might banish both her and Stella from his home and his sight.

After church ended, while Stella was being surrounded by adoring fans, Mama McCory held on to Olivia's arm and leaned around to speak to Neil.

"Neil," she said, "let's invite Edith and the pastor to have lunch with us."

"You must be feeling better," he said. Earlier she'd said she probably wouldn't eat out.

She gave a short laugh. "I've been revived."

His brief nod seemed to say he knew what she meant. Olivia, however, felt rather drained. She turned her attention to Mary Clayton who walked up with little Janie. Neil said he'd go speak to the pastor. Several others came up, raving about how much they enjoyed Stella's playing.

Olivia was grateful for the compliments, but she couldn't keep from glancing at the aisle where Hedda had a grip on Mama McCory's arm. Finally, Mama McCory shook her head, then turned and hastened away, quite quickly for a woman with a cane.

Hedda shot a glance at Olivia, making her wonder if Hedda had disapproved of Stella's playing.

Then she looked at her aunt, the center of attention. Yes, being around Stella was like watching a play all right—one in which you couldn't predict the ending.

Milton had a table reserved for them by the time they reached the restaurant. "I'm glad to have such talented ladies in my establishment." He smoothed the apron he wore over his church clothes. "Dessert's on me."

They thanked him, and waitresses brought the food. The Sunday meal was family style. Soon the table was filled with fried chicken, rice, gravy, biscuits, green beans, mashed potatoes, sliced tomatoes, and pickled cucumbers.

"Nothing against your preaching, Jacob," Mama McCory said after the pastor asked the blessing, "but it's about time we got some life back into our church. I remember when there was shouting and even some fainting when people felt the presence of the Lord."

He agreed. "You're right, Mama McCory. We need to get people more excited about the Lord than they are about the new telephones, automobiles, and running water."

Olivia's glance swept over Neil's face and sort of settled on those firm-looking lips of his. She tried to turn her mind to things of the Lord. But exactly what was she supposed to think about the Lord?

"I think the Lord was speaking to me this morning," Mama McCory said. "Again, no reflection on you, Jacob. But when Stella was playing, all we could do was just feel the music."

"I know what you mean." The pastor passed the food. "In church is a time for the Lord to speak, and it's not always through my sermon. Anyway, I'm kind of used to you speaking your mind."

"I liked your sermon," Stella said. "You talked about many things I'd never thought about."

The pastor seemed to bask in her praise. "Thank you. That's quite a compliment."

"Yes," Edith said. "Jacob and the Lord do sometimes speak in mysterious ways."

Olivia liked the way the pastor and Edith looked at each other then—he with a warning look and she with mischief. They all laughed. Olivia liked the throaty sound of Neil's laughter.

"Now that my wife has insulted me, let's move on," the pastor said. "What did the Lord say to you, Mama McCory?" He bit into a chicken leg.

"You know, after my Streun died, I quit hosting the Bible studies. Then when I thought I would start them up again, I had that stroke. I felt like life was over for me." She took a deep breath, put down her fork, and reached over to hold Olivia's hand. "There's new life in my house now." Her eyes grew moist.

Olivia looked at Neil. This is what he wanted. He sometimes glanced at her or looked for a brief moment, but this time their gazes held long enough that she saw the warmth and gratitude in his brown eyes. He finally looked down and poked his mashed potatoes with his fork.

Stella smiled at her fondly and gave her a slow wink.

Yes, it did appear she was doing her. . .job. . .well. But it wasn't just a job. She loved Mama McCory, and she didn't know a finer man than Neil.

"Mama McCory," Edith said, "do you want to start the Bible studies again?"

"If you will teach it."

Edith clasped her hands over her heart. "Oh yes. And there are so many ladies in the church who need this. We can announce it next Sunday. Then you want to start it on the following Tuesday?"

Mama McCory said she would. "Could you come up for the Bible study, Stella?"

"I would love to," she said so sincerely that Olivia suspected she meant it.

"Oh, this is wonderful," Edith said. "Should we have Juliet suggest our first topic?" The women agreed.

"Do you have a topic you'd like studied, dear?" Mama McCory asked.

"Yes," she said without having to think. "The Holy Ghost."

Chapter 14

Rain had fallen last weekend. Olivia feared it might again and Stella wouldn't be able to come. This Friday the weather was sunny, however, and the cooler mid-October temperatures had turned the West Virginia mountains into a spectacular array of red, gold, and yellow. The leaves were at their peak in color.

Stella hadn't been able to attend the first Bible study on Tuesday as the weekend rain made much of the road from Canaan Valley too muddy for travel. So Olivia was relieved when her aunt arrived at the inn shortly after sunset.

Hedda and Bart had left early to get home before dark, so Juliet served Stella, Neil, Mama McCory, and herself a piece of pineapple upside-down cake.

"I don't normally eat a lot of sweets before going to bed," Mama McCory said, "but Juliet is cooking up such good things nowadays. And, too,"—she reached over and patted Stella's hand—"when you visit, I don't want to miss a thing. There's always something new." She laughed. "You're wearing a tie."

Stella touched the green silk tie at her neck. "It's the style for women."

"Yes, I've noticed that. Amazing what is in the papers nowadays."

As if he, too, were thinking about another ad, Neil said, "I'm glad you're back to reading the papers again, Grandmother."

"I didn't have a reason to for a long time, Neil. When you're dying from a stroke and have a weak heart, that kind of becomes your world. Things have changed."

Stella returned her smile with her own affectionate one. "I'm sorry I didn't get to the Bible study."

"We had eight women," Mama McCory said. "Met in the parlor and had a good lesson and discussion."

"Maybe you could give me a summary of what you learned."

Mama McCory's eyes seemed to light up. "I'd love to, but first we must help clean up in here."

"There's not much to do," Olivia said. "You two go ahead. It won't take me any time to do this."

"Thank you, dear." Turning to Stella, Mama McCory said, "Let's retire to the parlor for our discussion so we'll be out of the way." The two women headed out the door, talking about the Bible class.

Neil stayed in the kitchen and helped Olivia clean up, although she protested.

"I'm glad to help, Juliet. You're busy from before sunup to late at night."

"I'm busy, yes," she agreed. "But it's not hard work. Anything I can do for Mama McCory is not work but a pleasure."

"That's fine," he said. "But I'm glad Stella is here and said she will help with breakfast in the morning. I'd be pleased if you could spend more time with the things you like to do. Like cooking, Bible study, playing the piano, reading. . ."

"I do those things," she said, handing him a plate to be dried.

"Good," he said. "I don't ever want you to feel like you're just. . .anything less than my wife."

Olivia let go of the plate and stuck her hands back into the soapy water. There was only one time each week when she felt less. And that's when he gave her the dollar she'd earned.

Neil thought she might say, "You decide," when he asked what she'd like to do on their day off that his grandmother and Stella had planned for them.

She responded, however, with a great deal of enthusiasm. "Could we take a hike? Everything is breathtakingly beautiful right here. But I'd like to see more. Fall is my favorite season."

"Mine, too." Neil liked finding out what she enjoyed. Maybe on this day off they could get to know each other better.

"Will we hike all the way to the top of the mountain?"

He laughed. "I think we'd better ride Sally. At least part of the way. It's a long way up there."

Her face was animated. "I'll make a picnic lunch." He felt rather pleased that she seemed to eat the rest of her breakfast with a great amount of zest, as if she couldn't wait to begin their day's adventure.

Yes, like his grandmother had said several times over the past few weeks, "Juliet's and Stella's enjoyment of life could be quite contagious."

He sat for a while longer, sipping another cup of coffee and stealing glances at Juliet making sandwiches for their lunch. If he did have a wife in the true sense of the word, he wouldn't want her thinking he'd married her only to manage an inn and be a companion to his grandmother. He would want to take time to show her that he. . .cared.

Then he should do the same for Juliet. After all, they were legally married.

Thirty minutes later, Neil stared at the young woman who walked out the back door wearing a shirtwaist much like she wore daily, a riding skirt, and sensible hiking boots. She came up to him and Sally. Her auburn hair was pulled back from her face and was fastened with a wide clasp at the back of her head.

It hung in waves to below her shoulders. He envied the early morning sunshine that caressed it with a touch of reddish gold.

With the discipline of a doctor trained not to say everything on his mind, he reached for the bag of lunch she'd prepared and fastened it to the side of the saddle. He mounted the horse, then looked down at her. "You can ride in front and I'll look over your head so we both see the views. Or you may ride behind me and stare at my back."

Her gaze moved toward heaven as if that were a ridiculous statement. Laughing, he hoisted her up in front of him. They rode along a trail marked for the inn's guests and tourists. A young couple moved aside to let them pass.

Olivia glanced around at him. "You think the hikers will appreciate a horse on the trail?"

"No, I don't." A short distance ahead he did what he'd intended all along. He left the trail, and Sally trotted along a familiar path.

Soon he stopped, dismounted, and held up his hands for Juliet. She gave him a questioning look, but he grinned at her and tied Sally to a tree limb in the completely wooded area. "This way." They walked onto a trail where they could peek through the myriad colored trees on their left and see the town below. On the right was the steep mountainside.

He heard the trickle of water about the time Juliet spied it and laughed gleefully. Water flowed over an outcropping of rocks like a miniature waterfall and formed a pool at the side of the trail. They cupped their hands and drank the cold, clear water.

Farther on, as the trailed curved up and around the slight incline, they passed others who were strolling along, enjoying the beauty of the day and the scenery.

She stopped. "Look how dark it is up there on that section of the trail."

"Look at this," he said, picking up a stick. He pointed with it to a muddy place on the side of the trail. "What kind of track do you think that is? Bear? Mountain lion?"

Her eyes widened. "Are you trying to scare me?"

"Yeah." He grinned at her.

She hit him on the arm and marched toward the dark, casting a glance over her shoulder that dared him to follow. He had no problem doing that. She slowed upon reaching the path into the section where rhododendron formed a canopy, allowing very little light into the area.

"There really are bears and mountain lions around here, aren't there, Neil?"

"Yes, but they try to stay out of our way."

All of a sudden something was upon them. Juliet let out a yelp, and Neil pulled her close to the side of the path and jumped out of the way. A young man apologized and kept running. That's when Neil thought he should take Juliet's hand in his, which he did. She didn't protest, but they let go when they walked into the light again.

They wound up and around, then stopped for a moment to look down, able to see the town that now looked even smaller.

Neil explained that the trail was almost parallel to the one they'd hiked. "We'll soon be back down to Sally."

Sally snorted, as if showing her disapproval of having been left in the forest. They mounted her, and after a time of winding up through the woods, the trees thinned. A sudden gust of wind whipped the tree branches, and soft yellow leaves fell on them like pieces of gold and blanketed their path.

Juliet held out her hand and laughed with delight. Suddenly her breath caught and all she could say was, "Oh."

That's how Neil felt whenever he came here.

They dismounted. While she walked toward the spectacular view of mountains below and beyond them, Neil secured Sally. He spread the saddle blanket out and set the bag of lunch on it, then walked up to Juliet.

"I've never seen anything so beautiful," she whispered, as if a voice might disturb the scenery. She looked over at him. "The colors, too, are more vivid than I've ever seen."

Hearing her appreciation of this spot that meant so much to him and looking into her eyes, he said, "Green is beautiful, too."

She blinked her eyes and looked again at the scenery. "I'm sure it's beautiful here anytime. And the town below is like a toy town."

Feeling he had made an error in implying something too personal, he turned and walked to the blanket. She followed, and soon they were eating the sandwiches, fruit, and cheese, and drinking from the canteens. All sounds were magnified. He could hear his own chewing. Sally whinnied, and he tossed his apple core for her to eat. Then Juliet did the same and quipped, "She didn't even have to step aside to get mine."

He straightened, pulling his knees up and hugging them. "Oh, was there a contest?"

"Yeah," she teased. "In case a bear shows up, somebody has to be able to hit him between the eyes."

Neil breathed easier, feeling that had eased the tension he had felt. "I've thought of building a house here someday."

She seemed surprised. "You don't plan to live in the inn?"

"Having the inn is grandmother's dream, not mine. I would like to have a home where friends can visit, but I'd like my home to be just for my family. Sunrise is becoming more of a tourist area every year. Hotels will be built. The town will become a city before long."

Juliet agreed. "The automobiles will come, too. Do you not want one?"

"They are the way of the future, contrary to what some are saying. The cities are filled with them. But for now, when I make house calls, the horse and buggy serves me better than an automobile. For one thing, we don't have the roads for them here."

"With a clinic and a hospital in town, I wouldn't think you'd make many house calls."

"I don't make a lot of them. But some of the people back in the mountains don't trust hospitals and clinics. That doesn't mean they shouldn't have a doctor caring for their needs."

Juliet looked out toward the spectacular view that went on for miles. "Has Kathleen seen this?"

"Yes." He closed their canteens and put them into the bag. "She still prefers the city."

Juliet stood. "But maybe she will prefer this when Sunrise becomes a city."

Neil picked up the blanket and shook it. "I don't think I want to marry a woman who rejects me because I won't live in the city." He laughed as if it didn't matter. "Maybe I could. . .hire a wife."

She walked alongside him toward Sally. "I think you already did that."

"Yes, but it's temporary."

"Right," she said. "If it wasn't, I wouldn't be getting paid. Humph." She stomped her foot. "Not only are women not allowed to vote, but they don't even get paid for all the housework they do."

Neil chuckled when she grinned. He could imagine her and Stella marching and speaking about a woman's right to vote. But more on his mind was her talking about getting paid for housework.

He'd hoped to find a way to ask if she might think of him not as an employer, but as one interested in her personally. He'd shared something of his future plans with her. Surely she would know he would not do that with a woman unless he thought her. . .special.

But he'd hired her to do a job and was paying her. It wouldn't be proper to pay a woman he was courting.

This was a predicament.

He thought of the Bible studies they'd started at the inn. If ever there was a time when he needed to study his Bible and pray, now was that time.

Chapter 15

The end of October brought fall rains, flooded areas, and winds that almost stripped the deciduous trees bare of their brown leaves. After the cold spell, the November sky cleared, leaving a crispness in the air.

Olivia was delighted, along with Neil, that Mama McCory wanted to make big plans for the holiday season that was quickly approaching. They spent many hours poring over recipe books and discussing how to decorate the inn.

Olivia was grateful that Stella had been invited to the inn for Thanksgiving and would join them for the Thanksgiving Day service at church.

After the special service, Edith and Pastor Whitfield joined them for dinner at the inn.

The inn smelled like roasted turkey, giblet gravy, yeast rolls, corn bread dressing, nutmeg, cinnamon, pumpkin pie, cranberry sauce, green peas, and buttery corn.

"I love the smell of Thanksgiving," Mama McCory said. "It's been a few years since we've cooked a turkey and all the trimmings. I have so much to be thankful for this year."

"I've missed these invitations to your dinners, too." Jacob frowned. "To not be alone, Edith and I had to go to Milton's at Thanksgiving or depend on some church member to invite us."

"But you don't look like you've missed a Thanksgiving dinner or any others for that matter," Mama McCory quipped. "No offense, Jacob."

"None taken." He patted his ample belly, smiled broadly, and reached for the gravy bowl.

Edith sighed. "Christmas will be here before we know it."

"Oh, I'm looking forward to it this year," Mama McCory said. "Why don't we go against tradition and decorate the day after Thanksgiving?"

"We could do that," Olivia said. "If you want to."

"Yes, we could, couldn't we? We've already planned how we want to decorate. And maybe Stella could stay and help."

"As long as you need me or want me. I don't do any more than put up a small tree with a few baubles and set out a few candles. But some years I went to my brother's house."

Olivia remembered when Stella came to their house, dressed so beautifully.

The two of them would go shopping downtown. They'd have fun, walking in the snow in their boots with fur-lined hoods around their faces. Stella would make hot chocolate when they returned to her father whose glass of Christmas cheer hadn't cheered him.

"It's a shame you have to stay down there all winter," Mama McCory said. "Do you have electricity?"

"No, but it's expected to reach that far in the spring."

Mama McCory scoffed. "You could freeze to death by then." She stared at Neil. Olivia watched them communicate without speaking.

The expression in Neil's eyes was warm. He smiled and gave a brief nod of understanding. Then he looked at Olivia. "My wife is the one to interview the hired help. Maybe she has something in mind."

Oh, Olivia could have kissed him.

No. . .she supposed she couldn't. . .or shouldn't.

"Mrs. Kevay," she said as dramatically and formally as she could, trying to hold back her excitement, "we have a position open for the winter. You may have free room and board in exchange for—" She paused and cleared her throat, waiting for everyone to look at her. "In exchange for your keeping the commodes clean."

They all laughed.

Stella said, "Honey, for the privilege of staying here with you wonderful people, I would keep the outhouses clean."

They laughed again. Stella and Olivia got up and hugged Mama McCory, then they hugged each other.

Olivia looked at Neil and mouthed a sincere "Thank you."

His gaze made her feel as warm as freshly baked bread. Edith Whitfield's voice finally got her attention. "Would you do that, Juliet?"

"Pardon?" She returned to her seat. "I didn't hear that."

"Oh, good. We all have just volunteered you and Stella to be in charge of the children's Christmas program."

She began to protest.

Edith wouldn't hear of it. "You must use your talents for the Lord."

"It's your Christian duty," the pastor added.

Olivia and Stella stared at each other. Since he put it that way, what recourse did they have?

As if that were settled, Mama McCory said, "Stella, you're part of the family, so there's no way you can stay in one of the servants' rooms on the lower floor. You can have one of the guest rooms upstairs."

Stella had a different idea. "That's so far from everything though. Why don't I take Neil's study? That way I'm close to the kitchen and dining rooms. Besides,

I'll be getting up early." She grinned at Neil. "I doubt he does much studying in there anyway."

Olivia thought he looked like he'd just been put out in the cold.

Finally, Neil found his voice and some color returned to his face. "That's fine. She's right. I don't really study in there." More color was in his face now. "I have my clinic, the parlor, the foyer"—he raised his hands and his eyes—"the second floor."

"Or even the lower floor with the laundry room and hired help," Stella said.

Neil grinned. "Now we know what it's going to be like, living with my mother-in-law."

They all laughed. Olivia loved the way Stella and Neil could tease each other.

——∾∾——

For a long time after the guests left and everyone had retired for the night, Stella and Olivia couldn't stop giggling.

"Did you see Neil's face when he thought I was taking his secret 'bedroom'?" Stella said.

"It was priceless," Olivia agreed.

"I think it finally dawned on him that he would still have his study as his bedroom and I'd be in here with you."

Olivia couldn't be happier about that. Sitting in bed eating popcorn, their conversation turned serious.

"What do you know about children's Christmas programs?" Stella asked.

Olivia thought. "I know Father sent gifts to the miners' children on Christmas. We had our own Christmas alone. Then after we moved to the city and before I went off to college, we went to some programs at church. I remember the choir sang and the preacher preached."

"About what?"

"I don't remember. But I do remember, as we left, everyone was given a paper bag filled with an apple, orange, some nuts, a candy cane, and some hard candy."

"If that's all you remember, it must have been boring," Stella said seriously.

"Well, I liked the candy."

They each tried to remember how much they knew about church.

"We can't ask the church members here. They'll think we're heathens."

Stella nodded. "Herman made me feel like I was not as good as church people, so I never went much."

"Father and I didn't go often," Olivia said. "There was only a traveling preacher when we lived at the mining area. Before she died, Mama told me about God and even read the Bible. But I remember very little of it."

190

"Your grandmother was like that. Mama McCory reminds me a lot of her. She used to talk about God like He was her friend."

After a thoughtful moment, Olivia said, "Pastor Whitfield said anybody can come to Jesus and that God invites anybody and we are to tell others that."

Stella nodded, a light replacing that question in her eyes. "I don't see any reason why we can't tell that to the children. I mean, it's like acting. You read what the scriptwriter puts on paper, you learn it, and then you act it out. I did that for twenty years."

Olivia wasn't so confident. "But I haven't."

"Posh!" Stella said. "I hadn't either when I started. And I didn't even go to acting school. I learned the hard way. Learned what it was like to feel rejected, alone, and criticized, and then acted it out on stage. You know those things. You can do it, too."

"You mean, we can just find something in the Bible, memorize what it says, teach it to the children, and have them act it out?"

"Sure. And it won't be like we're telling them something bad. We'll stick right by the script. Now what have I always told you?"

Nodding, Olivia felt a confidence that Stella often inspired in her. " 'All the world's a stage. . . .' "

"Exactly. Neil has to act in his job. He can't come right out and tell people their loved ones might be dying."

Seeing what she meant, Olivia could add to that. "I know Mama McCory and Hedda love cooking and serving the guests in the mornings. But sometimes Mama McCory's fingers are stiff and Hedda has a headache. But they act like everything is fine in front of the guests. So acting different than you feel isn't wrong, is it?"

"I don't think so. Remember that Sunday when Jacob Whitfield preached on love? He said it's not a feeling, it's an action. So, he's saying to act it out."

"Like I'm acting like I love Neil."

"Yes. And he's acting like you're his wife."

That made it sound all right. "So it will be good for us to act like good Christians in church?"

"Exactly," Stella said. "That's what they all do. We're going to church like other people. The motto?"

"Life's a stage, and we play many parts." Olivia felt better. "By the time I finish my year here, I may not need acting school."

"And," Stella added, "the pastor said if people do acts of love, they may learn to love the ones they do the acts for."

Olivia nodded. "Proof of that is my pretending to be Mama McCory's granddaughter-in-law. I really love her now."

"So do I," Stella said.

Olivia wondered why she was staring at her and grinning. Then something occurred to her—something she refused to say aloud.

That kind of reasoning didn't extend to Neil, of course. She pushed a piece of popcorn in her mouth and chewed. Acting like she loved Neil wouldn't make her love him.

Except as her *employer*.

Chapter 16

At breakfast the next morning, Stella arranged for her and Olivia to go to Canaan Valley for her things. "I can get everything in the wagon that I need for winter."

"Don't you have appointments on Friday?" Hedda asked.

Olivia saw Mama McCory give her a strange look. Maybe she thought that was too personal, coming from Hedda.

"I mean," Hedda said, "maybe you get your hair done?"

"I do my own hair." Stella studied her for a moment. "Would you like for me to do something with yours?"

"No." Hedda turned away and busied herself in the kitchen.

"Now, I might," Mama McCory said. "I like that new short style. I might even have you give me a bob."

"I'll hold you to that. But as far as my appointment on Fridays," Stella said, loud enough for Hedda to hear, "I can't very well do that and live here, too."

Olivia wondered if her aunt would really be able to give up her job in the theater.

Their plans for the day were settled. Olivia and Stella would go to Canaan Valley and bring back Stella's belongings. Hedda and Bart would go up into Mama McCory's attic and bring down boxes of Christmas decorations.

While in Canaan Valley, Olivia sent a letter to her father.

Father,

I am very happy with my new job. It keeps me busy, so I will not be home for Christmas. Please tell John and Sarah Merry Christmas for me. Stella is doing well. She sends her love. I love you, too.

Olivia

Olivia and Stella decided to get the Christmas spirit going with dinner that evening. After Neil came home, he, Olivia, Stella, and Mama McCory ate at a table in the dining room in front of a fire blazing in the fireplace. Stella had made a centerpiece of lighted candles, evergreen sprigs, and a few Christmas baubles. Olivia had lit candles on other tables, lending a cozy, romantic feel to the room.

"Streun and I used to do this," Mama McCory said wistfully. "Just the two of us."

Olivia could imagine that. She glanced at Neil who also was looking at the setting and wondered if he was thinking he would like a romantic evening with someone special. It suddenly occurred to her that he couldn't pursue another woman even if he found one he cared about. In his mind, he was a married man.

After the blessing, Neil mentioned the Christmas decorations in the parlor. "I see *someone* is going to be hanging and stringing."

"After *someone* brings in several big trees," Stella quipped.

"Several?"

"Yes. This is a big house."

The women were all nodding. He sighed. "I see I'm outnumbered."

Judging by the way he smiled, Olivia thought he didn't mind at all.

"Thinking of Christmas," Olivia said, eager to hear their ideas, "what kind of children's program has the church had in the past?"

"The usual," Neil said. "Children act out the Christmas story."

"Um, which one?" Stella asked. "My goodness, I've been thinking of Charles Dickens's *A Christmas Carol*."

"I saw *A Christmas Carol* a long time ago," Mama McCory recalled. "It's a good story. But I don't think we have enough people in the church who can do that. Maybe you should keep it simple and just do the birth of Jesus."

"The birth of Jesus." Stella nodded. "You have a script for that?"

"Well, no. I don't think they've ever had a script. Jacob usually reads the story. The children wear their little costumes and act it out. Edith should have costumes from last year."

"I can show you where it is in the Bible," Neil offered.

"I just thought of something." Mama McCory nodded, remembering. "Edith said they lost their star."

"Oh, I'm so sorry," Stella said. "What happened?"

Mama McCory shrugged. "Probably got thrown in the trash."

Disbelief crossed Stella's face. "I've heard of an audience throwing rotten tomatoes at the star, but I wouldn't think church people would do that, much less throw somebody in the trash over a poor performance."

Mama McCory began to shake.

Neil put his napkin over his mouth. Then he moved it. "I'm sorry," he said, but he couldn't hold back a hearty laugh.

Mama McCory laughed aloud then.

"You were joking, of course," Stella said.

Mama McCory couldn't talk but nodded. Finally, she said, "I'm not talking about the star of the play. But—" She paused as she had trouble getting the words out. "I'm talking about the kind of star that hangs in the sky."

Neil couldn't keep a straight face.

"Oh. Ohh." Stella began to laugh, and so did Olivia.

Finally, wiping the tears from her face, Mama McCory said, "You just tickle me to pieces."

"The star of the Christmas show," Neil informed them, still emitting a few chuckles, "is the baby Jesus."

Stella was nodding. "That gives me something to go on. I don't know if I can do this the way you're used to."

Mama McCory gave her a straightforward look. "I don't think anybody really expects that."

───※───

Neil had come to realize that Juliet and Stella knew less about the Bible and Christianity than he had assumed. But they were eager to learn and take part. At least his grandmother was having the time of her life. He knew she loved Juliet and adored Stella.

The days of December flew by, and the inn constantly had children in it practicing for the play, women meeting for Bible study, and cooking going on in the kitchen. Neil did his part, too. He, Bart, Stella, and Juliet went out on the mountainsides until the right sizes and number of trees were found.

The big one in the foyer was twice as tall as he. A smaller one was placed in the corner on the stair landing. There was one in the dining room, one in the parlor, and a small one on the table in his grandmother's bedroom that would shine from her front window.

Each evening, he'd say, "Is that it?"

"Almost," Stella would reply. "But we do need this garland hung along the stair banister."

Another time, one of them would say, "We must have some of that holly with red berries," and then look at him as if the temperatures hadn't dropped to below freezing.

"Hot cocoa will be waiting when you return," Juliet said.

He jokingly complained but loved every minute of it, even when they sent him off to find mistletoe.

Another evening, he strung beads, then stood back watching the transformation while the three women added candles, silver wire ornaments, glass baubles, and tinsel to the big tree in the foyer.

They stepped back, looked at each other, and nodded.

"It still needs something else."

They began to murmur about what it could need.

"Stella," Neil said, pointing to the top of the tree. "That's the spot for you."

Her hands went to her hips. "What are you talking about?"

"That's where the star goes. You're the star of this decorating show, so go on up."

She rushed over and beat him on the arm. "Oh, you keep that up and you'll find yourself in the trash can."

His grandmother found her cardboard star outlined with silver tinsel. He hung it while the others lit the candles.

Instead of in a trash can, he found himself encased in a world of glowing candlelight, vivid colors, the smell of cedar, and three beautiful women who made him laugh, brightened his days, and gave him a family to come home to at night.

His gaze fell on Juliet, with her face lifted, staring at the tree as if she'd never seen anything so beautiful.

He hadn't. Not with the way the candles seemed to make a halo around her hair, her face, and her eyes. *Why, why,* he asked himself, *when a man has so much, must he always long for. . .more?*

———

A week before Christmas, they went to the church for the children's program. When Neil saw the cows on the stage when the curtain opened, he figured it would be entertaining but not too spiritual.

However, after the scene of no room at the inn and the young couple in the stable, the cows were led off the stage and outside.

The children's program was a huge success. Stella, Juliet, and the women and men they'd engaged to help had done a professional job of it. They'd even added a curtain that could be drawn across the stage. It had become a theater, and the children were in costumes befitting real shepherds and kings.

There was no forgetting of lines or giggling over children making mistakes. The program turned out to be meaningful, with the focus on the birth of Christ. The children took it very seriously and so did everyone in the audience.

Every child had a part, from the youngest real baby in the manger to the oldest. The oldest said the words "This is the Savior of the world. This is Christ the Lord." The wonder of it came through.

Neil knew that Stella—this woman he suspected didn't know much about the Bible—was primarily responsible. Maybe it was her own wonder that caused it to come through in this performance. It was the old story presented in a fresh and awe-inspiring way.

The young actors questioned, "This baby is a king? Why is He born in a stable?" The participants asked more questions than they answered, causing the onlookers to think. "Why would God want us to bring these expensive gifts to this baby? Has anyone ever seen a star so bright? Why would an angel appear to us when we are just lowly shepherds?"

The musical ability of Stella and Juliet had to be what caused the children to sound like angels. Juliet played the piano, and Stella led them in her exuberant or quiet way, depending on the song.

At the end, Stella had everyone sing a hymn while leaving the church. The service had been solemn and worshipful. He reprimanded himself for having expected something rather outrageous to happen. All was quiet and peaceful.

All of a sudden, a loud crack disturbed his thoughts.

He and the pastor exchanged glances. They rushed to the door. Stella's wagon had been pulled up near the door. Bart and Carter stood in it, handing down paper bags.

Each one dipped into a bag, pulled out a Christmas cracker, and filled the night with pops, cracks, and laughter.

Neil took a bag and handed it to Juliet, then took his own. In it was an apple, an orange, nuts, a candy cane, pieces of hard candy, and a Christmas cracker. He and Juliet pulled the ends, popped theirs, and laughed. Their frosty breaths mingled in the cold December air and warmed his heart.

He spied his grandmother leaning against Stella for balance while she popped her cracker. She had refused to wear anything on her head, except the short haircut Stella had given her. It did look quite nice, but he feared she'd catch her death of cold. Soon she left with Stella in the wagon.

Neil and Juliet rode in the carriage. He tried to think of a way to express his gratitude. That weekly salary and ending their relationship in a year was becoming an albatross around his neck.

The stars were shining in the clear sky. The frosty air was invigorating, but not nearly so much as having this beautiful, talented, caring woman by his side. He'd warned himself not to say anything too personal. Maybe he could lead up to letting her know that her presence in his home—in his life—was far beyond any job offer he could imagine. Could she possibly be thinking along the same lines?

Finding his voice, he said, "I've never known the children's program to be so well done. I'm proud of you."

"Thank you. God gave us a beautiful story to work with." A touch of weariness seemed to have affected her voice.

"I suppose you're tired. You've worked so hard for this night."

"Oh, maybe a little," she said with a small smile. "But something is troubling me. Seeing the children and adults laughing and having so much fun on the church lawn tonight made me think of the children in the mining area. Just a paper bag with a few items in it would mean the world to them."

No, she hadn't been thinking of him. She was thinking of her unhappy childhood in the mining area. And after the wonderful reminder this night of what God had given the world, he should have been thinking of others, too.

"Should this be a church project?"

She nodded, and her smile lit up the night brighter than the soft moonlight that touched her face. He promptly turned the carriage around and drove to the pastor's house.

The Whitfields loved the idea, and by Tuesday morning the word had spread. The Bible study time turned into a time for goodies and toys being brought to the inn and bagged.

Neil came home for lunch to assist them, and in the evenings he helped some more. "I don't want to use only my money to buy toys and fruit," he said to Juliet. "I want to use my hands and heart in this project."

She nodded. "The pastor says it's more blessed to give than receive."

He smiled. All around him were happy faces. On Saturday he felt joyful when he and Juliet led the way up the mountain with a couple of wagons following.

Later, standing back and watching the miners' children excited about their gifts, parents looking on with happiness, and all laughing as they popped their Christmas crackers, he felt like he'd had an insight that had been missing.

He found fulfillment in being a doctor. Having watched his parents taken from him by the flu epidemic had enhanced his desire to help the sick. But that was also his profession. This—reaching out to the less fortunate—was not only a command of God, it was a heartwarming experience.

This wife of his was teaching him some important lessons. He couldn't remember a more meaningful Christmas.

After the worship service on Christmas Day, Neil started a fire in the parlor and lit the candles on the Christmas tree. He, Juliet, his grandmother, and Stella were to exchange gifts. He couldn't imagine getting anything to bring him any more joy than he already had.

He was especially pleased to see his grandmother enjoying herself and looking so well. Even in the times she was not well enough to get out of bed, she always had someone, probably Hedda or Bart, get a gift for him. But while the gifts were always nice, he mostly just missed having her to celebrate with. He marveled that this year she was in the parlor acting as excited as a child, tearing paper from her gifts and exclaiming her delight and thanks.

They all were opening presents at one time like eager children. Stella gave Mama McCory and Juliet headbands. Both promptly put them on. Neil slung a wool scarf around his neck and tried on a pair of gloves. Juliet draped a beautiful white-fringed shawl over his grandmother's shoulders.

He opened up the phonograph recordings Juliet got him, pleased that she must have remembered he'd commented how nice it was to have music in the house again.

She listened to the soft tinkling sound of the musical jewelry box he gave her. She liked it, but he didn't know how she would receive his other gift. Before she opened it, she exclaimed, "Oh, I only got you one gift."

"No," he said. "There are four recordings here."

She gave him that look. "It's only one gift."

"All right." He held out his hand. "Give it here."

She made a face and hugged it close. Then she began to tear off the paper and lifted the box lid. Her mouth opened in surprise. "Oh, you remembered."

Yes, he remembered the day she admired the black, jeweled purse in a shop window and wouldn't let him buy it for her.

While Stella and his grandmother admired it, Juliet looked at him with gratitude and said softly, "Thank you."

The gift that brought tears to her eyes, however, was the locket his grandmother gave her. "This is an heirloom," she said. "My and Streun's pictures were in here. Now it should have your and Neil's pictures."

Neil knew Juliet was touched by the gift. But he didn't know if the tears on her cheeks were because of the generosity of his grandmother or because she felt she had no right to accept it.

He wanted his expression to tell Juliet she had every right. But Juliet did not look directly at him again for a long, long time.

They all looked, however, when his grandmother handed him a legal document. "I don't want you to have to wait until I'm gone before you get this, Neil." It was the deed to the acres on the mountain where he'd often talked about building a house someday. The land he'd shown to Juliet in October—where he would like to someday settle down with his own family.

But it was not the gifts that touched his heart. In trying to make his grandmother's life more meaningful in her last months, he'd inadvertently done that for himself.

He would keep the memory of the togetherness, the caring, the reaching out to others—this Christmas—in his heart. . .forever.

Chapter 17

A big ice storm came at the end of January. That's when Carter came, almost frozen, saying a train had derailed going up a steep mountain curve from Canaan Valley to Sunrise. The injured were being taken to Sunrise Hospital. "It's bad," Carter said, shaking his head. "They need all the help they can get."

Olivia knew Neil hated to leave. Mama McCory had a bad cold she had been unable to shake. Even as he shrugged into his heavy coat, he gave instructions. "Make sure she gets her rest and takes her medication. When she's sick she won't always eat, but she needs to. And she needs plenty of water."

"We'll take good care of her," Stella promised.

He looked contrite. "I know you will. And"—he looked from one to the other—"take care of yourselves, too."

Without thinking, Olivia reached out and touched his sleeve. "You, too," she said softly. His gaze held hers for a long moment. He nodded, then pulled the hood up over his head and the gloves on his hands.

The ice and wind he went into were so cold that Olivia shuddered from having the door open only long enough for the doctors to leave. She turned, hugging her arms, and hurried to the parlor and stood in front of the fire. "Well," she said to Stella, "I guess it's just you and me."

"If anything happens to Mama. . ."

Olivia closed her eyes. "Don't even say it. I could never, never get over such a thing." She exhaled a deep breath. "Neil would never forgive us."

Stella put her arms around Olivia's shoulders. "You and I will become the best nurses ever." She brightened. "I played the part of a nurse one time."

Olivia hoped that would be good enough. "Let's go see our patient."

Keeping their patient in bed wasn't easy. By noon, Mama McCory was dressed and insisted on being up and around for lunch. "I was helpless for a long time," she said. "I don't mind resting, but I don't want to spend my life in bed if I don't have to."

"Fine," Stella said. "You stay in your room and read until lunch is ready."

Mama McCory agreed, with a look of triumph in her eyes.

"We can be as stubborn as she is," Stella growled. "She's not going to run around in this drafty house and blame us for getting worse."

They took the steaming chicken soup, slices of buttered bread made fresh that morning, and hot tea to the round table in front of her window. Olivia put another log in her fireplace. The three of them ate while looking out the window at the snow-covered ground. They agreed it looked beautiful but were concerned about the train wreck and wondered whether Neil was outside helping the injured or inside the hospital.

"I wish there was some way we could help," Olivia said, stacking their dishes after they'd eaten.

Suddenly, the sound of a horse's snort and whinny drew their attention to the window. Horses were struggling, pulling two creaking and groaning wagon-loads of people up the long drive.

"Looks like your wish is about to come true," Mama McCory said. "This kind of thing happened several years ago, but there's no time to get into that now. We'd better get these people in before they freeze to death."

"You stay in this room," Stella demanded.

"Would you?" She answered her own question. "You'd be up and helping if you could. I know enough to take care of myself."

Olivia laid the coats in a pile as the six men, three women, and four children shucked them off and warmed themselves by the parlor fire. They told fearful tales of having to climb out of the leaning train car. Others had not been so fortunate.

"We were told the hotel and boardinghouse were full," one middle-aged man said. "We're grateful we can come here."

After they were warmed, Mama McCory sent men to get cots from the basement. "Others may come."

Before the day was out, there were eighteen. Some had injured loved ones in the hospital. Cots were set up in the dining room for the men. Women and children had the second floor.

Olivia felt she learned more about running an inn that day than in the months before. Although the travelers pitched in, she knew that making sure rooms were clean, making breakfast, and insuring they had a good food supply would be simple after having this crowd to care for.

Mama McCory said they wouldn't charge them for staying. "They aren't paying guests but stranded travelers. But if they offer something for the food, we can accept it."

That sparked an idea in Stella. She was already delighting everyone by adding different ingredients to the muffins, cakes, and candy she made. They played a game of guessing the ingredients.

After the first day, she wrapped her sweets in waxed paper, set them on a table in the dining room, and sold them. The guests called them "Stella's Sweets."

Men kept the fires going and even set up an unused book-shelf in the dining room for Stella's Sweets. They shoveled snow from the driveway all the way to the main road, then came in for the hot cocoa Olivia made.

Mama McCory warned that the electricity often went off in the wintertime. Some of the travelers responded they didn't even have electricity in their homes yet, so that wouldn't bother them. It stayed on, however. The travelers were able to make telephone calls, and by the end of the week, word came that trains could leave Sunrise again.

Some of the women were afraid. "It's the safest way this time of year," a man said. "That's why we have more railroad tracks than roads in these parts. Accidents happen. The good Lord took care of us and gave us a warm place to stay."

One of the women expressed what had gone through Olivia's mind. "Why do things like this have to happen?"

The man shrugged, looking troubled. "The engineer might have been going too fast, a rail could have been loose, something could have been on the tracks..."

"And, too," Mama McCory said, "if things like that never happened, you would never know how to appreciate it when they didn't."

The man smiled. "Now there's wisdom."

They all seemed to accept that, and by the end of the week they had all gone except one woman who stayed a couple of days longer until she learned her husband was well enough to travel.

The first evening after all the "guests" were gone, the inn seemed strangely quiet. Olivia and Stella were cleaning up from supper, and Mama McCory sat at the table with a cup of coffee. Olivia heard male voices coming from the foyer. She hadn't heard the knocker on the door or the bell on the desk.

She walked into the foyer to find a man with a coat draped around his shoulders. His left arm was in a splint and a sling. He held a travel bag with his right hand. A bearded man, who accompanied the man with the splint, was leaning over the desk, looking at the open ledger that was turned toward him.

"Sir?" she said forcefully at such impoliteness. "Can I help you?"

The bearded man straightened and faced her. His eyes looked tired, but they held a trace of mischief. "Yes, ma'am."

That's when she realized he was wearing Neil's coat. And he had Neil's voice.

"Oh, Neil." She rushed over to him and grabbed the sleeves of his coat. "I'm so glad you're all right." She looked up into his face. The mischief was gone from his eyes. He just looked tired. But his hand had come up and lay against her waist.

"It's good to be home," he said. "But I need a bath, a shave, and something to eat. We have a guest." He stepped back and introduced her to the man with him. "This is my wife, Juliet McCory."

That's when Olivia realized she had rushed to Neil as if having every right to be enveloped in an embrace from her husband who had been away. She had to ask him to repeat the man's name, then turned to the ledger and wrote, "Danny Quinn." "He may have the trillium room."

"I'll take him up."

But that was her job, and Neil looked unkempt and weary. "You need to get cleaned up, remember?"

"Don't nag, woman." He shucked off his coat and handed it to her.

Oh, so he wanted to play the husband-wife teasing game. She'd try it. "You're just like your grandmother. You never slow down."

"You're one to talk," he scoffed. "I heard about what went on here while I was gone." A dimple formed in Danny Quinn's cheek as he began to follow Neil up the stairs.

Later Neil walked into the kitchen, looking and smelling clean. That weariness was still in his face, however, and he looked thinner than he had a week ago. He hugged his grandmother and Stella. "Good to be home."

He'd invited Danny to supper, saying they both had eaten hospital meals all week. Danny seemed polite and nice. He was very muscular and looked to be around forty.

After the men had eaten their second bowlful of beef and vegetable stew and buttered bread, Olivia poured them another cup of coffee, and Stella brought over some of her wrapped sweets.

"I know you took all those people in and made them feel at home. I'm proud of you. But, Grandmother," Neil scolded, "I suppose you gave them your cold since you didn't follow the doctor's orders and stay in bed."

She shushed him. "I don't need a doctor to tell me when to get out of bed. Anyway, a lot of sickness is right up here." She tapped the side of her head. "Why, there's nothing like a houseful of people to invigorate me."

They all laughed. Olivia saw Stella nod. She'd told Olivia before that she drew energy from the crowds who watched her perform. That seemed to be how Mama McCory felt about having people around her.

Danny began to praise the sweet he was eating. "I've never tasted anything as good as this. Where'd it come from?"

That led to the discussion of Stella's Sweets. "You could make a fortune selling these." His grin at Stella dimpled his cheek and gave him a cute, boyish look.

That night after she and Stella were in bed, propped up with their now-usual bowl of popped corn, Olivia said, "I think Danny took a shine to you."

"Oh, I know his kind. He has those dark curls falling over his forehead and looks at you with those big blue eyes and gets those dimples in his face and expects a woman to fall for him. They probably have. But I'm not taken in. Anyway, I think he's too young for me."

"No, he's not. He has a lot of gray hair in those dark curls you noticed. I wonder what kind of work he does. . . ."

The next morning at breakfast they learned that Danny was a logger. "I can't do that kind of work with a broken arm," he told them.

"You need to be around where I can check that arm every day for at least another week," Neil told him. "It was a nasty break, and if you get infection in it, you could even lose it."

"To be honest with you, I don't have the kind of money to stay in a place like this. But I'll make it. Have all my life." He looked at Neil. "Don't suppose you could use some help around here?"

"What can you do?"

"Lot of things a man can do with one hand. I can carry logs and a coal scuttle, clean out a fireplace, and lay a fire. I can take care of horses and clean out a stable." He looked around at the women. "I reckon I can dust if I have to. And sweep. Even crack an egg with one hand."

Neil studied him for a while. "Room and board for a week in exchange for work. That is, if the ladies agree. They usually only serve breakfast to guests."

Olivia and Mama McCory looked at Stella, since she'd taken over most of the cooking. Danny's big soulful eyes pled with her.

"Oh, all right," Stella said. "Just know it's the egg-cracking part that swayed me."

Over the next few days, Danny proved to be a good worker. Having a man around during the day, even with only one good arm, was better than Olivia and Stella having to try and fix things themselves. The slats on an upstairs bed had fallen out. A curtain needed to be taken down so the hem could be sewn. There was always something.

Danny was fun, too, and since there were no guests in the inn and he was having meals with them, Neil invited him to join them in the parlor after their dinners.

Olivia enjoyed seeing how Neil related to another man. They seemed to go beyond the doctor-patient relationship to being friends. They discussed the bigger issues of progress and politics, but what she liked most was their banter over baseball teams and which were the better trout streams for fishing. Each claimed to have caught the bigger fish.

Some evenings, Olivia and Stella took turns playing the piano. Olivia played sheet music and hymns. Stella entertained them with her rambunctious style of playing. "Best not to sing the words to these," she'd say.

The icy wind howled outside, but they were warm and cozy by the fire, singing and laughing.

After several nights, Danny seemed unusually serious. He thanked them for taking him in like he was a part of a family.

"Don't you have any family?" Mama McCory asked.

"I've been on my own since I was sixteen. I roamed around, had odd jobs until I finally found a girl I wanted to settle down with." Danny paused as if to compose himself for what he was about to tell. "She went out on a boat one day. Something happened, and it capsized." He grimaced with the memory. "She couldn't swim, and nobody could get to her in time. She wasn't the only one that day. . . ." His voice trailed off, but he seemed to shake himself out of that mood. "So"—he slapped his knees—"I've been all over since—seeing the world, so to speak."

"What did you find was the most interesting?" Stella asked.

He looked at her a long time, curiously, as if she might be making fun, but she just stared back. Finally, he nodded. "The circus, I guess. I wanted to be the lion tamer, but the one who had the job kept his head, so I never did get to do that." Danny laughed lightly. "I did some trapeze work and even cleared up after elephants. I'm experienced in a lot of things. I've also laid railroad tracks." He held up his hands. "Not the ones where the train derailed."

They laughed at that.

His serious mood returned as he said, "I have to leave tomorrow. There's business I have to take care of. You've all shown me what a real family should be like. I'll never forget it."

"You're welcome here anytime." Neil voiced what Olivia knew they all felt.

Chapter 18

Danny left the next morning after breakfast. His last words were, "I'll be back."

"He won't be back," Stella told Olivia when they were alone in the kitchen, cleaning up. "He's like many actors. They just can't stay in one place."

"You have for quite a while," Olivia said.

"It's all right for a man to travel around alone, but not for a woman when she gets a little age on her."

The house seemed cold, lifeless. There were no guests.

Olivia thought Neil missed Danny, too. They all obviously did, as it was much quieter during supper. They ate in the kitchen that was warm from the stove to avoid having to light fires in the dining room, making the house seem even colder.

After supper, Olivia expected they would all turn in early. Neil had enjoyed a male friend. He probably preferred that over having to pay attention to his "wife." She expected Neil would have her play something and probably suggest they all turn in early.

They did go to the parlor as usual after supper. Neil threw on another log, and soon the glow and warmth of the fire displaced the former chill of the room. Mama McCory settled on the couch with her embroidery.

When Neil went to the phonograph, Olivia thought he knew none of them felt like being too lively tonight. She saw him look through the recordings, then one she gave him for Christmas began to fill the room with the melodic tones of "Sweet Adeline."

Neil walked over to where she stood near the fire. "Shall we try our hand at a game of checkers?" he said, as if that were a usual night's event. It wasn't, of course.

Olivia nodded. She hadn't played in a long time.

He took first the checkerboard table then the two straight chairs away from the window and brought them closer to the fire and the couch, then sat.

Olivia looked at Mama McCory and Stella. They lifted their eyebrows and shrugged.

Neil opened the drawer in the checkerboard table. "Black or red?"

"Red." She sat and scooted up to the table.

He filled her side of the board with red, then started on his side with black. "On your mark, get set—"

"Are we running a race or playing checkers?"

"The goal is to win, fast or slow." He set down the last black checker with a sense of finality and moved closer to the table.

Olivia could hardly believe the challenge in his dark eyes. All right, so he played to win. Well, he would find out his meek and mild wife could be just as determined. She made her first move.

Before long, accompanied by "In the Shade of the Old Apple Tree," Neil leaned back and rubbed his hands together in victory.

"That was your lucky win."

"Two out of three, then."

He won the next one and wore a triumphant grin while placing the checkers.

"I need some hot chocolate," Olivia said. What she needed was to get her wits about her. She'd expected Neil to be sad that his new friend had left. Instead, he was acting like he wanted nothing more than an evening with his "wife" and family.

As they continued to play several games, he even joined in softly singing, "Ida, Sweet as Apple Cider."

Olivia stared at the board as if trying to figure out a move. Much of the time, however, she marveled at how sincere Stella sounded about embroidery. One would think she was simply a middle-aged mother enjoying a quiet evening.

"My mother taught me when I was a girl," Stella said. "But I haven't done this in years."

"Stella Kevay," Mama McCory scolded, "I know you heard Neil tell me to take up embroidery again because the exercise might be good for my fingers. Now you've become his nurse, making me use my hands."

Stella didn't deny it. "Sounds like a good reason to me."

The wood popped and crackled in the fireplace. Olivia felt the warmth and smelled the wood smoke mingled with hot chocolate when she lifted the cup to her lips. At least she did not smell that faint musky fragrance.

She could not sit there and think all night, so she made a move on the checkerboard and to her surprise was able to jump several of Neil's black men. "Crown me," she said.

He did. Finally, he was cornered. "You win," he said and sat back with his thumbs hooked into the armholes of his vest. He seemed pleased.

"It's about time," she said.

"All you needed was a good teacher. You've watched me win several times tonight, and you're finally getting the hang of it."

She scoffed. "Oh, so you're taking credit for my win."

"Of course."

Olivia shook her head and went over to look at the little bluebirds with pink ribbons in their beaks that the two women were embroidering on pillowcases. Soon, however, Mama McCory said she must turn in. "You know the saying that 'early to bed and early to rise makes one healthy, wealthy, and wise.'"

"I should try it," Stella said.

"Oh, but you must be very wise, having come from the mining area, raising your daughter alone, and even sending her to college. That must have been a great sacrifice for you."

"When Juliet went to college, she lived with my brother in the city. He paid for her education."

Olivia was glad Stella had not lied about that. She simply omitted the fact that her brother was also Olivia's father.

"That's good." Mama McCory was nodding. "Families should help out. That's what I've told Neil when he has said I've sacrificed for him. Trying to be a parent to Neil was never a burden. Oh, he could be a pistol at times, but it's still a joy to care for someone you love."

Olivia watched warmth come into Neil's eyes when he looked at his grandmother and smiled. They all seemed rather mesmerized as "By the Light of the Silvery Moon" permeated the room.

Then the music stopped.

Olivia realized she was toying with the locket Mama McCory had given her for Christmas. She often wore it, although there were no pictures of her and Neil inside. The locket was empty. She quickly moved her hand from the locket and with her glance saw the rings she wore.

It wasn't often she thought about it. But someday she'd take off the locket for the last time. She had no right to Mama McCory's locket, Neil's mother's engagement ring, or Neil's wedding band. Did he ever think of that?

He got up and put the screen close around the fireplace. There would be ashes by morning. Just like the warmth of this room, the laughter, the togetherness, the love. . .someday, those things, too, would be ashes.

Chapter 19

March winds whistled through the trees. Much of the landscape remained blanketed with snow and ice until the rains and floods of April washed them away. First came the white dogwood and yellow forsythia. Then tender red maple buds and tender green leaves made their appearance.

So did Danny.

His arm had healed and was getting stronger every day. Neil gave him a job and also the room on the lower floor that Bart and Hedda had in the summers when they stayed overnight at the inn.

Sunshine and longer days meant Danny would be painting or repairing until late. He still had time to comment on Stella's Sweets. "You could sell these all over."

"Fine," she huffed. "You get the stores to buy them, and I'll bake them."

So he did. Before long, he was acting as her promoter, selling her sweets to the general store, the Soda Shoppe, the bakery, the grocery store, and even the bakeries and shops down in Canaan Valley. He'd found out how to get paper with Stella's Sweets printed on it. Before long, he had her baking and packaging, and he sent her sweets on the train to the nearby cities.

Danny wasn't just a friend anymore, he was a full-time employee. *Like I am,* Olivia often thought. She and Stella, and even Mama McCory, spent time in the evenings in the flower beds making sure the inn would be spectacular for tourist season.

Danny began sitting beside Stella on the family pew at church. On Easter Sunday, Pastor Whitfield talked about Jesus, who grew to be a man and was sacrificed for everyone in the world who would believe in Him.

He said now that the mountains had thawed, new people would be moving in, so they needed to spread the gospel. And they could now baptize people in the river.

Later, when they were changing out of their Easter bonnets and fancy clothes, Stella asked Olivia, "You think we should get dipped in the river?"

"Do you understand all that? I mean, what they mean about Jesus coming into your heart?"

"I think it's a symbol, like baptism. The church members didn't have some kind of heart attack. It's ridiculous to think this little man, or big man, climbs in there and lives."

"That sounds funny," Olivia said. "But I'm not about to laugh. God might think I'm making fun of Him."

"I know," Stella said seriously. "I'm just trying to figure all this out, too. But if we're going to do this right, we have to do what the other church members do and learn to be good Christians."

Olivia sighed. "I keep hearing that we're supposed to have Jesus in our hearts, but nobody tells us how to do that."

Stella agreed. "We need to ask without sounding completely ignorant."

That evening when they, Neil, and Mama McCory had a light supper in the kitchen, Olivia approached the subject she and Stella had discussed. "Baptism," she began. "The church I went to in Davidson never mentioned it. But, um, Pastor Whitfield talked about being baptized in the river."

"Different churches have different symbols for showing a change has taken place inside someone," Neil said. "Pastor Whitfield likes to take believers down to the river and baptize them."

"I've heard of that," Stella said. "You mean he holds them underwater?"

Neil saw his grandmother put her hand to her mouth, and she chuckled. "Not hold them under," Neil said. "He just takes them under until they're covered with water, then brings them up. That symbolizes being dead to the old self and starting a new life living according to the teachings of Jesus."

"So, since Stella and I go to church and we are having the Bible studies again, should we be baptized? Otherwise, are we being hypocrites?"

Olivia didn't know what the ensuing silence meant. When her gaze met Mama McCory's, the woman said, "I'm thinking on this." She looked at her grandson. "Neil?"

Finally, Neil said, "You may be right. If the church people knew you hadn't been baptized, they might think you don't believe like we do. But," he said quickly, "baptism doesn't save you. It's a symbol of what you believe."

"Save?" Stella said. "From what?"

"From being eternally separated from God after you die."

"Oh-wee," Stella said forcefully. "Now there's a tragedy." Recovering, she gave a thin smile. "Would you explain what your church members believe about all that? I mean," she added quickly when a surprised look came onto Neil's face, "in case it's different from some other churches. We've had to move around so much, it's hard to remember it all."

Neil's eyes looked stuck on Stella.

Olivia's quick glance at Mama McCory revealed she must still be thinking. Her lips were clamped together, and she stared at her iced tea glass. Without looking up, she said, "All you have to do is believe in Jesus."

"That's true, Grandmother," Neil said. "But there's more to it. You do believe in Jesus, don't you?"

"Well, of course." Stella sounded insulted. "There has never been a time when I didn't believe in Jesus and whatever the Bible says."

Neil must have detected indignation. "I think," Neil finally said, "we should have Pastor Whitfield talk to you about what our church believes."

The following week, Danny walked down to the front of the church to ask Jesus into his heart, and they all went down to the river to see him and some others baptized.

"What's Danny's going to think about me," Stella said, "when he finds out I'm just pretending to be a good Christian?"

Olivia felt bad about it, too. "Maybe Neil is right. We need to talk to the preacher."

In May, when spring was alive in all its glory, workers returned to their work of building shops and homes. Roads were being built or improved.

Tourists arrived on the trains. Business at the inn was booming, along with Stella's Sweets. There was no time for special talks, with the preacher or anybody.

Chapter 20

Neil had an emergency and couldn't get away from the clinic in time for his grandmother's birthday party. When he arrived home after 3:30, he met the Whitfields, Mary and Janie Clayton, and some of the church women leaving in their carriages.

At least he got to greet Bart when he rode up to the stable and Danny took Sally's reins. "Those women of yours sure know how to have a good time," Danny said. Bart agreed and laughed.

Walking up to the house, Neil thought with pleasure how much he appreciated Juliet and Stella suggesting this party. These past months of activity had enlivened his grandmother. But hanging over their heads was still the specialists' diagnosis of her failing heart. This might be the last party she would ever have.

He walked right up to his grandmother who sat at one of the dining room tables with gifts in front of her. He sat beside her and handed her a book by her favorite author, Grace Livingston Hill.

"Oh, *The Finding of Jasper Holt*. I don't have that one." She kissed his cheek.

He was glad to see Hedda again. She, along with Juliet and Stella, slipped on their aprons and began to clean up from the party.

"I'll get you some tea and cake," Stella said.

Before she could, however, rushed footfalls sounded from someone coming into the inn from the main entrance. A middle-aged, well-dressed man appeared, his face scrunched like he was in pain.

Neil's first thought was that the man had been hurt. But that didn't make sense. Surely he would have gone to the hospital or clinic.

Neil stood when the man stepped farther inside the room, looking past him and around the room. He hadn't noticed the woman with the man until she stepped up and pulled on the man's arm, which he shrugged away.

Suddenly the man, in a booming voice, ground out, "So this is the kind of job you took? A waitress?"

Juliet squealed. She dropped a tray of dirty dishes, and it crashed onto the hardwood floor. Small china teacups broke. Stella rushed over and put her arms protectively around Juliet's shoulders.

The man glared at Stella. "I should have known the two of you would be in this together." With two long steps, he reached Juliet and took hold of her arm at the same time Neil reached him.

Neil grasped the man's arm. "Get your hands off her."

The man sneered. "I'll do as I please with my daughter."

Tightening his hold on the man's arm, Neil raised his right hand and circled the man's throat. "You will not do as you please with my wife. I'm a doctor. My fingers are on the pressure points that can have you on that floor before you can blink an eye."

Neil surprised himself with the intensity of his emotions. But he didn't back down. "And sir, that's the nice part of what I can do to you."

The man let go of Juliet. "I'm her father." He sounded like a man with a sore throat.

"I'm her husband." Neil glared at him. "Shall we sit down and discuss this like. . .civilized men?"

The man nodded. Neil looked at Juliet.

"It's all right," Juliet said in a small voice.

Her stark face and the fearful look in her eyes indicated everything was not all right. But Neil moved his hands away, still watching the man as he straightened his collar and tie.

"Now why don't you 'civilized' men sit down?" Stella said. "All you need is some tea. Everyone just calm down until I bring it." She looked around, smiling. "Would anyone like a tea cake?"

"No," Neil and the man ground out at the same time.

The woman with him said, "Yes, thank you. That would be nice." She put her arm through the man's. That's when her appearance registered. She looked to be around fifty, with a lot of gray in her hair that was pulled back in a neat roll. She looked pleasant and refined in a conservative dress and jacket.

Neil gestured toward the clean table next to the one where his grandmother sat. He was afraid such a confrontation might upset her, but her coloring looked good and her breathing seemed fine. In fact, she smiled as if enjoying the scene.

"Yes," Mama McCory said, "please, have a seat." She moved her chair around to see them better.

The pleasant woman stepped over to the table and turned her head toward the irate man. He exhaled heavily, then pulled out the chair for her. She thanked him. He sat in a chair next to her.

Hedda had picked up the dirty and broken dishes. "I'll be glad to serve the tea."

Stella took the seat next to the pleasant woman. Neil held out a chair and nodded for Juliet to sit next to Stella. He would be between Juliet and the man in case he needed to protect her.

"This is a nice place," the woman said, as if she had just dropped in on a friend for a cup of tea. "I've heard about it and have seen it advertised as one of the lovelier places to visit in Sunrise. But this is my first time here."

While Hedda served the tea, Stella agreed that it was a lovely place and spoke of travelers and tourists who made reservations to return at the same time each year.

Neil wondered how Stella could be so cordial to this woman. If this man was Juliet's father, like he said, wouldn't he be Stella's husband? But he was here with another woman. And Juliet's father was supposed to be a poor miner, wasn't he? This man's appearance was more like that of a prosperous businessman.

Stella stared at Hedda, who seemed to be taking an incredibly long time pouring the tea and bringing a tea cake to the woman. "Thank you," Stella said, and soon Hedda left the dining room.

"Now," Stella said in a commanding voice. "I'm probably the best one to explain everything since the men are acting like children competing for the last cookie in the jar."

The man made a sound like a growl deep in his throat. Neil glanced at him quickly. The man sighed and leaned forward with his forearms on the table as if resigned to some dastardly fate.

"It's simple." Stella lifted her hands. "She met and married Dr. Neil McCory." She pointed at Neil. "Married him last September." Her voice lowered. "Herman, she knew you would object, so she was afraid to tell you."

Neil watched the man's mouth move, from closed to open, closed to open. Finally, he said, "That's all I ever wanted for her—to settle down and marry someone and live like normal people."

"Well, I did," Juliet said.

The man sat back, seeming to relax. His eyes swept over the room and back again. "Then you're not working as a waitress?"

"Not that anything's wrong with that," Stella said with spirit. "I'll bet you've been served by many of them and enjoyed the meal."

A tinge of color came into the man's cheeks, as if he'd felt the brunt of her reprimand.

"But for your information," Stella continued, "she manages this inn. After all, she is the wife of Dr. McCory, which makes her the granddaughter-in-law of Mrs. McCory, who owns this place." Stella held out her hand toward Mama McCory, as if presenting her.

The man acknowledged Neil's grandmother with a polite nod. He seemed at a loss for words. Finally, he said, "This inn does have a fine reputation." He took a deep breath and exhaled. "And so do Stella's Sweets."

"This is delicious," said the woman eating the small cake. "I had one at the Canaan Valley bakery."

"That's how we found you," the man said. "I've sent letters that were never answered. I inquired at the post office and was told your mail had been picked up. I even visited your cabin after the weather cleared up. The baker said Stella's Sweets came from Sunrise."

"At the first store we stopped in," the woman said, "they knew who you were and said Herman could find you here."

The man looked smug. "So here we are."

"One big, happy family." Stella gave him a stony look.

He returned it, then snapped, "I don't know what you're doing, Stella." He looked at Juliet. "But I'm glad to see you're behaving responsibly."

Neil didn't care for the man's tone. "Please speak politely to the ladies, Mr. Kevay."

"The name's Easton."

Bewildered, Neil tried to make sense of it. He figured Stella and Mr. Easton must have divorced and then Stella married a Mr. Kevay, who adopted Juliet.

But this man's attitude wasn't like one who had given up rights to his daughter. The only Easton he'd ever heard of was the name of the coal that ran daily from the mining area to other parts of West Virginia.

The man spoke again, more politely this time. "Olivia, I'm pleased that you gave up that wild dream of yours and that you're married. I've worried about you and wanted to know that you were all right. And another reason I wanted to find you"—he touched the shoulder of the woman next to him—"I want you to meet the woman I'm going to marry."

Neil nodded at the woman Mr. Easton introduced as Evelyn James. But he was thinking about the man calling Juliet "Olivia."

Stella had told them that Juliet had lived with her brother in the city when she went to college. So this was Stella's brother? But he said he was Juliet's father. Had she called him her father when she had lived with him? He'd apparently cared about her, having her live with him while she attended college.

"Maybe I was too hard on you," Mr. Easton said to Juliet. He smiled with a more tender look than Neil expected. "Evelyn has pointed out some errors of my ways. She's a fine lady whose deceased husband was pastor of a church in Thurmond. She moved to Davidson after he died."

"I'm happy for you," Juliet said.

Mr. Easton spoke almost contritely. "I met her through friends but never thought we'd have anything in common. I soon discovered we didn't. But her faith, charity, and sweet spirit intrigued me. She's softened my heart in many ways." He took a deep breath. "You're my sister, Stella. I've been rough on you. I'm sorry. I do love you and hope you can forgive me."

The next thing Neil knew, Juliet, Stella, and Mr. Easton were standing and hugging, with tears in their eyes.

So this man was not Stella's ex-husband. He was her brother. Was Juliet's middle name, or first name, Olivia? Had Juliet and Stella decided to use a name different from what Mr. Easton had called her so they could stay hidden from him?

Now Mr. Easton was inviting them all to his wedding at his home in Davidson. Evelyn gave details and smiled at Juliet. "I would be so pleased if you would be my matron of honor."

Neil couldn't figure it all out. He stared at his cup of tea, cold now. Juliet, whom he would like to be his wife permanently, was the one to make explanations.

She was his wife, yes. . .but only for another two months. And she wasn't obligated to tell him anything.

That was not in the contract.

———

Olivia walked to the side window, watching as her father and Evelyn rode out of sight. She tried to concentrate on the trees outside, lush and green in the sunshine. The scenery became blurry, however, and there wasn't even any rain.

She wasn't sure what Neil and Mama McCory were thinking, but she could guess some of it. All she did know was that her father had said his name was "Easton" and he had called her "Olivia." What could she say?

Suddenly, she realized she couldn't tell Mama McCory anything. She was here in a binding contract with Dr. Neil McCory—her employer. She could offer no explanation to Mama McCory without his permission.

She was not even his legal wife, contrary to what he thought. She was nothing more than a hired hand, making a weekly salary.

"Juliet," Mama McCory called.

Olivia swiped at her eyes and turned. Neil and Stella had done the same, with concerned looks on their faces.

"Thank you all so much for the party. It's the nicest, most fun one I've ever had." Mama McCory smiled. "And you certainly surprised me."

Olivia held her breath. Did she mean she was surprised that somebody had apparently not been truthful with her? She'd been gracious in saying she was glad to meet Olivia's father and Evelyn. Was now the time for questions?

"It's been a long, interesting day," she said. "But I'd like to rest for a while."

Olivia waited for the next words. What would they be?

"If somebody would take my gifts to the parlor, we can all look at them after supper." Mama McCory grinned. "And you two girls will have to sing and dance that birthday song for Neil. He missed it. Hedda," she called, and Hedda stepped into the dining room.

Olivia suspected Hedda had been near enough to hear everything from the time the tray crashed to the floor and the dishes broke.

Mama McCory told Hedda, "I appreciate all of your help today.' The two women hugged.

"Are you. . .all right?" Hedda asked her.

"Never better," Mama McCory said.

Hedda looked as if she'd like to say something else, but Mama McCory turned to leave the room. Hedda then left the room herself.

Right after Hedda left, Neil took a deep breath, then exhaled. "I need to check Grandmother's vital signs." He followed Mama McCory to her room.

Without bothering with the dishes, Olivia and Stella went to their bedroom and propped up on the bed.

"That was quite a family reunion in the dining room," Stella said wryly. "You and I have finally gained Herman's approval."

Feeling helpless, Olivia sighed. "Think how mad he'll be when he learns the truth. He will never want to see me again."

Stella agreed. "He will blame me for this. I guess I am to blame. He always said actors were rogues and vagrants. Maybe I've proved that's true." Stella's face clouded. "Not in being an actor, but in what I've done to you."

"What you've done to me, Stella," Olivia said, "is given me the chance to save money for acting school. A chance to see what a real, loving family can be like. And a chance to grow up. I think I was a headstrong, rebellious girl. But so much has happened here. I've learned to care about other people instead of just what I want."

"I know what you mean. I've found a kind of meaning like I've never known when caring for Mama McCory, the inn, Stella's Sweets, the Bible studies, and. . .even Danny."

"Oh, Stella, I know he's crazy about you."

"He won't be when he finds out what I've done. He thinks all this is legitimate and that I'm your mother. He thinks we're a family—the kind he never had but would like to have." She sighed. "I've really messed up this time."

There seemed to be no solution. Then Olivia remembered something. "Do you suppose this is one of those times when forgiveness comes into play? Pastor Whitfield preached about it. If we tell the truth and ask forgiveness, wouldn't Mama McCory and Neil forgive us? They are good Christians, you know."

A sad expression crossed Stella's face. "Not if the truth causes Mama McCory to have another stroke."

Chapter 21

The inn was filled for the next couple of weeks with tourists and vacationers coming to the mountains to escape the heat of the cities. Neil was busy, too, since a lot of his patients couldn't come down the mountain during the winter and had their checkups in the summer. He deliberately made more visits to the hospital and house calls. He stayed later than necessary at the clinic, thinking and praying.

This was a busy time for Juliet and Stella, but he had the feeling they were as tense as he. His grandmother, who usually picked up on everything, didn't seem to notice that anything was different. Maybe her stroke had affected her brain. Or maybe she was ripe for another one.

Finally, Neil had to scoff at himself. He'd wanted to make the last months of his grandmother's life a happy time. He'd hired someone to do that, and that someone was doing her job well. He's the one who was failing to contribute to his grandmother's quality of life.

Was it really his business whether Mr. Easton was Juliet's father? Or her uncle? Stella's ex-husband? Or her brother?

Or if Juliet was Olivia? Or both? Or. . .neither?

He slammed his fists down on his desk in the clinic. Then, rubbing the sides of his hands, wondering if he'd broken a couple of bones, Neil berated himself. He had no right to harbor this attitude of having been betrayed by Juliet.

She owed him nothing. He owed her everything.

His actions should not be dependent upon what another person was or wasn't. Only what he, himself, was.

That evening he told Juliet he would accompany her to the wedding.

"I'll stay here," Stella said. "And I'll send Danny to ask Hedda to help out."

"Are you worried about seeing Mr. Easton again?" he asked when they were on the train Friday morning, headed for Davidson. Both he and Juliet had hardly spoken to each other during the past two weeks, except for casual conversation.

"No," she said. "I'm worried about what you think."

"I have no right to think anything." Immediately, he thought that might sound like she was nothing more than his employee. He looked over at her, so lovely in her tailored suit and pert little hat.

"Juliet," he began, wanting to explain, "I want to know all about you. Since we married, I've found out enough about you to know that you're a fine person. You're beautiful, you're kind, you're—"

"No," she stopped him. "I'm none of those things. I don't know if I can even tell you the truth about me."

"Whenever you're ready to confide in me, Juliet," he said, "I want to listen."

She nodded, and he thought she wiped a tear from her eye before she turned to look out the window where trees were less dense and flatter land appeared.

He'd called ahead so Mr. Easton would know when to expect them. What he didn't expect was to be met by a driver in a roadster who took their bags and put them into the automobile.

Neil climbed in after Juliet, grateful the three of them could fit in the two-seater. She pointed out various places as they traveled the roads and eventually along Main Street. He was somewhat familiar with Davidson. However, he had not been in this part of town.

When the driver pulled up in front of the impressive palatial house, Neil got a strange feeling he should have worn a more formal suit. This didn't fit the picture of a poor girl from a mining town. But it did fit the picture of a young woman whose uncle, or father, would pay her expenses to college. . .at least.

A housekeeper opened the door and addressed Juliet as "Miss Easton." Neil was welcomed warmly by Mr. Easton and met John and Sarah Easton, who were introduced as "Olivia's" brother and his wife.

When Mr. Easton said Mrs. Cooper would show them their room, Neil felt a moment of panic. How could he not have expected that? Now he supposed his bed that night would be a chair.

Juliet spoke up, however. "Oh, I was wondering if Sarah and I might share a room tonight. We've never spent much time together."

"Well, I was an old married woman when you were still a schoolgirl. It's about time we got together for some girl talk. And we have a lot to talk about." Her rather plain face took on a glow. "I have to tell it."

Having seen women patients act like that before, Neil had a good idea what she had to tell.

"I'm in the family way. We were beginning to think it would never happen."

Juliet reached out, and they hugged each other. "I'm going to be an aunt," Juliet said. "Yes, we have a lot to talk about."

During dinner, where Juliet was being served rather than serving others, what Neil suspected was confirmed. Herman Easton owned several mines and lumber mills. He was not surprised to learn that John, in his pleasant but formal manner and wearing eyeglasses, was an accountant for his father's businesses. Sarah taught piano lessons in her home.

Neil felt they were interested in and appreciated his medical practice in Sunrise. He was impressed anew with how articulate Juliet was about her responsibilities at the inn. Her enthusiastic rendering of her activities—learning to cook, playing piano at church, having Bible studies—seemed to impress them. Her sincere love for Stella and his grandmother was evident.

Mr. Easton seemed pleased. "I'm glad to hear that you and Stella have settled down and you got that foolishness out of your system."

Foolishness? Neil wondered what that foolishness was. Why had Juliet and Stella led him to believe they had been victims of abuse or poverty? He realized he had assumed many things that had not been explicitly stated. Just what was going on with this "wife" of his?

Neil didn't have an opportunity to question her about that, even if he had the right. After dinner they discussed the wedding, and Sarah played the music she would play the following day. John and Sarah had traveled a good portion of the day, so they wanted to retire early. They all decided to turn in early.

Midmorning on Saturday, they all took their places in the parlor, not larger but more luxurious than the one at Sunrise Inn. Neil sat on a couch with the pastor's wife, Evelyn James's sister, and her brother-in-law. The pastor stood in front of the fireplace that was hidden by pots of white flowers and a mantel decorated with white flowers and lighted candles. John stood on one side of the pastor beside Mr. Easton.

But Neil's eyes were only on Juliet. She looked so lovely in a soft blue dress, with her hair hanging below her shoulders, quite different than on the day they were married. She looked like she belonged here, not in that small cabin wearing an unimpressive dress.

Sarah began to play "The Wedding March," and Neil stood with the others as Evelyn walked in, wearing an ivory-colored lace gown. She kept looking at Mr. Easton with love-filled eyes. Juliet hadn't looked at him when they married.

Juliet held the orchid bouquet while Herman Easton slipped a ring on Evelyn's finger. In his wedding to Juliet, the bouquet had been smelly marigolds.

Who was that stranger standing there? Was she really his wife? The family relationship and background didn't match with what she and Stella had led him to believe.

Were they married or did she lie?

Why had she wanted the. . .job?

Was it all some kind of foolishness?

―∽∾∽―

A trip to the coast followed by their returning to West Virginia to see the sights of the state together is something Neil would liked to have done with Juliet. However, that was the trip planned by the newlyweds, Herman and Evelyn Easton.

Since their annulment was to take place in September, Neil had thought the ideal time would be in August. He had imagined standing above Blackwater Falls as it fell over rocks as high as a five-story building. Then he and Juliet would go deep into the earth and explore the caverns. The best place he would take Juliet would be to see the spectacular shower of stars. He would tell her she lit up his life like that and ask if they could make the marriage permanent.

Now, however, after the Eastons left on their honeymoon and John and Sarah left to return home, he and Juliet had nothing to say. Their train would leave in the afternoon. It seemed they had reverted, not as far back as to the day they first met, but to the second day, when each was so careful and uncertain about what to say or do.

That was decided for them when the telephone rang. Juliet picked up the receiver immediately. "Yes, this is she. Stella, what's wrong?"

She went so pale, Neil thought she might faint. But if Stella was making the phone call and something was wrong, he knew what it had to be.

Juliet didn't seem able to speak. Her eyes turned to him, and he saw her fear.

He took the phone from her. "Neil here. What is it, Stella?" He closed his eyes as he repeated what he thought she said. "Grandmother's in the hospital?" He listened to the skimpy details. Stella was usually in control of every situation. Now she sounded panicked. He knew this had to be bad. "I'll be there as soon as possible."

I? Neil realized he didn't say, "We."

Would this woman. . .Juliet Olivia Kevay Easton McCory. . .return with him?

She was a city girl; he saw that now. She'd done something that had displeased her father, uncle, foster parent, whomever, but the man had forgiven her and they were on good terms again.

He turned to her. "Grandmother's in the hospital."

She was shaking all over. "What happened?"

How many times had he asked that question of patients or someone who brought them into the clinic? There was always a story behind a fact. But he didn't know this one. He could only say, "She fell."

Juliet turned away. "I'll get my things."

Yes, she planned to return with him. After all, she was under contract—with the job—for another two months.

They all had been quieter at home—going through the motions, ignoring the tension—over the past two weeks since Mr. Easton came and called "Olivia" his daughter. Looking back, he could see that might well be the beginning of his grandmother's stroke, if that's what caused her to fall. His grandmother was smart enough to know the implications of that day. If Juliet was Olivia Easton, what did that mean?

After many miles of thinking and hearing the *chug-chug* of the train winding around the mountains, going higher, the forest becoming denser, he felt his mind became like the forest. The miles of thinking brought no answers.

Juliet looked miserable. But why? Was she like Kathleen, deciding she preferred city life now that she and Mr. Easton were on good terms? He could ask *something*. Whether she answered would be her choice.

"Juliet," he said, "who are you?"

"Olivia Easton."

"Not. . .Juliet Kevay?"

She shook her head.

Olivia Easton played on his mind with the sound and rhythm of the wheels on the track. . .going, going. *If she's not Juliet Kevay, then she's not Mrs. Neil McCory.*

She didn't move. He watched her profile as she stared out the window, seeing. . .what? "Were you mistreated at. . ." He didn't even know what the relationship really was. Was Herman Easton her father? Uncle? Foster parent? What? He tried again. "At the Easton home?"

He thought she wouldn't answer.

Finally, her stark face turned toward him, but she didn't raise her eyes to his. "I thought I was."

He strained to hear her words.

"As far back as I can remember, I wanted to be an actress. Father refused to support me if I pursued that. I took this. . .job to save money so I could go to acting school in New York this fall."

He had told her at the beginning that he wanted her to pretend for his grandmother's sake. Was their entire relationship a pretense on her part? He'd begun to believe she cared for him. Maybe because that's what he wanted to believe. They seemed right for each other.

Now he knew it was all an act. An act that he had begun to believe. Soon the curtain would close. Many times he'd thought of her name that represented one of the great love stories of all times. Now he realized just how fitting it was.

Shakespeare's *Romeo and Juliet* ended in tragedy.

Chapter 22

The prognosis was inconclusive. The only thing the specialists seemed to know for sure was that Mama McCory had extensive bruising and a couple of cracked ribs from the fall.

Neil could have told them that.

What he did know was that she looked helpless and frail, her face and hair as white as the sheets on which she lay. He knew the doctors were keeping her heavily sedated. She would moan sometimes from the pain of even a shallow breath but never open her eyes. Neil feared she might never do that again. Pneumonia was also a concern, and she was allowed no visitors.

After several days, the specialists were still trying to determine if a heart attack or stroke caused the fall. They needed more tests. Neil felt they were not as open as they had been when she had her stroke and they discovered her weak heart. He feared the worst.

When the doctors said they would be consulting with another specialist, Neil could only nod. Here he was a doctor but helpless to do anything for his own grandmother except pray and wonder what they were doing in her room so much of the time.

Carter assured him he was taking care of the patients at the clinic. Neil visited his patients in the hospital and sat in the waiting room—not as a doctor but as a helpless person concerned about a loved one in the hospital. He wasn't allowed to stay in her room at night, so he slept in an empty room with the promise he'd be called if any change took place.

On one of the rare times when they weren't poking, prodding, testing, or consulting, Neil sat by her bedside, held her cold, thin hand in his, and confessed that he had deceived her. His intentions were good and the results had been good, but he had not been completely honest with her. Although she couldn't hear him, he asked her forgiveness.

Finally, he was told she could have regular visitors. Her pain medication had been lessened and she was lucid at times, but most of the time she slept.

"Her breathing is not as painful now that her ribs are healing," one specialist said with a reassuring smile.

Neil wasn't reassured. Why did they keep talking about ribs? They should be more concerned about the bigger issues of stroke and heart disease. He knew from experience, a doctor wouldn't tell you any more than he wanted to.

"Is she recovering?" Neil asked.

"We can't answer you yet, Neil."

That's when he feared something even more threatening was taking place in his grandmother's frail body, in addition to her weak heartbeat and aftermath of a stroke.

Perhaps they were allowing visitors because she was failing fast.

Stella and Olivia came right after he called home. He wouldn't prevent this visit. His grandmother loved them, regardless of what deception had taken place. Hedda accompanied them. They came in quietly and stood near the door, staring at the quiet, still figure in the bed.

"It's my fault."

Neil could hardly believe who said that. "Hedda, how can you blame yourself for something like this?"

"I knew things," she said, "about Stella. We were arguing about it that day."

"No, it's my fault if anybody's," Stella said.

Olivia began to refute that, and so did Neil. They stopped suddenly when a moan sounded from the bed.

Neil went over and spoke to his grandmother, but she didn't respond. He looked at the women. "If we've hurt her, all we can do now is ask forgiveness. It's too late for blame and explanations."

"No it's not," came a feeble sound. Grandmother struggled to open her eyes but couldn't make it. "You just keep talking and talking, and I'm trying to get a good breath. That's what's killing me." She struggled. Her words were slurred. "I want to hear it all. Let's try again when I can sit up without my ribs hurting."

Neil had seen enough illness to know that sometimes a patient revived shortly before he or she died. He feared this was the case with his grandmother.

———

His grandmother seemed to feel better daily, but the doctors still claimed their tests and consultations were inconclusive. They wanted to keep her in the hospital until they were sure. Neil was a doctor—he knew that kind of talk was always bad news.

Finally, Grandmother was ready to hear everything. Neil, Olivia, Stella, and Hedda gathered outside her room. Neil went in while the others remained at the door.

His grandmother was propped up on pillows. "The doctors have their diagnosis," she said.

They hadn't told him. What was this? Neil opened his mouth to speak.

"No, Neil. I told them not to tell it until after I've talked to each of you." She gave an audible breath. "This still hurts, so don't make me talk too much. You're to do the talking."

Neil couldn't believe the doctors wouldn't have talked with him. Last year, they'd said she was dying. Why this secrecy now? "But. . .Grandmother—"

"Neil, I made them promise to not say anything yet. Before you hear it, I want the truth about what's being going on."

She motioned for the three women, still standing at the door to sit on her bed.

Olivia and Hedda did. Stella held up a small bag. "I brought things to fix you up."

His grandmother nodded. Stella leaned over the bed and began to brush her hair. She held his grandmother's head out a little to get the back, then brushed and fluffed the waves around her face. Stella looked around. "Any of you can start at any time."

His grandmother let out a sound like a laugh turned into a yelp. "Eew, that hurt." She rolled her eyes up at Stella. "Don't make me laugh."

Hedda began. "We were arguing. She didn't want to hear it, but I kept on. To get away from me, she turned too quick and struck her hip on the corner of the kitchen table. Her cane slipped, and she fell across the table trying to catch herself. But she lost her balance and fell on the floor."

"Tell what we argued about, Hedda."

Hedda squeaked. "In front of them?"

"We're here to tell the truth, Hedda," Neil said. At least he hoped so. But how would he know the truth? Nothing was like he thought for the past ten months. Olivia was an actress, and he had no idea who or what Stella might be.

Hedda kept her head down. "It started the first day they came to the inn. I knew I'd seen Stella somewhere. Then I remembered. When me and Bart went down to Canaan Valley last year to visit our son and his wife, we went to the nickelodeon. Sure enough, there she was, playing the piano big as life."

That didn't surprise Neil. It sort of put some things in perspective. His grandmother's expression didn't change, and her eyes were closed.

"I felt it was my Christian duty to tell Mama McCory. The first time Stella played the piano at church, I told her I'd seen Stella play the piano in that nickelodeon. That it just wasn't right to come and sit on that piano bench in church and play the piano. I said that was being a hypocrite." She began to sob.

"Tell what I said about that, Hedda. It hurts my ribs to say too much."

"Yes, I'll tell it all." She took a handkerchief from her skirt pocket and made use of it. "Mama McCory said, 'Hedda sits in a nickelodeon while Stella plays the piano. Hedda sits in a church while Stella plays the piano. Now why is Stella a hypocrite and Hedda is not?' That's what she said." Her sobs were louder and her handkerchief wetter.

Stella turned and patted Hedda's shoulder. "I am a hypocrite."

"*We* are," Olivia said.

Stella nodded. "We're not good Christians. When we went to church, we pretended."

His grandmother held her ribs. "I told you not to do that." She turned her face toward Neil and gestured.

He would try. "I think what Grandmother means is that's what we all do in church. That's not bad, but it's what you do at home, at work, and in private that shows who you really are."

His grandmother nodded, so he must be doing all right. "But you don't do things to be a Christian. You do things because you are a Christian."

Stella's eyes got big. "So we weren't sinning?"

"Well...I...no...but...far as I know." He cleared his throat. "Basically, being a Christian is being a follower of Christ."

"Having Jesus in your heart?" Stella asked.

"Yes."

She shook her head. "Then we were sinning. We didn't get that done."

"Are you finished with me?" his grandmother asked.

"Oh. No." Stella finished her hair. "Now the truth about me. I'm a retired actress. And I'm not Olivia's mother; I'm her aunt—the sister of her father, Herman Easton."

"Hmm, I didn't know that part."

Neil wondered what "part" his grandmother did know.

Olivia spoke up. "My mother died when I was very young. Stella has been like a mother to me."

"Yes," his grandmother said, "I know the love you two have for each other. I saw it that first day, and it's never wavered. That isn't pretended."

"Now, I guess we get to the ad in the paper?" Stella asked.

Neil exhaled heavily. "That's where I come in."

His grandmother gave him a look. "I've known about that advertisement all along. Hedda showed it to me."

Hedda looked like she'd been wrung out. "She didn't want me to say anything. But things weren't right. I kept nagging about it. I kept saying the ladies weren't what they seemed to be." She wailed. "And all that time, I was being judgmental even though Mama McCory was so happy. I'm sorry. Please, everybody forgive me."

Everyone murmured his or her forgiveness.

"I don't understand, Grandmother. How could you know about the ad and not say anything?"

"Maybe we're cut from the same cloth, Neil." That look again. "At first I was shocked. Then I got to thinking. That gave me something to think about instead of lying in bed dying. I couldn't wait to see who in the world you'd bring home. I planned to expose you before you went through with any wedding."

"Why didn't you?"

She waited awhile before answering. Giving him a sidelong look and smiling, she finally said, "I liked Juliet. . .um, Olivia. If that delightful girl wanted the job of being my companion, I was all for it. I was ready to say, 'Let her have the job; you don't have to marry her.'"

Again, he asked, "Why didn't you?"

"When she served your cup of tea and you looked into her beautiful eyes, I felt like you were seeing a new world—one where Kathleen didn't live, one filled with possibilities. This girl was for you."

Was she? Olivia wasn't looking at anyone.

"At first I thought it would be wrong to marry for any reason but love. But I got to thinking further. In some countries the parents arrange the marriage. Why, right here in West Virginia, there was a time when mail-order brides came in. So I knew if you thought a girl would make me happy, that meant deep in your heart, even if you didn't know it, she would make you happy, too."

She patted Stella's hand. "Oh, and as for Stella, who wouldn't want this vivacious woman around? I felt like I'd found a new friend." They smiled fondly at each other. "There's something else you don't know."

Neil thought this was supposed to be their confession. It looked as if it was his grandmother's. "If you remember, when I looked at Stella, I said her eyes were unforgettable. Well, I knew exactly where I'd seen her, and it wasn't the nickelodeon. About fifteen years ago, a traveling troupe of actors came through here. Streun and I went to the performance. There was this beautiful young woman with long red hair and the greenest eyes imaginable, kicking up her heels and singing to beat the band. She made these mountains ring with music. When I remembered that, I realized who she was and thought that Olivia looked a lot like that young woman."

Neil could hardly believe what he was hearing, but Grandmother wasn't finished.

"Oh, I was already middle-aged when I saw her. But I thought if I was a young woman, I'd like to do that. I envied her. Then to have her in my house, being entertained by that famous actress every day has been such a joy."

She looked at Olivia. "And anyone would have to love this young lady."

"I didn't mean to do anything wrong," Olivia said.

Neil listened as she told of her dream to be an actress and said that her name was Olivia Easton. Her breath caught.

Stella interjected, "What's she's saying is that she's not legally married to Neil."

Neil felt it and knew it, but to hear it stated was like a knife in the heart.

"I came here for a job," Olivia said. "And from the beginning, I wanted to be your companion. I didn't realize anyone would be hurt."

"I'm not hurt," his grandmother assured her. "I would have done anything to be an actress, too, if I was young like you. I think it's time this job with Neil ended."

He nodded, and his grandmother continued.

"If you want to stay on at the inn, I will hire you. If you want to go on to acting school, I would love to help out with that, too. I love you."

Neil had to leave the room. A man could take only so much of women hugging and crying all over each other.

Out walking the halls, he thought of his grandmother saying, *"And anyone would have to love this young lady."*

Neil didn't know about that. He didn't know Olivia Easton.

He'd fallen in love with an actress playing a part, not a real woman who returned his affection. How did one deal with being in love with a character in a play?

Chapter 23

That afternoon Olivia said she was going for a walk and would be back soon. She hadn't really planned to go and see the pastor. It just seemed like the thing to do.

She didn't want Neil blamed at all but wanted Pastor Whitfield to know why she must leave Sunrise. She told him the entire story. "I'm sorry for pretending to be a fine Christian woman when I wasn't even sure what I believed."

"Olivia, I can't condone misrepresentation. But I can't condemn you either. If we place blame, we must also give credit. You've been good for Neil. He hasn't been this happy in years. You and Stella have brought laughter into people's lives. Mama McCory has lived longer than expected. The specialists said she would never be up and around again like she has been since you and Stella came."

"Stella says she and I can go back and live in her cabin if we need to. Do you think," she said, "if I confess to my father, who will probably disown me again, that I can clean up my life and be a good Christian?"

Olivia was shocked when he said, "No."

"Oh." She placed her hand on her heart.

Her feeling of devastation must have shown. He smiled kindly. "What I mean is that you don't need to wait until you clean up your life. First, just ask Jesus into your heart."

"I don't know how," she confessed.

"Just tell Him that you're sorry for your sins and ask Him to come into your heart."

"That's. . .all?"

"That's the first step. If you really mean it, then you'll want to live the way He tells us to live in the Bible. You pray and ask Him to show you how to live each day."

"I want to do that."

"Then pray after me."

She did. After they finished, she waited for a long time. Finally, she said, "I don't feel any different."

He smiled kindly. "It's not a magic potion. But you asked Jesus into your heart. He's there. You're a baby Christian right now."

"I think I understand," she said. "The Bible is my script. I need to read it and learn it and follow instructions on how to act on it."

"Exactly. And you'll find out that having Jesus in your heart isn't just a feeling. It's a knowing. You're now a part of God's family. And it's not just your heart; it's your life."

———

When Neil walked into the church, he saw Olivia and the pastor standing at the front. She was wiping tears from her face.

He started to turn. "Come on in, Neil," the pastor said.

"I can come back later."

"No," Olivia said, "I was just leaving." When she passed him in the aisle, she said, "I told the pastor everything. I'm sorry." She hurried out.

Neil and the pastor both sat on the front row. Although Olivia had said she told him everything, Neil told his side of it.

"Neil, like I told Olivia, I'm not here to condone or condemn. I know good has come of this situation. But if you feel you've done wrong, you can always ask God's forgiveness. He's in that business, you know."

Neil gave a self-conscious laugh and nodded.

They prayed.

Afterward, the pastor said, "Olivia has given her life to Jesus."

Then she was a part of God's church, which Jesus called "His bride." It was much more important for Olivia to be "the bride of Christ" than the bride of Dr. Neil McCory. Maybe some great good would come out of this situation. Perhaps God's plan for her life was for her to be a shining light in the acting world.

He could survive, although he didn't expect to ever love again. "Do I need to confess to the church?"

"Wait awhile," the pastor said. "Olivia said she may go to her father's. Who knows, she might decide to return and work at the inn. After all, the Lord works in mysterious ways."

Looking into the sympathetic eyes of the pastor, Neil knew he hadn't hidden his broken heart.

———

Although it seemed all the truth was out now, including her having given her heart to the Lord, Olivia dreaded hearing the prognosis about Mama McCory. She and Stella sat on the bed and Neil in the chair when two doctors came in.

They were wearing long white smocks and carrying clipboards. "This has taken so long because we had to be sure. That's why all the tests, consultations, and waiting."

Olivia felt as stark as Neil and Stella looked. All the color seemed drained from them. Mama McCory looked fine, as if she could hold up under anything. Olivia admired her strength.

"It seems," the doctor said, "she's improving."

The moment of stunned silence was suddenly filled with their exclamations of joy and wonder and laughter.

Mama McCory smiled broadly. "I was afraid to say anything. Afraid it wouldn't be true. Oh, I knew I felt better after you two came, but anyone would. There was music, laughter, and love in the house again."

Olivia could only praise God. Yes, this must be what it felt like to have Jesus in one's heart.

They wept together. Even the doctors had moist eyes.

After the doctors left, Olivia said she was trying to be truthful to everyone now. She needed to go and see her father. Knowing that she had to do it, she laid Mama McCory's locket in her hand.

"Remember, Olivia," she said, clasping the locket. "I'm your friend. And I know your heart is breaking. But whatever you decide to do, I'll be praying for you. Don't forget me."

"Oh, I could never do that."

She knew she could never forget Neil either. But there was no way she could stay at the inn. Mama McCory knew her heart ached for Neil. She would never be a good enough actress to hide that from him. She had to leave.

"I can't keep the money I made," she told Stella later as she was packing.

Stella nodded. "I know." Without either having to say it, she knew that Stella was aware she was in love with Neil. She left the money, rings, music box, and little black, jeweled handbag on the desk in Neil's study.

Olivia didn't want to see Neil, so Stella took her to the depot. Neil must have felt the same way, because he hadn't been there for breakfast. Not until the train left Sunrise far behind did Olivia allow the tears to fall.

When Olivia arrived at her father's house, he and Evelyn greeted her warmly, although they gave her curious glances when she said Neil wasn't with her.

When they were settled in the parlor, Olivia said, "I need to talk."

Evelyn said softly, "I'll get us something to drink."

"No," Olivia said. "I can't let you be hospitable to me. This is not just a visit. You both need to hear what I have to say."

She told the whole story in the face of wide-eyed disbelief. She let none of that stop her. When she finished, her father stood and stared at her for a long time. He paced in front of her. She and Evelyn glanced at each other guardedly.

Finally, he turned and hit the palm of his hand with his fist. "That took courage."

Courage? She'd be quaking in her boots if she hadn't been wearing her pointy-toed shoes.

He returned to a chair across from her. "I'm to blame, too, Olivia."

She couldn't believe it. He wasn't calling her a liar? Saying she was worse than a rogue and vagrant?

"I see now how much acting means to you. When I gave you an ultimatum, I thought you'd give in, give up the idea of being an actress. I thought I was protecting you."

He surprised her further by saying she was welcome to stay there as long as she wished. "Evelyn and I will go with you to New York and help you get settled there. You have our blessing."

Olivia should have been the happiest girl in the world, having come to know the Lord and now having her father's approval for an acting career. But she wasn't.

She thought and questioned and prayed for several days, then came to the conclusion that acting was not what she wanted after all. She wanted a real life, like managing an inn and having a husband and children.

She called Stella. First she asked about Mama McCory.

"She's improving every day," Stella said brightly. Then she told about going to the preacher and giving her own heart to Jesus. "Maybe we can be baptized together."

"Maybe someday," Olivia said. "But I've had a change in plans. Right now I don't feel like going to that acting school. I don't know what I'll do. For now, I need to study my Bible, attend church with Dad and Evelyn, and pray." She took a deep breath. "How is Neil?"

"Like all of us," Stella said, "he misses you."

"How do you know?"

"I'm smart."

They laughed, and Olivia said no more about it. Maybe Neil did miss her. She had done a good *job*.

―⁂―

Neil didn't feel as thankful this Thanksgiving as he had a year before.

"Holidays can be a sad time," Stella said when he sat heavily, thoughtfully, at the kitchen table and accepted a cup of coffee from her. She poured herself a cup and sat in front of him. "I heard from Olivia."

He stared at his cup. He wouldn't even act excited. She was probably in New York, living her dream.

"She's studying the Bible and has a good relationship with her father and Evelyn."

"That's good," Neil said blandly. He was glad about that, but self-pity seemed to take precedence. He'd had to reprimand himself for being glad people's illnesses kept him almost too busy to think. That didn't speak well for his own Christian life.

Suddenly Stella blurted out, "I have a confession."

Neil braced himself. What was it now? That he would lose this brightness in his life, too—along with Danny Quinn?

Stella sounded repentant as she told about the influence she had over Olivia. "I've basked in the admiration of Olivia—one of the few people, aside from actors, who thought I was in a respectable line of work."

Neil realized Stella wasn't acting but was being very honest and open with him. "I wanted to feel important in someone's eyes, and Olivia has been that someone to me."

"I know Olivia loves you very much."

Stella nodded. He saw the tears form in her eyes. "I believe, Neil, that part of her wanting to be an actress is her identifying with me. I have tried to take on a mother role for her, maybe selfishly because I never had a child. She needed someone after her mother died."

"Just so you know, Stella," Neil said. "I think now that Olivia has given her heart to the Lord, she could do a lot of good as a Christian actress." He scoffed. "I remember that she wouldn't even look at me that first day, and I came to the conclusion she was cross-eyed."

"You think of her often?"

Neil heard that intimation in her voice. He was tired of acting. "Yes, I do. Stella, she loved my grandmother. I really believed she was legally my wife, and in pretending, I sometimes forgot she wasn't."

"I think Olivia has had enough acting to last her for a lifetime. I've set her straight on a few things. The life of an actress has its disadvantages, too. I couldn't have done anything else. But I have suspected Olivia wanted to be like me more than she wanted to be an actress. She's reconsidering."

His head came up. "Reconsidering?"

"Yes. When a girl gets a taste of what a good husband can be like, it sort of takes precedence over a career."

"Is she. . .interested in someone?"

"Neil, I think that's for you to find out—since you are in love with her."

"But *she's* not in love with *me*." He looked at Stella for confirmation, but Stella simply looked at the ceiling and sighed as if she were bored to tears.

"I don't know if she cares for me that way," he added.

"You lived here with her for almost a year, Neil. You two liked each other. Do you think it was all an act?"

"I was trying to act like a dutiful, loving husband myself," he said. "Yet I condemned her for doing what I hired her to do." He gave an ironic laugh. "It's just that she did it better than I could have imagined."

"At least you can laugh about it now."

"That's all I can do," he said. "She gave back everything I gave to her. I can't just show up on her doorstep and expect her to greet me with open arms."

When she didn't answer, he asked, "Can I?"

Stella scoffed. "I should hope not. With an adventurous, imaginative girl like Olivia, that would seem so old-fashioned and dull."

Chapter 24

Olivia got letters from Mama McCory at least once a week. She would tell what was going on with her, with the church, and with the inn. While reading her long, detailed letters, she could imagine all that Mama McCory described. Oh, how she would love to be there herself.

On Tuesday, Olivia called Stella. "You must come to Dad's for Christmas. You know you're welcome now. He's such a different person."

"I suppose we all are, Olivia," Stella said. "A lot will depend on the weather. You know how the snows are up here, and sometimes even the trains don't run. And you'll never believe this—Danny and I have talked seriously about getting married."

"You would leave the inn?"

"Oh no. Danny and I both love it here. We'll stay as long as Mama McCory and Neil want us. And they say we're family and must never leave."

"I'm so glad for you, Stella. But. . .I thought you never wanted to marry again."

"Well, nobody does until the right one comes along. We girls make our plans, then *boom!* Some man comes along and changes them."

Olivia laughed lightly, but she felt a tug on her heartstrings. She knew exactly what Stella meant. "So, is Neil doing all right?"

"The usual, of course. He's busy at the hospital and clinic, and he still makes some house calls. With these telephones beginning to reach even up into the mountains, he's more in demand than ever."

"That's good, I guess. And I guess you're cooking the breakfasts for the guests."

"Yes, and Danny helps since Hedda and Bart have officially retired. We have occasional, temporary help, but by the time a girl or woman gets trained, she leaves, like always. Neil is looking for help. There should be an ad in all the Sunday papers."

"What kind of help? A manager?"

"Oh dear. It's Bible study time, and here come the ladies. I'll talk to you later, dear. I love you."

"I love you, too," Olivia said almost absently. She did, of course, but she kept thinking how blessed Stella was to be at Sunrise Inn. Sometimes Olivia thought she was being punished because she had been deceptive to Mama McCory, all the people of Sunrise, and even Neil.

But Stella had been deceptive, too. She'd apparently been forgiven, for she surely was blessed now. She was living at the inn and had someone who wanted to marry her.

Olivia lectured herself often. She'd asked God to lead her into the kind of life that would be a blessing to others and would serve Him. Evelyn told her just to be patient and continue her Bible studies. God would let her know what He had for her when He was ready.

Olivia didn't find a lot of comfort in that. God might decide He wanted her to go somewhere far away from Sunrise Inn...and Neil.

After church on Sunday, she waited impatiently until her dad had finished with the newspaper, laid his head back in his chair, and closed his eyes while Evelyn sat before the fire with her needlepoint.

Olivia picked up the paper and whispered to Evelyn that she would be upstairs in her sitting room. Evelyn nodded sweetly and smiled. Although the thought made her even lonelier, Olivia was glad her dad had found a woman like Evelyn who complemented and perhaps even tamed him with her gentle nature.

As soon as she sat in the chair next to the window, Olivia turned to the classifieds and searched the columns. Her mouth opened and she gasped. There it was, in much larger print than the other ads:

WANTED: A beautiful young woman with the initials J.K. or O.E.
to marry an established man and live in a house large enough for a big
family. Several months' experience necessary. Payment is love for a lifetime.
If interested, please respond to DNMC, General Delivery, Post Office,
Sunrise, West Virginia.

On Monday, after making rounds at the hospital, Neil went to the post office, although he knew it was too soon for a response. He'd hoped Olivia would read the ad, think it clever, and respond.

By Tuesday, he felt like an idiot. On Wednesday, since Stella had errands to run in town, he asked her to check for a response. Stella stopped in and said there was no mail. "I could call her."

"No," Neil said. For the rest of the day he forced himself to concentrate on his patients. On the way home, he shivered in the cold and prayed for God to help him regain his joy. He'd accomplished what he'd set out to do, and that was to make his grandmother's last weeks and months happy ones. The Lord had allowed that. Not only had that made her happy, it had apparently given her an extended life, with no end in sight. Olivia had given his grandmother a new heart to live, but when she had left, she had taken his heart with her.

Danny came out to tend Sally when Neil arrived at the stable. Scrunching into his jacket and with head ducked to shield his face from the blustery cold wind, he made his way to the back door of the house, took off his gloves, and rubbed his hands together. He went into the kitchen where Stella was fixing supper. The aroma of baked bread and cake filled the room.

"Mama McCory and I thought we'd eat in the dining room tonight," she said. "Maybe that will cheer you up. Danny's having supper with us, and we want to talk to you about our business venture we've mentioned before. It should be ready by the time you're washed up."

Although he felt washed up already, Neil nodded. Winters and cold weather could be hard. Stella was lively and interesting, but it just wasn't the same without his "wife."

Having no secrets now, they'd shown his grandmother his "wanted" ad. She had said and kept saying, "The Lord will work out what's His will."

"The Lord can be awfully slow sometimes," Stella had quipped.

When he returned to the dining room, he thought the table looked especially nice, as if they were having company. The flickering candles emitted a comforting glow. He walked over to the fire and held out his hands, still feeling chilled.

"Um, Neil," he heard.

Without turning, he said, "Yes, Stella?"

"You didn't get a letter at the post office, but a young woman did come in by train. Her initials are J. O."

Neil felt his hands shake and told himself not to hope.

"Her name is Jenelle Owings."

Neil closed his eyes for a moment. No, he mustn't hope. That would be no stranger than some of the letters he'd gotten when he first put an ad in the paper. He took a deep breath, and slowly his head turned and he looked over his shoulder.

He felt like his eyes might pop out and he couldn't close his mouth. He couldn't even breathe. Standing between his grandmother and Stella was a pitiful-looking creature dressed in the most awful brown dress he'd ever seen—except once. Her hair was back in a tight bun, and she wore the most grotesque spectacles on her eyes that almost covered her entire face.

Stella's hand was over her mouth. Danny and Grandmother were chuckling. Neil took a few steps closer, and that's when he saw her crossed eyes behind those spectacles. He could only shake his head and try his best to give her a threatening look.

Before he could say anything, she whined, "Am I...beautiful enough?"

"To me, you're the most beautiful person in the world."

"Fine," Olivia said. "I'll stay this way."

"Will you now?" Neil spoke threateningly and walked closer. Her eyes uncrossed and widened. He reached up, took off the spectacles, and handed them to Stella.

Stella turned to Danny and Neil's grandmother. "I think we'd better get out of here."

They did, and Neil took Olivia in his arms, afraid to do more than brush his lips against her warm, soft ones. He then held her head close to his chest, feeling as if his heart might beat out of him. "I love you, Olivia."

"I love you, too, Dr. McCory," she said softly, and this time she looked very serious.

"I'll be back," he said.

Soon he returned with the others following. They all sat at the table and waited.

Neil came to her and fell to his knees. "Olivia," he said. "I have a proposal for you. I love you and I want you to be my wife."

"I accept." She looked as happy as he felt.

He took her hand and slipped his mother's engagement ring on her finger.

"Aren't you going to kiss her?" Danny said.

Neil rose. "I prefer to do that in private." He remembered the fake wedding in Stella's cabin. This time, however, he wouldn't just stand there and look over Olivia's head.

Chapter 25

As if no one wanted any secrets anymore, they openly discussed wedding plans over the supper table.

"Do you want a big church wedding in Davidson?" Neil asked.

"I don't," Olivia said. "I would like a small ceremony at Sunrise Church, performed by Pastor Whitfield."

They all agreed that would be ideal. During the following days, Stella and Mama McCory would not tell Olivia or Neil what they were doing at church.

Olivia's dad and Evelyn came the day before the wedding to help. John and Sarah were unable to attend, as her baby was due in only a few weeks.

Finally, the big day arrived. The week before Christmas, Olivia stood in the doorway of the church. Neil walked to the front. Olivia's dad removed her coat from around her shoulders and laid it across a back pew.

The sanctuary was stunning. Red poinsettias were set all across the front. An arbor was set up in the center of the stage, decorated with greenery and white ribbons. A white rug lay on the floor in front of it.

Olivia felt breathless. All the people she loved so much were there, except for John and Sarah. The pastor, Neil, and Danny wore black suits, white shirts, and bow ties. Stella, standing as her matron of honor, looked beautiful in a green satin dress. Mama McCory wore a fur coat over her lace dress. She had returned the locket to Olivia as "something old." Evelyn, Bart, and Hedda sat next to Mama McCory on the front row.

Edith began to play "The Wedding March," and Olivia was in her white satin dress adorned with lace and seed pearls. She did not put the veil over her face but wanted to see her fiancé as she walked down the aisle, escorted by her dad.

She and Stella exchanged a sly glance when she handed her the bridal bouquet—a far cry from stinky marigolds. Evelyn said Herman had ordered the roses, and they'd come just in time. They looked beautiful against a background of green leaves and white baby's breath and tied with a white satin ribbon.

Olivia and Neil said their vows, the wedding band was slipped on her finger, and the preacher said, "I now pronounce you man and wife. You may kiss the bride."

Finally, the congratulations, hugs, and kisses ended. Her dad had rented a suite of rooms at the hotel for him, Evelyn, Stella, and Mama McCory. "I expect

Stella and Mama here to show us what Sunrise is all about," her dad said. "I'd like to see the hospital and your clinic, Neil."

"We'll show him," Stella said.

"Expect us when you see us," Mama McCory said, waving at them as she left the church, seeming to be having the time of her life.

"I'm riding ahead of you two, and I'll take care of the horse and carriage," Danny said. "I'm staying with a buddy tonight. Your father's invited me to go with them tomorrow."

On the way to the inn, snow began to fall, as if showering a blanket of blessing on their wedding day. When the carriage pulled up in front of the inn, Olivia and Neil laughed. On a post, large as life, was a sign: No Room at the Inn.

They alighted from the carriage, and Danny appeared to take it out back. Olivia linked her arm through Neil's as they stood for a moment while the snow softly fell, turning the scenery into a winter wonderland.

Neil unlocked the door, then turned and brushed, not rice, but snow from her hair. His lips met hers for a moment. Cold as they were, they warmed her heart.

He swooped her up and set her inside the foyer, lighted only by the lamp on the desk. Laughing, they removed their coats, hung them in the entry closet, and headed for the parlor to get warm.

The fire only needed to be stoked. He did that. She lit the candles on the Christmas tree, and the room danced with the firelight and glow from the tree.

She walked to the middle of the room, not quite certain what to do next. He came to her and looked up. She then looked. Overhead, hanging from the chandelier, was a ball of mistletoe.

With him standing so near and looking at her with eyes of love, she didn't need that as a cue to kiss her husband. Her arms encircled his neck as his hands came around her waist. She lifted her face to his. The musky fragrance was there as his head bent and his lips were a breath away.

She wanted no more pretenses. She preferred the reality of being in love and basking in the arms of her beloved who once had a bride idea.

YVONNE LEHMAN is an award-winning, bestselling author of forty-eight books, including mainstream, mystery, romance, young adult, and women's fiction. Her recent books are *North Carolina Weddings* and *Aloha Love,* the first in a series of three historical Hawaiian Heartsongs. The other two books in the series are *Picture Bride* and *Love from Ashes.* Recent novellas are in the collections *Schoolhouse Brides* and *Carolina Carpenter Brides.* Founder and director of her own writers' conference for twenty-five years, she now directs the Blue Ridge "Autumn in the Mountains" Novel Retreat: (www.lifeway.com/novelretreat. She is also co-director of the Honored Authors of Gideon Media Arts Festival (www.gideon-filmfestival.com). Her Web site is www.yvonnelehman.com.

SENECA SHADOWS

Lauralee Bliss

Dedication

To my father-in-law, Ken Bliss, with grateful thanks for his wisdom, his prayers, and his service to our country.

Acknowledgments

With grateful thanks to Shirley Yokum for her discriptions of life by Seneca Rocks, West Virginia, during the training of the doliders.

Chapter 1

Summer 1943

The gentle rush of the North Fork River played a soothing melody to Lucy Bland. She tucked a section of hair behind one ear and tentatively took a few steps forward, hoping her sneakers wouldn't slip on the wet rocks.

"Watch yourself there, Lucy!" a voice called out. "I was out here just a few days ago, and the river nearly carried me off."

Lucy sighed. *Oh, to be carried away,* she thought. But not by a wild river rapid that came on the heels of some terrific thunderstorm. She had seen the valley drowned by rising waters. It often happened in the springtime with the melting snows and the onslaught of rainy weather. When the fields became engulfed by water, her family would seek her uncle's farm to pasture the horses and cattle.

No, not carried away by the river, but to be swept away by a man, safe in his strong arms—that was a different story. He would place her on his white steed and take her to his castle in the sky. What a wonderful romantic tale that would make. If only it would come true. She glanced back while teetering precariously on a rock with the river dancing at her feet. Her prince of the field was approaching her now. Short. Stocky. His red hair ignited by the fierce sunlight. He wore a brown shirt and stained trousers that had seen better days. Allen Hopper, the childhood friend she had known as far back as she could remember, the same one who used to steal her sweater at recess and her apple at lunch. Was he the person she longed for, her knight in shining armor?

"What are you doing, Lucy?" he demanded. "I said I had to talk to you about something important, and you take off on me."

"I want to cross the river, Allen," she said. "Let's go up in the woods across the way, toward my favorite place by the rocks. I just love the view from up there. It's so beautiful."

Allen shielded his eyes to glance at the famous rocks hovering above them, like pointed sentinels standing guard over the valley. "We're going way up there?" he complained.

She took another hop forward on the rock. How could she tell him that up there, among the pointy rocks, with the valley spread out before her, she felt as if she could touch heaven? Especially when clouds enshrouded the land.

"C'mon, don't do that." He came to the bank. "Am I gonna have to come in there after you?"

Lucy giggled at the thought. Maybe there were ways to make one's dream of being carried off to some distant land a reality. Momma often told her that her head lay more in the clouds than in the real world. Lucy admitted that sometimes she thought of the rocks as some great castle and herself as the queen of the gate. Some time ago, her younger brothers once caught her pretending to be a regal woman before the mirror.

"What are you doing, Lucy, acting dumb?" they had chided. As if to say she couldn't be anyone else but Lucy Bland, as bland and boring as her name.

Just then she felt a hand brush hers. Startled at the sudden touch, she screamed as she lurched away and slipped on the rock, landing on her knees in the rushing water. The chill shocked her, and she drew in a sharp breath. "Oh, now look at what you did!"

"I'm sorry, Lucy, but I told you to come out of there. I have something important to tell you."

She accepted his hand and slowly made her way back to the riverbank. Her overalls felt like they weighed a ton after the mishap in the river. She began to shake from the heavy, cold fabric against her skin.

"If you're cold, I'll give you my shirt," Allen said, starting to unbutton it.

Just the thought of seeing him without his shirt on made her blush. "No, I'll be fine," she managed to say. "It's my overalls that are wet. I'd better go home and change."

Allen blew out a sigh of dismay. "When are we ever gonna have some peace to ourselves, Lucy? Am I gonna have to kidnap you or something to get some time alone with you? There's always something that keeps us apart."

Kidnapped and carried off. She couldn't help but smile until she saw the look of irritation on his face. "I'm sorry, Allen. I guess I need to. . ."

Just then she heard a roar echo in the valley, bouncing between the two ridges of mountains that flanked them on either side. She glanced upward to see a perfectly blue sky without a hint of clouds. It couldn't be a storm brewing. Then she saw a procession of olive green trucks rumbling down the main road running through the valley. One of the trucks veered off the road and headed into the field, directly toward her and Allen.

"C'mon," Allen urged, taking her by the hand. Her sopping wet clothing did little to help her move any quicker. The roar of the truck grew deafening. Its brakes suddenly squealed and the truck came to a halt. The acrid stench of exhaust filled her nostrils.

"No need to be afraid," announced a friendly voice. From out of the truck came two men dressed in olive green fatigues and caps.

Lucy stared. "Oh no," she whispered and found herself stepping toward Allen for protection.

"What's going on here?" Allen demanded. "Why are you driving on this land?"

"Don't mean to alarm you," the man said. He offered his hand. "I'm Captain Nick Landers. And this is Sergeant Fred Watkins. We're with the MTG."

"The what?" Allen asked.

"The MTG. Sorry. It stands for Mountain Training Group. We're out of Camp Hale, Colorado."

"Never heard of it—or you, for that matter."

Lucy continued to stare at the soldiers standing before her, from the top of the olive green caps on their heads, to the uniforms they wore, to the military boots that clad their feet. What could the military possibly want in this part of the valley? "I never thought I looked like a German," Lucy suddenly remarked. "In fact, my family has English roots."

Loud laughter emanated from the man who had introduced himself as Captain Nick Landers. "I'm sure," he said. "Though if you were German, you'd be the prettiest one in the East."

Lucy felt the heat enter her cheeks as Allen's hand tightened around her arm. "What do you want here, soldier?" Allen asked.

"Didn't you hear the news? The military has set up a base of operations in this part of West Virginia. We have men here that have already established a climbing school over in Elkins. My job is to train groups of soldiers to climb those rocks there." He pointed toward Lucy's beloved castle in the distance.

"You mean you're going to climb Seneca Rocks?" Lucy asked in disbelief.

"That and much more. At least we will be training in that general area. There are divisions in different regions that will be doing other types of training maneuvers like working with artillery. The sergeant here and I came early to scout the area for the best place to set up a base camp from where the soldiers can begin climbing exercises." He gestured toward the green fields beyond. "And this looks like an excellent place. By the end of the week, you'll see tents scattered all over this field."

Lucy wasn't sure she liked the prospect of strange men running around the valley and invading her beloved rocks. Though she had to admit she did like Nick's smile, and his laughter nearly made her laugh with him.

"Well, this is my family's field. Who gave you permission to trespass on our property and set up a bunch of tents?" Allen demanded.

Nick stared at him. "He's called Uncle Sam. The military selected this location because of its topography; it's ideal for training troops for conditions in Europe. Climbing studs set in a wall wouldn't give our troops the invaluable practice on the type of real terrain we expect to encounter in battle. Maybe we can even encourage you to enlist and help us with our training, Mister. . ."

"Hopper. Allen Hopper. My family owns a good deal of the land here. And the only country store in these parts, too. And I will tell you right now, my dad never said anything about you military men coming here and invading our land. Or driving your truck across it. Look at how you dug it up." He pointed at the deep tire tracks made in the soft ground.

"You might want to ask him again. We sent out maneuver permission cards about our plans. They alerted folks here about what we are doing and how long we'll be staying. Cards were sent to other places, as well, where other training will be conducted. And I'm sure good, upstanding citizens like yourselves believe that anything to help give us victory is worth a little inconvenience and some tire tracks, don't you think?"

Lucy could feel the tension rising out of this encounter. She tugged on Allen's hand. "Let's go, Allen. They have to do what they have to do. There's no sense arguing about it. I need to change into some dry clothes."

"There's plenty of other places they can do their training, like those rocks north of here," he muttered. "They'll only end up leaving this place a mess. I'm gonna talk to Dad about this and see what's going on."

Lucy glanced back at the two men who were already retracing their steps toward their truck. Suddenly Captain Landers paused, turned, and gave her one last once-over. She thought she saw the crease of a smile break his smoothly shaven face. Why would he be smiling at her? Maybe he found her humorous. Plenty of city people had come through the valley, looking on the residents here as simple-minded country folk. She lifted her head and turned away, linking her arm with Allen's. Again she thought she heard Nick's infectious laugher, but only the sound of the truck's engine revving up met her ears. Exhaust blew on the wind, replacing the sweet scent of flowers and green grass with the odor of oil.

Allen took off his hat and fanned away the fumes, coughing all the while. "I'm gonna find out what's happening, all right," he declared, watching the truck make a U-turn and head for the road. "Just look at how those truck tires tore up the ground. And with a bunch of men camping here, this place will never be the same. How are we gonna graze our livestock?"

"Nothing is the same since Pearl Harbor," Lucy mused. "All Daddy talks about is the war. You hear it on the radio or at the picture shows. And all those men dying. It's awful." She glanced back wistfully as the truck disappeared into the distance. "Maybe it's a good idea to let them do what they want, Allen. I mean, we're helping the war effort, like that captain said."

"We're already helping the war effort. Dad sells war bonds at the store. And we've started rationing."

"Momma just got a ration book for sugar, too. She says we can't use sugar like we used to. And that means I can't make muffins anytime I want."

"I can get you all the sugar you need and you know it," Allen said. "So you keep on making your muffins."

"Yes, but that's not being honest, Allen. So many others can't have it. Momma says we need to do our part and use the coupons. Just like everyone else."

"Yeah, Dad's even gotten involved in that training to become one of those air raid wardens. Not that we would ever get bombs dropping on us here, of all places." He paused. "Though with those soldiers running around, who knows what could happen? They may drop their own bombs on us from the looks of it."

"Don't say those things, Allen. You're scaring me. They're just here to train on the rocks. And we should help them feel at home."

Allen fell silent. Lucy wasn't certain why he reacted the way he did toward the soldiers. Maybe the fact that he hadn't joined the army like others his age had left him with a guilty conscience. His father had been able to keep him from enlisting, claiming a need for Allen's help at the store. Not that she wanted Allen to join the army. No one knew what the future held or when the government would send troops into harm's way to drive out the enemy. Even though the war still seemed a long way away from West Virginia, the sights and sounds on the radio and on the newsreels made it real. Now, with soldiers arriving in Seneca Rocks, the war had come directly to their front doorstep. Lucy trembled despite the warm summer temperatures, more from nerves than her wet overalls.

When they reached her home, Allen turned and took her hand in his. "I still need to talk to you about something important," he said. "But I guess this isn't the time or the place. You need to get into some dry clothes."

"I'm sorry it didn't work out today, Allen."

He sighed. "It's all right. I have to get ready to go on a business trip to Elkins for Dad. When I get back, I'll take you to Petersburg for an ice-cream soda and we'll talk then. How does that sound?"

"Sounds real nice," she said with a smile. He returned the smile and leaned over, poised to plant a kiss on her lips. At the last moment, she turned her face so his lips found her cheek instead. He drew back with a look of surprise. Lucy hurried into the house before he could say anything. She banged the door shut even though she heard him calling for her.

"What's going on, Lucy? And what happened to your overalls?"

Lucy looked over at Momma, who stood holding a mixing bowl against her frilled apron.

"I slipped in the river, but I'm fine."

"Oh, Lucy. I don't know why you insist on traipsing around like you were some man."

"We saw some soldiers today," she said hastily, hoping to change the subject.

"Yes, I heard some neighboring boys just joined up. Did you know your classmate, Henry Glass, is one of them? I must say I'm thankful Carl and Tim are too young. Can you imagine waiting to hear when they might have to go over and face those terrible Japanese or the Germans? I couldn't bear the thought of it. I'd worry day and night. I don't know how others do it."

"No, I mean we saw soldiers *here*. They're going to train on Seneca Rocks. They're planning to make camp right on the Hoppers' field. We met a couple of them today while Allen and I were at the river."

Momma set down her bowl and glanced out between the parted cotton curtains. "Oh dear, I wish they didn't have to come here. Not that I'm against our fighting men, but things are so difficult with the war right now." She stared a bit longer. "Lucy, why is Allen sitting on our front porch? Did you leave him there without inviting him in?"

Lucy felt the warmth rush into her cheeks. She looked out the window and saw Allen sitting on the steps, a pencil and slip of paper in his hand, writing a note.

"Go see if he would like a glass of lemonade."

Lucy knew what he really wanted, but she wasn't about to let him kiss her for real. Nor did she know when she would ever be ready for that. At least not with Allen. "It's all right, Momma. I—I think it would be better for me not to talk to him right now."

Momma gave her a quizzical look. "Now what? Don't tell me you two had an argument."

"No. I need to change out of these wet overalls. Excuse me." Lucy headed for the stairs and her room, thankful to have escaped another encounter with Allen on the front porch. She just couldn't imagine being kissed on the lips by the man. He was a childhood friend, after all. A buddy. Not the man she should kiss and then marry. She flopped down on the bed and stared up at the ceiling. Instead of Allen, she suddenly envisioned the handsome army captain named Nick Landers coming toward her with a bunch of flowers in his hand. He would give them to her, accompanied by his ever-ready smile and a hearty laugh that tickled her insides. His tall frame would tower over her. And then he would stoop and ever so slowly, with great emotion, kiss her full on the lips.

"Lucy, Allen is downstairs!" Momma called up.

She sighed and tossed a bed pillow. *Oh please, not now.* "I have a headache!" she called back. It was true. Already she felt the tension creeping up her neck and into the back of her head from her emotional turmoil. After a few anxious minutes, she heard the front door shut, then footsteps on the stairs. The door to her room opened a crack.

"Really, Lucy," Momma admonished, handing her a note. "I don't know what's gotten into you. Do you really have a headache or is something else bothering you?"

"I don't know, Momma. Thank you for bringing me the note."

Momma gave her one last look before heading down the stairs. Lucy unfolded the paper and read Allen's message—which included many misspellings. It said he would be in Elkins for a week and when he returned, to be ready for a wonderful night out to finish what they had started today. She refolded the note and set it on the lamp table. *What is it we're supposed to finish, Allen?* she thought. *Have we really started anything? I mean, I like you and all. We've been friends since we learned to talk. But are we really supposed to be together? Am I supposed to be your girl? Even marry you? Or should we just stay friends?*

Lucy began to shiver again like she had back at the river. Only then did she realize she was still wearing her wet overalls. When she stood up, a damp impression remained on the bedspread. *Now I am losing my mind. But why? Can it all be because of those soldiers we met in the fields today, and especially one named Captain Nick Landers?*

Chapter 2

Nick Landers loosened his laces and yanked off the stiff boots, thankful for the cool air that refreshed his aching toes. He should be used to this military show by now, but every day yielded surprises in one form or another. And after today's encounter in the fields, he sensed his time here at Seneca Rocks would be no different.

Nick glanced up and squinted. From where Fred had hastily erected their tent for the evening, he could see the darkened scales of rock jutting toward the sky. They weren't much compared to the mountain terrain where he grew up and where he'd trained—the Rocky Mountains of Colorado, which had year-round snow at the uppermost peaks. He loved those mountains. On such peaks, adventure loomed all year. Skiing, climbing, camping—all the things he loved to do and had perfected with time. When he heard from his ski instructor that the army was looking for men to help train outdoor and survival techniques to enlisted men, Nick knew he had the skill to do it. But he hadn't imagined it would lead him here, to the backwoods of West Virginia where vertical sheets of rock would become a training ground for numerous soldiers before they left for Europe.

But he didn't have anything drawing his heart back to Colorado. There was no woman waiting for him. Donna had been jealous of the mountains and the way they affected him, the mountains she insisted stole Nick from her.

"You keep skiing and climbing like this and we'll have to say our good-byes," Donna once threatened. He never took her seriously, until that day at the soda fountain. They were supposed to be sipping ice-cream floats and having a nice conversation about the future. Instead, she turned the meeting into a Dear John encounter, minus the letter. Nick never saw it coming, though thinking back on it, he should have. Donna had dropped enough hints. Yet when she told him they were through, he balked.

"I don't understand. I thought you liked what I do. You never said anything otherwise."

"You never have enough time for me, Nick," she complained. "And if you remember anything at all, I did say plenty about it. You just never stopped to listen."

"I asked you to come out and see what I do."

"Like your mountaineering is some baseball game, and I'm supposed to be the lovesick girl swooning in the stands," she grumbled. "Don't you understand that girls want to feel special? That we don't want to feel like we have to chase you men around all the time, especially not up some mountain? That sometimes we want to be the ones chased?"

Nick remembered the ice cream melting into his soda until it had turned into a white, frothy film floating on top. Never had he imagined Donna was so unhappy. She'd always had a smile on her face for him—or so it appeared. She talked about everything happening in her life. They went to dances. They would take walks in the woods. Did she really have that much discontent in her, simmering like some pot of stew, ready to boil over at the least provocation? Or maybe it was something else altogether. Like another man.

When he broached the subject, she turned as red as an apple. Her hand clenched her purse, as if she might clobber him with it. She rose from the counter in a fury. "How dare you even say that, Nicholas Landers! As if you think you're some king of the mountain. Let me tell you, you're no king. You—you're a—a— regular nincompoop!" With that she stalked out of the shop.

He saw her once after that, on a street corner, before he left for Camp Hale. She looked at him, a stony expression on her face. He could tell right away things had irrevocably collapsed between them. She then spun about on one high heel and disappeared.

And that was that.

For a while he thought about her words, pondering whether the mountains had become some obsession in his life, keeping him away from her and life in general. Soon after that he'd had little time to ponder its significance. He poured all his energy into readying himself and the men from Camp Hale to head east, to this area where he would be teaching them rock climbing techniques. Now he had one job and one job alone: to train the men to climb Seneca Rocks with courage and ease.

Nick had never been east of the Mississippi before coming to West Virginia. Denver had always been his home. His family still lived there. When he first arrived here, he marveled at how small the Appalachian Mountains were. And they were thick with vegetation. Trees lined the very summits, unlike the bare peaks above the tree line of the Rockies.

Then today, he'd had his first encounter with the natives. West Virginian folk like the young woman he saw by the river, clad in wet overalls, holding on to the arm of a freckle-faced, red-haired young man who looked like he might have been running a lemonade stand. Nick had casually glanced at the materials that had been given to him—a book on mountain lore, describing the people who lived here. It was as if the higher-ups were readying them to enter another culture, even though they were still in the United States. But the people weren't backward, not by any means. He'd found the young woman in her wet overalls to be the adventurous type, even if she was uncertain about their presence. And she hadn't complained once about her damp clothing. As far as he knew, Donna had never worn a pair of pants in her life, let alone overalls soaked in a mountain river. But this woman wore them all right, hitched up enough to expose a portion of her calves. Most of all, she had spunk. He liked the picture.

"I said, have you finished looking over our supply list?" a voice spoke loudly in his ear.

Nick jumped and turned, only to see his friend, Fred, staring at him with a funny smirk on his face. "Actually, no."

"I could tell. You'd better come down off your mountaintop there, Captain, and back to solid ground. And we haven't even started climbing and rappelling yet."

"I was thinking about those people we met by the river earlier today."

Fred hooted. "They didn't look too eager to make anyone's acquaintance. Especially ours."

"Yes, but they live in this area. They know it well and probably know the terrain like the backs of their hands. Maybe we should try to find them. We could use a guide or two to show us where to access the rocks. Scouting out all the trails and such will take a lot of time. And maybe we can make some friends with the locals."

"Are you joking? We need to do it ourselves. Like I said, that fellow there looked about ready to spit nails. The dame was kind of cute, I'll have to admit, even if she was dressed in overalls. A perfect picture of country living, the two of them, don't you think?"

"I think we just startled them is all. I mean, how would you like it if you were by the river, having a grand old time, maybe even ready for a kiss, then suddenly a huge army truck comes barreling down at you?"

"I'd have jumped out of the way and offered a salute."

Nick slapped his friend on the shoulder. "Sure you would. Since when do rules and regulations mean that much to you?"

"What? They mean plenty to me. We'd have no army without them. And if we're going to defeat the enemy, we'd better make sure we're following the rules."

"Good point. As it is, you and I have been a little lax about fraternization. We'll have to be more careful about that," Nick said thoughtfully, then smiled. "So here's a direct order from your commanding officer: We will go track down that young couple to find out more about this area, Sergeant Watkins. And make new friends, too."

"Friends, sure," he murmured.

"I'd like to hear you say, 'Yes, sir. On the double, sir.'"

"I lost that with you long ago, don't you remember?" he said with a grin. "Hey, I may still be heading up raw recruits, trying to get them ready to scale rocks as thin as gingersnaps. But as far as the 'sir' routine with you, I thought we'd dealt with that. Like on that icy cliff back in Colorado when I saved you, and you said rank didn't matter." He paused. "But it was a while ago, I suppose. I'll offer a salute if that will help."

Nick shook his head, though he couldn't help the slight smile creasing his face. How typical of Fred's personality. "So, getting back to my original order—can I count on you, Sergeant Watkins, to help me find the guides we need?"

Fred righted himself and offered a salute, accompanied by a mischievous smile.

Nick waved him on. "Let's get going then. That fellow said his father owned the only store around here. I'm sure we can find it."

"Sure, I'll come along, Captain. There isn't much around here to keep me busy. It will be a few days before the boys arrive."

Nick reached for his boots and jammed them back onto his feet, ignoring the pain of having his toes crammed once more into a tight space with no room to spare. He and Fred then started across the tall fields of grass, inhaling the fresh air. What a pleasant place this was, even if it was West Virginia. No, the mountains weren't like the Rockies, but they were mountains in their own right and quite beautiful. Especially the site where they would be training—nearly nine hundred vertical feet of jagged stone.

Looking back at the face of Seneca Rocks, Nick felt a sudden desire to head over there with his gear and begin climbing. He could tell Fred they needed to try out some climbing routes before the troops arrived.

Nick refused to think about what might happen to them once their training was complete. For all he knew, they could be shipped to Europe, perhaps never to return. He held the idea of that possibility down in a deep reservoir inside himself, along with his fear of the unknown. He would take it one day at a time. And right now, his job was seeking out the young woman in the overalls—and perhaps her ill-mannered boyfriend—to find out more about the rocks he planned to scale with his trainees.

As Nick and Fred walked along the main road, they received many stares from people in the automobiles that passed them by. One gray-haired woman tugged on her elderly husband's arm and pointed. "Look at the soldiers, Barnaby!" she exclaimed.

"We seem to be causing quite a stir with the local folks," Fred mused. "Like they don't know there's a war going on."

"Maybe they don't. This isn't Main Street, America. Look where they live, out in the middle of nowhere. They probably lead sheltered lives. I don't even know if there's a theater around here. And who knows if they get any of the radio broadcasts."

"Well, if they don't know about the war by now, then they really are living in a hole in the ground. Everyone's heard about Pearl Harbor."

Just then another automobile drove by. The horn honked, and the driver waved.

"See?" Nick pointed out. "There's some support to be had around here. Someone knows about us."

"It's probably the general, arriving incognito for a surprise inspection," Fred added.

Nick snickered. Soon they came to a fork in the road with a store sitting at the junction.

"There it is. Hopper General Store. That was easy." He inhaled a breath. "Now comes the hard part." He headed toward the establishment with Fred following close behind. Several young men standing on the front porch ceased their chatter and stared. A little girl ran to her daddy, pointing back at the soldiers. Nick felt as if he were an invader on these people's land rather than a defender of freedom. When they entered the store, an older woman was standing at the counter with several items. She turned and gasped at the sight of Nick towering over her. "Land sakes, what are you men doing here? Are the Japanese coming here?"

"No, ma'am. We're just here to do some training on the rocks."

"Whatever for?"

"Well, there are lots of rocks and cliffs over in Europe. So we're going to train our soldiers how to climb them so they'll be ready to drive away the enemy when the orders are given."

She blinked, looking as if she didn't quite comprehend what he was saying before finishing her purchase.

"I need your coupon for the sugar, Matilda," said the man behind the counter.

She opened her pocketbook and fumbled through its contents. "Oh dear. I must have left it at home. I'll bring it tomorrow."

The man looked at her and then at Nick and Fred. "Sorry, Matilda. Got to have it. We have military men among us. Need to go by the rules or it looks bad."

Fred laughed. "If I wanted to go into police work, I sure wouldn't be here." He paused. "Not to say this isn't a nice place, even if it is located in the middle of nowhere."

"We're pretty proud of our home," the man said, offering his hand. "Ed Hopper. I heard you boys were coming. Saw the announcement."

Nick breathed a sigh of relief. "That's good to know word got around. From what your son said, he didn't seem to know anything about it."

"Well, folks might know but sometimes it doesn't sink in. They kind of lead their own lives here, you see. So you met Allen?"

"By the river earlier today. He didn't seem too happy that we were on your land."

Ed Hopper waved his hand. He then shoved the sugar, canned meat, and other staples into a paper bag. "Bring that coupon tomorrow, Matilda, all right?"

"Thank you kindly," she said, sidestepping away from Nick and Fred.

"Allen doesn't know a good deal about what's happening," the father continued. "He's got his mind set on one thing. His girl. That's all he thinks about."

"Sure, that happens to many young fellows in love," Fred mused. "The captain here knows all about that. His girl didn't appreciate his first love. Mountain climbing, that is."

Ed smiled. "Around here we all like the mountains. They're a part of life. And I hope they do well for you."

Nick began to relax. At last God had led them to someone who not only understood the importance of why the soldiers were here but was giving them encouragement.

Suddenly Ed Hopper stepped out from behind the counter and fetched two cold sodas from a large red case. "Welcome to Seneca Rocks."

"Thank you, sir!" Fred said with enthusiasm, using the bottle opener mounted on the side of the counter, then taking a long swig. "That hits the spot."

"Mr. Hopper, we need assistance from someone who knows the rocks," Nick said. "Someone who could show us around, perhaps? I was hoping maybe your son and even his girl could help us out. They looked like they know this place pretty well."

"Well, Allen just left to run some errands for me in Elkins, and he'll be gone all week. Lucy knows the land around here. Lived here all her life, just like many of us. But I'm not sure her folks would take kindly to her traipsing off with military fellers all by herself."

"Certainly not, and I wouldn't want her to. What about her father? Could he be of help?"

"Sure. Dick Bland would help you out if he's not busy at the mill. They live up the road there, about a half mile. White house with a front porch. Can't miss it."

"Thank you. And thanks for the soda."

Ed nodded, turning his attention to another customer who had ventured forward to make a purchase. Nick and Fred wandered up the road. By the time the house materialized in the distance, the sun had begun its departure behind the ridge of mountains. Evening shadows seeped across the land. "We may need to continue this another time," Fred commented. "It'll be dark soon."

"We can at least introduce ourselves and see if anyone is willing to help." Nick slowly mounted the porch steps. A dog bounded out from behind the house and latched on to Nick's pant leg. "Hey!" he shouted at the snarling canine. "Ouch! Let go!"

Faces peered out from behind the parted curtains. He could hear the voices of boys calling for their mother. The door opened a crack and a woman peered out. "Can I help you?"

"Sorry to disturb you, ma'am," Fred began, removing his cap while Nick continued trying to shake his leg free from the dog's toothy grip.

"Carl, Jeepers got off his rope again!" the woman yelled. "Come tie him up!"

"Jeepers knows better than that," another female voice said as a young woman stepped out from behind the woman. She stopped short and stared. "You again! What are you doing here?"

"Lucy, you know these men?" the woman asked.

"No, Momma. Well, in a way. Allen and I—we—we saw them by the river earlier today." She lowered her head and stared down at her feet as if embarrassed to reveal the fact. Her damp overalls had been replaced by a fresh pair. Her hands now slid into the front pockets of her new overalls, where they remained.

"Do you need something?" the mother now directed to Nick and Fred as Lucy brushed by them to retrieve the dog. Nick couldn't help watching Lucy interact with the dog, speaking kindly to it, scratching the pooch around the ears as she led the dog away. Meanwhile, Fred tried to explain their need for a guide.

"I think you've come to the wrong place," the woman said. "We don't climb those rocks."

"I know about the rocks, Momma!" piped up a young boy.

"That's enough, Tim. It's getting dark and soon it will be time for bed."

"Momma!" he protested.

At this point, Fred yanked on Nick's sleeve and shook his head. "I think this is a dead end," he whispered, retreating off the porch stairs. "Sorry to have bothered you, ma'am. We'll ask around maybe in the morning."

She nodded and closed the door. The men turned to leave but not before Nick spied Lucy standing nearby, having completed her duty with the dog. "Sorry we startled you out there in the field today," he said. "I hope you didn't get hurt in the river."

"I didn't. Allen was the one who caused me to fall in the river."

Nick hesitated. "You go there a lot?"

She laughed. "All the time. I live here, you know. And our cattle graze right next to the Hoppers' land."

"Ever been up to the rocks?"

"Of course. They're wonderful. It's like a different world up there."

"Maybe you know someone who could help us look around for trails and climbing routes to the top?" he asked hopefully.

She shook her head. "I've never climbed them. They're too dangerous. You could fall off."

"Not with the right equipment. You'd be surprised what you can do these days." Nick felt Fred nudge him again. "Well, if you think of someone who could help us out, let me know. We're down at the camp in the field." Nick wheeled and headed for the road.

Soon the sound of Fred's silly singsong interrupted the quiet evening. "Do you know the rocks here, m'dear, oh m'dear? Do you know them? Do you know the river clear, m'dear, oh m'dear? Do you know them?"

"What are you doing?"

"I'm singing a ballad about an elite mountain climber and a mountain dame from the wilds of West Virginia, Captain."

"You've got some strange ideas roaming about in your mind, friend. I was trying to find someone who could help us."

"Of course, sir. I don't suppose we'll mention some of the other things you were trying to find out, too."

"You're right, we won't, because there wasn't anything. Besides, she has a boyfriend already. You saw him."

"Of course. Whatever you say."

Nick said no more, hoping Fred would likewise forget the whole thing. But he had to admit he liked the idea of knowing a young woman who enjoyed the mountains as much as he did. Donna had never set one foot on them. Lucy, as her mother called her, seemed to breathe them. Just as he did. He shook his head. There was no sense pondering it. They were only here a few weeks and then he would be gone. Where to, he didn't know. But there certainly was no time to think of another woman, not after his experience with Donna. Even if this Lucy loved the mountains. . .just like he did.

Chapter 3

Of course I would love to show you the rocks, Captain Landers. What? Alone? Well, it's not like we're really alone now, are we? God is watching over us. And I know we can find what you need to know, sure enough." Lucy then grinned her fullest, her teeth gleaming back from her reflection in the mirror. Her hand slid through the length of her bobbed brown hair. She smiled again, turned to one side, and smiled once more. *This is no good. I can't stand here pretending to have a man fall in love with me, dressed in overalls.* She went over to the wardrobe and pulled out a cotton dress. After taking off her blouse and overalls, she slipped the dress up and over her head and then returned to the mirror, grinning broadly at her beaming reflection. She took the folds of the dress in her hands and spun around. "Oh, this old thing? Well, thank you, Captain Landers. It's so nice of you to say so."

"Hee hee hee."

"Ah ha ha ha!"

Lucy whirled to find thirteen-year-old Carl and eleven-year-old Tim peeking around the door. "How dare you!" she shouted at them, throwing open the door. They scattered like squirrels, racing for the stairs.

"Can't catch us!" Tim shouted in glee.

"I don't plan to catch you. I have better things to do with my time."

"Yeah, like pretending that soldier is your sweetheart or something," Carl sneered. Then in a high, squeaky voice, his fist planted against his cheek, he continued. "Oh, honey, sure I'll take you to the rocks. Whatever your little ol' heart wants! In fact, let's just pucker up while we're at it!" He laughed. "Bet Allen gets real mad when he finds out."

"Why, you little snitch. Don't you dare say anything to Allen. And I—I don't even know the soldier anyway. I'm just having some fun." She shut the door, then turned back, staring at the mirror once more and the dress that hung on her thin form. Angry tears burned her eyes. She took off the dress, wondering what in the world had possessed her to put it on, knowing her two nosy brothers were always spying on her. Lucy hung the dress carefully in the wardrobe.

What was she doing, fantasizing about a military man like Nick Landers? She paused to think about that one. Like she told her brothers, she didn't know the first thing about the man, except that he was here to climb her beloved rocks.

On the other hand, she did know Allen inside and out—everything about him, it seemed. His likes and dislikes. His emotions. His internal battles that sometimes raged more than she cared to see. But to her, Allen was a friend. A childhood playmate. Someone she had grown up with. Not a hero by any means, though he had offered to give her his shirt after she had fallen into the river—not that the shirt would have made her feel any drier.

Allen had always been around. He'd once brought lilies from his mother's garden when Lucy was sick. He was always able to obtain supplies from the store for her family if ever the need arose. And she had agreed on a date at the soda fountain with him when he returned from Elkins, to go over some important news.

Lucy began to tremble. What if that important news signaled his desire for a deeper commitment between them—like marriage? "How can I marry Allen?" she said aloud. She couldn't even picture him as a father, taking up the reins of the family as the head of the house with her by his side. The picture she saw instead was the two of them sharing an ice-cream cone while climbing up to the viewpoint just below the rocky summit, chatting about the neighbors or sharing some memory from grade school.

Lucy put on her blouse and overalls once more. Slowly she went downstairs to find the house was empty. Everyone had disappeared. Momma had gone to help sew a quilt with the elderly Mrs. Sampson. The boys probably went next door to play with the neighbor's children. Daddy had left at dawn to work at the lumber mill. She was all alone.

Stepping outside, the bright sunshine greeted her from another pleasant summer day. Nearby in the corral, a horse nickered at her. A fine day for a ride. Maybe she could head toward Seneca Rocks, just to see what might be happening with the soldiers who had been arriving this past week. She had seen many trucks rumbling along the road, bringing men and equipment to the valley. "How about a ride, Maple Sugar?" she asked the tan-colored mare. The horse bobbed its head as if nodding in agreement. Lucy saddled the horse, one of two their family owned. Later that evening the boys would go round up the few head of cattle Daddy still owned. Momma often asked him when he was going to sell them. But with the onset of war, he'd decided to hold on to them as their bread and butter should things go awry.

Lucy rode Maple Sugar down the road, waved at the driver of an automobile who honked a friendly greeting her way. She passed the Hoppers' store, where the usual neighbors gathered on the porch to swap tales. Then she caught sight of the mountains, looming above her in all their grandeur, just as she'd seen them all her life. Seneca Rocks. What a spectacle to behold, and one that still caused her to draw in a breath of awe. A natural wonder chiseled by the hand of God. She couldn't fathom how the touch of His hand had made these rocks jut into the air. Nor could she comprehend how men like Nick Landers could go way up there and climb the rocky faces. The closest she had been to them was a point near the rocks where the forest opened to reveal a spectacular view. She was too scared to venture any farther. Now she couldn't help but marvel at Nick's bravery.

The thought of him made her guide the horse down the road. When Lucy reached the fields, she observed the array of green tents standing in rows, one after the other, as if the tents themselves were part of some vast company ready for inspection. The sight proved strange on a field normally occupied by cattle and horses. For now, the animals had been moved to a separate part of the pasture, behind a row of fencing. She wondered what Allen would think of this massive intrusion on the family land when he returned from Elkins.

Lucy dismounted and tied up the horse, ready to investigate the sight. Men moved about in groups, appearing like ants, hard at work at various tasks. About twenty of them were constructing a strange wooden contraption, the likes of which she had never seen. It looked to her like some gigantic beehive. *What could that be?*

Curiosity got the better of her. Momma often scolded Lucy for the way she snooped around, saying she was always far too interested in what was happening. Today was no different. Lucy simply had to know what they were building and why.

Approaching the outskirts of the camp on foot, Lucy was suddenly stopped by two guards. Their helmets boasted the large white letters *MP*. "Sorry, miss, but you can't come through here. This area is off-limits to civilians."

"But my friend owns this land," she said. "In fact, our cattle are grazing right over there. It's the Hopper family's."

"Sorry. It's the rules."

"Would it help if I said that Captain Nick Landers asked me to come?"

The two guards looked at each other. "You have proof of that?"

"He came just the other day to my house. He and some other man. They were looking for someone to guide them to Seneca Rocks where he's gonna be climbing. He told me all about it." She placed her hands on her hips. "If you don't believe me, go ask him yourself. Tell him Lucy Bland has come with information about the rocks."

The guards conversed with each other. Finally, one of them headed off in the direction of the wooden beehive. Lucy could see men exchanging words. One of the men stepped away from the group and straightened, as if straining to see in her direction. The man, dressed in a gray T-shirt and green pants, lumbered over, accompanied by the guard.

"Miss Bland, what are you doing here?"

Nick Landers looked even better than what she'd imagined that morning in front of the mirror. The T-shirt he wore displayed his strong muscles. Sweat glistened on his limbs and face. How she wished she were wearing that pretty dress instead of dingy overalls that made her feel unkempt and immature.

"Hello, Captain Landers. You said if I knew of someone who could guide you to Seneca Rocks that I was to find you."

"She's all right," he informed the guards. "Thank you." They saluted and moved off. "Okay, so who did you find?"

Lucy couldn't help grinning. She slid her hands into the pockets of her overalls. "Why, me, of course."

"You."

"Certainly. Who else?"

He scratched the top of his head. "I'm sorry, Miss Bland, but I don't think it would be proper for a fine young woman like you to take a bunch of gritty soldiers on a grand tour of the rocks. Not that I doubt your knowledge or experience. I was hoping maybe you had talked to your daddy or someone else about doing it. Or maybe an uncle or a friend. Even that fellow who was with you."

"Allen would sooner show you a copperhead, I think. We have a lot of them around here, you know. Good thing you all wear those boots. You never know when you might stumble onto one of them."

"I'll have to remember that, thank you. I guess you'd better not ask him then. Sure don't want any more hard feelings."

"He's gone to Elkins. Hey, what is that thing they're building?"

"What?" He followed her finger as she pointed out the large beehive in the distance. "Oh. You mean the corncrib."

Lucy laughed long and loud, which spawned a smile on his face. "That is no corncrib, Captain Landers. I ought to know what a corncrib looks like. That looks more like a huge wooden beehive. Or tower of some sort."

"I've never heard it called a beehive. That's a new one." He began to walk toward it.

Lucy followed eagerly, past some tents and a few soldiers milling about. They all stared at her. Some smiled. Others looked inquisitive, as if wondering why one of their training leaders was conversing with the likes of her. It felt strange to be walking through a military camp. Lucy had seen pictures of such things, of course. Now with soldiers and their equipment nearly in her own backyard, she felt as if the war had become very personal. In a way it left her anxious. With Nick by her side, though, she felt strangely protected, as if he might give his life for her if the enemy were to invade. She liked the feeling. Not that Allen didn't protect her at times or show his concern. But there were things about Nick that were different. His strength of purpose. His determination. He wasn't a friendly soul like Allen but someone completely different. And maybe by spending this time with him, she would find out exactly who he was.

"This is our corncrib, beehive, tower, or whatever you want to call it," he said rather proudly as he gestured to the officer supervising the construction.

The officer nodded, issued an order to his men, and the group moved away.

Lucy studied the contraption made of wood. "I'm afraid to ask what you might be doing with this, Captain Landers. Dare I?"

He smiled. "Dare away. We'll soon have plenty of green recruits who have never even used climbing gear, much less climb rocks like you have here. So we plan to have the boys first climbed the wooden tower to give them a feel for the ropes and the techniques involved in rock climbing. They'll learn how to climb and rappel while becoming familiar with the commands we use. Climbers need to understand all the technical aspects before making an actual climb along a marked pitch. That's a steep portion of a vertical rock that requires the use of ropes for safety. Or belaying, where a climber protects a fellow climber as he ascends by holding a safety rope."

Lucy listened intently. "I wouldn't need any fancy climbing gear to climb a tower like that," she said. Impulsively, she brushed by him, placing one foot on the wooden slats of the structure to begin hoisting herself up.

"Miss Bland, please don't go any farther," he said as he reached out to her. "I'm sure you can climb this without being roped in, but I don't want anything to happen to you. As it is, it's still not completed. Please come down."

Just hearing him speak such words of concern sent Lucy stepping back down off the wooden contraption, directly into Nick Landers's arms. She inhaled a breath, trying to steady the rapid beating of her heart.

Almost as quickly he stepped back, adjusting the cap he wore. "I guess that's enough excitement for one day," he said rather sheepishly. He glanced over at several men standing in the distance, observing them with interest.

Suddenly, a whistle pierced the air. "Fred," he muttered.

"What was that, Captain Landers?"

He shook his head. "Nothing, nothing at all, Miss Bland."

"Could you just call me Lucy? The last time I was called Miss Bland was by my sixth grade teacher who didn't like the way I wrote my paper on what I want to do when I grow up."

"What did you write about?"

His question caught her off guard. No one ever asked what she wanted to do with her life. At that moment she didn't know, either, except to go with Nick up to the rocks. "I'm not sure what I wrote. It was a long time ago. I guess what every girl wants. Be a wife and mother. Maybe a teacher or a nurse. That kind of thing. By the way, can I call you Nick?"

"Well, uh…" He glanced toward the men, including the one who had visited her house with Nick. They began to disperse under his glaring eye to engage in other duties. "I suppose while I'm here in camp, my title would be best. You see, I need the men to respect me, and using my rank helps accomplish that. It's a matter of military protocol."

"Of course," Lucy purred.

A bit of red filled in the tips of his ears, as if the familiarity of being on a first-name basis somehow made him shy. But Nick Landers was far from being shy when it came to life. His life seemed filled with adventure. What must he have experienced that brought him to this place and time, to begin training soldiers on Seneca Rocks? How she would love to know more about him. She didn't want to intrude on his privacy, yet she found him fascinating enough to want to know everything. "So what did you want to do back when you were in sixth grade?"

"What I'm doing right now. That is, anything to do with the mountains. Hiking them. Climbing them. Skiing them."

"People do those things here. I've never even been on a pair of skis. But I do like to climb mountains, using the trails, of course. That's why I thought I could help you and your men at Seneca Rocks. I know the area really well."

He smiled once more. "Lucy, I appreciate the offer, but again, I think it might be better if we find a man to help out. Not that you couldn't do it. I know," he added hastily. "I just don't want your father or that young man of yours coming after me with a shotgun because you're leading a bunch of rough military men up the side of a mountain."

Lucy giggled. "It's not like I haven't gone up the mountain with a man before." Now it was her turn to feel the warmth in her face and running down her neck. "What I meant to say is, Allen and I have gone up there near the summit of the rocks plenty of times."

"You mean you've gone up there with your boyfriend?"

"He's not my boyfriend. Not really, though he might think he is. We're just friends. We've known each other since we were born, practically." She shuffled her feet, her gaze taking in the rows of green tents before her. "So where do you stay? I hope not in one of those tiny tents."

"We have an officers' tent, one of the bigger ones. But I've stayed in small tents. Even went without a tent once, in a blizzard, of all things."

Lucy stared. "How did you keep from freezing?"

"Snow is actually quite an effective insulator. It kept me pretty warm. You can make a shelter of sorts with it. That's part of the survival techniques one should learn before going into the mountains."

Lucy considered the idea of camping in a tent made of snow and trembled at the thought. "I'm sorry, but a snow tent is not my idea of a fine shelter. I'd need a solid roof over my head in a storm like that. We get some good snows here. The mountains are very pretty with snow on them, especially Seneca Rocks. They look like upside-down icicles."

For a moment neither of them said anything. Nick's gaze wandered from her to the tent city and back again, as if he were preoccupied by something. How she wished she knew what he was thinking. Maybe one day those deep thoughts he had would become audible. At least he didn't seem to mind conversing with a girl dressed in overalls, although she would have preferred to be wearing a dress right now. Maybe one day she and Nick could make their escape to the viewpoint just below the rocky summit with a picnic lunch and take in the scenery together.

The man Nick called Fred came up then, tentatively at first, to show Nick some paperwork he had hidden behind his back. "You remember Fred—er, Sergeant Watkins, don't you, Lucy?" Nick asked.

"Yes. How are you?"

"Oh, just fine, miss." Then turning to Nick he said, "Excuse me for interrupting, Captain, but I have some things here I need to go over with you."

"I need to get going, Lucy. Duty calls."

"Of course. Thank you for showing me your, uh, corncrib–beehive contraption, Captain Landers. If you need anything now, just let me know. Anything at all. We all want to make you feel at home."

"Thanks. I appreciate it."

Lucy wandered off, looking over her shoulder at the men now jabbering away, about what she couldn't tell. Her feet were slow to return to where she had left Maple Sugar tied to a fence post. All good things must come to an end, though she wished they wouldn't. But she knew Nick was here for one duty and one duty only. It wasn't to make eyes at her. Or ask her out on a date. Or become her man. He was here to train his men. But things could change. Maybe after this meeting, Nick would feel differently about her. There were other mountains to conquer besides those he could see with his eyes. She would be most willing to have him climb the mountain of love with her if the opportunity arose.

Chapter 4

Whoever thought you would go for some mountain dame from the wilds of West Virginia? Then again, when you think about it, it makes complete sense. The mountains are your life. Why not have a wife from the mountains? It would be the perfect complement, like gravy with mashed potatoes."

Nick tried to ignore the gibes of his friend and concentrate on the tasks before him. Instead, Fred took every opportunity to make remarks about Lucy's impromptu visit. In Nick's eyes, Lucy was a young lady looking to make a friendly impression on the soldiers who had come to her valley. And yes, her visit had made an impression on him, though he would never let Fred know. "She was just being friendly. Let it go."

"Well, it looks to me like she considers a certain climbing captain more than just a friend," Fred continued. "You could see it. When she came here, you should have told her to leave, that you were too busy. Instead you gave her the grand tour and then some. An interesting way to feed an appetite, don't you think?"

"You must be missing Alice," Nick retorted, thrusting the paperwork into Fred's hands. "It's the only reason I can think of for this continued pestering of your CO. Unless there's some jealousy mixed in there, too?"

"Have you forgotten that I know you? That we went through blizzards and rocks in Colorado? That I saved your neck more than once, my friend if you remember?"

"That's why I make certain you're on the other end of the climbing rope, Fred. You've never let go, even when you've been tempted to, no doubt. So when's the last time you heard from Alice?"

Fred shook his head and strode off, muttering to himself. Nick knew he'd hit a sore spot by mentioning Fred's girl. For several weeks now, Fred had worried that Alice was about to send him a Dear John letter. Many of the men had received them or been dumped like Nick had when Donna discarded him like an empty milk bottle on the doorstep, all on account of his interest in mountain adventures. He rubbed his chin, thinking of Lucy's eagerness to show him anything having to do with the mountains.

What a difference between Lucy and Donna. Like night and day. Donna had become like a storm cloud. For certain, Lucy was like sunshine and he'd come all this way, to a beautiful place in the middle of nowhere in the wilds of West Virginia, before finally meeting her. If only he had met Lucy in Colorado, instead of Donna. Sadly, he would only be here for a few weeks and then the training would end. From there, he couldn't begin to fathom what might happen or where he might end up.

Nick pushed the thoughts aside when a line of soldiers marched up—the first of the raw recruits they would begin training in rock climbing techniques. With their youthful faces, they looked like schoolboys to Nick. They seemed fearful and anxious. All of them were probably wondering what they would be doing in the days ahead.

Several of the privates offered meager salutes to Nick. Fred began barking at them to stand at attention. "At ease," Nick said with an elbow toward Fred.

"Sir, excuse me, sir, but are we gonna climb that?" a baby-faced soldier inquired in a tremulous voice, pointing to the distant rocks.

"You certainly are, Private."

All of the recruits stared in shock and dismay. Some shook their heads. Assorted whispers filled the air. "No way can I do that." "Are they crazy?" "They can't make me do that. Fighting the enemy is bad enough."

"You'll do all of it and more. Sergeant Watkins and I are going to be there to guide you every step of the way."

"Excuse me, sir, but I was scared to even climb the loft in our barn."

Nick wanted to encourage the men with a verse that helped him when his courage waned. He straightened and placed his hands behind his back. "Men, I've done a lot of work on the rocks. I've been in snows higher than your heads. Through it all, I've come to believe in the protection of a mighty God over my life. I know He is with me. And I believe I can do all things through Him who gives me strength. Make that your motto in life, and you will surely succeed in everything you put your mind to. Like climbing these rocks."

Nick didn't know if the words affected the men, but he found strength just by speaking the verse. He indeed wanted to do all things but only through Him who imparted the strength he needed, even when the going got difficult. Like when he was lost, frozen, and nearly found his toes sacrificed to frostbite. Or had men freeze on the rocks or go off trail. And for himself, when love began to wane and he wondered what the future held, especially with the tide of war and not knowing how they would all be involved in this affair, the strength of that scripture sustained him.

"Now that that's taken care of, let's get you assigned," Fred said, giving Nick a sideways glance. Nick knew his friend disliked anything with a religious connotation to it. Much like his remarks about Lucy, Fred had often ribbed Nick about his faith. How could God let the Japanese bomb Pearl Harbor and kill so many sailors? Or let the Germans overrun countries and hurt innocent people like the Jews? At times Nick felt confused by these events, too. But he could not relinquish his faith, especially when it came to matters he did not understand. God had His purposes. As simple human beings, they could never understand the whole picture. Maybe Nick wouldn't understand this either until they were in Europe, driving away the enemy, liberating besieged towns. Maybe then he would understand it all.

Nick felt a new determination surge through him then, determination to conquer the rocks here and then the rocks in Italy or wherever the high command sent them. He would help the men overcome their doubts and fears. He would teach them how to rise to the occasion and overcome the mountains, both within and without. And they would march forth, proclaiming victory, setting the captives free.

When Fred returned from assigning the men to their respective companies, he plunked himself down. Nick had spread out a topography map before him to study the terrain. "So what was all that about?" Fred asked.

"What?"

"That display of religiosity before the men. C'mon, Nick."

"Captain Landers, Sergeant."

Fred threw up his hands.

Nick set down his pencil where he had been taking notes. "Look, I saw the fear in those young men's eyes. We need to come across as confident leaders if we want them to do things that maybe none of them have ever done before. And I know that without God, I couldn't begin to do the things I'm called to do."

"I'm just asking why you have to bring God into everything, Captain, sir. I thought we would keep religion separate from our duties here."

"Anyone who separates duty from God is foolish. Without God there is no sense of duty. You were the one commenting on the need for rules and regulations so we can defeat the enemy. If you can't believe and devote your life to a Higher Being, then why have rules in the first place? Why follow the high command? Why defeat an enemy? Why be good even? Why not do whatever you want?"

Fred stared. "Look, religious or not, you have to admit the Germans and the Japanese need to be run out of town. It doesn't take a belief in God to come to that conclusion."

"But why? What good does it do?"

"Maybe because your God didn't do a good enough job of keeping the bad guys from killing innocent people. Maybe He needs a little help running them out of town, maybe even off this earth." Fred muttered a few more choice words. "Anyway, what are we gonna do with these green GIs, Captain? Where do you plan on taking them, since we still need to plot out the climbing routes?"

Nick folded the map. "They are going to work on the tower with the other officers. You and I are going on a scouting mission come morning. We can head out early tomorrow, scout the route, and lay in the pitons."

"You mean by ourselves? What about that mountain dame who wanted to help?"

Nick pondered that silently. He would dearly love a guide, and yes, he wouldn't mind if it were Lucy. She seemed so eager to lend a hand. He recalled her large eyes, dark brown and misty, her lips parted, her cheeks colored pink, looking as if she might guide him to the ends of the earth if he asked. Maybe it was just infatuation on her part, as Fred claimed. Right now he was only interested in what needed to be done. His duty, the duty of seeing these men trained for whatever mission the military sent them to complete. And if Lucy could help him accomplish this task, so be it.

He shook his head at Fred's inquiry, which bordered on teasing. "We have a map of the region. We know enough about climbing. We can figure out where to go, at least for now."

Fred chuckled. "I'm sure you would love an escort, but I guess we'll do what needs to be done."

Nick folded the map. "Lucy seems very intelligent and helpful, but that's it."

"You sure about that, sir? You two were getting along really well the other day."

"I was only feeding her interest in our operation. Nothing more. Remember, we need to keep the residents happy, to make friends when we can. We are invaders in their valley, so to speak. We need them on our side to be successful here. And as you well know, Lucy has a boyfriend who doesn't lack in his opinions." Nick began filling a green canvas backpack with some supplies. "So what do you say we head out early tomorrow morning and scout out the route?"

"I'm at your command," Fred acknowledged with a half-hearted salute.

Nick frowned. He hoped in the coming days Fred would show him the respect deserving of his rank now that the men had arrived. He hadn't minded the laxness in previous adventures together. They had been through quite a bit, from the time they both were caught on the mountain in a Colorado blizzard and survived in a snow cave. There, Nick had thrown titles and rank to the wind. But this was different. The men would be watching their every move when it came to tackling the rocks, especially when it came to respecting the chain of command and following orders. Leadership and discipline were crucial to making all this work. That and plenty of prayer.

—⁓—

Nick lay in his tent that night, listening to the raindrops splatter on the canvas like tiny feet. In one corner of the tent, the dampness had already begun to seep inside. Fred elected to stay in a separate tent rather than force Nick to share it with a lowly enlisted man, as he put it. Nick wanted to tell Fred to come join him but knew the separate quarters were in keeping with protocol now that the soldiers had arrived. Still, he missed the man's camaraderie and their conversations about their adventures in Colorado. Nick found himself alone in this massive tent with only his thoughts to keep him company as the rain fell harder.

He rolled over on the narrow cot, careful not to tumble to the ground below. He could think of more pleasant places to be, especially when stuck in a tent that did not keep the elements at bay. But he'd suffered through worse in his life. Like the snow shelter he once constructed to stay alive. Or the other tents he'd found himself in, perched on some rocky outcropping high in the Colorado Rockies, wondering if he might be found frozen to death come morning.

All were part of his survival skills and training that had eventually led him to the Mountain Training Group. He loved the adventure, but he wondered where it was taking him on this path of life and where he would end up. This could very well provide Nick his ticket to the front, from what he had been hearing. Rumors flew that the United States would soon become embroiled in the war in Europe. Already, troops were beginning to amass in Britain once their training was completed. It would be a long and nasty conflict, driving a fierce enemy from lands it had conquered over the last few years. There was no time to think about life here. Like relationships. Marriage. Family. It seemed so out of reach, even if the conversations with Lucy and seeing a glimpse of her home life brought it to the forefront of his mind. The war did affect some of the people here but not nearly as much as those training for it. Lucy, her young man, and the other members of her family lived their lives apart from it all. Certainly the army's presence gave them a taste of reality. But Lucy didn't seem to mind having them here. In fact, she was quite willing to embrace it as part of life, and Nick with it.

The wind began to shake the tent. Raindrops flew and settled on him. He pulled the scratchy wool blanket over his head to protect himself from the dampness. If only he had the materials to construct a barracks. But that was impractical, given the short amount of time they had here. He wondered then what Donna would say about his rustic accommodations. He could picture her face wrinkling up, her nose in the air.

"This is perfectly awful, Nick!" she would say. "How can you sleep in some tent with the rain leaking in and everything? You'll catch your death of cold, maybe even come down with pneumonia or something."

And then he imagined Lucy's reaction.

"Here, Captain Landers. This is just what you need." She would then produce a large umbrella to situate over his head.

Nick laughed in spite of his circumstances. *Yes, that's exactly what she would do.* And the next day she would trudge alongside him, through the muck and the mire created by the rains, then across the swollen river to the rocks that she loved. Maybe he should seek out her help. So it wasn't very becoming for her to tag along with two rough men. But acting as their guide, it wouldn't be so unseemly. She knew the Seneca Rocks area. He could learn a great deal and make the time here easier.

The rain finally began to let up, but Nick still felt damp. The situation was not pleasant, but his thoughts were. Thoughts of Lucy warmed him more than anything he could think of at that moment.

The next morning, bright sunshine greeted Nick as he emerged from the tent, tired from the lack of sleep and a night of contemplation. Fred met up with him, toting his backpack, ready for the scouting expedition to the rocks.

"All they have is baby food around here this morning," Fred grumbled, referring to the cereal issued for the breakfast. "What I wouldn't give for a plate of ham and eggs. Bet the families around here know how to put on a good meal. How about that mountain dame's family? Maybe we can head over there, plead starvation, and ask them to give us some good food? I mean, she likes you and all."

Nick said nothing as he adjusted the belt around his waist that contained the equipment for the day's expedition. He slipped a pair of binoculars over his head.

"You gonna eat anything, Captain? Can I get you some of that great food?"

"I'm not hungry," Nick said. "Just tired. The tent leaked last night."

Fred hooted. "You should have stayed in that warm building in Elkins with all the other COs, Captain. You'd be living it up just fine."

"Then I wouldn't be available to accomplish our mission here. Let's get going."

Fred shrugged and accompanied him. A mist hung over the open fields beyond the encampment. Sunshine made the droplets of rain glisten like jewels on the grass. The scents of the land came out in full force after the rains. Everything was fresh and new. If Nick must suffer through a drenching night in a soggy tent to witness the wonder of a new day, he didn't mind the storm in the least.

"Land ho!" Fred suddenly called out.

Nick readied his binoculars. "What? Did you find something already?"

"At ten o'clock, Captain. See for yourself."

Nick looked through the binoculars. First he saw woods, the grassy fields, and then a few cows. Working among the cows, he saw two figures in overalls. "What about it?"

"Looks like mountain people to me. Maybe even that dame you like so much. And it looks like she's ready to lead you into the wild blue yonder after all."

Nick handed the binoculars to Fred. "Take a look for yourself, Sergeant. Looks to me like two young fellows doing their morning chores." He began to walk swiftly across the field, refusing to glance back at the cattle or the people hard at work, hoping he would appear invisible. Right now he had a job to do. "Let's keep going. Hopefully, they won't see us."

"Mister! Hey, mister!" a young voice shouted from across the field.

Fred eyed Nick. A smile crept across his face. "So much for slipping past unnoticed, Captain."

Two young boys ran swiftly toward them, their eyes wide. "Are you the men who are gonna climb the rocks?" one asked breathlessly.

"In a few days. Right now we're just doing some scouting and topography work."

The boy scrunched up his face. "What's that mean?"

"We're finding out the lay of the land, elevation changes, things like that." Nick withdrew his map and compass. "These tools help us figure out where to go. Then we hope to find a good climbing route up the rocks."

"Wow. Hey, we know about the rocks 'cause we live here. I'm Carl Bland. This here's my younger brother, Tim."

Nick straightened in interest. "You wouldn't happen to be Lucy's brothers?"

"Sure are! Hey, are you the soldier she's taken a shine to?"

Fred chuckled, even as Nick felt his throat constrict and his face heat up. "I'm not sure what you mean by that. Your sister just stopped by the camp as a friendly gesture. There doesn't seem to be that many friendly faces around here."

"Lucy's real friendly. You don't have to worry about that. So are you heading to the rocks up there?"

"Yep, got some routes we need to plan out. We'll be taking the men climbing very soon."

"Wish I could do that," Carl said wistfully. "You think you could teach me how to rock climb sometime?"

Nick smiled. "Wish we could, young fellow, but as it is we have our hands full with these enlisted men, many of whom are not happy about climbing. I think it will take us time to get them acquainted to it all. The techniques, the equipment..."

The boys began peppering them with questions about the equipment needed to scale the rocks. Nick shook his head, explaining that they needed to get going, but maybe sometime they would like to come and watch one of the exercises.

The boys' faces brightened at this suggestion. "Sure thing!" they both said at once. "That would be great."

When the two boys had scampered off, Fred laughed long and loud, as if he had just witnessed a great comedy act. "It seems to me, my dear Captain, that you are linked to this Bland family in more ways than one. There's just no escaping them, is there?"

Nick wanted to contradict Fred but could not. In fact, he couldn't help silently agreeing.

Chapter 5

Lucy wiped the sweat from her face, which had already begun accumulating from the warm summer day. Momma had given her instructions to do the gardening that Lucy had allowed to slip these past few days. Not that she wanted to admit her preoccupation, but ever since the soldiers had arrived in the valley, her thoughts turned to them night and day. When she arrived home from the personal tour Nick had given her of the camp, Momma immediately confronted her, especially at seeing the rip in the knee of her overalls.

"What are you doing, Lucy? First you get your overalls wet, and now they're ripped."

Lucy looked at the tear in dismay, realizing she must have done it on that corncrib or beehive or whatever the contraption was that Nick showed her. If he had let her, she would have proven herself on the thing, showing him there was more to her name than Bland, that she could do whatever he asked of her and more. Perhaps she could still convince Nick to allow her to help them navigate the rocks, if he would just forget the notion that having her along was unseemly. She was up to the challenge. Maybe if she convinced him of her outdoor skill, he would think her worthy enough to pursue. Maybe he would suggest an outing to the picture show or the soda fountain in Petersburg.

Lucy stuttered as she tried to explain to her mother how she had ripped her overalls unknowingly. Lucy then fetched the sewing box and immediately set about mending the tear. "I think I'd rather wear dresses from now on," she informed Momma. "Overalls are getting too hot with summer here."

"You *are* going to wear overalls when you do the gardening, aren't you? I need the last of the broccoli picked today and the tomatoes hoed. The weeds are already crowding them in."

Lucy sighed in exasperation. At times she wished she had her own home to look after. She was twenty, after all. Plenty old enough to be married and caring for a place. Staying here with two rambunctious brothers underfoot and being under the watchful eyes of her parents was getting to be too much. When would they allow her to venture out on her own, to make something of her life? She'd once asked Daddy if he would teach her how to drive, hoping it would give her some freedom. He thought up some excuse, even suggesting that Allen could teach her one day, maybe after they had tied the knot.

Lucy cut off a large broccoli head and placed it in the basket. She shivered at the thought. Marrying Allen was the farthest thing from her mind. She hoped that somehow his business at Elkins would keep him beyond the week he had said he would be gone. *What a thought, Lucy,* she chastised herself. *Allen has been a good friend. A good friend, yes, but never a man like Nick. Dear Nick, broad-shouldered and handsome, standing there in his gray T-shirt.* She sighed. *A picture-perfect man with whom to spend a lifetime.*

"Lu, hey, Lu!" a voice cried out.

Lucy twisted around to see Carl running up with Tim following close behind. "You know you're never supposed to call me Lu!" she shouted back, picking up the basket of broccoli heads to take back to the house.

"Ha! Then I won't tell you who we saw today in the pasture."

She hesitated. "Who?"

Carl gave her a sheepish grin. "Wouldn't you like to know? What will you give me if I tell you?"

"How about I tell Daddy what you're up to and let him tan your britches?"

"You don't scare me, old Lu-Lu. If you knew who it was we talked to, you'd be hightailing it over there faster than any jackrabbit. Wouldn't she, Tim?" He poked his younger brother.

"What, you mean that soldier she likes?"

Carl pushed him. "You weren't supposed to blab! It was our secret."

Lucy nearly dropped the basket. "You mean you saw Nick? I mean, Captain Landers?"

"I don't know his name. There were two of them. They were gonna go scout out the rocks."

"What did he look like, Tim?" She coddled her youngest brother. "C'mon. Buy you a grape soda at the store if you tell me."

"Don't say a thing," Carl warned.

"He wasn't anyone special," Tim said. "Just some soldier. But he asked if we were your brothers. And he talked about you visiting the camp. When did you go, anyway? And how come you didn't take me? I'd love to see everything, like the guns and trucks and stuff."

Lucy never answered his question. Instead she raced back to the house, forgetting everything, even the basket of broccoli and the faint voice of Tim asking when she was going to buy him that bottle of grape soda. *This might be my only chance to see Nick while he is scouting the rocks. I know he doesn't want me there, but if I go, he'll have no choice but to let me come along. Then I'll get to spend more time with him.* She struggled out of the overalls and blouse, rushing into the bathroom to wash up. Her face was marred by dirt. Dark circles surrounded her eyes from her sleepless night of reminiscing about the encounter at the camp. Every waking moment seemed to be filled with visions of Nick Landers. Why, she didn't know. This might give her the opportunity to find out. She had to know if God was drawing them together or if she truly was lost in a maze of wild emotion.

Lucy threw open the doors to the wardrobe and settled on a navy print dress. No overalls for this venture. She must look nice if she had any hope of grabbing his attention. She fingered the material for a moment before slipping it over her head. She and Momma had sewn the dress for church wear. She loved the way the skirt flared and the belt accentuated her slim waist. She hoped Nick would love it, too.

Lucy picked up her purse, ready to head down the stairs, when she suddenly stopped. *What am I doing? Those men are heading for the rocks. How can I climb a hillside wearing a dress?* She sighed in exasperation and returned to her room. Reluctantly she put her blouse back on, then the overalls, even though they were covered in dirt from her work in the garden and had a mended knee. This is how she would appear to Nick—Lucy Bland, in her customary overalls, her hair tied up in two ponytails, but with a heart willing to do anything for him. She hoped he would look beyond her appearance to what lay inside.

At the last moment she sighted the blueberry muffins she had made for breakfast. One by one she put them in a basket when Carl and Tim rushed into the kitchen.

"Hey, I'm hungry," Tim shouted.

"Don't take them all, Lu!" Carl protested. "Give me some."

"Here, you can each have one. I'm taking them over to the soldiers. I'm sure they have a hankering for some fresh baked goods. Army food must be nasty."

"You just want that Nick person to turn sweet on you," Carl said, spitting out muffin crumbs as he spoke.

"And you just want to make a nuisance out of yourself."

"At least we told you about him," Carl reminded her. "Or rather Tim spilled the beans about it."

"Yeah, and you still have to buy me a grape soda, Lu," Tim added, his mouth full of muffin.

"You keep calling me Lu and you won't get anything." She covered the basket with a hand towel. "Don't tell Momma where I've gone." She knew that wouldn't happen, but she still hoped to avoid more confrontations, especially where her mother was concerned.

On her way down the road, she waved to a passerby riding a bicycle. Above her, Seneca Rocks reigned supreme with the gray and black stone against the backdrop of a sapphire sky. She envisioned herself and Nick perched near those rocks, singing a hymn to God and enjoying each other's company. "Rock of Ages" would seem appropriate.

Lucy paused. She hadn't even considered whether Nick was a Christian. Momma talked a great deal about finding a husband who trusted in their Lord and Savior. She had no idea if Nick felt the same way. If he didn't, what would she do?

I'll just have to convince him, that's all. Invite him to church. Have the pastor speak to him. Pray like crazy. She grew nervous just thinking about it. How sad it would be if she found out he wasn't a Christian and all this had been in vain. The feelings she had. The sleepless nights. The blueberry muffins that Momma was sure to wonder about when she found them missing, knowing that sugar was a prized commodity. *He must be a Christian,* she reasoned. *He is a nice and courteous man, after all.* Lucy knew quite well that being nice didn't make one a Christian, not by any means. As the pastor often said, "No one does good, not one. All our works are but filthy rags, lest you've put your faith in the Lord Jesus." Yet there were things about Nick that led her to believe he might be. *Oh Lord, I pray Nick has put his faith in Jesus. Lord, please show me his true heart.*

Lucy looked up at the rocks, wondering where the men might have gone. She sighed, hoping her brothers hadn't made up some wild tale about meeting the men. She wouldn't put it past them to do such a thing, especially the way Carl had been teasing her these last few days. Lucy searched for a place to ford the North Fork River, choosing the same rocky area where she had taken a spill before meeting Nick. Using a large stick, Lucy maneuvered her way across the slippery rocks, some teetering beneath her feet. She murmured a quick prayer for safety and, in particular, the safety of the muffins she was sure would win Nick's heart. Once across, she ventured up the foot trail she and Allen had used many times to access the viewpoint just below the summit of Seneca Rocks. There she caught sight of two military men about halfway up the hillside, surveying the terrain.

Suddenly they wheeled about. To her astonishment, one drew a pistol and aimed it in her direction. "Who goes there? Identify yourself!"

Lucy froze for an instant. She dropped her stick and scampered back down the trail, too scared to even think.

"Put that away!" a voice shouted. She then heard, "Wait a minute!" echo down to her, accompanied by the sound of footsteps.

Her limbs shook. Perspiration dripped down her face. Dizzy and weak from fright, she felt she might faint. *Don't look back! Oh God, please help me! Please don't let him shoot me.*

"Lucy? Lucy, please wait!"

She heard her name and stopped. The voice belonged to Nick. His face was etched with concern. "I'm sorry about that. Fred overreacted. Guess he's getting ready to meet the Germans or something."

"Like there are enemies around here, Captain L–Landers," she sputtered, trying to catch her breath. "How can you scare a person like that?"

"I didn't even know Fred had his pistol on him. Please, it's all right."

She plopped down on a rock by the edge of the river, breathing rapidly. "I've never had a gun pointed at me," she murmured, wiping a stray tear from her face. "Daddy would go hunting, but that was just to get a critter or two. I'm not used to all this, you men in your uniforms, pointing guns, making wooden towers. It's like what Allen said. We've been invaded."

"I'm sorry, Lucy," he said again. A second pair of footsteps approached—Nick's friend Fred, whom Lucy was beginning to dislike more and more.

"You scared her to death," Nick told him.

"Well, she sure didn't do anything to announce herself, Captain. Sorry about that."

Fred had tucked the pistol back into its holster, but Lucy couldn't keep her eyes off it, wondering if he really would have used it on her.

"I didn't know I had to announce myself in my own hometown and in my own country," she told the man flatly. "After all, you're the ones who are trespassing here with your trucks and your tents everywhere. Now you're pointing guns at civilians."

"Well, if you had just—"

"Sergeant Watkins, do you mind?" Nick interrupted. "We left our topography materials up there on the ridge. Go ahead and finish plotting the trail on the map, and I'll catch up with you."

Fred stared at Nick, then Lucy. He gave a stiff salute, wheeled on one foot, and marched back up the hill. Lucy dried one last tear as Nick slid onto a rock beside her.

"I'm sorry again for what happened, Lucy. I hope you'll forgive us."

His close proximity and gentle words imparted comfort. *Nick, I would forgive everything, especially if you put your huge arms around me.* She cast the thought aside and surveyed the river flowing gently by on its way to a much larger river. Actually, she was glad his friend had pointed the pistol. She soaked in Nick's concern for her like parched ground absorbing the gentle rain. How nice it was to have someone so apologetic and caring sitting close beside her. If only she knew what else made up the man who called himself Nick Landers. What were his hopes and dreams? His plans? He had an aura of ruggedness about him, as if the mountains and he were one. He was bold and adventuresome. He scaled great heights. He camped out in blizzards. But what were his thoughts on life? And love? And did he trust in the Lord of heaven and earth?

"You look like you're deep in thought," he observed. "I'm not sure what else I can say to calm your worry. Unfortunately, you will probably see more things around here that might alarm you. We are instructed to take the utmost care among the civilians. We will only do what is necessary but with your safety in mind. I know the display you saw doesn't give you much confidence, but I hope my apology helps in some way."

"It helps a little, thanks." She opened the basket to show him the blueberry muffins. "I thought army food might be getting to you right about now, so I brought these."

"Why, thank you!" he said with enthusiasm, helping himself. "This is terrific."

"So you really like to rock climb?" she suddenly asked, picking up a rock and tossing it into the river.

"I love it. I've scaled plenty of rocks, some a lot more challenging than these here. I just have to convince the new GIs that they can do it, too."

"Where else have you climbed?"

"The Rocky Mountains. That's where I'm from. Colorado, to be exact."

"I've never been anywhere except here. I've studied other parts of the country, in school. Someday I would like to see the ocean and many other places. But I don't know if I will ever leave here."

"Why not? You have to leave sometime. There's so much to see. God made a great place when He made the United States. Maybe you'll even get to Colorado someday."

Lucy inhaled a swift breath, glancing at him out of the corner of her eye to see the sincerity in his face. He had mentioned God. Not that this was a sign of his Christianity, but at least he didn't shun the name of God. He spoke it quite naturally, in fact. *Oh Lord, can it be? Is he a Christian?* "I know I often think about how God made Seneca Rocks. The rocks here are different compared to other mountains. They look more like scales on a lizard."

Nick chuckled. He glanced over his shoulder, toward the rocks high on the hillside behind them. "It is amazing. I think of the Rocky Mountains, too; a whole line of them with ridges one after the other in a rippling effect. On the summits it can snow year-round."

"You talked about staying in some kind of snow shelter. I can't even imagine it, though I know some Eskimos way up north live in igloos. Imagine, homes built out of big blocks of ice. Did you ever want to live like that?"

Nick laughed. "No. A snow shelter for one night is enough for me. As it is, I do miss a good, sturdy shelter. My tent leaked during the storm last night—made me wish for a solid roof over my head."

Lucy shook her head. "That's awful. Once our roof leaked, and Daddy was up there at once, fixing it. Thankfully only the rug got wet. I can't imagine sleeping in a damp bed. Were you cold?"

"No. Fortunately it's summer. I wouldn't have wanted it to be leaking during freezing weather, though."

Lucy fell silent, thinking of Nick shivering in some cold, leaky tent. "Wish I'd known—I would've brought you an umbrella," she remarked.

His sudden laugher made her jerk around in a start. "Now that is very funny, Lucy. I have to admit, while I was lying there, I thought about that very thing. What's the one thing Lucy Bland might have brought me in a storm like this? A good old umbrella to hide under."

Lucy stared in amazement and awe. Nick had been thinking about her in his time of trial, with the rain beating above his head and leaking over his bed? This was more than she could have hoped or dreamed. *Oh God, I'm in heaven. Just to know that Nick thought of me coming to his aid.* And here she thought she'd made a feeble impression on him that day in the camp. More of a nuisance than anything. He must have seen something redeeming in her, worthy enough to think of her in the darkest night as if she were a lamp set high on a hill.

Nick looked sheepishly toward the river. He sat there in quiet contemplation while the river rushed by. "Ever go fishing?" he finally asked.

"Sometimes. We get trout mostly. Sometimes bass."

Again they sat in silence until a holler came from the hillside. "Sounds like my sergeant found something good," he said, slowly standing to his feet.

"I could take you up to the viewpoint near the top of the rocks," she offered once more. "You can see the whole valley from there. I know the way."

"How about you point me in the right direction?"

"Okay. Follow the trail you've been on. You'll come to a fork. Take the right trail. It starts getting kind of steep just before it comes out on the rocks."

"So the trail only goes to the top of the rocks?"

"Well, not all the way to the top. The rocks are too narrow at the top for that. But it does end at a pretty viewpoint. You can see everything."

"I was also hoping for a trail that went to the base where the rocks begin. The sergeant and I were going to check out climbing routes up the rock faces. The pitches I talked about on our tour, remember, where you need ropes to climb?"

"You'll have to go downriver for that, beyond where the cattle are grazing. Another trail goes to just below the rocks. I haven't been there in a long time, though. I always go to the viewpoint."

"Thanks, Lucy. Without you, this whole day might have been wasted. Though I'm sure the view from up top is great, we do need to check out the other trail." He stretched his arms over his head. "I'd better go find my sergeant." She watched Nick ascend the trail effortlessly, calling for his companion. He was tall and strong, like a great tree gripping the hillside, unmoved by the wind and rain. She thought of leaving them to their venture and returning home but instead waited for them to come down. Even if he didn't want her guiding them to the rocks, she could still show him the cut-off trail. Maybe one day all this would point the way for his heart.

When the men came stumbling back down the trail, Fred complained of twisting his ankle on the steep terrain. "If this is any idea of what we have to face, Captain, I'm not sure anyone is going to be able to do it."

"Of course you will," Lucy said, standing to her feet. "If I can do it, anybody can."

Fred glanced over at her, his face flushed. "Didn't realize you were standing there, missy. I thought you'd gone back to your horses and cattle."

"I thought maybe I could at least show you where the trail is, Captain Landers. If that's all right."

Nick nodded. "That's a good idea since Sergeant Watkins here probably couldn't make it if we had to traipse around looking for it."

"Old Sergeant Fred is just fine and dandy, Captain, sir, even if my ankle is a little sore. I can do whatever you need." He shook his leg and began to cross the river, followed by Lucy and Nick.

Lucy felt Nick close behind her, like a strong shield ready to protect her from harm. How she wished he would suggest a date somewhere—to the theater or even a walk in the cool of the evening. Instead, he waited on her as she led the way downriver. "I haven't been there much," she said. "Maybe once or twice." She paused, pointing to a trail opposite the river. "There it is. Sorry you have to cross back over the river again. And there aren't many stepping-stones, so it will be deeper here."

"We should have stayed on the opposite side of the bank and bushwhacked to the trail," Fred grumbled. He plodded headlong back into the river. Water nearly came up to his knees. "Always wanted to see if my boots could float. Guess they'll get a good test."

"Thanks for your help, Lucy," Nick offered with a smile.

Lucy sucked in her breath at the sweet way he said her name. Gently, with tenderness. Without even thinking she blurted out, "Do you ever get time off, Captain Landers? Like in the evenings? I mean, I'm sure Momma would be happy to have you over for dinner sometime. Daddy would like to hear any news you have about the war."

He hesitated, then shook his head. "With the recruits here, I'd better stick close to camp until everything is set with them. But thanks for the invitation."

Lucy dug her hands into the pockets of her overalls, hoping to conceal her disappointment. "Oh, sure, I understand." She gave a lopsided smile as he began his trek across the river in pursuit of his friend. *Lucy, why couldn't you be more patient?* she lamented silently. *Now he thinks you're some brazen woman.* All the encouraging thoughts she'd had about their encounter quickly faded. She tried not to let the tears surface as she turned away, refusing to look back at the men. *God, maybe we are too different and this is just a silly dream of mine. But, oh, I do like him. Only You can make my dream come true, if I'm patient enough to let You do the work. Dear Lord, help me wait on Your timing.*

Chapter 6

Patience was a virtue, or so she had been taught. Patience when life threw curve balls and she was trying to catch them. Patience with Nick Landers. Ever since meeting him, Lucy felt like she was chasing curve balls. While she believed Nick did have an interest in her, at the same time he held himself back, as if unwilling to move forward. Maybe he already had a girl back in Colorado. Or he wondered about Allen. Or because he knew he would only be here a few weeks and pursuing a relationship was not something he had the time or the will to do. If only she could read his thoughts and determine where his true feelings lie. After all, she had been in his thoughts that rainy night. She perceived a sincere look in his eye and heard the gentleness in his voice. She cupped her cheek with her hand. Maybe all this was some dream without any basis in reality. But to her, Nick Landers couldn't be more genuine, even if she still knew very little about him. If only she could discover more.

Lucy contemplated seeking him out again, but Momma had given her a list of unending chores to complete. More weeding in the garden. Mending the boys' socks. Going over to the store for some staples. She left that errand for last. Any day now Allen would be returning from his errand in Elkins. She hardly knew what she'd say if she saw him, even though she had agreed to meet with him when he returned. What if he sensed something was going on in her heart—that she had grown interested in another man? How would he react to such news?

Lucy didn't want to think about it as she unwound more thread to fix a hole in Tim's sock. Thankfully, Momma had gotten the boys out of her hair, charging them with the duty of cleaning out the barn. At times she thought she could hear them arguing. No doubt Carl was upset that Tim wasn't pulling his weight, as often happened when they worked together.

"You seem quiet today," Momma observed.

Lucy looked up. She hadn't even heard her mother come in, so soft were her footsteps. Either that or Lucy was completely preoccupied. No doubt the latter. "Oh, just thinking."

"I heard Tim and Carl talking about some soldier, the one who came here a few days ago, looking for a guide. They said you've been sneaking out to see him?"

Lucy put down the mending. *I'm gonna get them for that,* she thought, pressing her lips tightly together. "Momma, all I've been doing is making sure they know their way around here. That's why they came to the house the other day. They had no idea how to get to the base of the rocks, so I just showed them the trail."

"Hmm. That's not what Carl says, but he's also known to make up some interesting stories."

"Yes, he does." She returned to the mending, hoping her mother wouldn't notice her heated face.

"I do wish, though, that you had let Daddy know about them wanting to find the trails. I don't like the idea of you keeping company with men like that."

"They're just soldiers, Momma."

"Yes, but they are men, too. Far away from home and maybe even looking for trouble. I've already heard about one soldier in Elkins and how he was going after a farmer's gal. I won't even say what happened. But you are not to go to the soldier camp alone anymore. It's too dangerous."

Lucy sighed. "Momma, it's all right."

"Yes, it will be all right if you stay here and don't go traipsing off by yourself, at least not until Allen returns and can escort you. By the way, isn't he supposed to be coming back soon? The week is nearly up."

"Something like that," she answered carelessly, tugging at the thread with the needle. Her mother stared at her thoughtfully before moving off into the kitchen. Lucy sighed and stood to her feet, throwing the socks into the mending basket. At least she could deal with one matter right now—her unruly brothers and their big mouths, which had nearly landed her in the middle of another firestorm.

Lucy heard the rise of young voices debating about the work inside the barn when she entered. In the darkness, she nearly tripped over a pitchfork and rake. "What are you doing leaving these tools in the middle of the floor?" she shouted at them. "I could have hurt myself."

"Help me move this, Tim," Carl was saying, handling a wooden barrel.

Lucy came instead and helped Carl move it to the opposite side of the barn. "Now, would you like to tell me what you said to Momma about the soldiers?"

"Not a thing," he told her with a sly smile on his face.

"You know that isn't true, Carl Matthew. You've been blabbing to everyone about my business. And quite frankly, I'm getting tired of it."

"I just want to know when you plan on telling Allen that you've got another boyfriend."

Lucy ground her teeth. "I do not have another boyfriend. I was only helping guide the men to the rocks—if it's any of your business."

"I could have done that myself," Carl retorted. "I know those rocks real well. I've even done some climbing myself. I could tell them everything they need to know."

"You have never climbed them."

"Have so. Not with equipment and stuff, but I've gone up them. I know a lot more than you know. I don't know why you'd want to help them except to take peeks at the captain there."

"You're impossible! I'm warning you right now not to be telling Momma or anyone else my business. Or I'll tell Daddy what I saw in your room the other day."

Carl stood with his arms crossed. "What? You didn't see nothing. You're making it up."

"You know very well. A cigarette." Lucy turned on her heel, preparing to head out into the yard when she heard Carl call for her.

"Don't you dare say anything about that," he hissed. "I wasn't gonna smoke it. I–I'm keeping it for a friend."

"Sure you are." She held out her hand. "I think we have an agreement, don't we?"

Carl stared at her hand as if it were on fire before reluctantly shaking it.

"And you'd better get rid of that cigarette, too. All it does is make your breath bad and make you sick. It isn't glamorous at all, even if a lot of people do it nowadays."

Lucy whirled and returned to the house. At least she could claim a small victory, but to what end, she remained uncertain. She knew things were happening between her and Nick, and one day soon she would have to reconcile those feelings. For now she continued to dream about the future. *Captain and Mrs. Nicholas Landers. Mrs. Lucy Landers.* She paused. *Lucy Landers!* She shuddered. *Oh no. Two Ls.* She giggled. It didn't matter. She would be proud to carry that name as his wife. If only she could convince Nick, or more importantly, if God could change his heart toward her. There must be something there, after all. Nick had thought of her during that long, dreary night in his tent. If that wasn't the beginning of love, what was? Since the moment he'd revealed that fact, Lucy had clung to his words, even when doubt began to creep in and she felt a million miles from him—though the camp was only a mile or two down the road. She would recall how he thought of her in his most depressing hour. The thought sustained her more than anything else.

But with Momma knowing of her trips and the boys sticking their noses into her business, she would have to be more careful. Maybe she could volunteer to take in the cattle on the pasture adjoining the camp. Or feign a need to go to Petersburg that would take her right by the camp on the main road. Or what about writing Nick a letter? Carl and Tim would never know about it. Nor would Momma. There must be errand boys running from the store or other places to keep the camp well stocked with supplies. She could write the letter and have someone deliver it. Or try sending it through the regular mail. *Oh, why didn't I think of this sooner?*

Lucy immediately went to her room to locate paper and a pencil. She hadn't written much since her school days, but this day, armed and ready, the words just flowed out of her very being.

My dearest Nick,

    Oh, how I love to write those words because you are dear—dear to me, that is. I know you don't know much about me, but I feel like I have known you forever. And I do want us to be together. Whatever it takes, I want to become your wife. I would make you a wonderful home and be there for you always. No matter where we are or what happens, I am here for you and you alone.

Lucy paused to reread it. This type of letter would never do, at least in the stage they were in. She could just picture his reaction—his dark eyes widening, his cheeks turning ruddy as his sergeant friend teased him about some enraptured young woman of the hills with her claws in him. Lucy placed the letter in the drawer of her desk and took out another sheet of paper.

Dear Captain Landers,

    I'm not sure when I will see you again, but I wanted to thank you for all you're doing for our country. It makes me proud when I see men like you here to protect us. I know the training on Seneca Rocks will go very well, because I'm sure you're very good at what you do. The men are blessed to have you. If you need anything, I know our family would be happy to help. Thank you also for the tour of the camp. Maybe we will be able to talk again before you leave.

                          Sincerely,
                          Lucy Bland

She read it over and sighed. Cordial and considerate if not bland-sounding, like her name. In no way did it reveal her true feelings, but at least nothing in it should cause him to turn away. Maybe it would be enough to draw a bit of interest, to let him know that she wasn't some lovesick girl waiting for him to sweep her into her arms and give her a kiss. Even if she did feel that way.

Lucy slid the letter into an envelope and addressed it with the words *Captain Nicholas Landers, Seneca Rocks Camp.* "Now to find someone at the Hoppers' store who can deliver this."

Lucy changed out of her overalls and into a dress. She didn't want to go to the store to deliver an important note looking like a ragamuffin. She checked her appearance. For all she knew, Nick might even come by the store and she could hand him the letter personally. Maybe he would suggest a picnic by the North Fork River as a thank-you. *My, how my imagination can run away with me.* For now, she would relish in whatever came of this letter, even if he were to simply smile or send his own note of thanks. Any sign of encouragement would be welcomed with open arms and an open heart.

Lucy quickly headed down the road toward the store. As usual, Seneca Rocks stood before her in all its beauty. She wondered if Nick was yet climbing the rocky pinnacles. Maybe even now he was looking down at her from some lofty perch, staring through his binoculars. Maybe he saw her in the navy print dress and thought to himself, *Now there's a sweet dish I'd like to take somewhere—maybe to the movie house in Petersburg.* Lucy sighed. *If only.*

She mounted the steps to the general store, nodding at several neighbors who bid her a good afternoon. Ed Hopper gave her a huge smile when he saw her. "You're in luck, Lucy."

Is Nick in here buying something? She nearly popped the question before stopping herself. How could she even think of asking Allen's father such a thing when he knew nothing of the man? "Why is that, Mr. Hopper?"

"Allen just got in this morning. In fact, I'll fetch him right now. He'll sure be glad to see you. It's been Lucy this, Lucy that."

Lucy stared, first at the open door where Mr. Hopper had exited, then at the letter still in her hand. She tucked the envelope hastily in the pocket of her dress, just before the door opened and Allen rushed in.

"Boy, how I missed you, Lucy!" he said, curling his arms around her. "And don't you look nice! Wow, what a greeting. Makes a feller just want to come running home."

"Hi, Allen." She gave him a swift embrace before slowly stepping out of his arms. "So how was the trip to Elkins?"

"Boring, but don't tell Daddy I said that," he whispered. He took her hand, gently escorting her outside. "I just did the normal things. Checked out inventory for the store to see what's available and what isn't anymore with the war going on. But boy, Elkins is hopping."

"What do you mean?"

"Soldiers. I mean they are everywhere. It's like an invasion. In the stores. On the road. Asking directions. Some even had guns. I saw a few who claimed they belonged to that camp by Seneca Rocks." He looked beyond the parking lot of the store to the rocks. "I see they already have some kind of tent city set up down there."

Lucy tentatively touched the letter in her pocket. "Yes, they do."

"Have you been back there? What's going on?"

"Oh, nothing much. They plan on climbing the rocks. A couple of them came around asking if you wanted to help them find some climbing routes. In fact, they were the same two soldiers we met that day by the river."

Allen raised his eyebrow. "You mean the ones who drove that truck over my dad's land? I thought they would've hightailed it in the other direction after the meeting we had. Like I would show them where to climb. Ha!"

"Allen, they're only doing it to help our country. Nick says it's to train for the war in Europe. They are not here to cause harm but to help."

Allen stared at her quietly for moment or two. "Sounds to me like you've had more than just a little one- or two-word conversation with these GIs."

"Well, they came by the house, looking for a guide. What was I supposed to do, ignore them? I mean, they're fighting for our country. I think they deserve as much help and respect as we can give them."

"Well, I'm helping, too," Allen said defensively. "Trying to make sure you still have sugar and other supplies before they're all gone. And speaking of that, I got something for you while I was in Elkins."

Lucy prayed with all her might it wouldn't be what she feared. When he returned with a thin square package, she breathed a sigh of relief.

"I heard from some other shopkeepers that this kind of thing will soon be gone," Allen was saying as she opened the package to reveal a pair of nylons. "All the women like 'em and they are getting scarce. So I thought you'd want some. Got some for your mother, too, and mine."

"Thank you, Allen. That's real sweet of you." She gave him her best smile, all the while thinking what Nick would say if he saw her in a pretty polka dot dress complete with nylons and heels. She pushed away such a thought as Allen continued to stare at her.

"You look like you're a million miles away. So, are you up for going to Petersburg? We still have to finish where we left off when I had to leave for Elkins."

Lucy swallowed hard. "Actually, Allen, I have some chores to finish up at home."

"I'm sure that can wait. Especially if your mother knows I just got home. If you want, I'll go and ask her if it's all right."

Lucy bit her lip, imagining her brothers coming out of the barn to greet Allen and then spouting off to him what had happened this past week. She could see his ears turning red and a slow rage building inside him. Even if she did make an agreement with Carl not to say anything, Tim was known to speak up at the least provocation. He would tell Allen how she had sneaked out to the camp a couple of times to visit the soldiers. And she knew Allen would be upset if he found out. He wouldn't understand one bit. Oh, how she wanted to break down and tell him the truth—that she had fallen in love with Nick Landers, a man with hopes and dreams, a dazzling smile, and laughter that warmed her heart. But compared to Allen, she still knew so little about Nick. And she didn't know where Nick's heart stood, either. For now, any confession must wait.

"Really, I do need to finish the list Momma gave me to do," she said instead. "Maybe we can go another day. After all, you just got back from one trip. I don't think you'd want to leave on another."

"Believe me, this is a trip I've wanted to take for a very long time." He picked up her hand. "Maybe I should just come right out and say it now rather than later."

"Here?" She looked about nervously as customers drove up, exchanging friendly chatter with each other or heading into the store to make their purchases.

"You're right, this isn't a good place," he agreed. "Okay, we'll settle on a place and then I'll have your attention at last. What day?"

"What day?" Lucy repeated. Suddenly she caught sight of the mailman coming to pick up the daily mail. Again her hand tentatively touched the letter. "Excuse me just a minute, Allen." She rushed over to deposit the letter in the man's pouch. "I don't really have an address for this person," she told the man, "but he's at the army camp by Seneca Rocks."

"Just so long as his name's on it and he's at that camp, it will get to him."

Lucy nodded. When she returned, Allen was pacing with his hands stuffed inside the pockets of his trousers, looking at her curiously.

"That's one errand done," she said nonchalantly. "I almost forgot to mail the letter."

"Anyway, what day should we get together for our outing, Lucy? How about Friday?"

Lucy thought hard and fast. She could agree to a date and then have something come up. At least it would give her some time to think up a good excuse, if not the truth. Besides, if she didn't agree on a day, Allen would only grow suspicious that something had happened during his absence. She sighed. If only she were more confident about her chances with Nick, that he liked her as much as she liked him. But without that confidence, she had nothing to hold on to and everything to lose. And she didn't want to lose it all. "I think Friday will be good, but I'll have to let you know if something suddenly comes up."

"That's an interesting answer, but I guess I'll take it for what it's worth." He again took her hand. His thumb stroked her skin. "I really did miss you, Lucy. At least I won't have to go away now for a long time."

Lucy glanced back toward Seneca Rocks, hoping he wouldn't try to kiss her like that day on the porch. There was no doubt Allen was a sweet guy. She cherished their friendship, their rambles, and the times they played in the river or took walks up to the rocks. But she could not let go of the fact that he was just a friend to her. And in his absence she had met an honest-to-goodness man of flesh and bone with a kind spirit she loved. "You really are a million miles away," he said again. "Well, I need to go talk to Dad about the trip. I'll stop by and see you when I can. Hopefully next time we'll be able to talk more."

Lucy watched him meander back to the store, his head low, his feet scuffing up the dirt, clearly vexed by their meeting. She did feel bad misleading him like this. If only she could be sure about everything, that God would clear these muddy rivers, that she would know which direction to turn. *Oh God, I need to know somehow.* She took to her feet then, slowly continuing her walk down the road, gazing transfixed at the rocks before her and then the tiny green army tents in the distance. No doubt Nick had his hands full with all the new soldiers. She wondered if he had managed to find the routes he needed up to the rocks. She wondered, too, if he'd had time to think about her in the midst of his duty.

Just then she heard a whistle of appreciation. A truckload of soldiers came rattling down the road, some of them waving and calling out. Lucy looked away shyly. All this attention was new to her. Nick would never do anything so unseemly, but if he did whistle, it would be fine with her. It would give her something else to hold on to. *At least you will read the letter,* she thought, stooping to pluck a daisy by the side of the road. She twirled the flower in her fingers. *I would love to have sent you the first version, but maybe appreciation and encouragement will be enough to make something happen and soon. . .before Friday comes.*

Chapter 7

Nick glanced down at his dinner that night at the mess tent. He refused to say what others called the monstrosity served up on the aluminum plates—the slivers of dried beef in some sauce that tasted like wallpaper paste, all thrown over dry bread. Fred was quick to make the first comment about the unmentionable stuff served "on a shingle," and in front of the men, much to Nick's disgust. For himself, Nick stole away with the plate in hand, eating only a few bites before dumping the rest on the ground for the critters to consume. In no time a stray dog came wandering about the camp and ate Nick's meal in two huge gulps. Nick laughed, watching the hound lick his lips and wag his tail in the hope of a second helping.

"Believe me, you don't want to eat any more of that stuff," he told the dog. He missed the meals he'd enjoyed back at Camp Hale in Colorado. Sometimes it would be hearty beef steaks right off the Colorado range. Or chicken. Real beef stew. Chili. The cooks here were still trying to get adequate supplies lined up from the local farms. He had seen a few trucks come by with fresh produce. Maybe things would turn around and good meals would soon be forthcoming.

Right now Nick's stomach rumbled at the thought of Lucy's blueberry muffins. He missed them now more than ever. If only she would come by with a new batch, hot out of the oven, accompanied by her shy smile and dressed in her overalls as if ready for a ramble. Sometimes he would go out to the sentry post, salute the guards on duty, and casually search the neighboring fields with his binoculars for any sign of her. Much to his dismay, he always came up empty. He decided he had put her off that day by the river. She had been nice enough to invite him to a meal at her folks' place. Now he regretted not jumping up and agreeing to a wonderful home-cooked meal and with a real family to boot. What was he thinking? Even if she might have some kind of infatuation for him, what did it matter? Instead he had to contend with lousy camp food, Fred's obnoxious ways, and the green GIs commenting on the wooden tower they had to climb and wondering why they were forced to do things beyond their capability.

Nick came to his feet and again headed toward the sentry post. They would wonder what he was up to, most likely. He assured them, as he did most evenings, that nothing was amiss, and then he ventured beyond the camp perimeter to the fencing that separated the camp from the pasture. This night the fields were empty. The Bland boys must have finished their chores early. He wondered what their mother gave them to eat for dinner tonight. Maybe slices of smoked ham and heaps of mashed sweet potatoes that they washed down with cups of fresh milk.

Get a hold of yourself, Nick. Bad food is part of army life. But he couldn't get used to it, not after Lucy had begun spoiling him. And how did he return her favor? A slap on her wrist by some dissuading comment. Maybe he had offered a smile or two, but little else to show her how much her kind ways had affected him. Especially now when he had nothing.

"There you are!" a voice startled him. He turned to see Fred, still holding a plate of the evening fare, gobbling it down as if he had not tasted food in ages. "You sure got done eating in a hurry, Captain."

"It's not my favorite meal."

"What? You mean the..." he began, then proceeded to call it by the expletive the soldiers used to describe the dish.

"I could do without the cursing, Fred," Nick said.

"Oops. Pardon me, sir. You know I'm not holy like you."

"Believe me, by myself I am not holy. But my trust in God help make me holy. Not by anything I can do. It's by His grace alone."

Fred rolled his eyes. "Here we go on another religious ramble. Must we do this, sir?"

"Sorry, but my religious rambling does more for me than anything else. And when I get over to Europe, I'll be ready for whatever comes at me."

"Like the bullets? People get killed, you know. It could just as easily be you or me."

Nick looked at his friend with what he hoped was a challenge. "In that case, you'd better make sure you know whose side you're on and where you will end up if death does come knocking. That's why I don't need to worry about it. I know where I'm going."

"You mean in a trench with everyone else, listed as missing in action. Unless they can identify you. Then maybe you'll get to come home."

The fear from those words met Nick full force, like cold wind brushing over his soul. He refused to yield to its cruel touch. He knew there was much more to life than death. "The ground is where the old, worn-out body goes. But my spirit will be in heaven."

"You're always so sure about everything. I don't understand it. You think you have everything all mapped out, like that climbing route where we stuck in those pitons yesterday. But you don't, Nick. You have no idea what's going to happen, nor do you really know what happens when you die. You go by some book that dictates how to run your life. But no one really knows."

Nick sensed his friend's growing animosity was wrought out of conviction. He was glad for it and even gladder there was this time to talk to Fred. They had been so busy with tasks, preparations for climbing, and a myriad of other responsibilities. He'd prayed for Fred that morning in his devotions, and it seemed God had opened a door. If only his friend would have the blinders removed from his eyes and face reality. That what Fred said was true, that death was the final chapter for those who had no hope. But there was hope after death for those who believed. Hope that ran afresh, like rivers bubbling with water from the mountain rains. Hope in eternal life.

"Actually, Fred, someone did return to tell us about death. Jesus, who rose from the dead. His disciples were eyewitnesses to His resurrection. And they knew there was more to life than just the finality of death. There's something to hold on to. Something to trust in when you go marching up a hill while the enemy is blasting away at you. To know that if a bullet does get you, there is something beyond the grave. Eternity."

"You believe in a story is all, Captain. I sure hope you see how miserable it all is out there."

"And what about you, Fred? What will happen to you when you die?"

To Nick's astonishment, Fred's face broke open into a grin. "Why, I guess I'll just turn into a grassy field for the cows to eat, won't I?" He sauntered away, whistling, to Nick's dismay. At that moment he couldn't help but feel sadness for the man. And marvel at his ignorance. If only Nick could persuade Fred to reconsider his beliefs and his choices.

Nick observed the fields before him. *Dust thou art, and unto dust shalt thou return.* "But there is more to this than just dust, Lord. Much more. You revealed it all in Your Word. The hope of eternal life with You. If only You could reveal it to Fred and others." He wondered then what Lucy thought of it. If God was as real to her as He was to him. How he would like to find out. And if so, it would be good to talk with someone like-minded.

He recalled how she'd mentioned God making Seneca Rocks. She had a "God consciousness," so to speak. But he knew of many, at least in the camps, who had talked about God. It was another thing to actually serve God and live one's life for God alone. Whenever the challenge came forth, and Nick proclaimed that life belonged to God, many shirked the issue or looked at him strangely. Others proudly espoused their own invincibility.

God, I can't do any of this without You. I know there are adventurers out there who don't ever acknowledge Your hand in their lives. They do things out of their own strength and belief that their lives are in their own hands. Don't they realize it can take one misstep, one slip of the rope, one thing to go wrong, and that no amount of bravado will save them in the end? They could very well meet eternity, then what will happen?

A warm breeze blew up then. The grasses waved back and forth as if God's breath signaled His favor and grace. Nick sighed. He was here for a purpose, even if a few soldiers like Fred scoffed at his faith. He would show through word and deed the reality of God, which in the end could be their saving grace.

Just then, Nick heard someone call his name. Another of the sergeants marched up with the mail call. Who would be sending him a letter here, of all places? For all he knew, his parents weren't even sure of his whereabouts. Nick and his father had never been close. Dad disapproved of his adventuresome ways, wanting Nick instead to help at the family clothing store. As a youngster, the lure of the mountains had drawn Nick's heart, even when he tried to learn the art of tailoring to fit eager customers with a new wardrobe. Day after day his father would shout at him to get his mind off the mountaintop and back where it belonged.

But for Nick, his mind was always on that mountain summit, and he had no plans to come down from it. He told his dad what he wanted to do with his life. Angry words followed. His father then turned to Nick's younger brother, Phil, who was a natural at the business side of things. For himself, Nick took off for the mountains and never looked back. As far as he knew, no one had told them about this trip to West Virginia. He decided that when he returned to Colorado he should at least let his mother know what was happening, especially before the army sent him anywhere else. She always worried for his safety. And he knew she prayed for him.

Nick stared at the unfamiliar handwriting spelling out his name and the camp of Seneca Rocks. He liked the cursive writing. Large and flowery, as if the person was cheerful at heart. Ripping it open, he unfolded the paper to find a message from Lucy Bland. It was short, simple, and kind. He tucked it into the pocket of his shirt. He should write her back tonight if he didn't forget. Tell her how much he enjoyed their visits. Ask her when she would come by with more fresh muffins. In response, his stomach complained from the lack of dinner. Striding back toward camp, he touched the letter over his chest. Dear little Lucy. She wasn't little, by no means. She was a robust, grown woman with eyes of fire, eager to help him with anything. If only he knew what to do. Surely he couldn't handle a relationship right now. That was out of the question. But a friendship would work. A person could always use friends. Especially when his own friendship with Fred teetered on the brink of dissolution. Lucy would fit the bill nicely.

The next day, Nick called for a meeting with Fred. "What's up?" Fred asked.

"We're going to take a few of the experienced men out and test climb the route."

"Sure thing, Nick ol' boy. I'm ready to get going."

"Good. And another thing. You will address me as Captain Landers. One more infraction like that and I'll have to write you up. This is serious business, and we must conduct ourselves properly. Do you understand, Sergeant?"

Fred whirled, his eyes wide, his mouth gaping in astonishment. He appeared ready to issue a rebuke but wisely clamped his lips shut.

Nick rattled off the names of the men he wanted to accompany them—several privates who had previous climbing experience. "Fall in," Nick ordered when the men arrived. They stood in a single line of formation, their eyes focused straight ahead. "We're going to do a test climb of the main pitch today. You're the best we have, so I know you'll do what is expected of you. In turn, you will instruct the others on proper climbing protocol."

"What exactly are we climbing, sir?"

Nick pointed to the crest of rocks reaching toward the sky. "That. Seneca Rocks."

The men observed the rocks with curiosity and trepidation. One or two murmured their anxiety while the majority nodded, their facial expressions as stony as the rocks, determined to meet whatever challenge was thrown at them. Nick recalled a time not long ago when he'd stood before a commanding officer with an eagerness to prove himself and did so with determination. He hoped the men would have the same determination to succeed, and afterward, he would lead them to victory on future hillsides yet to be determined.

Fred returned and stood by the privates. He looked off into the distance, refusing to meet Nick's eye. With coils of rope over each shoulder, carabiners clinking, Nick led the group through the grassy fields toward the rocky faces. He tried not to think about Fred, who brought up the rear of the group, though his anger was palpable. Nick sighed. If only things weren't so complicated in life. He wanted to maintain order and discipline, but he also needed companionship and the camaraderie of a friend. Then with Lucy thrown into all this, it had become an entangled web of mixed feelings, to say the least.

Nick sighed. For now he couldn't worry about it. He had a job to do. He must devote his energy to the route they would face today, an easy three-pitch climb that he and Fred had laid out with pitons yesterday. He'd done the lead climbing to hammer in the pitons while Fred held the safety rope and belayed him. He was glad he and Fred hadn't had a falling-out then or he might have been a bit concerned with Fred on the other end of the rope. But Fred had always been there, no matter what. Like during that blizzard in the Rockies and when they did other training exercises. Nick did not doubt the man's abilities or will-ingness to keep him safe.

Suddenly Nick heard what sounded like a youngster crying. He took off toward the base of the cliff where a young boy stood. The boy's face was wet with tears. "What's the matter, young fellow? Are you hurt?"

"It's Carl," the boy said, pointing up at the jagged rocks. "He's stuck up there and can't get down. What are we gonna do? He'll die!"

Nick squinted to see another boy hovering near a rocky precipice nearly sixty feet up. "Carl!" he shouted. "Can you hear me?"

"I—I can't get down," a tremulous voice answered. "Help me. I—I don't know what to do. I think I'm gonna fall."

"Just stay calm. Keep away from the ledge. Is there a bush or tree near you?"

"Y—yes. A couple of those stubby trees."

"Okay. Now Carl, I want you to go ahead and grab hold of one of the trees and stay put. Don't let go for any reason until I come and get you. Okay?" Nick paused for a moment to listen, even as his heart began to race.

"O—okay," came the faint voice. "I found a tree."

By this time the other men had arrived, breathless from following Nick's lead through the dense underbrush to the base of the rocks. "What's that young boy doing way up there?" Fred exclaimed, shielding his eyes from the glare of the sun off the rocky face.

"I don't know how he got up there, but we have to get him down. I'm going to have to lay in pitons, Fred, just like yesterday. You okay with belaying?"

"Of course, Captain."

Nick stared into his friend's face, knowing he could trust Fred even if they had a difference of opinion on other matters. "I'll have to carry up another hundred feet of rope."

"You up to this?" Fred asked.

"It's good training. And good for the other men, as well." Nick tied himself in with the rope to form a harness. He attached extra pitons on a sling and tucked in a hammer to pound them in.

"Take a drink." Fred offered him his canteen. Nick took a healthy swallow while assessing the task that lay before him. Handing the canteen back to Fred, he positioned himself. "Okay, Carl, I'm climbing up to get you," he shouted. "Are you hanging on to that tree like I told you?"

"Y—yeah. Hurry!"

"Okay. Don't let go, no matter what." Turning to Fred he called out, "On belay?"

"Belay on," Fred told him, the rope secured around his own waist but slack in his hands.

"Climbing." Nick began the perilous ascent, looking for hand- and footholds. When he came to a healthy crack in the rock, he pounded in a piton with a piton hammer, fastened a carabiner to it, and connected his rope.

"Climb on," Fred reassured him from below.

Sweat poured off Nick's face. How he wished he could enjoy the climb, thinking of the beauty of the valley unfolding below him. But all he could think about was that young boy and how close to death he had come. Whatever possessed him to climb this far on his own? Nick hammered in five more pitons until he reached the ledge. There, clinging to a stubby tree, was a boy about twelve or thirteen, shaking like a branch caught in a stiff wind. The boy suddenly let go and came toward Nick.

"No, stay where you are. Hang on to that tree. I'm going to fasten the rope to it." When Nick had the rope anchored, he called down to Fred. "Off belay! Give me some slack." Then turning to Carl, he said, "Okay, Carl, I'm going to tie this other rope around you, and we're going to lower you to the ground. It's not really like rappelling, but it will give you a little taste of it. Want to try?"

"I—I guess. I just want to get down from here. I didn't know I wouldn't be able to get down."

Nick secured one end of the rope to Carl's skinny waist, the other end to the tree. He made a figure eight in the rope a few feet from the tree and, using a carabiner, attached the rope to his harness for stability. "Okay, I'm going to let you down nice and easy. It will be like walking down the side of a rock wall. Just use your feet and pretend like you can walk down it. Okay?"

"Okay."

With a prayer on his lips, Nick slowly began to lower Carl toward Fred's position. The boy took small steps against the rock wall, bouncing as he did while Nick guided the rope. When he heard an exclamation from below, Nick breathed a sigh of relief and thanked God for His hand of protection. He then checked the anchor of the rope tied off on the tree and rappelled down to where the two boys stood.

"Whew, I'm glad you're safe," he said to Carl, wiping the sweat from his face before taking up Fred's canteen. "Whatever gave you the idea of going up there without safety equipment?"

"I don't know, sir. It looked really easy to me. And. . .I wanted to do what you do."

Nick sighed, looking at the boys. It dawned on him then who they were, now that the rescue had been complete. They were none other than Lucy's brothers, the same ones he had met in the field the other day. "I'm glad you two boys are safe, but now I need to get you back to where you belong. The Bland household, right?"

"Yeah, but we can find our own way back home," Carl said, scooting away from Nick's grasp.

Nick took hold of his shirtsleeve. "Not so fast. I intend to take you there myself." To Fred he said, "Think you all can manage the climb? Might as well do this section for starters."

Fred saluted. "We've got a handle on it, Captain. See you back at camp."

Nick stepped aside and whispered, "Thanks for your help, Fred. I appreciate it."

The man gave him the semblance of a smile before redirecting his attention to the other soldiers and began shouting orders.

Nick's gaze diverted to Carl and Tim, who looked more scared now than when he'd first arrived at the rocks. "Okay, boys. Let's get you home."

"Really, sir, we know the way," Carl protested. "Don't you have other things to do?"

"Plenty. But after a situation like this, I need your parents to know what happened and to make sure you don't do anything like that again. You were blessed this time. Next time you may not be. Rock climbing can be deadly if you don't know what you're doing. And even people who do know have been killed by a piton breaking loose, a rope giving way, or slipping on the rocks. This kind of climbing can never be taken lightly."

Carl stared at the ground, scuffing up the grass with his shoes. "Daddy won't let me out of the house if you tell on me," he mumbled. "Just tell him we got lost or something. Please?"

"Is that being honest?"

"It beats getting a whipping."

"Well, maybe a whipping isn't such a bad idea, considering what could have happened to the both of you. Like getting yourselves killed. C'mon." Nick moved swiftly through the fields with the two boys dragging their feet. How glad he was that everything worked out all right for the Bland boys.

Just then, he remembered a comment Fred uttered the day they first encountered the boys in the pasture.

It seems to me, my dear Captain, that you are linked to this Bland family in more ways than one. There's just no escaping them.

Truer now than ever, Lord, Nick added silently. *But I have to wonder where all this will lead in the end.*

Chapter 8

Lucy looked in the oven at the dish she'd prepared—chicken and dumplings, her father's favorite. Daddy was coming home for the noon meal, a rarity as the lumber mill often kept him away for hours on end, sometimes late into the evening. But with his expected arrival today at noon, Momma had decided to have the main meal then so he could enjoy it before his business took him away again. Lucy promptly set to work making the dish as soon as her mother informed her of the plan.

She now took the casserole out of the oven to find it nicely browned, the gravy bubbling through the cracker crust, when a commotion erupted in the front yard. "Must be Carl and Tim," she told Momma, untying her apron. "They can smell cooking a mile away."

She came to the window, prepared to see them racing each other to the porch, flinging open the screen door, waving their soiled hands in her face while their voices begged for food. Instead, to her amazement, she saw Nick enter the yard, leading each boy by the arm. Both brothers had flushed and downcast faces. Neither said a word. She opened the screen door. "Captain Landers, what happened?"

"Are your folks at home, Lucy?"

She stepped aside as Momma came to the door.

"What's this about? Carl, Tim, where have you been?"

"It wasn't anything," Carl began.

"You sure about that?" Nick said, nudging him slightly.

"I just wanted to try it out. It wasn't anything."

Nick frowned. "Getting stranded on a ledge sixty feet up with no safety equipment and no way down is hardly nothing. And especially when others had to stop their own business to come up there and rescue you."

"Oh no!" Momma cried, just as Daddy walked into the room. "Did you hear what happened, Dick? Carl and Tim were up there on Seneca Rocks and this soldier had to rescue them."

"What's this?" Daddy came forward, the morning paper in his hand. Nick quickly unfolded the details. "I don't believe it. The one day I get off at noon and you boys have to do something like this."

"I didn't get stuck up there," Tim declared. "Carl did."

"You could've been hurt!" Momma wailed.

"Killed is more like it," Daddy said in a matter-of-fact tone that sent another wail from Momma's lips. "We're very thankful, Mister. . ."

"Landers, sir. Captain Nick Landers with the Mountain Training Group."

"Thank you, Captain Landers. I'm much obliged. Now surely you can come in and share the noon meal with us. It's the least we can do to thank you."

Lucy's heart nearly skipped a beat as she watched Nick look beyond her father to the table in the dining room and the dish of chicken and dumplings, its steamy aroma wafting through the house. "Well. . .I do have things to do, but I left my sergeant in charge. I suppose he can handle it."

"Good. Come on in then, and make yourself at home."

Lucy thought she had died and gone to heaven. The man she dreamed of day and night now stood in the foyer of her humble home. His gaze settled on her for a brief moment before taking in the sights of the home. "The washroom is over there if you want to clean up," she said, pointing the way.

"Thanks." He whistled a tune Lucy didn't recognize. He washed and then tried to scoop up a mound of his dark hair and comb it back with his fingers. "Here's a comb," she added from the hallway, offering him one of her father's old ones.

He seemed startled, then took it. "Thanks." In several swift strokes he had his hair neatly parted to one side and combed back.

"Sorry my brothers gave you such a headache today," she said when he stepped out of the washroom.

"Backache is more like it. I think I pulled something on the last part of that pitch."

He followed her to the table where the two boys stared down at their plates in silence, refusing to acknowledge anyone. Lucy nearly chuckled when she saw the guilt written on both their faces, especially on the outspoken Carl. It was rare to see him so silent. No doubt Daddy's presence fueled their despondency as he glared at the two boys from the head of the table.

"I'd send them to their rooms," Daddy said, "but I don't like hungry boys under my roof. I think there are other punishments better than an empty belly, don't you think, Captain Landers?"

"Please call me Nick, sir. And yes, I'm sure there are. In fact, locking oneself away in a room for a time to think things through can be a good idea."

Daddy offered a prayer for the meal, then served Nick a huge mound of chicken and dumplings. "I think Captain Landers has made a good suggestion, boys. After your chores are done, you will go to your room and think about what you did today."

The boys said nothing but picked at their food.

"I remember being in their shoes when I was their age," Nick added. "I loved the mountains. One time, I got lost up there and hadn't come home by dinnertime. My mother was frantic. When Dad finally did find me, he sent me to my room for a week."

"A whole week!" Carl said in alarm. "Why a week?"

" 'Cause I could've been hurt badly. It made me think real hard about what I had done. They let me out for meals, of course. And the chores. But it did me good. I think about that time often when I'm mountaineering, to make sure I'm always careful and not to glorify myself in what I do. It's good to be humbled once in a while. Pride comes before the fall, you know, and you don't want to be caught falling off some cliff. It's a long way down."

Lucy said nothing but quietly enjoyed listening to Nick's conversation. He ate the food she'd prepared as if savoring a gourmet meal. She imagined herself as his wife then, preparing the evening meal, making sure he had a comb ready to do up his hair. She'd even wash and iron his clothes if he'd let her. Anything, so long as she could relish the time spent with him and become a part of his world, a world that still seemed so far away.

"This is excellent," Nick said, helping himself to another portion. "I have to say, I haven't been able to eat much of the camp food recently. Hopefully that will be changing as some of the good folks around here bring supplies to the camp."

"What do you eat?" Carl wondered, his mouth full of biscuit.

"Oh, stews and soups mostly. We had chipped beef on bread the other day."

"Yum."

Nick chuckled. "You wouldn't have said 'yum' to this, I'll tell you. More like 'ugh.' That is, unless you enjoy salty strips mixed with paste—the cook's attempt at making it resemble chipped beef in gravy." He hesitated. "I suppose I shouldn't be complaining about the food. There are plenty of people in other places who have nothing."

"Why not?" Daddy said. "You have every right to complain. They ought to be feeding you men the best food there is, with the sacrifices you're making."

"They're probably trying to save money for the war effort," Momma added, passing the chicken and dumplings to Nick.

"That is no excuse. Of course, I'm no cook, Captain Landers. Now Lucy here, her mother taught her well. She makes the best food. In fact, she made this meal today."

Again Nick's gaze fell on her and lingered there for a time, as if appreciating this tidbit of news. He then dished up his third helping and took a fourth biscuit. He winked in her direction as if to say he loved her cooking. She felt warmth rise in her cheeks and a sudden shyness. If only she could meet his steady gaze with one of her own, one she hoped would reveal her innermost heart. Instead she felt like a schoolgirl on the playground, her feet scuffing up dirt, wondering what to say to the most popular boy in the class.

"She's a great cook," Nick agreed. "She made me the best blueberry muffins."

"Really," Daddy said. "So you two have already met?"

Oh no, Lucy thought. At once her shyness was replaced by decisiveness. "Well, I thought it was a nice gesture, Daddy, seeing as what kind of food the men have to put up with at that camp."

"Your daughter was kind enough to also show my sergeant and me the way to the base of the rocks for our climbing maneuvers," Nick added. "If it hadn't been for her help, we might have spent valuable time wandering around and not had the opportunity to promptly begin the training. It's these acts of kindness that help us accomplish what we need to do."

Daddy nodded. Lucy caught the slight smile on Nick's face, as if he were trying to soothe her nerves.

"We all need to do our part in this effort," Daddy said. "Bring out the tea, Jane, will you? I'm sure the captain here would like a good cup of hot tea."

Nick wiped his mouth with his napkin. "Well, I must say, that was a great dinner. Best I've had in years." Again came his smile of appreciation in Lucy's direction. How she would love to pull him aside for a chat on the front porch. Instead he stood to his feet and dropped his napkin on the table. "I hate to eat and run, but I left my contingent of men by the rocks. I should go check on them."

"So where are you staying, Captain Landers?" Daddy asked. "I hear there are officers staying in Elkins. Pretty nice accommodations, as well."

"I'm staying in the tent barracks by Seneca Rocks, sir."

Daddy took a swig of tea, sat back, and shook his head. "That's no place for men like you with your kind of responsibility. We need to do what's right to keep our officers healthy. We have a spare bedroom here. You're welcome to stay with us. We're just down the road from the camp, so you'd be pretty much near your men if the need arises. And I'm sure your sergeants can help, as well."

Lucy thought she might collapse if not for sitting in a chair. Her heart began to take off like a mare racing across the field. *This can't be happening.* Daddy had actually invited Nick Landers to dwell under their roof? Was this heaven sent? God's answer to all her questioning of late?

"That's thoughtful of you, sir, but I wouldn't want to impose."

"It's no imposition. I'm sure we can learn a lot about what's happening. It would do the boys some good to have a soldier here to keep them in line. Eh, Carl and Tim?"

The boys stared at him with wide eyes. "Well, I'm not so sure," Carl began.

Daddy laughed. "You see? I believe it's settled, that is, if you agree, Captain Landers."

"I would be a fool to say no, sir, seeing as my tent did leak in the rainstorm last week."

"Good. Then we will expect you for dinner unless you want more of that food you were describing. Unfortunately, I won't be here some evenings, but I know the missus and Lucy will make you feel at home."

"Thank you again for your kind offer and for the delicious meal." Nick shook Daddy's hand and then began making his way to the front door.

Lucy slipped out of the dining room and followed Nick to the porch. "I guess we'll see you later," she said, hoping she didn't sound too eager. She didn't want to chase him away him because of some obsession. She wanted their relationship to be real, to mature naturally in God's perfect timing.

"Yes. And thanks for the great meal. You're quite a cook." He nodded, offered her another dazzling smile, and headed for the road. Lucy did her best to contain the happiness welling up within her. This couldn't have been planned any better if she'd tried. "I just need to let it go and let God take control," she murmured.

Just then, she caught sight of Carl making his way to the stairs and his room. "Carl, you're the best!" Lucy called up to him.

"What?"

"For getting yourself trapped on that cliff. If that hadn't happened, Captain Landers would never have come here. And now he's our houseguest. I owe it all to you."

"Goodie, goodie for you," Carl muttered, climbing the stairs one by one.

It's more than good. It's a blessing. And maybe I'll find out all that I need to know, especially about the man who has conquered my heart. Thank You, God! She raced back outside to the porch, hoping to catch one last glimpse of Nick walking down the road, heading for the camp. He had since vanished, but she knew he would return tonight. And she would make plans for a wonderful welcome-to-our-home meal, complete with plenty of biscuits. There may even be time for conversation afterward, perhaps during a moonlit walk. Lucy leaned against the porch railing. Everything was slowly coming together and before the meeting with Allen on Friday. She still wasn't sure how she would talk herself out of the date they had agreed on. Maybe honesty was the way she should go. Be forthright and tell him about Nick.

Tell Allen what? That I'm in love with Nick, but I still don't know how he feels about me? That I could be imagining some relationship and then be left out in the cold when he leaves with his troops? That Allen could be angry with me forever and others gossiping around town, wondering what I'm doing? Lucy straightened. She would take everything as it came. And right now, she planned to make Nick Landers feel so welcome, he would never want to leave her side.

Chapter 9

Friday came, and with it, nervous jitters as Lucy waited all day for Allen to stop by the house and ask about their planned date in Petersburg. She'd stayed up most of the night, rehearsing what she would say when the time came. Since that day when she talked to Allen at the store, Lucy had not seen hide nor hair of him. She wasn't sure what to make of it. Maybe Carl had gotten hold of him and told him right off that Nick was their houseguest. At times she considered moseying on down to the store to see what was afoot. After all, this not knowing was driving her crazy. Not that she wanted a date with Allen or have him push her into a corner she couldn't get out of. But she did want to know his intentions and if they could at least remain friends.

Momma glanced into the room just as Lucy was finishing the speech she might need to give later. Momma stared with a quizzical look before shaking her head. "Really, Lucy. Will you never get your head out of the clouds? Ever since those soldiers came, I don't know what's come over you."

"I'm fine, Momma. I was wondering. . .has anyone—have you heard or seen any messages or anyone stop by asking for me?"

"Should I have?"

"Allen said something about getting together today, but I haven't heard from him all week."

Was it just her imagination or did her mother's face brighten? Lucy never knew Momma cared that much for Allen. Though that time Allen brought her home and she left him standing on the porch, Momma had come to his defense. She hoped Momma and Daddy weren't assuming that she'd marry the man. Other things were at work right now. Like Nick Landers, who gave her a quick good-bye that morning after drinking down a cup of coffee and eating three crullers Lucy had fried up the night before.

"No, I haven't heard any news about Allen. I did see him heading out of town on Wednesday. Maybe something came up."

"He didn't say he was going out of town."

Momma stood in the doorway, her arms folded. "I just wonder if he's up to something. Sneaking off without telling anyone doesn't seem like the Allen I know. Maybe he's getting ready for something big."

Lucy didn't want to dive into speculations right now, even if Momma hinted at them. She prayed silently that Allen wasn't going off to buy an engagement ring. She couldn't bear the thought of confronting him while he stood there with a gift box in hand and a look of expectation on his face.

"I'm sure there's a good reason," Lucy said quickly, spinning about to avoid seeing Momma's questioning expression. How she wished she could confide in Momma about her feelings for Nick, but she didn't really know what her mother thought of the handsome soldier. Momma had said little since Nick arrived, even if Daddy peppered the man with questions about the war effort and the soldiers he trained. In turn, Nick entertained them with his experiences in leading the men on the rocks and his adventures in Colorado.

When Momma disappeared, Lucy contemplated a new set of worries. If Allen was indeed planning a marriage proposal, she would have to act soon. But first she must know Nick's intentions. As far as she knew, he had no romantic inclinations. His contact with her had only been congenial at best. Lucy blew out a sigh that ruffled her bangs. If only she could corner him, maybe on some moonlit road, and find out what he wanted for the future besides adventure. If he ever thought of finding a woman special enough to marry. Or if he had someone special back in Colorado. Then she might have a better idea what to do about Allen.

"I'm going to the store, Lucy!" Momma called up the stairs. "Be back soon."

Oh no, she thought, rushing to the window as Momma headed down the porch steps. She bit her lip. What if Momma told Mr. Hopper what she'd said about Allen? That nonsense about expecting a date tonight? Lucy sighed in exasperation. If only she hadn't found herself lost in some dark alley of confusion with two men mixed up in it. If only these men would make up their minds the way she wanted.

Lucy, when have you taken the time to ask God about His *way? What* He *wants for your life? Not your will, but* His *will be done.* Again she bit her lip. What if God wanted her to be with Allen? Could she accept it? Could she say good-bye to Nick? If so, then why had He opened the door for Nick to come and live under their roof—providing a situation that only added to the attraction she felt for him in her heart? Surely God wouldn't do this unless there was some plan.

Lucy tried to busy herself with mundane activities while waiting for her mother's return. When she finally heard the front door close, she stepped out into the foyer, pushing strands of hair behind one ear. "How was your errand?"

"You can help me with this," Momma said, handing her a paper bag full of groceries. "Having another hungry man in the house sure makes the food go fast."

"Nick told me he tried to give Daddy money for his room and board, but Daddy refused."

"It's just our way of helping the cause," Momma said. "With your brothers too young to enlist, I guess your father felt this was one small way we could help."

"I'm sure you're glad that Carl and Tim are too young," Lucy remarked.

"Some days I am very glad. Other days, especially when they find themselves in a whirl of mischief, I think having them in the army might do them some good. Though having Captain Landers under our roof has seemed to put them on their best behavior. It's good to have another man here, especially with your father working late at the mill on odd days. I feel more secure, too."

Lucy took out the packages of flour and sugar to stow away in the cupboard. "Any other news?" she hedged.

"Leslie Watson had her baby. Mrs. Sampson has something wrong with her heart, or so she says. Others are moaning about the soldiers that are everywhere. I had one man ask me why we are keeping a soldier under our roof. I asked him what he's doing to help the cause." Momma chuckled. "Guess I can speak my mind when I need to." She paused. "And speaking of that, I asked Mr. Hopper about Allen. It seems Allen had to go out of town unexpectedly. His grandfather on his mother's side has taken ill. You remember him, I'm sure, the one who lives in Charleston."

"Yes, I remember him." Lucy recalled the older gentleman who'd stayed for several years when she and Allen were young. Allen was named after his grandfather and they were close. He called him Grandpa Al, and they would often go fishing together in the North Fork River. "I hope he's all right."

Momma shook her head. "Not from what Ed says. They don't think he will live much longer, which is why Allen left to go visit him. No sense in seeing someone after they're dead. You should see them when they're alive so you can say your good-byes."

For some reason, the statement saddened Lucy. She had only thought of life, after all, here by Seneca Rocks, watching soldiers like Nick train and carry on with their duties. It hadn't truly dawned on her until now that those men trained to go into the heat of battle. And battles meant death. Many of them might never return. She shuddered and turned away.

"I didn't mean to upset you, Lucy. I know how you all used to do things together when his grandfather came to visit."

"Yes," she said absently, still thinking of Nick. What would she do if the army called him away to that dreadful war in Europe? Was it right for her to marry someone like Nick, only to see their love die on some distant battlefield? How could she bear being a widow? Her throat began to close over at the thought, making her choke with emotion.

"I'm sorry." Momma came and wrapped her arm around Lucy. "I know it must be hard."

Lucy wanted to confide in her mother that while she was sorry for Allen's grandfather, it was Nick and their future that left her choked up with worry. Nick wounded or lost or even killed. Life without Nick by her side. Perhaps these were the birth pangs of true love.

"I'll make some tea," Momma offered. "We can sit on the porch and say a prayer for his recovery."

Lucy said nothing as she fetched two teacups and the tea strainer while Momma put the kettle on to boil. If only she had the courage to express her thoughts. If only there were someone to talk to about her feelings. After the kettle sang, Momma poured the steaming water into cups.

"This is nice," she said with a smile, carrying out the tea. Lucy followed with a small plate of crullers left over from breakfast. "We should do this more often, but there's always things to do, it seems. Now with that soldier around here, everything is so hectic."

"You don't sound as if you like Nick that much, Momma," Lucy noted carefully.

"On the contrary, he's a very nice man. And, of course, he rescued Carl and Tim from the rocks. Like I said before, those boys have been angels with him around." Momma sipped her tea while Lucy stared into hers, watching the tiny fragments of tea leaves chase each other around. "Come, let's say a prayer for Allen's granddad."

Lucy obediently set her cup down and closed her eyes. Not only did she pray for the elderly man but also for Nick, that his day would go well and that he would come home in a jovial mood. That she would know beyond a shadow of a doubt whether they had a future together.

"Amen," Momma said. "I'm sure he will feel better soon. The Lord has answered my prayers so many times. Just as I've prayed for you, Lucy."

Lucy looked at her mother curiously. "What have you prayed for?"

"Oh, many things. Mostly that you will find a nice man to marry. And I think soon you may get your wish."

Lucy returned her gaze to the cup. "Why do you say that?"

"Oh, just a feeling. Mother's intuition, I suppose. I think you will make someone a fine wife, Lucy."

She opened her mouth, ready to inform her mother how she would love to be a certain army captain's wife and live with him in Colorado, but she could not speak the words. Instead she finished her tea and told Momma she was going for a walk. Momma said nothing, though Lucy could tell her sudden withdrawal had surprised her mother. She wished everything could be spelled out clearly, but matters of the heart were the most difficult to discuss. Especially when one's heart wasn't sure which way to turn on the path of life.

That evening Lucy waited anxiously for Nick's return. In a way she looked forward to seeing him again, but in another way, she felt shy and reserved, especially considering her thoughts of late. If she weren't so nervous, she might be tempted to come right out and ask Nick if he had feelings for her. If he had any notion of a relationship or even marriage or if she should accept the proposal she was sure Allen had waiting for her upon his return. But the thoughts stayed buried. She knew she couldn't bring herself to ask Nick such personal, forward questions. It must come naturally from the heart, something that God birthed within the both of them. Maybe tonight there would be some glimpse into the inner workings of Nick's heart. Something that would guide her decision making and spark hope for the future.

Nick arrived late that evening, much to her dismay. Dinner was already on the table, being enjoyed by the family, when he came trudging in. Lucy listened to him enter the foyer, moan, and retreat out the door. She excused herself to see what the trouble was. She found him outside, trying to remove his mud-caked boots. Chunks of mud lay scattered on the wooden floor of the foyer. She fetched the broom as she heard him fumbling outside on the porch, knocking mud off of his boots. The door opened and suddenly she and Nick collided.

"Oops, I'm sorry." He stepped back when he saw her standing there with the broom. "You don't need to clean up after me. I can do it. I forgot to take off my boots."

"It's nothing."

"I figured I'm probably too late for dinner. Sorry about that. I would be happy with a sandwich or something."

"You're not too late. Though you'd better get in there before Carl and Tim eat it all."

He walked past her, stopped, and turned. "Are you coming, too, or did you eat already?"

She looked up, surprised at his concern. At this point she was willing to take any inkling of concern for her well-being as a sign of hope. "I had a little, but I'm not that hungry tonight."

He stood there, silent for a moment, then walked into the dining room where Lucy heard the greetings, including Daddy's welcome. Daddy took great pleasure in having the officer under his roof. He seemed to radiate with pride, as if his hospitality would earn him a medal. No doubt Daddy also liked bragging to his coworkers about his contribution to the war effort by housing one of the higher-ups. Lucy couldn't care less about such things. She only wanted to know which man she should marry.

When Lucy finished her duty, she entered the dining room to see Nick with a heap of stew on his plate. Carl was asking questions about the day's activities. Nick looked right at home among her family. He smiled and chatted as if he had known them for years. He would make a wonderful son-in-law and brother-in-law. Perfect to keep her unruly brothers in line and for Daddy who enjoyed his presence. And Momma would go along with whatever Daddy said. It all seemed so right. But one thing was lacking. A commitment on Nick's part. A sense of adoration. The knowledge that he loved her.

"A great meal once again," Nick said with satisfaction as Momma placed a cup of tea before him. "I do hope, though, you will allow me to at least offer a bit of support toward my room and board."

"I won't hear of it," Daddy told him. "We're just glad we can help. So long as you are able to do your job, training those boys of yours."

"It is a job, that's for sure," he agreed. "Especially trying to get them to do what I want. Many of them are scared, and I guess rightly so. It takes a lot of calm words and prayer to get some of them to even put one foot in a foothold on the rock and to trust that the ropes won't give way. But I like to think how it compares to our walk of faith. It takes faith to trust God with the things in our lives. Things that seem too difficult, hoping He won't let us fall. I think more than anything else, I'm learning about God and His Word as I instruct."

Lucy marveled. Nick was so much more spiritual than Allen. Allen went to church, yes. He did pray sometimes. But he hardly mentioned God in his conversations. Nick talked about the Lord as if He were his closest companion, there for him always, a friend in times of need. Nick trusted God with everything.

When the family retired to the living room to hear the evening radio programs, Lucy began clearing the table. Suddenly she saw Nick's beefy hands reach out to pick up a few bowls. "No sense leaving you with all this to clean up," he said.

"Oh, it's no bother. I'm used to it."

He stood there holding the bowls, appearing thoughtful. "Is something bothering you, Lucy?"

Caught off guard by his question, she trembled. "Why do you say that?"

"I don't know, but ever since I came here, you seem kind of put out. Like my presence bothers you or something."

"Of course not," she said, trying to look relaxed even as her voice shook when she said the words.

"I don't want you to feel that way. I hope I'm not making more work for you."

"Of course not. I guess I have a lot on my mind these days."

He nodded as if he understood, though she couldn't figure out how he would know what was on her mind. He continued to help clear the table and then armed himself with a towel while she proceeded to wash the dishes. "You don't need to do this," she said again.

"Believe me, this is a nice change from what I do every day. Being with a bunch of rough, gritty soldiers can get to you. And they certainly don't smell as nice as you do."

Lucy felt her cheeks heat up. "I know after Daddy and the boys come in from work, they do tend to smell like the great outdoors. But so do I, after I come in from the garden."

"I don't know, but there's something about women. They never smell bad." He laughed. "Not sure why I'm on that topic. Like I go sniffing around or something, which I don't."

Lucy chuckled in spite of herself. "I'm sure a nice man like you has a girlfriend, though. Maybe in Colorado?"

"Used to. She hated my mountaineering. But it seems your boyfriend likes the mountains."

Again her cheeks flamed. "Allen is just a friend. We've known each other since we were children. That's all."

Nick said little else. After the dishes were done, he joined the family in the sitting room where they sat listening to the radio. Lucy stood in the doorway watching him amid her family. How well he fit in—as if he were meant to be there. His gaze then met hers. She stepped back into the hallway, suddenly embarrassed. What would he think of her staring at him? Maybe it was time he knew how she felt. Maybe she could bring out that first letter she wrote and slip it under his pillow while he was away at camp. Or tuck it into his shirt pocket as he slept; the pocket that sat directly over his heart. He would find it the next day and the words would seal their future. If only the time were now.

Chapter 10

That's it for today, men," Nick announced when the last of the team had safely rappelled to firm ground. A round of cheers rose up from the group. Some slapped each other on the back, congratulating each other on a job well done. One young man, still trembling from the encounter with the rocks that day, could only peel off his helmet, wipe the perspiration dribbling down his face, and claim he was glad the day was finished.

"Sure hope I don't have to do that again," he murmured. "Once is enough for me."

"Sorry to be the bearer of bad news, but we'll be doing it again tomorrow," Nick reminded them. "So don't relax too much. Just remember all we've done. The next time it will be as easy as pie."

The men laughed, except for the nervous private. They talked with one another about their adventure as they made their way back to camp. Nick watched Fred silently gather up the equipment. Since their falling out, Fred had said little to Nick. At times, Nick regretted the harsh tone he had used with his friend, especially threatening to report him for disregarding the use of titles. But Nick knew he had to maintain clear authority. The young GIs would respect him if the chain of command remained intact. So far it had worked well, but he wondered if it had been worth sacrificing the only true friend he had in the entire outfit.

"So how do you think the day went, Sergeant Watkins?" Nick asked.

Fred glanced up, his eyes wide. "You talking to me, Captain?"

"There's no one else here by that name. I noticed you haven't said hardly a word to me for days."

Fred heaved a coil of rope over his shoulder. "Just trying not to say the wrong thing so I don't get written up, sir."

Nick paused. "What if I said, since the men are gone, that you can have a personal 'at ease' during our conversation?"

"I'd say that once I get going, I probably would never end it at the appropriate time. And I might get into trouble with my CO, which I don't want to do."

Nick frowned as his friend began the slow trek back toward camp. At that instant, he felt entirely alone. Despite their ranks and their differences, Fred was still his friend. They had been through the good and the ugly together, working

312

first in the mountains of Colorado and now undertaking this mission. Nick enjoyed the talks they had when they sat up nights, trying to figure out what to do with the men. But ever since the training program began, there had been no such talks. There was no one to confide in but God. Not that there was anything wrong with that, but Nick missed the human interaction. The friendship.

He took up his backpack and helmet and hurried to join Fred. "Hey, Fred, if I could get you a dinner invitation, would you be interested?"

"What? I like the food served in camp, Captain. I'm not picky like some soldiers who will remain nameless."

Nick had to chuckle. "Quite true, and yes, I'm picky. But what if I said I know someone who's serving up a good smoked ham tonight? And biscuits that melt in your mouth. Could you be enticed to come?"

Fred stopped in his tracks. He tipped up his helmet and glanced at Nick. "What are you trying to do, Captain?"

"I'm trying to accomplish what I need to succeed, Sergeant. I wanted us to be a team by preserving the chain of command when we are with the other men. But at the same time, I could also use a friend."

"Like I said, you should have gone with the other COs to Elkins. Instead you take up at that mountain dame's home to be with her and her kid brothers. You're never around here anymore. I end up having to play cards with a bunch of privates who don't know a club from a spade."

"Let's just say that my association with the family can now get you a good meal. You even complained about the 'baby food' they serve here. So how about it?"

Fred's face erupted into a grin. "You know I'd be a fool to refuse a ham dinner, Captain Landers."

"Good. If you don't mind then, I'm going to make your presence known to the family before you get there. You know the house, the same one we visited when we first arrived, the white one with the porch."

"I know it. Hope they tie up that dog of theirs."

"They have been, so don't worry. Come around seven."

"Seven." He adjusted the rope he carried. "And thanks for thinking of me, Captain." Fred trudged on, but Nick saw those steps leading them back to the path they had once trod together, the path of friendship that he needed more and more. Even if they were different men with different ranks, and yes, different beliefs, they were friends for a reason. And Nick would preserve that friendship to the best of his ability. Now as he looked back toward the Blands' home, he hoped Lucy would agree to the plan.

———

"You sure were right about the food, Captain Landers," Fred said with a sigh, patting his stomach. "That was the best meal I've had since I entered the army.

Years, in fact. It was excellent."

Nick glanced across the table and saw the slow flush of appreciation high-light Lucy's cheeks. He never saw anyone looking prettier. She then stood to her feet to perform her customary duty of clearing the dishes. Nick flew to his feet, as well. "Allow me," he said, taking the plates from her hand. "You've done plenty tonight." He ignored the looks circulating around the table, from Fred to Lucy's parents, then to the boys, who poked each other in glee. He didn't care what they thought. This young woman did more than anyone. He sensed her silence the last few days was because of the ceaseless chores. Though he disliked the idea of making more work by having Fred join in, he needed to reestablish a rapport with the man. Maybe once the dishes were done he could take Lucy aside and explain why he'd invited Fred—that she was helping a good cause by reaching out to a man whose heart was as far away from God as a heart could be.

Mrs. Bland brought out her rose print teapot and cups for the evening round of tea. When Nick finished drying the dishes, he took his seat opposite Fred and asked for the sugar bowl.

"It's going well, sir," Fred was saying to a question posed by Mr. Bland. "Of course, you get some boys who can't seem to remember when's the last time they climbed a haystack. I mean, we all were climbers way back when. I'm sure your two boys have done their share of climbing apple trees." He looked over at Carl and Tim, who perked up at having been addressed.

"Why, sure," Carl said. "In fact, I'm a good climber."

"You proved that on the cliff when Nick had to come rescue you," Lucy murmured.

Carl shot her a look. "I could have gotten myself down," he said defensively. "But it was good practice for you, wasn't it, Captain Landers?"

Nick winked at Lucy over his cup. "Sure. Good practice. It isn't every day I get to rescue a young boy trapped on a cliff. Keeps my skills sharp."

"Well, you won't have to worry about that anymore as the boys still aren't allowed to leave the property," Mr. Bland said with a warning in his voice. "You men need to do what's important without having to rescue ill-mannered boys." He drank down his tea. "But you men must get some time to yourselves, don't you? Or are you here to work only and then leave when everything is finished?"

"As long as we get in the training we need, we can take off an evening," Nick said. "In fact, I've been thinking about some way to congratulate the men who have mastered some of the more difficult climbs. A reward, I guess you could say. I have about six or so that have done very well. They are even helping to train the younger GIs."

"I'd be glad to help," said Mr. Bland. "I was thinking you soldiers might want an evening of fun. I could drive you over in the truck to see a picture show in

Petersburg, maybe. Then you can get yourselves an ice-cream soda while you're in town."

"Sounds good to me," Fred said. "What about you, Captain?"

"How soon can we go, sir?"

"Well, I can do it tomorrow night. I won't be working at the mill late."

"Tomorrow night," Nick said. Only then did he catch Lucy's eye. Again he sensed trouble brewing in that stare of hers. He saw her come to her feet and leave the room. He vowed then to find out if he was the cause of her discontent and prayed that God would show him what to say and do to make things right.

While Fred was engaged in a healthy conversation with Mr. Bland, Nick moseyed on outside and found Lucy lingering by the barn. He watched her for a few moments. She had on a cute dress this evening that accentuated her womanly figure. He liked the way her bobbed hair swayed around her shoulders with the evening breeze. Her hand swept the stiff boards of the barn wall as she walked about, staring up at the starlit sky.

He shoved his hands into the pockets of his trousers and ventured forward. "Nice evening."

She whirled as if his greeting had startled her. "Yes, yes it is."

"Lucy, I've been meaning to talk to you. I know it seems like all I do is eat, sleep, and run off to the camp."

"You have your work to do. I understand."

"I know, but I have a feeling that you think I'm ignoring you. That I don't appreciate everything you've done for me since I came here. But I do appreciate it, more than words can say."

She kept her gaze averted as if embarrassed by the fact. Nick sighed, wondering what else he could say to change the mood of the evening. "Also, I was thinking. I'm not a big picture show person. How about you and I get an ice-cream soda at the fountain while the others are watching the movie? I'd much rather take the time to talk to a real person over ice cream than see others talking on a screen."

Her head lifted and her gaze finally settled on him. He couldn't see her reaction well in the fading twilight, but he thought she looked pleased. "That's very nice of you to ask me, Nick, but you don't have to."

"I don't have to, but I want to. That is, unless you have other plans with your friend."

"No. I mean, he's not here. His grandfather is very ill, so he's been away to Charleston." She paused as if lost in thought. "I think it would be nice to get away for a change. I feel like I've been cooped up here. Not because of you or anything, but I haven't done anything fun in a long time and—"

"Good. I'm looking forward to it."

"I am, too."

Silence followed, but in that silence he heard things speaking loud and clear to his heart. For once he could cast aside mountaineering and army life and things military to concentrate on people. Like Lucy, who looked as if she could use a friend. And he needed a friend, as well. Someone like-minded, someone with whom he could share those hopes and dreams that God whispered in the middle of the night. Someone who would understand his beliefs and not ridicule them. And Lucy, he knew, would never ridicule anything. In fact, she would stand by closer than any friend. Or maybe she was becoming more than just a friend. If only she didn't have her other friend standing in the way.

After the soldiers were dropped off at the picture show, Nick and Lucy hurried away before anyone could say anything, heading for the soda fountain around the corner. Lucy appeared relaxed and happy, chattering about the community, the shops, and the places where she used to come as a little girl. Nick preferred hearing her sweet feminine voice over the gruff voices of soldiers complaining about this or that. Once inside the shop, they settled on revolving stools at the counter with their sodas. Her chatter came to an abrupt end as she played with her straw. Nick wondered about it. At least he didn't have to worry about this being a Dear John encounter like he'd had with Donna. Instead, he hoped this might be the beginning of something special in his life. Away from the mountains and his work, he could take time to concentrate on things that he had sacrificed to duty, like the woman sitting beside him.

"So your family lives in Colorado?" Lucy finally asked, still playing with the straw in her soda. "You probably don't see them much."

"Not very often. We've never been close, not since I took up with mountaineering and then joined the army. Dad wanted me to work in his clothing business. But I had no interest in it. Can you see me in a shop, working as a tailor?"

Lucy giggled. "Not at all. You look like you belong in the mountains. You have such confidence in everything you do. Though you must get scared sometimes, don't you? I mean, it's not all fun, is it?"

"Everyone has their fears and their times of trouble. That's why I try to tell the men about God, even though it irritates Fred. He doesn't believe, you see. He thinks religion is a lot of hogwash. But I think one day he might change his mind, especially when we head over and see what's happening with the war."

"You think you will be sent to Europe soon?"

"From what I've been hearing, it's a good possibility. Rumors are running wild about a major invasion to take place in the future. It has to come sometime. Someday we'll have to drive the enemy out of those countries. When that happens, they're going to need every man."

Lucy dipped her straw down in the tall glass. "I'll miss you, Nick. I mean, I'll miss you when you leave to go back to Colorado or wherever you go. You probably will soon, won't you? The training is only supposed to last for a few weeks, if I remember."

"We may have another week or two. Depends on how quickly the men progress. There may be more units coming in with fresh instructors. But yes, my time here will eventually come to an end." For some reason, the fact saddened him. He was enjoying his stay—the simplistic lifestyle, the beauty of Seneca Rocks and the surrounding mountains, even if the mountains weren't the rugged Rockies he knew so well. He liked mountains he could easily conquer without having to push himself to the limit. And he enjoyed the people, like Lucy and her family, who blessed him with their hospitality. God had provided for him every step of the way. How he wished he could do something in return for the Bland family, who had given him so much. But what? They had refused money. Maybe this time spent with Lucy would give him a chance to convey some measure of gratefulness for all she and her family had done.

"Let's take a walk around the town," Lucy suggested when they finished their sodas.

Nick jumped at the suggestion, took up her sweater, and helped her put it on. Lucy seemed surprised and pleased by the gesture, offering a shy "Thank you" in response. They slipped outside where people roamed the sidewalks, including a few military personnel.

"It looks like the U.S. Army has definitely set up residence here," Lucy observed. "We never saw anything like this a month ago. Hard to believe that our little corner of West Virginia could attract this much attention."

"This is a great area of the country for training, Lucy, not only at Seneca Rocks but in other remote places, as well. But it won't be for long. Soon we'll all be gone and it will just be a memory." Again he didn't know why the fact of his departure saddened him. Lucy must be affecting him more than he realized. He had tried to push away any thought of a relationship because of his work and her friend who seemed set in his ways. But Lucy had said many times that she and the man were only friends from long ago. There were no romantic entanglements to be had. And in all honesty, his work was well in hand. He should offer his feelings before God to see if something else was at work in his heart.

Lucy talked of the time she had come to town when her brothers were lost. The family spent a whole afternoon looking for them. "We found them in the candy store with the sheriff," she said. "Carl had been caught trying to steal candy."

"Those two have a knack for getting into trouble," Nick observed.

They continued walking until the road eventually led out of the business section of town and into a quiet area. A few homes stood near the banks of the

North Fork River. Just then, Nick heard a rooster crow. He laughed. "I think that bird is a little late. Either that or very early."

Lucy chuckled. "I don't know, Nick, but every time you laugh, I just have to laugh, too. It's such a hearty laugh. I hope you never lose it, no matter where you go. Laughter is as good as medicine, or so the Bible says."

Nick paused in his steps. Lucy continued on, unaware he had stopped until she turned around. "Nick? Why are you back there?"

"Lucy, I wish we had more time to spend together. I wish I didn't have to go back to camp every day. I think you're a fascinating, wonderful woman who's been overlooked by her family because of a busy lifestyle and two brothers who don't know anything but mischief."

"It's not that bad," she began.

Nick came forward. The urge to comfort her was too great. She needed to know that someone cared for her as a person. That most of all, *he* cared. His arms surrounded her. She did not stir or even quake but seemed to melt in his arms as if she had been anticipating the encounter. When they kissed, he felt more alive than ever before. This was much better than conquering a steep mountain slope. He felt renewed. If only he didn't sense despair at the same time. How could he fall in love with Lucy when he might never see her again? How could this be right?

Lucy said nothing as they turned and began heading back toward the business section of town. When her hand slipped into his, he knew she didn't mind what was happening between them and even welcomed it. He welcomed it, too—for the time being—and prayed that God would give him peace, despite an uncertain future.

Chapter 11

Lucy felt as if she were floating on a cloud. All the doubts, the wondering, the questions about how Nick felt were answered in one starlit evening in Petersburg. She thought about it all that night and all the next day. Earlier that morning she'd gotten up to make Nick a special breakfast. He offered his usual bright smile at the fluffy pancakes and sausage waiting for him. He whispered what a special night it was for him. She told him it was for her, too. And when she saw him off to camp, he gave her a small peck on the cheek. It was nothing like the kiss they shared the evening before in Petersburg, but it still held a measure of love that welled up with each passing moment.

A song of praise filled her lips as she went about the morning chores. Nothing about the day seemed cumbersome at all with love like sugar racing through her. Thankfully, Momma said nothing about her cheerful mood. Even her brothers managed to stay out of the way. Daddy had given them the chore of digging a new garden patch for next year. All was peaceful. Her heart overflowed with joy. The doubts had been laid to rest. Nick was her love for life.

Lucy had just pulled out the jar of flour to make some muffins when she saw Carl running across the front yard and to the house. "Oh, Lu! You got a visitor!"

In an instant, she thought Nick had returned to say they'd given him the day off and to ask if she would like to go somewhere. Maybe to Smoke Hole and the cave there or up into the mountains for a day all to themselves. She wiped her hands on a towel and went to the front door. Standing behind the screen with a smile on his face was Allen, all dressed up in a suit. In his hand he held a bouquet of flowers. Immediately, the sense of peace drained out of her and was quickly replaced by anxiety. Her knees grew weak. She held on to the doorway to steady herself. "Allen," she managed to choke out.

"I'm back, Lucy. Finally." He gave her the bunch of daisies.

"Thank you. How—how is your granddad?"

"He's doing better. We all thought he was going to pass away at any moment, but he has a will to live. He says he wants to see us married." Allen cracked a grin. "Guess that was reason enough to keep him in the land of the living."

Suddenly the flowers lay on the ground at her feet. Lucy hurried to gather them up. "I don't know why he would think that," she murmured, heading off the kitchen to place the bouquet in a glass of water.

Allen followed. "What do you mean? Of course I've been thinking about it for weeks now, though nothing has worked out the way I planned. But today is a new day." He smiled. "So put on your best dress, Lucy. I'm taking you for a ride in the country and then to a nice dinner. I saw your mother on my way here, and she agreed to give you the day off."

Oh no! Dear God, what am I going to do? Help me. She glanced out the window, wishing Nick were here to take her in his arms and tell Allen the news—that they were in love. Heat filled her cheeks, and they felt as if they were on fire. "I–I'm surprised she would say that. I have a lot of work to do."

Allen pulled up a chair and plunked down at the kitchen table. "You always have work to do, Lucy. That's why you need some time away. With me. I need time, too. We've been apart for too long now. And I plan to have things work out, to have that date I promised you and everything else, if you catch my meaning."

"I understand that things can happen, Allen. Things change. People change, too." *Other loves can come up. Oh, how I wish you'd fallen for another girl. One in Elkins or your granddad's next-door neighbor in Charleston. Anything.*

She heard the door bump open. Carl came trotting in, looking for something to drink. "Hey, Allen! Boy, are you all fancied up."

"Sure am. I plan to take your sister to a nice place for dinner tonight. After a drive in the country."

Carl laughed. "You'd better stand in line then."

Allen chuckled. "Oh, really? What's that supposed to mean?"

"It means that Carl had better get back outside right now or Daddy's sure to find out he hasn't done the work he's supposed to do," Lucy said, throwing Carl what she hoped was a look of warning.

"I can get something to drink if I want," he retorted. "So did you tell Allen about the soldier we got staying here, Lucy? And how you went out with him to the movie last night?"

"That's enough." Lucy pushed Carl out of the kitchen. "Just for that, I'll tell Daddy everything about your cigarettes," she hissed.

Carl said no more but left abruptly with a cunning smile plastered on his youthful face. When Lucy returned to the kitchen, she felt Allen's gaze burrowing into her. "What was that all about?"

"You know Carl. He makes mountains out of molehills. Daddy took some soldiers into town last night to see a picture show. And I went along for the ride. I wanted to do something different."

Allen said nothing for a moment or two as he studied Lucy. He began to stir in his seat. "So you have some soldier living here?"

"Just temporarily. It was all Daddy's idea. He wanted to do something for the cause. He invited one of the officers to stay here at the house so he wouldn't have to sleep in a leaky tent. It's nothing to worry about."

"Well, I do worry when I hear that you were out with another man. So tell me it isn't true, Lucy, that you didn't go out with some soldier. We can forget what Carl said—he's just a nuisance anyway—and we can have ourselves a fine day."

Oh God, it wasn't supposed to happen like this. But what other way is there? I have to be honest with Allen. I can't go on deceiving him. "Okay. I'll tell you the truth, Allen. This is hard for me to say. I value our friendship so much. We've been through everything together. You're my best friend in so many ways. I've known you forever, it seems. But when Nick came along. . ."

Allen flew to his feet. His face turned red. He clenched his hand.

Oh God, help me. "A–Allen, you and I are the best of friends," she managed to continue. "I—I want to stay on being good friends. But that's all."

"You can't mean that," he began. "You knew all along I was going to propose to you. That I meant to propose to you that day by the river when those two soldiers came and ruined everything." He stopped. "It's one of them you're sweet on, isn't it?" He whirled on one foot, striding out into the foyer.

"Allen, please. I do love you, but it's not a love that one can build a marriage on. I love our friendship, the great times we've had together, and our long talks. You're a great friend."

"I don't want to be your friend, Lucy. I—I want to be your husband."

"Allen, I'm so sorry. It just isn't meant to be."

"No." He looked at her, his eyes blazing. "It's not true. It can't be true. Lucy, we've known each other since we were kids. Everyone expects us to get married. My parents, Granddad, the neighbors who come to my dad's store—even your mother. They're all talking about it." His voice began to tremble. "You'll put Granddad in his grave if he hears this. He's staying alive just to see us get married."

"Allen, you can't say that. It isn't right."

"It isn't right what you're doing, either. You walk around like you're blind. You've been hoodwinked by that soldier. Some big man who climbs a bunch of rocks. And where does that leave you? He's gonna be gone, you know. He won't be around. He may even get himself killed. And then what? You want to give up our relationship to be with someone like that? Someone who won't even be there for you?" He shook his head.

"But Nick will be there. In a different way."

Once more his fist tightened. "No. We're supposed to be together, and that's the way it's gonna be." He hurried out, the screen door slamming behind him.

Lucy collapsed into the nearest chair. Tears filled her eyes. *Oh God, what should I do? I don't know what to do.*

———

Despite the day's promising start—a wholesome breakfast and a heartwarming farewell from Lucy—Nick had his hands full at the rocks. Today he was starting a new group, and the men proved more challenging than any group he'd worked with. Nearly every man balked at climbing the first pitch, despite the preparations back at the camp and the words of encouragement.

"Private Stacy, you did fine on the wooden corncrib," Nick said, trying not to sound exasperated. "This is no different, except this is made of rock not wood. In fact, it's unmovable."

"It's a lot different, sir. One slip and that's the end. I never thought I would die on a rock. Maybe on a battlefield, but not like this. And it looks really steep."

Nick wanted to scold him for an attitude that only bred fear. He told them no one was going to die, that they would be roped in and with a safety rope as a backup. The man still hesitated, so much so that Nick panicked over the loss of time. Just as he managed to convince the soldier to try the climb, another private broke down from the stress, the tears running down his cheeks. Nick sighed, his hand sifting through his hair. He wished at that moment he was back at the soda fountain with Lucy, sipping a cold float and talking about their future.

"So what are we gonna do about them, Captain?" Fred asked, puffing from the work of belaying. "Personally, I think they should be written up. When they became part of the MTG, they knew what they were getting into."

Nick gazed up at the rock face before him. Maybe he could find a shorter, easier route. An area that could be done without the ropes, yet they would use the ropes for safety and security. Something to instill confidence so the men would be able to tackle a pitch of this degree.

"Yes, I could write them up, but that won't accomplish much, will it? Will it make them climb? No. I'll try an easier route first. You work with the ones who have already demonstrated good technique. I'll take the other men with me and see what I can find that they will be able to climb."

"You're going to need me to hold the safety rope when they get caught up there and you're left hauling them back down," Fred retorted over his shoulder.

Nick didn't even want think about having to do another rescue if one of the men froze. There had to be an easy route for them to gain their confidence. He acknowledged the two privates still discussing their fears and anxieties with each other. He ordered them to pick up their gear and follow him. Nick retraced the steps back down the path and along a narrow stretch of trail that circled the base of the rocks.

"What are we gonna do, Captain?" asked one of privates.

"We're going to climb these rocks. That's what we're here to do. But I also know it takes practice. Sometimes it's better to start with something easier. We're going to find a pitch that can be done just like the tower back at camp. Then you can say you did it, right?"

The men looked at each other and nodded. "Yes, sir."

Nick sighed, praying that God would show him the right rock. He halted then before a cliff face. Pitons had already been driven in from an earlier climb. The pitch was only about thirty feet up. Easy to negotiate and easy to get out of if necessary. He began unwinding the rope. "Looks like we have a good one here to start with, men."

"I think someone's coming, sir," one of the privates said.

Nick glanced over his shoulder to find a man quickly approaching on the trail, puffing hard from the ascent. He was dressed in a suit. *Another newspaper reporter,* Nick noted in dismay. He'd heard of reporters from the big cities, making their way to the rural area, looking to cover the training going on in the East. "Can I help you?"

"I'm looking for someone named Nick. The one staying at the Blands' house?"

"That's me. If you're here for an interview, I can talk with you later when we return to camp. I'm assisting these men with the climb right now."

Before he realized what was happening, the man rushed forward. Nick felt a sharp pain in his face. The punch drove him to the ground. The next thing he knew, he was looking up at the sky, which then became hidden by the man's snarling face. Dazed by the blow, Nick felt his shirtfront pulled taut and the man's fist pummeling him until the privates managed to drag the man away. Nick slowly sat up, his head throbbing, pain radiating from his jaw. He tasted blood and felt fragments of tooth in his mouth.

The man fought his way out of the privates' grasps. "That's a warning, soldier boy," he growled. "Lucy is my fiancée, and I won't have you anywhere near her. Stay away from my girl or next time you'll get my shotgun." The man whirled and took off down the trail.

Nick sat on the ground, rubbing his bruised jaw as the privates stared down at him in bewilderment. "Are you all right, sir? Should we go back down to the camp and get the MP? Or fetch the medic?"

"No." Slowly, Nick stood to his feet. His legs began to buckle. Everything was spinning. "Sorry, men, but I—I can't take you on the rocks. Go back to Sergeant Watkins over on the other side."

"Sir, are you sure we shouldn't get some help?"

"No. I need to head back down to camp." Nick managed to grab his backpack and the rope before stumbling down the trail. Everything was a blur. He could barely see the trail in front of him. His jaw was on fire. His tongue ran over the jagged edges of the broken tooth. He felt stunned and confused. Never had anything like this happened to him before. And right in front of the other GIs... He paused, squeezing his eyes shut. The humiliation of the event was worse than the pain in his battered jaw. He stumbled on, nearly tripping over the roots and brambles in his way. Even with all the mountain climbing he had done and the excruciating physical demands on his body, he'd never felt worse than he did at this moment.

Once Nick arrived at the camp and was examined, the medic told him he had suffered a concussion when he fell. The medic pulled what was left of Nick's broken tooth, then found an ice pack for his face. Nick was ordered to rest in the hospital tent for the remainder of the day. Several times the medic came and flashed a light in his eyes while asking him dumb questions. The ice felt good, but his heart felt broken. How could he have allowed things to come to this?

Later that evening, Fred popped in to check on him. "How are you doing, Captain?"

"I have a bruised jaw, a missing tooth, and a whopping headache."

Fred shook his head. "I heard what happened. What did you do to land yourself in a pickle jar like that, Captain? Why did that man come after you?"

Nick refused to tell Fred what happened last night in Petersburg. He would only rub it in his face and tell him he deserved it. Instead he stayed silent.

"Were you and that dame cozying up or something? I mean. . .it was the same fellow we met in that field when we first got here, right?"

"Just leave it alone, Fred."

"I'm sorry, Captain, but the whole camp is buzzing over what happened— how you got yourself hooked up with a local girl, the one whose house you're staying at. Some are even accusing you of shacking up with her."

At this, Nick struggled to sit up on the cot. The ice pack fell into his lap. "None of that is true! Whoever is spreading that kind of bald-faced lie, I'll write them up. Who are they, Fred?"

"Everyone is going a bit crazy with this thing. And those two raw privates who saw it all are telling everyone about it. Captain, speaking as your friend, this is one big mess you've gotten yourself into. I heard they're going to have another trainer transferred from Elkins to take your place for a few days while you recover. Your rock climbing escapades are over for now."

Nick lay back down and closed his eyes. "Thanks for all the good news. Right now I need to rest and think things through."

"Okay, sure. Take it easy."

Nick did not reply. There was nothing to say. Nothing but regret. How could he have let this happen? Why didn't he press Lucy for more information about her relationship with this man, a supposed friend who was really her fiancé? He'd had an inkling that a relationship with her might be unwise. Now he had the bruises to prove it.

Nick sighed. He didn't know where to begin or end or even what to do. Only life had been stopped dead in its tracks by a fist and threats from an angry soul. Confusion and turmoil reigned in his heart.

Chapter 12

I'm sorry, God. I let You down. I should have never opened myself up like I did without knowing everything. I should have never kissed Lucy. It was wrong. If I had known she was engaged, I never would have done it. He said it repeatedly to himself, but none of the words brought comfort. All he felt was pain. Looking in the mirror, the agony within matched the huge bruise extending across his jaw, which was rapidly turning black and purple. It was a stain on his being, a mark that everyone could see. He'd never felt so ashamed. He was always the proud Nick Landers, conquering hero to the masses. But he couldn't conquer this mountain. It proved too steep, too difficult, even for him. Maybe it wasn't meant to be conquered. Maybe he had deluded himself into thinking that Lucy could be his, that she was free and could even one day be his wife. All his dreams had been shattered by a fist and the humiliation it brought.

Nick found it difficult coming out of the tent the next morning. When he did, he was met with stares. Some who had not heard what happened asked if the bruise came from a tumble on the rocks. When he told them no, his voice harsher than he intended, the privates scurried away like frightened mice into the corners of the camp.

Nick sat at the table, alone in the mess tent, nursing a cup of coffee and trying to cope with the stress that seemed to follow him everywhere. He only looked up when Fred took a seat opposite him. "I'm in no mood for a lecture," he muttered.

"I don't intend to say anything, Captain. I'm only here to inquire about the day's training since your substitute hasn't arrived yet. And to ask how you're doing."

Nick hadn't given the training a thought. The men needed to continue their routine, of course. There was still his duty as an officer and to the men he vowed he would train. Without proper instruction, their lives could be placed in peril. He swallowed down some coffee. "Just do the same thing as yesterday. And try to get those other boys to do the climb."

"They actually did make the climb, you know. After you left, Private Stacy and the other fellow even did the more difficult one. I was rather surprised, I must say. So do you think you're well enough to lead?"

Nick shrugged. His heart and mind certainly weren't, even if the dizziness had subsided. The medic cleared him to observe but not to rock climb. "The medic said I need to take a few days to recover, what with the concussion and all. You'll have to wait for another trainer to help out."

"They're sending someone from the climbing school in Elkins." Fred slowly ate the cereal that resembled mush in his bowl. "It won't be the same, though." He set down his spoon. "I know we've had our differences in the past, sir. But I will admit that I admire you and your skill. Okay, so I ragged on your religion. But all in all, you're an excellent officer. I won't have anyone tell you otherwise, either, or I'll punch him in the nose."

Nick stared into the eyes of his friend. A genuineness radiated from them. He had never heard Fred speak this way. He figured the man would only ridicule him for getting involved in a local spat over a girl. This new side of Fred was a surprise, to say the least—almost as much as being slugged by Lucy's irate fiancé. "I appreciate that, Fred."

Fred picked up his bowl and stood to his feet. "I just wanted you to know."

"Thanks," he said again. "It means a lot to me." The comments did cheer him, even if he remained plagued by his circumstances.

Now he considered the day's duties. He wondered what the members of the Bland family would think with him not returning to their home last night. He would have to go back to the house and retrieve his belongings. Looking at his watch, he saw he had plenty of time. The men would be engaged in their morning routine. Drill and a climb up the wooden beehive, as Lucy called it.

Nick closed his eyes. *Lucy, why didn't you tell me you were engaged?* His anger rose. *Why did you open yourself up like that? Why tell me the man was just a friend when he was your fiancé?* He couldn't help the anger of betrayal and especially from one who professed to being a Christian. How could she deceive him like this?

Nick rose weightily to his feet. He would go right now to the Blands' house to fetch his duffel bag and anything else he'd left there. And when he left Seneca Rocks of West Virginia, he would never look back.

———

On the way to the Blands' house, Nick thought about what he might say or do should he encounter any of the family. Everyone must know by now what had happened. He prayed the family would be busy so he could sneak inside the place and grab his belongings without a confrontation. When he arrived he hid behind a tree, observing the house. Not long ago he saw Mrs. Bland and the two boys leave. He hadn't seen Lucy. He might be able to deal with her if the need arose. But what he really wanted to do was disappear and pretend none of this had ever happened.

After waiting for a bit, Nick decided to enter the house through a side door.

He had a key but found the door unlocked. Walking softly upstairs, he found his belongings where he had left them and quickly stuffed them into the duffel bag. He thought of leaving a note of thanks but decided against it. He would write to the family once he returned to camp. If he could avoid seeing anyone, all the better. Glancing around the room, his gaze fell on the mirror and the ugly bruise on his jaw. He shuddered and turned away, heading down the stairs.

"Captain Landers?"

Nick froze on the landing. The deep voice came from the kitchen area. He glanced around the corner to see Mr. Bland sitting at the table, looking at a newspaper.

"Come in and have a cup of coffee with me."

"I, uh. . ." He paused. "I really need to get back to camp, sir. I have things to do and—"

"You have a few moments to spare, I'm sure." Mr. Bland folded the newspaper and gestured toward the chair opposite him.

Nick didn't know what to do. He could leave, but his spirit told him to remain, to confront the man and whatever lay before him. He sought for the words to speak as he slowly walked over and sunk down into a chair.

"That's a nasty bruise you've got there," Mr. Bland observed, pouring him a cup of coffee. He pushed the sugar and milk toward Nick. "I guess I shouldn't ask how you got it."

"That would be better, sir," Nick said dolefully, dumping cream and sugar into the cup.

"And how are the troops progressing on the rocks?"

"Pretty well, sir. Of course, there are a few who would rather be doing something else." *Like me*, he added silently, wishing he were anywhere but here conversing with Lucy's father.

"I think that's always the case when someone tries something new. I've had a few men who didn't want to work the saw at the mill. Afraid it would cut off their hand or something, I suppose. Once I showed them how to work it, taking it all step by step, they learned. And now they run it better than me." He chuckled. "Of course, I didn't plan to be replaced by the younger ones. But they can quickly develop a talent for things. Just as I know you have a talent for what you do."

Nick wasn't sure where this conversation was heading.

"You know, things aren't always as they appear to be. I'm sure you've come to realize that, not only in the army but in life in general. Like with climbing rocks. They look tough, but there are ways to master them."

"Yes, sir. One needs to learn the technique."

"I guess one can say that for relationships, as well. Take, for instance, my daughter, Lucy."

He felt a shiver race through him and then heat build up. He set down the coffee cup, fighting to control the tremors in his hands.

"There are ways to handle relationships," he went on. "Ways to be a gentleman in all things."

"Yes, sir. I agree."

"And there are ways that can harm and even destroy the virtue of an innocent woman."

Nick sensed the rising condemnation. "Sir, let me say right now that I did nothing improper concerning your daughter. We only went for a walk that evening in Petersburg. While I confess we shared one kiss, I would have never done it had I known she was engaged."

Mr. Bland sat back. "Engaged? Lucy? To whom, may I ask?"

"Why, that fellow there. That friend of hers. I think his name is Allen."

Mr. Bland shook his head. "Lucy isn't engaged. I don't know where you came up with that idea."

"He told me they were. After he landed one on me, saying if I didn't stop seeing her, I'd be greeted with a shotgun next. Mr. Bland, I'm not here to cause trouble. I deeply regret it if I have." He stood to his feet. "You have no reason to be afraid for your daughter's virtue, at least not from me. I will take my things and go back to camp where I belong. I appreciate very much your hospitality, but I don't want to cause any more pain in your family."

Mr. Bland began to unfold the newspaper once more. "All right. But I'm wondering when you plan on telling Lucy you're leaving."

Nick stood still, blinking in astonishment, wondering if he'd heard him right. "Excuse me, sir?"

"I think you owe her that, don't you? Especially since she's been caught between two men—one she thinks of as a friend, like Allen, and one she thinks she might want to marry one day. And I'm sure after giving her that kiss, you were thinking along the same line, weren't you? I mean, I don't take kissing lightly. I think of it as the start of a commitment, you see. Many young people here, they kiss and carry on without even thinking about a commitment. But I'm a believer of commitment. I believe when you decide on that kind of contact, that you mean it to last."

"I. . ." Nick didn't know what to say for fear he might offend the man even more. "I'm not sure, sir. I know for a fact that Lucy cared about my mission here. She did her best to make me feel welcome. At first I thought it was some kind of infatuation. But I believed God was doing something greater. That is, until Allen came after me yesterday."

"Allen and Lucy have known each other a long time. He likely felt he was defending her, wrong or not. And I'm sure you know, as a Christian man, that you need to forgive him for what he did to you."

"Yes, I realize that."

"If you can find the strength to forgive him, you can forgive Lucy, as well, for any hurt you think she may have caused. And before you leave for wherever the Lord sends you, you will at least say something to her about all this and where it has led the two of you." He then turned to scan the paper once more.

Nick pondered Mr. Bland's advice for a moment before setting the house key on the table, issuing a quiet "thank you," and moving off to the back door. He couldn't quite believe the conversation. Here he had thought Lucy's father would supplement the blow Allen had delivered, with a rain of harsh words—that Mr. Bland considered him a vulture, implanting talons in his daughter's heart. But it seemed Mr. Bland liked the idea of their being together, that things were not as they appeared. And Lucy felt the same way.

Nick returned to camp, wondering where to go from here. Forget training the men for the moment. He still had a tough climb ahead of him, one of the soul and spirit. He had to decide what tactics he would need to master this steep pitch of emotion. Vanish into thin air as he had proposed to do before he met with Mr. Bland? Or seek out Lucy after the day's events were complete to try to figure out the future? Should he use tactics of kindness and gentle persuasion? Or come right out and ask her intentions?

Nick decided to check on how the training was progressing at Seneca Rocks. In the distance, he spotted the men positioned along the rocks like a line of ants, becoming ever clearer as he approached. When he arrived, Fred was on the safety rope as usual. He said nothing, even when Fred gave him a questioning glance, until the last climber had safely reached the first pitch and the command "off belay" was given.

Fred loosened the rope twisted around his waist. "Where were you off to? I noticed you had disappeared."

"I went to get my duffel bag from the Blands' house."

Fred raised an eyebrow. "That must have been an adventure. You didn't run into that fellow again, did you?"

"No. Only Lucy's father."

Fred whistled while reaching for his canteen to take a swallow of water. "That must have been an interesting encounter."

"Actually, it was. It appears he's not entirely against Lucy and I being together."

"What?"

"At least that's what I gathered from the conversation. And Lucy is not engaged, even though Allen said they were."

"I guess that lets you breathe a little easier, eh, Captain?"

"Not much," Nick admitted. "I still need to figure out what to do. He wants me to talk to Lucy. But I know we'll soon be leaving, Fred. I can't continue a relationship from across the country or even the ocean. If we get sent to the front, which seems likely, then there really isn't a reason to pursue this."

"Then, my friend, you should have never started anything to begin with." Fred twisted the cap back on the canteen. He handed the rope off to Nick. "I know you can't climb, but are you up to holding the safety rope and belaying this short pitch for me? The other trainer is on the opposite side of the rocks."

Nick did so, trying to keep his attention focused as his friend began the climb to where the other men waited. Nick looked on as Fred felt for each hand- and foothold, using the piton to connect his carabiner, careful to do all that was required to maintain the utmost safety. He began to pray, too, that God would likewise lead him as he tried to navigate the precarious foot- and handholds in his relationship with Lucy, until he reached solid ground.

Chapter 13

Lucy could not imagine the changes in fortune, sending her from one extreme of emotion to the other. After the evening in Petersburg with Nick, when she'd felt the strength of his arms around her and his lips on hers, she was flying on a cloud. And now suddenly she felt herself tumbling out of control after the encounter with Allen. Whispers abounded soon after. She had not seen Allen since the meeting when he first learned of her preference for Nick over him. Nor had she seen Nick for that matter. She felt certain the two men had met somehow. When she glanced in Nick's room the next morning, she saw he had not slept in his bed, though his belongings were still there. Then when she arrived back after visiting a friend, she found all his personal items gone. A knot formed in her stomach. Somehow Allen had driven Nick away, just like he said he would. She simply had to find out what happened.

Lucy put on her polka dot dress and even a touch of color to her lips. She wanted to look her best when she went to confront Allen. She needed confidence. Picking up her purse, she rushed out the back door, hoping no one in her family would see her. She didn't want to have to explain her every move to them. She was on God's path now, and a path she felt certain Nick and she were to walk, even if everyone else thought otherwise.

When she arrived at the store, she met a few of her neighbors, including Mrs. Sampson who gave her a bright smile. "Well, I hear it's soon to be official, Lucy!"

She blinked. "What's that, Mrs. Sampson?"

"About you and Allen. Of course, I knew it all along. You two just seemed to be a pair. I guess because I saw you two together when you were still in diapers." She chuckled.

A sick feeling came over Lucy. What was Allen telling everyone? A wave of anger gripped her as she pushed open the door. Allen stood behind the counter, his back to her, putting items on the shelf. "Allen."

He spun, the boxes he had put up on the shelf tumbling down in a shower. "Lucy, you can't come sneaking up on me like that." He began picking up boxes from the floor.

"Well, you can't be telling lies."

He looked at her over the counter and quickly stood to his feet. "Excuse me?"

Lucy put her purse on the counter. "You heard me. You're telling everyone that we're getting married."

"I didn't tell everyone. No one but the goody-goody soldier, that is. He needed to know where things stood."

Lucy stared wide eyed. "Why did you tell Nick that?"

"Because it's the truth." He looked over at a few customers who stood in the aisles, gawking at them. "Can you keep your voice down, Lucy? You're scaring the customers."

"You'd better find your father or someone to take over, because you have some explaining to do." Lucy took her purse off the counter and marched outside, plunking herself down on a bench. She nodded at the customers that entered the store. Now her gaze fell on Seneca Rocks. Dark clouds began to drift over them. She couldn't help the tears that flooded her eyes. How could Allen have done something like this—tell Nick that they were engaged? Now it made sense why Nick had left their home in such a hurry. And how he must dislike her, too, for thinking she had kept this secret from him, only to have them kiss on a street in Petersburg. She couldn't help the anger foaming up within. *Oh God, why did this have to happen?* When she thought about it, though, she realized most of this was her fault. If she had been open and honest with Allen about her feelings from the beginning, all of this might have been avoided.

The door to the store bumped open, and Allen stumbled out. "I really need to watch the store, Lucy. Dad said he could take over for ten minutes, but that's it."

She patted the seat next to her. "Allen, come here. I need to say something."

He raised an eyebrow but he followed her lead and sat down cautiously beside her.

"I wanted to say I'm sorry I wasn't honest about Nick right out. All that talk about getting together and everything. I wasn't being truthful. I should have told you that I loved Nick. Like I said, you're my best friend in so many ways. But he's different. He isn't a friend. He's more like—"

"He's nothing," Allen muttered.

"No. He's everything I need in a husband. You're everything I need in a friend. You both fill different roles, and roles that are both dear to me."

Allen stood to his feet. "You think he's better than me, don't you? Just because he can climb an old rock. Well let me tell you, he sure can't defend himself. He's a fish. Weak. Can't even stand up for himself like a man. I don't know what you see in him."

Lucy stared.

"I told him to stay away from you. That we. . ." Allen paused. "You know we're supposed to be engaged, Lucy. I just jumped the gun a bit and told him that. But he needed to know that I wanted him out of your house and your life."

Lucy flew to her feet, clutching her purse to herself. "You can't do things like that, Allen. You can't speak for me or about the plans God has for my life. And I can say that friends don't do this to one another. They don't twist arms and hearts. They understand and care for each other. They are there for each other, no matter what. I've come to realize this even more after my own error. But if you can't see it, too, then this really needs to be good-bye."

Lucy headed down the stairs of the store and out to the road. She had no idea where she was going. At this point, she didn't care. Her mind lay in a fog. She had lost everything. Allen's friendship. Nick's love. She had nothing left. She tried not to look at the rocks that only added to the misery in her heart. She didn't even look at the rows of tents in the distance that began to materialize. Even when raindrops began falling in earnest from the darkened skies, she walked on. She would continue until there was no more pain. She didn't care where she ended up, either. Even if it was in the next county.

Suddenly a horn sounded. She wiped the strings of her damp hair out of her eyes and continued walking, ignoring the vehicle that crept up beside her.

"Lucy?" a voice called out from the passenger window.

She looked up even though the rain fell harder, making it difficult to see. She couldn't believe her eyes. The voice belonged to Nick.

"What are you doing out here? Where are you going?"

"Nowhere," she said, looking away.

Nick said something to the driver, who obliged and pulled the military jeep over to the side of the road a hundred feet ahead of her. Nick jumped out. Lucy looked at him and saw a nasty bruise on his face. Her breath caught at the sight.

"You shouldn't be walking out here in the rain. And you're already starting to shiver. Come on and get into the jeep."

She shook her head. "N–no. Just go ahead, Nick. Leave me alone. That's what you did. Left me alone."

Instead of answering her, he took her by the hand and led her over to the jeep, then opened the back door. "Please get in. Stan, go ahead and drive back to the barracks. Then I will take this young lady home."

The driver obliged, taking them to the tent city where he exited the jeep. Nick took the wheel and pointed to the passenger seat beside him. Lucy slowly moved from the back to the front seat, refusing to look Nick in the eye, even if his bruised face did spawn questions. He put the vehicle into gear and sped down the road. "Where are we going?" Lucy asked. "I don't intend to go home right now."

"I'm taking you to a place where I can get you a cup of coffee. You need something warm in you before you catch cold."

"I'm not cold."

He gave her a sideways glance. "So why were you walking out there?"

"I'll give you three reasons."

"I take it I'm one of the reasons."

She paused at his honesty. "Well, yes. You left without saying a word. You just packed up your things and left. You blame me for what Allen said, and it isn't right."

"Lucy, I don't blame you."

"Yes, you do. And I had nothing to do with it. I can't help it if Allen got angry and went and told you we were engaged when he knew it wasn't the truth."

"I know. Your dad told me."

At this, Lucy stared in disbelief. "You talked to Daddy?"

"It was a very good conversation. He's quite a wise man. And. . .I think he likes me."

Lucy couldn't help cracking a smile. "He's enjoyed having you at the house. He reads the paper all the time about the war. I think it's been good for him to talk to a soldier who's training for it. If he were younger, I'm sure he would have signed up. He holds nothing but the highest regard for you."

"I could sense it. It was like the best tonic I could get. It's hard to get any respect these days. You try to gain the respect of your soldiers. But I have to admit, since the whole incident, I've lost the respect of my men. Everyone looks at me strangely. Even with the men I used to command, there's a difference in the way they respond to me."

Lucy shook her head in confusion. "I don't understand why you're having such trouble."

"I guess you didn't hear. Your friend Allen hunted me down at the cliffs and gave me a present, right in front of my men." Nick pointed to the bruise that decorated his face.

Lucy gasped. "Oh no! Allen did that?"

"And he told me he would come after me with a shotgun if I ever got near you again. Not that I was about to leave you on the side of the road in the rain today, even if he does come after me. I'm willing to take the risk."

"Oh, Nick, I'm so sorry. I don't know what to say."

"You don't have anything to be sorry for."

Tears welled up in her eyes. "Yes, I do. If I had been open and honest with Allen about my feelings, none of this would have happened. I led Allen on. I didn't have the courage to tell him I had fallen in love with you." There. She'd said it at last. She didn't care what Nick thought of it, either. It was all out in the open, before both men, to digest at will. No more secrets lay between any of them now.

Nick said nothing for a few moments. Finally he responded in a quiet voice. "Lucy, I'm speechless."

"You don't have to say anything. I just had to say it myself, because it's been bottled up inside me since the first day I laid eyes on you. I can't explain why, but you're someone very special to me, Nick. I know you don't feel the same way, but that's okay. I want you to know that I care about you. With everything in my heart." She hesitated. "But I think you care a little bit, too, or else you wouldn't have kissed me the other night."

Nick chuckled as he steered the jeep into a parking place at the corner diner. "Lucy, you're worth kissing. You're a wonderful, caring woman. I'll have to admit, on that street, all I wanted to do was reassure you, to let you know that I see everything you do here, even if you feel buried by the roles you play at home. Honestly, I hadn't intended to kiss you. But it seemed the right thing to do, and I still believe it was."

Before Lucy could say anything else, Nick leaned over, his face close, his lips once again seeking hers.

"Nick?" she managed to say when he withdrew, her lips still tingling from the kiss.

"I guess it was the right thing to do again, Lucy," he said with a laugh. His fingers reached out to touch her face. "You have such a sweet spirit. I only wish. . ."

"What?"

"Never mind." He pocketed the jeep key. "Let's get you that cup of coffee."

Moments later, Lucy sat at the booth, nursing a cup of coffee with the steam warming her cheeks. Not that she needed any more warmth after the tender moment with Nick in the jeep. He had also ordered a coffee and laced it with cream and sugar, four teaspoons' worth. When Lucy commented on the amount, he only shrugged. "I like my drinks sweet," he explained. "Just like my girls."

"So you've had other girls?"

"Just one. I think I told you about her. She never liked the mountains. She wasn't the rugged type. I couldn't see her putting on overalls and crossing rivers with a basket of muffins over one arm." He grinned before taking a drink of coffee.

"So where do we go from here, Nick?"

He sat back in his seat, his gaze never leaving her. "Once my mission here is accomplished, I move on, Lucy. Probably back to Colorado."

Lucy leaned forward. "Then take me with you. I think I would love Colorado, from what you've described."

Nick shook his head, fingering the cup handle. "I can't do that, Lucy. I don't know how long I will even be at Camp Hale when the call comes up. I could end up leaving for Europe. You won't know anyone in Colorado. You're better off here, with your family and the people you know. And, of course, the rocks."

Lucy sighed. "So I wait here not knowing." She then righted herself. "Then at least marry me before you leave."

Nick's mouth fell open. His hand jerked so he nearly upset his coffee cup. "Marry you?"

"Yes. Why not? At least we can have a few days of married life together. We can have a simple ceremony, maybe even at the rocks. Then I will wait for you to come back from the war."

Nick shook his head, much to her disappointment. "Lucy, don't you think you're rushing this?"

"No. There isn't any time. I don't want to lose you, Nick. And it would settle things once and for all, as far as Allen is concerned. Please. Let's just do this before your duty and the war tear us apart."

Nick downed the rest of his coffee. "Again you leave me speechless, Miss Lucy Bland. I don't know what I can say to something like that. In fact, normally the fellow asks for the girl's hand in marriage. I don't even have a ring and—"

"I don't care. Rings don't matter to me. I don't even own any jewelry. Please, let's just do this."

Nick wiped his hand across his face and sighed. "Lucy, I wish I could come right out and say yes. But I don't know the future. You don't know the future. You could be making the worst mistake of your life."

"I trust God, Nick. And I know you do, too."

"I trust Him also with times and seasons. And when the time is right for a commitment. I—I don't believe it's that time, Lucy. We've only known each other a few weeks. You can't say you know enough about me."

"That's not true. I know you well enough to want to marry you."

"Lucy, you can't say that. Neither of us can. Only time can help."

"But it can't, Nick, don't you see? There is no time. Soon you'll be gone."

Nick came to his feet. "Speaking of which, it's getting late. I need to be heading back. I hope you understand what I need to do—that other things take priority right now."

"Of course. Duty calls." She grabbed her purse. "I only wish you would consider other duties, too, Nick. Duties that can be just as important as your rock climbing. Like duties to people." She paused. "Maybe I know now why that other girl left you. It's hard to compete with a rock wall, both on the inside and the out." To her surprise, Nick said nothing. The ride back to her home was made in silence. When she walked in the front door to the sound of the jeep driving away, the family pounced. Momma scolded Lucy for her damp dress. Carl and Tim asked about the jeep in the front yard. Daddy inquired what happened.

"Nothing, Daddy," Lucy said glumly. "Not a thing." She went to her room and flopped down on the bed. It couldn't end this way, not after all they had been through, even if it had been a mere few weeks. There had to be love there. But how could love remain, especially after her comments this night? She wished she had not said those angry words to Nick. That she had given him time to consider her request. She had been too impulsive once again, acting out of desperation propelled by anxiety. She wanted so much to marry Nick and not risk losing him. Now she may have lost him anyway.

Lucy rose from the bed and went to the desk drawer, taking out the first letter she had ever written to Nick. She found an envelope and addressed it as before. *Captain Nicholas Landers, Seneca Rocks Camp.* "At least this note will tell you my true heart, Nick," she murmured, giving the note a light kiss. "Even if there's nothing else left to hope for."

A week later, Nick was gone. There was no note from him. No word at all. Lucy looked at Seneca Rocks with a thick lump in her throat, her heart heavy like stone. But the tears refused to come. Nick had made his decision. And she had made hers.

She would wait as long as she had to, just as her letter said.

Chapter 14

Summer 1945

Two years had come and gone. Lucy still couldn't believe how much time had slipped by. In all that time she'd only received a few letters from Nick, mostly having to do with his work in Colorado and expressing his thanks to her family for its hospitality. Nothing about the encounter at the diner where she'd confessed her true feelings or the kisses they'd shared or her plea that they marry. Nothing about the letter she sent, even, or what the future may hold. It seemed everything they had nurtured during his short time at Seneca Rocks had disappeared, as if nothing had ever happened.

Allen asked repeatedly for her to forgive him and to accept his proposal of marriage. Lucy politely refused, though she had met him for an occasional soda at the shop. Other men had come around, asking for dates. She had refused them, as well.

Instead, Lucy took long walks along the North Fork River. She ventured to the base of the rocks to view the pitons still there, hammered in by Nick's hand. Her feet traced the paths in the fields where tents and the massive beehive once stood. She paid homage to the place where Nick first greeted her with his dazzling smile. And then she came to the road in Petersburg where he had announced his love with a kiss. Had it all been real or just a dream? Maybe it was simply a dream and she should stop living in the past.

At least Daddy had caught wind of her unhappiness and tried to help. He taught her how to drive. He gave her a little bungalow that she could call her own. She fixed it up with some of Momma's old linens and a few pieces of furniture the family no longer needed. Lucy was glad for the tiny home that provided her a place of refuge to think about her life and her future, however bleak it seemed. Many days she would think back to that time nearly two years ago—had it been that long?—when the military men first came to climb the rocks. And dear Nick, who remained vivid in her thoughts, his words reverberating in her ears, his kiss on her lips, still fresh and inviting. Momma and Daddy had suggested many times that she let go of the past and embrace the idea of her future with another man. Even Daddy knew of a few men at the mill who wanted to ask her out on a date. But Lucy couldn't. Not until she had confirmation that

Nick had indeed moved on with his life, whether by marriage to another woman or because of the war.

Eventually, Nick's letters had trickled down to nothing. Lucy had tried to discover what may have happened to him by traveling to Elkins with Daddy. There she'd sought out town officials who had records of the military units who came back from the war. With that Lucy was able to find the address for Camp Hale and wrote Nick letters. When they came back *Return to Sender*, she tried calling officials in Colorado. They could tell her nothing until late in the fall of 1944. It was then she learned the division would be sent to Italy. They took her name and address and said someone would be in touch if there was any news about Captain Nicholas Landers. All she could do from that moment on was cling to the news reports in Daddy's paper, listen to the radio, or watch the newsreels at the theater for any hint of Nick's possible whereabouts. Lucy lived her life by Seneca Rocks, waiting for any news whether good or bad.

Today she went about her duties as usual, which included watering the flowers she had planted not too long ago. Momma and she had gone into the woods and dug up wildflower roots to plant in a little garden near her tiny home. It was hard to believe that God had provided her this quaint dwelling just up the road from her parents. The house had belonged to a man who worked at the mill, and when he died of a heart attack last year, his relatives gave the bungalow to Daddy as a gift. In turn it became Lucy's.

"Wanna go for a walk, Lu?" a voice greeted her.

Lucy looked up and saw Tim standing near the road. He had grown up these past two years. Tall, with an ever-ready smile, his voice was slowly changing as he entered his teen years. While nearly sixteen-year-old Carl was entertaining a new girlfriend or asking Daddy about driving an automobile, Tim would stop by and ask to do something with her. He was still of the age to enjoy a sibling relationship. And she'd never found him as much of a nuisance as Carl. Tim had an innocence about him that she liked. She cherished their sibling bond, especially during these lonely months. "You know better than to call me Lu," Lucy warned him with a smile.

"Yeah, I know. Just wanted to see your reaction."

"I guess I could go for a walk. Let me finish watering the flowers." Lucy emptied the rest of the watering can on the plants, then set the can down by the steps. They took off down the road, heading toward Hopper General Store. Before her rose the familiar sight of Seneca Rocks. At least the rocks didn't bother Lucy as much as they had when Nick first left. She could barely look at the rocks then without shedding a tear. Now the sight had become commonplace again, just as it was before Nick had ever set foot here. A settling of things inside her heart, she'd decided.

"Let's go into the Hoppers' store," Tim said. "I want a soda. I'm thirsty."

Lucy obliged. She didn't mind going into the store now that Allen was engaged to a girl named Susan. Allen and Lucy still talked to each other, though things were never the same after the episode with Nick. As it was, Lucy had just received an invitation to Allen's wedding. At least things weren't too bad if Allen felt inclined to invite her. She thought she might have been excluded or he would be bitter over the way things ended. There was a bright spot to be had in all this, and he didn't look down on her for what she'd decided.

At that moment she did wonder about her decision. Waiting for some ghost of a man, whom she had no idea where he was or if he still existed. It seemed ludicrous. Maybe she needed to move on with her life. She had waited two years, after all. Two years of her life pining away for a man she was never meant to have. She sighed and vowed the next time a man asked her out on a date, she would accept.

Several automobiles were parked by the storefront when they arrived. People milled about sharing news. A car door opened, and a lanky man stood up. Lucy wouldn't have taken any notice except the man withdrew a pair of crutches from the backseat. Upon closer inspection, she saw that part of his leg was missing.

"He's back, Lu," Tim said with a grin. "Ha, ha! See! Gotcha good! And you didn't even see it coming."

"What are you talking about, silly?" Lucy continued walking until a voice stopped her short.

"Hi, Lucy."

She turned. The man with the crutches had greeted her. She blinked. "Do I know you?"

"Are you daft, Lu?" Tim chided, elbowing her. "He's your soldier, the one who stayed with us! That captain is back. I ran into him when I came to the store earlier. He told me to come fetch you. Surprise!"

Lucy could only stand there like a statue. Was this thin and ragged man with a scraggly beard and using crutches because of a missing leg, Nicholas Landers? Her Nick? It didn't seem real. Maybe this was just another dream like the ones she often had at night, wondering what he looked like years later.

He hobbled over on the crutches. "I know this must come as a shock," he began.

Lucy didn't know what to say or do. Finally she opened her purse and gave Tim some money to buy a few sodas. "Take your time."

"Sure." Tim winked.

They moved off to sit on a bench in front of the store. "I don't blame you for not speaking to me," Nick said, easing himself down on the bench and propping the crutches against the wall. "I decided to come back. I had to see you again."

Once more she tried to think of the words to say. Only questions filled her mind. Why did he leave without saying good-bye? Why did he cease responding to her letters? Why was there so little in the way of communication from him for almost two years? Why? But she asked none of them. She only sat in silence.

"I also wanted to come back and thank your parents for everything they did for me. You all were such a big part of my life two years ago. You were like family to me. I owed you at least that." He paused. "I know what you're going to say: that family doesn't do these kinds of things to each other. They don't leave without a word about where they are going or what is happening. They stay in communication. They pray for each other." He looked down at the ground. "I did pray, Lucy. I could do nothing else but pray. My life was in God's hands."

"What—what happened?" she finally managed to choke out.

He glanced at his leg. "You mean this? It happened in Italy. We were under heavy enemy fire. A mortar blasted into a trench about fifty feet away. Should have taken me out. Instead the shrapnel tore off my leg. I saw my leg there and my foot, lying in the trench. An awful sight."

Lucy shivered and looked away.

"Sorry. I guess I shouldn't have gotten so descriptive. It was hard. I thought I would die, there was so much blood. I looked over at Fred and asked him to get me the medic and maybe my leg while he was at it. It was a sick joke, I know. It was so surreal. . . He didn't answer me. I said, 'Fred, c'mon, I need that medic now. I lost my leg.'" Nick hesitated. "Then I saw the blood coming from under his helmet. He had taken one in the head. He was gone."

"I'm so sorry, Nick. I know he was your friend."

Tears filled his eyes. "He was gone, just like that. Talking to me one moment. Telling me the mortar blasts were getting awfully close and asking if we should abandon our position. And then he was gone."

"I'm sorry, Nick," she said again.

"But you know, he accepted the Lord only a few months before that. We were still in Colorado. He was on a ledge and a piton came loose. He was dangling there, a couple hundred feet above the ground. He said he saw his life flash before his eyes. And he saw how black and cold it was. After that we talked. He wanted assurance he would see life after death. So I talked to him about accepting the Lord and the gift of eternity."

"I'm so glad, Nick. That must give you comfort."

"It does a little. At least Fred is in a good place. I just wish I had gone there with him, that the mortar had taken out my heart and not my leg."

"Why?"

The question seemed to catch him off guard. She saw the confusion in his eyes. He suddenly turned quiet.

At that moment Tim returned with cold sodas for each. "So how is the reunion going? Bet you're glad you don't have to fight anymore, huh, Nick?"

"I suppose. The battlefield is a terrible place, I must say. Even in my dreams, I can still hear the grenades and mortars going off. If I hear a loud truck, I think it's enemy tanks crossing the breach."

"Well, there's no enemy here," Tim said matter-of-factly. "And guess what? Did you know Lucy's been waiting for you all this time? Did you tell him, Lu, how you refused to go on any dates, even with men from Daddy's sawmill? That all you did was wait? Even Allen finally gave up and now he's getting married in a few months. We just got the invitation for it."

Lucy wanted to silence Tim, who never had any trouble sharing everything he knew in life. Yet the look Nick gave her stilled her heart. A look of wonder and maybe of gratitude. Though why he would be grateful, she wasn't certain. He'd abandoned her, after all. But looking down at his devastating wound, how could she be angry for what he'd done? She began to drink her soda. Try as she might to find mercy in this situation, the words were still hard to say.

"So how are you?" he finally asked her.

"All right. Daddy taught me how to drive. Someone at his mill died and left him this small house, which he lets me use. So now I have my own place."

"Good for you. I know how much you wanted to be out on your own."

"Do you want to see it? Can you walk that far?"

"I can walk as far as I need to," he said a bit gruffly, as if her challenge had sparked defiance in him. She told Tim she would see him later and headed out with Nick, pleased he was able to keep pace with her on his crutches. She marveled at his strength. After all his rock climbing, he must have developed strong arm muscles to pull himself up so many cliff faces. She thought about that fact and suddenly became somber. He would never be able to do those things again. He could never maneuver himself with crutches up the steep mountain trail to the top of Seneca Rocks. And certainly he wasn't in the army any longer. She glanced out the corner of her eye at his civilian shirt and navy blue trousers, so different from the green she was accustomed to him wearing. Everything had changed.

When they arrived, he was panting. Sweat rolled down his face. Lucy immediately went to fetch him a glass of water, which he accepted. "Nice place," he noted, easing himself down on the front step.

"I can bring out some chairs," Lucy began.

"I'm fine. Even if I look like I can't do anything anymore, I can do plenty."

Lucy bit her lip at the accusation his words implied. "I didn't mean—"

"I know. I'm sorry that came out the way it did. I'm just tired of people seeing me as a cripple in need of special care. My mother spent the last few months babying me. Fetching me everything. I tried to tell her I could do things for myself. She spent the day by my side, crying." He paused then. "Mourning her poor crippled son's loss, I guess."

"You aren't poor, Nick, not with the Lord on your side."

For an instant he grimaced. Lucy wondered about his response. Was Nick angry with God for what had happened? He didn't say it, but his reaction spoke volumes. Finally he murmured, "I guess," before downing the rest of his water.

"I plan to get a job," Lucy continued. "Now that I know how to drive, Daddy said there might be jobs near the mill. So I'm going to look around. I need money to get things for the house. Momma gave me a few things to get me started."

"You really have changed," he noted. "I mean, having your own house and everything. You seem to know where you're going in life, and that's good."

"What about you, Nick? Are you going to stay in Colorado?"

He snorted. "Living next to mountains I can never climb again is like having a perpetual pin stuck in me. It's nice to look at, but the idea I can't do the only thing I love—it hurts too much."

"I'm sure once you get a prosthesis, you will be able to do more."

He shrugged. "I suppose."

"I mean it won't be the same as having a real leg. But then you can get around better."

"You always were the optimist," he said with a smirk. "Lucy coming to feed hungry soldiers with her muffins. Lucy offering to help guide. Lucy, who's always been there for me when I needed her most."

But you weren't there for me, Nick. You left me two years ago. You said nothing to me. Did you ever think of me during all that time? Did you ever wonder what I was doing? Did you have any feelings for me at all?

"But I'm not here to gain sympathy," Nick was quick to add. "I just wanted to come back and thank you all for everything. For making it a special time in my life that I will never forget."

"I'm sure Daddy and Momma would like to see you. You don't have to be anywhere, do you?"

"I'm staying with a friend in Elkins. I need to tell him I'm here somehow and what I'm doing. He's visiting a cousin who lives near here. Sadie Mahone."

"I know Sadie. We can call her on the telephone and let her know that you will be staying for supper, and she can give the information to your friend. Then he can come by and pick you up. If that's all right."

Nick nodded. "That would be great, Lucy. Kind of like old times. . ." He hesitated, then added, "Having a meal together and all." He took up his crutches and maneuvered himself to a standing position. Lucy couldn't help watching. She bit her lip to keep her emotions at bay. Maybe it was better that they had this final good-bye. Or was it really good-bye? Maybe it was really a "Hello, I'm back to stay." *If you will only forgive, Lucy, and open your heart up to a man who has lost so much.* She did not know what the outcome might be. Once again her future lay with God and with Nick.

<hr>

Nick's presence in the Blands' home seemed to humble them all. Carl, in particular, appeared upset by what had happened to Nick. At first, Carl wanted to hear all the news of the war. When he learned the details of Nick's wound and Fred's death, he turned silent. Tim was the more positive one out of them all, encouraging Nick to get a prosthesis and keep living life to the fullest. Lucy marveled at how her brothers had changed since the days when they were nothing but trouble.

Daddy and Momma both sat and listened carefully to everything Nick shared, offering a sympathetic ear and plenty of good food, which Nick appeared to enjoy. Yet a distinct sadness prevailed. Nick had changed so much. It was not only the wound to his leg that ailed him but some untold wound to his soul.

After the meal, Momma shooed Lucy out of the kitchen, claiming she would do the dishes. Daddy also left them alone and went seeking his paper. Lucy and Nick took seats outside on the porch to enjoy the nice evening.

"It was good to see everyone again," he commented. "Carl and Tim have grown up quite a bit."

"Yes. I think life itself got them thinking about where they are going and what they will do."

"War is also an eye-opener. I didn't really know what I was getting myself into. I thought all my skill in mountaineering would save me. But when the fire rains down, nothing can save you except the hand of God. I guess I should be happy that I'm alive. But right now, I'm not sure what I'm living for."

"God isn't done with you yet, Nick Landers. He still has a plan for your life."

Nick sighed. "I'm not sure what a one-legged man can do. The life I used to know is gone forever. Hard to believe. Sometimes I can't quite believe it myself. But I know I have to wake up one day and accept it."

Lucy sat still for a moment, praying for the words to say. From here she could make out the image of Seneca Rocks through the tree branches. "The rocks are still the same, no matter what happens," she commented.

"What?"

"Seneca Rocks. They stay the same. Even when it snows, rains, or the sun is shining on them, they never change. They may look different, but in essence they remain the same. You're still the same, Nick. You may have gone through storms. You may have only one leg right now. But the same Nick is there, the man God made. And the same man God can still use, if you let Him. The trials get us ready for a greater purpose. You're still the same man who trained all those young men to get over their fears. The same man who helped lead a lost person to Christ before he died. And the same man who still has so much to live for."

Silence met her ears except for the occasional scraping of a few branches against the side of the house. Lucy thought she heard a sniff. Was Nick crying? She looked over, but the shadows of the falling dusk masked his face.

Just then, a car pulled up. Nick slowly came to his feet. "My ride.'

"Will I see you tomorrow?" Lucy asked.

For a moment he stood there, balancing on the crutches, weighing everything. Her heart began to patter. She knew he was considering everything—the past, the present, the future. He stared off toward Seneca Rocks as if studying them. He took a step forward. Her heart began to flutter. Then just as quickly, he shook his head. "I can't, Lucy. Thanks for everything. I mean it sincerely."

Her heart sank. Tears welled up in her eyes as he hobbled away. When the car door slammed shut, she knew he had shut the door for the last time. There was no turning back or going forward. "Good-bye forever, Nick," she whispered and ran off to shed her tears.

Chapter 15

Lucy thought it a fine plan that sunny afternoon a few days later—to take a picnic lunch and make peace with her troubled heart by the rocks she had known all her life. Seneca Rocks. The rocks that had brought Nick to her and then suddenly sent him away. But it was not really the rocks that did it. Or her. Or even God. It was meant to be this way. She believed it. She had kept her end of the bargain. She had waited until they were reunited. Nick had come back alive, even if he was missing a part of his limb and his heart. And he had made his decision.

Lucy folded a red gingham cloth to cover the contents of the basket. It seemed hard to believe she'd decided to bring food with her on this journey, as if she could eat one bite. But it seemed the right thing to do. She'd even baked a few muffins. Packed bread and cheese. A bottle of milk. The basket was heavy, but she would bear it. She would offer it all to God and find her happiness and her worth in Him as she broke bread.

Picking up the handle to the basket, Lucy began the trek toward the famous rocks that seemed to beckon to her. She felt strength surge through her. Suddenly the basket didn't feel as heavy anymore. She felt light on her feet. God was already doing a work of restoration. Giving her the oil of joy for mourning. Giving her a thankful heart.

Just then, Lucy heard a car horn sound. She prayed it wasn't a neighbor looking to spy on her and ask her questions. Or Allen, though she had not seen him for quite a while. She turned to see who it was and caught sight of a familiar face in the passenger seat.

Nick.

Her heart nearly stopped.

The car pulled over. Nick whispered something to the driver, then opened the door.

"Wherever you plan on going, I'd sure like to come along."

Lucy stared as he took out the crutches. She didn't know what to say. Finally, she blurted out, "I—I was going on a picnic."

"Really. With whom?"

"With no one. No one, that is, except God. I mean, He isn't no one, but, oh, never mind."

His face broke into a smile. Oh, how she loved his smile. It was in her every dream from the first day she'd laid eyes on him. "I wonder if I dare ask if it's all right for me to come along."

"I'm sure He won't mind."

Nick turned to address the driver. When they came to some manner of agreement, he rose out of the car using his crutches. As they entered the field, Nick kept up with her pace for pace. When they reached the river, he found a rock to sit down on. "Need a little breather," he said.

"This is as good a spot as any." Lucy announced, spreading the red gingham cloth onto the grass and placing food upon it. When she produced the muffins, Nick stared in shock and amazement.

"You didn't know I was still around, did you?"

"No. I made them for me. Well, and for God. Sort of a peace offering. I was going to come here and. . ." She hesitated. What was she going to do? "I was going to offer everything to God. Everything from the last few years." She hesitated. "But I thought—I thought you were leaving for good."

"I considered it. Where would I go, really? Then I said to myself, how can I leave the one woman who cared for me? Why should I abandon her again and hurt her heart and mine? I would be throwing everything away. I've already lost enough. I wasn't going to lose you, too. Then it really would have been the end of me. Because, Lucy Bland, you mean everything to me."

Lucy blushed and handed him a muffin. "Here."

"I don't suppose you would mind a trade?"

Lucy stared wide-eyed as he withdrew a simple box from his pocket. She couldn't believe she was actually seeing this. "That isn't what I think it is," she began.

"It's just an idea I have. I know we haven't spoken much since I left. That we still have a lot to learn about each other. But this is a token of a promise and one I intend to keep with all my heart, if you'll let me." He showed her the ring. "This is my promise like the one you made me. That I will be there for you always, Lucy. I won't turn away. I will do whatever I must to fulfill my destiny, with you by my side. And I believe the mountains can still be a part of it all."

"Oh, Nick," Lucy said softly, taking the ring. "It's so beautiful."

"I bought it back in Colorado," he confessed.

"What? In Colorado? But. . ." His statement confused her. He had left the first time without even saying good-bye. They had hardly remained in contact but for a few scant letters. And hadn't he said good-bye just the other day at her parents' home?

"In fact, it was not long after I got out of the hospital that I bought it for you. I didn't know what you would say or do when I came back here. But I bought it as a leap of faith. And I knew you. I knew you would wait, like your letter said. So I decided to take my own leap. And I prayed—'God, if You can make this come to pass, I will be the happiest man alive. If not, I'll know it is Your will.' But I trusted you, Lucy. I knew you would wait for me. You are the most honest and devoted woman there is."

"But why did you leave the other night?"

He blew out a sigh. "I wanted to wait for the right time and place to give you the ring. I'm sorry if it seemed like I was abandoning you. But I wanted to give this to you all along."

Lucy ran her finger over the small diamond set in a silver base.

"I love you, Lucy. Please forgive me for any hurt I've caused you. For not being there. But I will be here for you. Always. All I want to do is spend the rest of my life with you. . . ."

She gazed at the ring, thinking how perfect everything seemed here, with the river running by her feet. When she slipped the ring on her finger, he laughed as his arms swept her up in a tender embrace.

"Glory be," he murmured, nuzzling his face in her hair. "And you will have a whole man, Lucy. I promise."

"I have a whole man. His name is Nick Landers. He's more whole than any man there is, because God is with him."

Nick kissed her and then took up his muffin. "Now I'll have my end of the bargain." He bit into it. "Excellent as always, Lucy. Just as I remember. And that's all I remembered, even when I was over in Italy. I'd be in my tent, listening to the enemy fire and thinking of you and the times we had. Wondering what you were doing. Hoping and praying that if I survived, God would somehow reunite us. And I'm glad He's faithful, or I'd be one miserable and lonely person, knowing I might have lost the best woman in the world for me."

Lucy sighed. At that moment everything else faded but the man sitting before her and the miracle that God had wrought. Her tears began to flow. Tears from all the time spent waiting and wondering. And now to this special moment, with a ring on her finger and the promise of a man who wanted to spend his life with her.

"Are you okay, Lucy?" Nick asked, curling his arm around her.

"Yes. I'm just so happy."

⸻

Eight weeks later, Nick and Lucy stood before the shadow cast by Seneca Rocks in the green pasture and celebrated their marriage with family and friends. Nick stood on two legs for the ceremony, having obtained a prosthesis. Lucy wore her mother's wedding dress and her grandmother's pearls. The ceremony was simple but everything Lucy had ever dreamed it would be.

When the wedding ceremony concluded, everyone headed back to the Blands' home where Momma and Daddy put on a nice reception in the backyard, complete with plenty of miniature muffins and, of course, a wedding cake that Momma made from scratch. Lucy and Nick chatted with friends old and new. Just then, a shy man ventured forward. He sheepishly shook the hand Nick offered.

"You probably don't remember me, Captain Landers," he said slowly. "Sergeant Matthew Stacy. I was a private when we met. I liked this place so much, I came back here to live after the war. And I became friends with Lucy's brother, Carl."

"Private Stacy," Nick repeated, his eyebrows furrowing. "I don't know. . ."

"I was one of the men you were trying to get to climb those rocks there. In fact, I told you it couldn't be done. You were gonna take me and Private Alexander on another climbing route to help us get over our fears when that man came and socked you in the face."

Nick nodded. "Oh yes. I remember you now."

It was then that Matthew brought out a medal. "I want you to have this, sir. I guess you could call it a wedding gift. But this really belongs to you. You gave me the courage to make it up those rocks, even when I didn't want to. You know, after that incident at the rocks, I climbed them without any difficulty. I guess it was the idea of seeing an enemy attacking you that got me going. There was no more fear. And because of your training, I was able to help a few fellow soldiers get up those cliffs when we were in Italy. They gave me this medal."

"You keep it. You earned it."

Matthew shook his head, pressing the medal into Nick's hand. "No, sir. You earned it, for all of us. Please."

Nick slowly took the medal. Lucy could see his lips trembling and tears glazing his eyes. "Thank you. This means a great deal to me."

"I was sorry to hear about your leg. And about Sergeant Watkins. I know, and many of the privates agreed, if you hadn't done the training you did here, we couldn't have been victorious in Italy. And more of us would have died. Thank you." He shuffled off then and disappeared into the crowd that had gathered.

"Oh, Nick," Lucy said in wonder, gently rubbing a circle of comfort on his back as he stared at the medal in the palm of his hand. "God is so good."

Nick sniffed, drawing a finger over his eye. "Yes, He is all good, Lucy. All good."

She kissed him on the cheek and turned, only to find Allen staring at her. She froze. "Allen, hi. Thanks for coming."

"Lucy. I—I wanted to thank you for inviting me and Susan to your wedding. It was a real nice wedding."

"Thank you, Allen."

He hesitated. "And I just wanted to say—look, I know it's long overdue, but I want to apologize for hitting you that day, Captain, sir."

Nick looked at him in surprise.

"I mean, it was wrong of me. I see now that God has His plans for everyone. They just weren't my plans. And I'm glad we have stayed friends, Lucy. My wife, Susan, could use a friend, too. She doesn't know a whole lot of people around here."

"I'd love to get to know her, Allen," Lucy said. "Tell her to come over so I can meet her."

"She had to leave early. But here's a gift that she made for you."

Lucy took it with a trembling hand. She fought to steady it even as she undid the wrapper. It was a sampler with their wedding date and a message: *I can do all things through Christ which strengtheneth me.* "Thank you so much, Allen. I will treasure this always."

He scuffed his foot in the grass, then meandered off.

Lucy turned to see Nick looking first at the medal, then Allen, and finally the rocks of Seneca. "This is a day of miracles," he murmured. "Who would have thought?"

"God knew that this would be a day of miracles. And reconciliation."

"And a day when those who were separated are united forever as one. Right, Mrs. Landers?"

"Forever, my dear sweet Captain."

Lucy stood on her toes for a kiss that she gladly gave with all her heart.

LAURALEE BLISS, is a published author of over a dozen historical and contemporary novels and novellas. Lauralee enjoys writing books where readers can come away with both an entertaining story and a lesson that ministers to the heart. Besides writing, Lauralee enjoys hiking in the great outdoors, traveling to do research on her upcoming novels, and gardening. She invites you to visit her Web site at lauraleebliss.com.

A Letter to Our Readers

Dear Reader

In order that   , we
would appreci   ving
questions. Wh   itor,
Barbour Publi

1. Did you en
   ❏ Very muc
   ❏ Moderate

2. What influe
   (Check thos
   ❏ Cover
   ❏ Friends

3. Which story
   ❏ *Mountains*
   ❏ *A Bride Idea*

4. Please check y
   ❏ Under 18
   ❏ 35–45

5. How many hou

DATE DUE

Demco, Inc. 38-293

Name _____

Occupation _____

Address _____

City _____ State _____ Zip _____

E-mail _____